second
chance

L.B. DUNBAR

www.lbdunbar.com

ROMANCE. FOR SEXY SILVER FOX LOVERS.

Second Chance
Copyright © 2019 Laura Dunbar
L.B. Dunbar Writes, Ltd.
https://www.lbdunbar.com/

Cover Design: Shannon Passmore/Shanoff Formats
Cover Image: Shutterstock
Content Editor: Melissa Shank
Editor: Mitzi Carroll/Mitzi Carroll Editing
Proofread: Karen Fischer
2022 Re-proof: Gemma Brocato

Other Books by L.B. Dunbar

Road Trips & Romance
Hauling Ashe
Merging Wright
Rhode Trip

Lakeside Cottage
Living at 40
Loving at 40
Learning at 40
Letting Go at 40

The Silver Foxes of Blue Ridge
Silver Brewer
Silver Player
Silver Mayor
Silver Biker

Silver Fox Former Rock Stars
After Care
Midlife Crisis
Restored Dreams
Second Chance
Wine&Dine

Collision novellas
Collide
Caught

Smartypants Romance (an imprint of Penny Reid)
Love in Due Time
Love in Deed
Love in a Pickle

The World of True North (an imprint of Sarina Bowen)
Cowboy
Studfinder

Rom-com for the over 40
The Sex Education of M.E.

3

L.B. Dunbar

The Heart Collection
Speak from the Heart
Read with your Heart
Look with your Heart
Fight from the Heart
View with your Heart

A Heart Collection Spin-off
The Heart Remembers

THE EARLY YEARS
The Legendary Rock Star Series
The Legend of Arturo King
The Story of Lansing Lotte
The Quest of Perkins Vale
The Truth of Tristan Lyons
The Trials of Guinevere DeGrance

Paradise Stories
Abel
Cain

The Island Duet
Redemption Island
Return to the Island

Modern Descendants – writing as elda lore
Hades
Solis
Heph

Dedication

For Tammi Hart (Mati Rath)
and
my girls (and guys) in Loving L.B.
Thank you for loving romance over 40.

L.B. Dunbar

1

The Letter

Dear Mati,

If you're reading this, something has happened to me. Hopefully, it wasn't something long and drawn out, but quick and peaceful. Baby, I'm also hoping it didn't take you, too, although you know I'd find you in heaven if you are here with me.

So, you've made it to cleaning out my office, which you've been asking me to do for years. I never was the neat one.

Reassure the boys I'm watching over them. I have faith that the two halves of us will find their way in the world, hopefully as fathers, as fatherhood has been one of the greater joys of my life.

The greatest joy has been your love, Mati. I know you gave it to me willingly, in sickness and in health, for richer or poorer. We know we've covered all four areas. Death does not part us, but I don't want it to stop you from living. We promised each other, young or old, whichever one of us went first, the other would continue to enjoy the gift of life. It's an adventure. Ours has certainly hit some bumps, taken curves, and ridden steep hills, but we enjoyed the ride, right? Don't stop now. You're the driver, Mati. A new road awaits.

I want you to do me a favor. Just consider it before you get mad at me. (Those vows should have included in moments of conflict and peace.) Contact Denton. He was one of our best friends. He loved you as I did, only I'm the luckier man. Despite riches and fame, I won you. I had your ear and your heart and your body. You might need someone to talk to, and he could be the ear for you. I have no doubt his heart is still open to yours. As for your body, well, I'd be a selfish man, deserving hell instead

7

L.B. Dunbar

of heaven, if I expected it to waste on earth without attention. We gave each other permission, in vows outside our wedding, babe. I expect you to accept them. For once, don't argue with me.

Live life.
Love from heaven,
Chris

2
Death Does Not Become Me

[Denton]

"Mama's dying."

The words hang in the air. My mother. The woman I tried to protect when she didn't protect me. The woman who never left *him* despite all he did to her. Eventually, it was him or me. I chose me when she didn't.

"Denton, did you hear me?"

I nod before I remember my older sister can't see me through the phone.

"I heard you." I swallow the lump in my throat, torn between the emotions of love and disappointment.

"You need to come home this time." My sister never asks me for anything. She tackled our worthless father's death alone. She understood my reasons for not attending his funeral. She'd been a witness to all that wasn't right, but thankfully, she was not a victim. Her plea for me to return to a place I hadn't called home in twenty-seven years punches me in the stomach.

"It's time, Denton. Besides, she's alone."

"Don't bring Mati into this," I groan, my mind instantly going to someone who should no longer hold me back, but Dolores is quick to correct me.

"Not Mati," she huffs. "Mom."

I curse my thoughts.

Mom, not Mati. Not Mati Harrington.

Lion-red hair, body like an hourglass, scented like a pomegranate, Mati. Of course, Mati isn't really alone. She got the man of her dreams, the children she wanted, and a house in the hills. I'm the one alone all these years later.

I scrub a hand down my face and flinch when cool fingers touch my lower back.

9

"Everything all right?" The feminine voice behind me forces my eyes to close. How did I get here? Not literally—too much scotch landed me in this bed—but in this position of nights with meaningless sex filled with women who mean even less to me. I shake my head and stand from the edge of the bed, ignoring last night's too-easy conquest.

"How long?" I ask Dolores, as I pace to the window overlooking the Los Angeles skyline. This place holds the dreams of my lost soul. This is my playground. This city is my home.

I don't know if I *can* go back after all the time that's passed.

"Ten days. Maybe two weeks at the most, the doctors say." Why didn't she tell me sooner? The answer comes quickly. I don't pick up most of her calls. Besides, what do doctors know? Sighing, I scrub down my face one more time. I need a shave. I don't like the scruff despite modern popularity.

It's been long enough, I tell myself. Only memory can hurt me now—not him. But there's one memory still burning like the hot tip of Dad's cigarettes. The girl who wasn't mine. Can I see her after all this time? When the soft mousy voice of last night's lay calls out my name, I have my answer.

"I'll be there."

3
Taking a Chance

[Mati]

I hug the letter to my chest, tears flowing down my cheeks. *Dammit, Christopher.* Why did you have to bring up Denton? Why do you feel the need to direct me, even after death? I chuckle through the salty streams on my face, swiping briskly. *Don't fight me on this.* He knows me well, stubborn to the core. We didn't have a push-pull relationship. We had compromise. We were good like that. Christopher was levelheaded and methodical while I was wild and spontaneous. We worked. For twenty-five years of marriage, and the years before those as high school sweethearts.

He's been gone a year, and I still feel a little incomplete. A cog sprung loose from a well-oiled machine—a coach missing her team. The thought forces me to wipe my face once more and check the time. I have practice at three-fifteen. I don't know why I decided to tackle the last of Christopher's home office today, but it just felt like the time was right. It was a year ago August, and with the holidays only months away, I want them to be special. Jax is expecting a child in November, and I want only joy for the new little life, not tears over death.

I fold the letter and take the second envelope with me to my bedroom. I can't tackle another read—besides, this envelope isn't addressed to me.

In twenty minutes, I'm at the high school gymnasium, my second home and center of the Blue Ridge Girls' Volleyball team I coach. I claim these young women as family since I have no girls of my own. Jordan and Jax are my boys, both grown into men of twenty-six years old. *Twins.* What a shock it had been when the doctor said there were two of them. More shocking than the fact I was pregnant at eighteen. The fright of delivery and surgery to remove them forced me to rethink my dream of a team of children. I wanted ten. I'm happy with two. It's hard

11

L.B. Dunbar

to believe I'm on the verge of *grand*motherhood. Jeez. That's what happens when you have boys who can't keep it in their pants, though.

The school bell signals the end of the day, and I anxiously await my girls. Team tryouts earlier in the month resulted in who I hope will be a winning combination for the fall season. I've coached here for years, after being a player myself at this very high school. My thoughts flash back to the mention of Denton in Chris's letter.

Denton Chance.

All-star athlete. Hidden talent as a musician. Too big for this small town.

One of our oldest friends who would laugh if he discovered I still live here, working for the high school we attended. We went to school together our entire lives. Denton had been the boy next door. On the outside, our homes were picturesque Americana in the mountain ridges of Georgia, but behind the closed door of the mayor's home, a darkness lurked for the Chances.

I shiver with the memory. As I stand in the gym awaiting my team, my eyes glance up at his name stitched in the banners, highlighting his achievements, or those of the teams he played on. Football. Basketball. Baseball. You can participate in it all in a small town, but music had been his passion. The whisper of his voice singing in my ear inside this gym makes me shiver again. Distant images flash through my mind like an old photobook, calling out for a second glance. Like the cabinets in Christopher's old office, filled with years of history, collected on paper, and stashed in a long-forgotten drawer, the simple mention of Denton's name in Chris's letter opens the memories locked away nearly twenty-seven years ago.

I chuckle as I scan the dates on the banner. Has it been that long? *Yep.* Twenty-seven years since I graduated from this high school and I'm right where I was back then. Only Chris was my high school sweetheart, and he's dead. Denton had been our best friend, and he abandoned us. I shake my head at the silliness of reminiscing. No good comes of it. The past is the past.

+ + +

12

Hours later, I'm rethinking things. I don't wish to dredge up what happened or why. I just want to be faithful to Chris's command, but I don't know how to reach Denton. I could ask his sister Dolores who runs the local diner, but that would open a can of worms I won't even go fishing with.

My fingers tap on the edge of the keyboard as I sit at Chris's desk. *I'm doing this because Chris wants me to reach out to him,* I tell myself. *That's it. He asked me to deliver this final message.*

I'm not big on social media. I mean, the school has a page with the teams' accomplishments. Our family-owned microbrew pub has a page for specials and events. My personal page I don't often use because, well, in a small town, I see everyone I want to see, and avoid those I don't. I have no need to be a busybody on Facebook. However, tonight, I'm searching for a name—Denton Chance.

Former classmate, I mutter to myself.

People do this all the time, I think.

I'm not stalking.

I'm mentally talking to myself, cheering myself on to complete the task at hand. Silently, I'm hoping I won't find him. He might not even be on social media. My attempt to search him might be futile. Then I laugh. As famous as he is, he probably has multiple pages and accounts, and people who run them for him. I type in the search bar, and low and behold, there he is.

Denton Chance. Former rockstar. Current photog. Model.

Even with his age, there's no denying it's him. Rich, dark eyes. A face like a Hollywood actor. His hair isn't dark brown any longer, but a light almond color mixed with white at the temples. Barely-there stubble graces his jaw with a hint of inky black and silver. He looks more like someone from a famous boyband than a rock band. He also looks good. *Damn good* for forty-five. I want to curse him for aging so well, but I don't. Instead, the old feeling returns—the one I suppressed each time he was around me. The butterflies take flight, but I swat at them with an imaginary net, hoping to catch them before they fill me.

I loved Chris, but I always crushed on Denton.

I click the link to Denton's name and my breath hitches as I'm accosted with an image of him. Smiling mischievously—his jaw edgy and hard—he looks every bit the rockstar he was and the model he is.

I don't necessarily want to friend him, but I need to send a message. I hover over the Add Friend button, circling it like I'm highlighting something in my playbook.

"Aw, fuck it," I say aloud and click. Instantly, I follow through to the message center and type:

Hey Denton. I'm pretty certain I have the right man. It's Mati Rathstone. If you have a second, can you message me back?

I stare at the words as if I'm writing the greatest sentences known to mankind. It's only a greeting, I admonish of the beginning. You need to introduce yourself, I remind myself. A question leaves the ball on his side of the net. If he responds, he responds, and if he doesn't, I've done what Chris asked. I click the mouse, and the message sends.

Then the butterflies flutter up to my throat, and I nearly gag.

What have I done?

4

Road Trips

[Denton]

"Denton Chance? Well, fuck me." The strong hand of Hank Paige connects with mine for a firm shake. It's been a long time since I've seen him—any of them. With Kit Carrigan's death, and the band falling apart around her diagnosis, I mentally walked away long before I quit.

"It's been a long time," I state, and Hank nods to agree. It's an awkward moment. How did I spend more than twenty years with this guy, call him family, and not know what to say?

"Did you hear Tommy settled down?" I hadn't heard. Tommy and Kit Carrigan are family by blood, my cousins as their mother is my mother's sister. Hearing his name reminds me why I'm at Hank's garage in the first place.

"I hadn't heard," I say, swiping a hand over my hair. "I don't talk to family much." Hank's eyes narrow at me. It seems to be my MO. Dumped my family. Dumped the band. Dumped my friends. I'm pathetic.

"He got married last New Year's, and I got married this summer." My mouth falls open. I'm stunned. Speechless. Lawson Colt, aka Thomas Lawson Carrigan—songwriter, guitarist, breaker of hearts—is married as well as Hank, drummer extraordinaire who was so focused on one woman he couldn't think straight. What has the world come to if these two fell in love?

"Wow…just wow. Congratulations, man." I reach out again to shake his hand and tug him to me for a Hollywood hug—chest bump, slap on the back, and step away quickly.

"Thanks," Hank mutters, scratching up the back of his neck. "It's been amazing."

Another tense moment passes.

L.B. Dunbar

"So, what can I do for you?" He tips his chin, noting my car in the lot outside the window. The Beast. A 1967 Ford Shelby GT500 Super Snake. White with blue striping. *Nice midlife crisis car*, his pop joked. *Ha*, I replied when I bought it some twenty-years ago. *This baby will keep me young forever*, I teased back. Suddenly, though, I feel very old at forty-five.

"I'm going on a trip, and I want to make sure she's sound to handle a long ride."

"Oh yeah, where you going?" Hank asks, reaching for a tablet and motioning for me to follow him out the waiting room door.

"I'm heading home." The words feel thick and strange in my mouth. Hank's head shoots up, and he looks at me.

"Everything all right?" Without asking for clarification, he reads in my expression which home I mean. Blue Ridge, Georgia. A train stop through the scenic Appalachian Mountains of northeast Georgia. I don't deserve the concern in his tone or the empathy in his eyes. We haven't been friends for a long time.

"My mother's dying," I say aloud for the first time. *My mother is dying*. It hasn't really hit me. It's still a simple statement.

"I'm sorry, man. Does Tommy know?"

I shake my head. I should have kept in touch with the guys, but when I walked away, I didn't want to ever look back. It's the same way I felt when I left Blue Ridge. Only now, I'll be barreling backward in time—a ride in reverse—and I'm curious how much of the past remains.

+ + +

I decide to road trip home to give myself time to adjust to my decision. Not to mention, I haven't cruised the country in forever. It's how I originally got from Georgia to California. I couldn't wait to graduate high school and escape my small town. I had big dreams, and they took me across the states, where I picked up a few stranglers on my way. My cousin Tommy Carrigan begged me to come get him in Texas. We always promised each other when we were ready to blow, we'd go together. And I went—the day after commencement. A new beginning,

16

the word suggests. Only I thought I'd have someone else along for the ride.

I hate the fact Dolores's phone call brings along a wave of memories. Backroads. Bonfires. Late nights. The wrong girls. My best friend had the right one, and I let him have her.

I take a long pull off the blunt between my fingers. Been a long while since I smoked, but today I need the hit. I'll claim it's medicinal. The highway before me is empty like my head should be. Instead, my mind wanders like the deserted pavement ahead of me, curving and swerving.

I wonder if she was really happy with him.

I laugh out loud, knowing full well the answer. Of course, she was happy. He gave her everything. The house. The kids. The steady income.

Mati Harrington, now Rathstone, didn't need the income. Blue Ridge royalty, her parents owned a microbrewery, producing illegal beer way back when, until finally getting it legalized around the time her grandfather inherited the family business. She had more money than most. A real socialite, except she renounced being a princess. A tomboy at heart, her mother hated that her two best friends were boys.

Chris and Denton. *Can't you pick a better set of friends?*

I can almost hear the screechy drawl of her mother's voice in my head, and I take another drag of the sweet weed. Elaina Harrington was no sip of Southern sweet tea. Then again, she was practically my second mother, offering safe harbor to Dolores and me as she knew all our secrets. The wealthy all lived on the same lane—Mountain Spring Lane. A mouthful to say, it was shortened to The Lane. Nothing less would be acceptable for the mayor of Blue Ridge than to live between the notorious illegal brewers and the local lodge owners. Old money was old money. History was history, and Kip Chance wanted to be part of history in Blue Ridge.

He made his mark. I snort without humor. He made many.

+ + +

L.B. Dunbar

My first pit stop is in Arizona. I'm taking the long route home, knowing if I went through Vegas I might not continue east. At the service station, I load up on junk food I typically wouldn't eat to feed my buzz. As I walk back out to my car, a bag of snacks in my arm, I tap my phone. I'm relieved to see no calls or texts from Dolores. I told her my plan, and she knows it might take me three days to get home. *Home.* The last place I want to go, and yet I know deep down, it's time. Dolores has handled everything for long enough. She inherited our grandmother's diner after our mother disowned it. She's also been in charge of our mother's well-being since our father died.

I toss my bag of goodies on the front seat, ready to drop the phone in as well when something stops me—a Facebook notification.

Now what? I think. I told the girls I'd be out of town for a few weeks. I cleared my current shoots and my social calendar. Only the most important people know I'm heading home which consists solely of: my neighbor, Garrett; Abigail, my personal assistant; and Madelyn, my agent at MetroModeling. The rest of my "peeps" I can disconnect from for a bit. Still, something draws me to tap the app and wait as the connection drags. Messenger opens and the first name I see I can't believe. I read it twice.

Mati Rath.

My thumb quivers as it hovers over her name, the full message incomplete until I open it. I tap the message, and the words stare up at me.

Hey Denton. I'm pretty certain I have the right man. It's Mati Rathstone. If you have a second, can you message me back?

Rathstone? I chuckle at the full last name. No one called him Rathstone. He'd always gone by Rath, his nickname.

Mati Rathstone, I type. **I don't know a Rathstone, but once upon a time, I knew a Mati Rath.** I glare at the statement. This isn't true. I don't know Mati Rath any more than I know Mati Rathstone. I left before they married.

I erase the message up to a point.

Mati Rathstone? I only know a Mati Harrington.

18

Will she know I'm teasing her? She used to tell me I was such a prankster. Actually, she'd say I was a prickster. My lip curls with the memory, and then I force them to flatten. Pranking is how she lost everything, but I remind myself I no longer care.

What do you want? I almost type instead, but then I decide to leave it as I said. I don't know this woman. I gaze at the letters like they might jump off the screen and Mati will slap me, like she once did. I wonder if she looks the same. Piercing brown eyes. Wild lion-red mane. A personality to match. I shake my head, tossing the phone through the open window.

"She's probably gotten fat," I curse under my breath, circling the car for the gas dispenser.

"I bet she's gone gray and became a blonde to cover it up," I mutter to myself as I return the nozzle.

I enter the Beast and twist the key, listening to the engine roar to life.

"Fuck it," I stammer aloud, reaching for the phone one more time and tapping the message to open the link to her personal page.

And there she is.

Mati. My Mati, looking everything like I remember, and yet a little bit different. She isn't fat. She isn't gray. She's goddamn gorgeous. *Shit.*

5

Private Messages

[Mati]

The Blue Ridge Microbrewery and Pub is busy for a Monday afternoon. *A family run business since before Georgia was official*—that's our tagline. I've never felt confident enough, nor do I desire, to run the business side of the brewery. Instead, my brother Billy—the third of my four older brothers—is the manager of the pub. My contribution is human resources, which means I'm the head waitress and in charge of managing the waitstaff and event coordinator, which simply means I'm the brains behind special activities to bring in customers. All my responsibilities shift when it's girls' volleyball season as my varsity team has been state champions three of the last five years. It's important to the community, which makes it important to my family.

The Harringtons. We've been here since before Georgia was official. My great, great, great something established the crafting of beer long before it was legal in Georgia. Daddy likes to brag we've been here— since the beginning, *thank you great grandfathers*—and yet the state took until 2017 to get on board with selling bottled beer from craft breweries. If we wanted to be in the bottled beverage industry, the Harringtons should have settled in Atlanta and developed a soda pop. Of course, I never would say something like that to my daddy. It doesn't matter, though, as my oldest brother George is the CEO of the production and distribution of our product. Giant is his nickname which makes sense since the official brand name of our beer is Giant Beer…from Georgia.

Don't even get me started.

I only have a few hours before my shift ends. I prefer coaching to pub work, but it's the family business, and I'm obligated. When my boys were babies, I didn't work. Having twins was difficult, and I stayed home while Chris struggled to complete college and earn his law degree. I played the good wife then. As the boys grew older, it was either society

Second Chance

functions to appease my mother or join the pub business to make my daddy happy. I always chose Daddy. He understood me better. He didn't fuss because his little girl wasn't all feminine and genteel. He understood I had four brothers and a nagging mother. His disappointment came when I announced I was pregnant, at eighteen, and marrying Chris Rathstone.

The rushed wedding was an attempt to disguise my "indiscretion," but you can't hide twins for long, especially on a petite-framed body. I'm five-six which isn't small, but small enough to not be able to disguise the bump of two babies. Short enough to not play college volleyball, which was my initial dream. I lost that shot for other reasons than a teenage pregnancy and a too-young marriage, though. The thought brings me back to Denton.

I don't use my phone for social media, so it won't be until I'm home before I know if he's answered me, but I feel the weight of waiting. Did I find the right man? Will he respond? Does he remember me? The last question makes me laugh. I have no doubt he remembers me, us, the town. He's just chosen to ignore it all. Yet, his sister is in on all Blue Ridge's gossip. Not one to spread it, Dolores is aware of the town happenings as her diner is a central place for locals to gather. I have no doubt she's kept her younger brother informed of a few things.

Like Chris's death. The funeral Denton didn't attend.

The memory makes me angry, and I almost drop my tray of beers. A round tray with five tallboys isn't difficult to balance, but I'm off today.

Before I know it, I stand at my kitchen sink and eat a dinner consisting of what I call an adult Lunchable—sausage and cheese with bread biscuit crackers. It's tasty.

Then I decide I've stalled long enough, and I check Facebook. The lights remain off in Chris's office, although I don't know why I keep referring to it as his. He isn't here any longer, and the thought makes me sad. Not as sad as I know I've been with his loss but still filled with sorrow. I also feel a little…guilty, risky, sly…like I'm doing something I shouldn't be doing although my husband is gone, and he asked me to make contact with his best friend. Our *ex*-best friend.

L.B. Dunbar

I see the message instantly.

Mati Rathstone? I only know a Mati Harrington. I stare at the words. *Is he kidding me?* He has to be. Rathstone is Chris's official last name although he always hated it. Sounded too pretentious, albeit fitting for an attorney. He went by Rath at school. Our boys went by Rath. I'm even called Coach Rath. But Rathstone is the name, and I don't know if he's mocking me or not. Mati Harrington, on the other hand, was his neighbor. The girl next door who he came to in time of trouble, needing comfort, and…

I refuse to think of the other things. We were kids. We were innocent. Hell, even my parents let him spend the night in my bed when we were young. When we were older, they just didn't know he still ended up there some nights—avoiding or hiding—depending on whose interpretation you wanted to believe. The town believed in the mayor, Kip Chance, whose personae was smooth, well-meaning, and a real family man, until he was seen with his young secretary or found hanging at the biker bar twenty minutes outside of town.

I shake at thoughts of Denton's father and stare at the second message sent.

So, what's up?

What's up? What are we, teenagers? What's up?! My fingers itch to type: *What's up is Chris is dead, and for some reason, he thought of you in the end. He still considered you his best friend although you dumped us and never looked back. AND he has a letter for your sorry ass.*

But I don't type those words. Instead, I type: **As you may know, Chris passed away**. I swallow back the lump in my throat at the formality, but I've mastered this part of my speech. I continue.

He left some things behind, and I thought you might like them. No pressure, though. However, he had something specific he wanted you to receive, and I'd like to know where to send it if you don't mind sharing an address.

I don't hesitate. I hit return and let the message go. I don't have patience for the LA-snob Denton Chance. I imagine he's stuck-up and egotistical from all the acclaim he's received. The diner hails his images like he's some kind of hero, yet he didn't save anyone from anything. He saved himself. I don't fault him—not really—but I might still be a teeny-tiny-bit bitter that he didn't allow Chris and me to share in his success by supporting him, cheering him on like we would have done. Instead, he cut us off. He disappeared, but we couldn't avoid him. His band was famous, and their songs filled the radio for years. Every girl wanted to be Kit Carrigan and hang out with her band Chrome Teardrops.

Denton Chance was the bass guitarist. His cousin and Kit's brother, Lawson Colt—whose real name I think was Tommy—was the second singer, working duets with his sister, plus playing guitar. They also had a drummer, but I don't remember who he was. Either way, they were the *it* band when rock chick bands were a thing. Their end was a sad story. Cancer sucks. We've had it take a member of our family as well. I sigh with thoughts of my deceased sister-in-law.

I'm ready to close the laptop when a popping sound comes through the speaker, and I notice one message in the box.

Hey.

That's it—another Hollywood greeting. I imagine him tipping up his chin with *What's up?* Then a nod with *Hey.* What the hell?

Hey.

I know, I'm lame.

I heard about Chris. I'm sorry I wasn't able to make it. What does he have for me? Maybe it's something you'd like to keep instead?

My eyes blink at the brightness of the screen and ponder his questions. If he doesn't want Chris's stuff, why doesn't he say so? *Keep his shit.* We already went through all Chris's personal effects: clothing, crap in the garage, business items. I have all I'll ever need of Chris's belongings. Some old high school memorabilia for the boys. Photographs of years together. A favorite sweatshirt or two. Most of all I had Chris's love and his children, something I can't measure or keep in a box.

I'm frustrated with Denton's attitude although I don't even know him—this version of him anyway—and I really should excuse social media as it's hard to read tone and intention in messaging. Still…

23

L.B. Dunbar

I'm not certain what it is. It's sealed in an envelope. Chris asked me to send it to you. I'm just following through with his wishes.

I pause a moment as three dots appear like he's reading the message. Another thought occurs, and I type a second response.

If you're worried about size, it isn't too large. And if you decide you don't want it, you can dispose of it afterward. That would be up to you.

Words appear almost instantly.

Still following whatever Chris wants. A smiley face follows, and I assume it's to soften the blow of his comment. It stings a bit.

Just do your own thing, Mati. Make up your mind for you.

He wasn't wrong; he just didn't see how many times I did make decisions that were centered around myself. He also wasn't wrong that many times I didn't act on those decisions.

I'm ready to type a retort when another message appears.

Sealed envelope? Sounds mysterious. Maybe you should just open it and tell me what it is. I give you permission.

I hear his demanding voice in my head, the one I remember from twenty-seven years ago.

Jump. I'll catch you.

Another message appears.

As for size, there's no such thing as too big.

My mouth falls open. He can't possibly…is he…did he just…he can't be teasing me. I stare blankly at the screen.

As for disposing of it, I've never gotten rid of anything which had to do with you or Chris. I've held on to everything.

I sit back in the chair, astonished at his words. What does he mean? Am I reading too much into this? Is there an innuendo there? He was hurt when he left all those years ago, but so was I.

I think of the gifts over the years. Handmade cards. Personal jokes. Little tokens. Denton hated the holidays. I loved them. However, I can't think of a single thing worth keeping in the sense of past presents.

Deciding I have no idea what he means, I'm ready to respond again when another message flashes.

Hello? Still there? Did the too big comment scare you off?

24

My lips twist at his audacity, and then I laugh. *Damnit Denton.*

I'm still here, though I've gotta go. In your dreams are things too big. And nothing scares me, remember?

I hesitate on the last question but hit enter too quickly. The message is permanent. Darn it, why can't there be an edit button in the message box?

Oh, I remember, lion cat. I remember everything. As for too big, that might be in <your> dreams. Gotta go? Have a hot date?

My eyes widen, stunned. Did he just call me *lion cat*, a nickname I hadn't heard in years? Too big in my dreams. Snort. I don't have dreams. They dashed a long time ago. Although, if I think about it, I have been dreaming of Denton lately. At least, he's been *in* my dreams, but they don't make sense. I brush them off in the morning as my subconscious pulling him forward because I reached out to him. It's all memory tricking me. As for a hot date, it's the first issue I respond to.

I don't date, so very funny.

That might have been inappropriate. Sorry about that.

Why was he sorry? Should I not date? Is it still inappropriate? Mother said I needed to mourn a year, but I was still young enough to find a good man. My now best friend Cora tells me I need to get back out there. I don't know where *there* is—or where I'd go. I don't do social media, so all those virtual dating slash matchmaking places are out. I know every man in this town and most are married. The few eligible bachelors happen to include my brothers and some of their single friends, so that's just a big double *ew.*

Where would I even go to find a hot date if I wanted one?

Do I want one?

Why does my head rush to thoughts of dating Denton?

I realize I'm talking to myself again, asking these questions aloud and I clamp my mouth shut.

Well, you always were inappropriate, so glad to read things haven't changed. As for needing to go, some of us work…real jobs…like during the day and need sleep at night. Just let me know where to send the envelope. I'll take care of it as soon as you do.

25

L.B. Dunbar

Rockstars don't have day jobs, and I roll my eyes at the thought. I imagine being a photographer and model doesn't provide him a regular schedule either like us working class minions. I scroll back through the conversation until something catches my eyes.

I remember everything.

Does he? I'm hoping he doesn't, and I convince myself he's just saying it to rattle me. Another message hits the chat box.

I'd be a fool to think anything stayed the same, lion cat. I guess I lied about remembering everything because, from your profile picture, I see you've changed.

My mouth pops open. *What is he saying?* I know I'm older, a little rounder, my hair a lot lighter. I've had babies, for Christ's sake. I live in a small town where we like to eat—my heart races at the potential insult. *Fuck off, Denton*, I scream in my head until another message hits the screen.

I don't remember you being so gorgeous.

6

A Bit Much or Not Enough

[Denton]

The last comment might have been a bit much. I'd like to say she started it with her comment about large things, but I'm sensing Mati's missing her former sense of humor and her dirty mind. Too bad. She was quite the hellcat as a teen. It's part of the nickname. Her hair reminds me of a lion's mane, the color rich like burnt sunshine. It also framed her face in a wild manner. She would never qualify as strawberry blonde. No, that would be too cute for her. Her personality was all lioness. Protective. Mothering. Safe.

She was a high school star on the girls' volleyball team, the Mountain Cats. Other schools had a field day with the name. Mountain Pussy was among my favorite. Peaked Kitties, mocked to titties, was another good one. Mati would never have been considered a kitten, though. She was too fierce. As for pussy, just try to accuse her of being one and a fist might meet your face.

I chuckle to myself and type: **Night, Mati. Dream of big things.**

There's no response and something in my chest burns. I hadn't realized how much I missed our banter. Or her.

We separated on rough terms. For all my accusations of her doing what Chris asked, I'd done the same thing. He was my best friend, and I loved him.

Tell her you don't want her to go.

Chris's voice rings through my head. I hurt her, but I did what he wanted.

I'm staring at the ceiling with my memories swirling like the fan above me. I'm somewhere off I-10E in New Mexico, and I can practically feel the Mexican border calling me, but I don't have the patience to deal with that kind of shit tonight. Still, I could get some good weed there and a nice lay. Then again, I don't need a disease. My dick

L.B. Dunbar

doesn't even get hard at the thought of some sweet Mexican pussy. I think of Mati, instead. The semi-wood surprises me. I shouldn't be thinking of her like this. I shouldn't be thinking of her like anything.

Funny thing about memories, though. Once they start, more tumble forth, and within seconds, I'm remembering sharing a bed with Mati as a teen. Pre-Chris. Pre-Kristy. It was another night of fighting off my dad, or maybe it was one of those nights I chose to ignore him completely and didn't go home. I'd face his wrath the following day, but some nights I needed the reprieve. The beating could wait until morning.

I was fourteen. We were freshmen. Mati was wrapped around me, holding me to her chest which had developed quite a bit over the last year. She's busty for a small thing, her mother would say, often publicly, and much to Mati's dismay. Mati hated to be reminded she was a girl.

As she stroked through my hair, mothering me with whispers, I nuzzled into her breasts. Her fingers stilled, and my hand came to her hip. I remember shaking, my fingers fumbling as they climbed the outline of her body.

"Denton," she whispered, my name an exhale.

I remember pulling back, lifting my eyes to hers.

"Kiss me, Mati," I begged. I wanted to know what it felt like to have lips love me, instead of hating me, like the insults my father slung.

Her brow pinched. She hesitated, and for a moment, I thought she'd tell me to fuck off in true Mati fashion. Chris and I each flirted with her, but it was all in good fun. Neither of us would ever get with her. This was Mati, our best friend.

However, that night she must have seen something, something deep within me. Maybe she only took pity on me. Maybe she was curious herself. Whatever her reasons, she leaned forward, and our lips met. It wasn't one of those overly passionate kisses at first, but it was more than kissing my best friend. Our mouths started slow, our lips lingering for a second before they moved. Hesitant. Curious. Sweet. Then the kiss deepened. We found a pattern to sucking at each other's lips. Our mouths opened, and our tongues met. Mati giggled against me, and I smiled around her mouth. My hands moved up to her hair, a ray of burnt sunshine in the dark, and the kiss deepened. I grew hungry like I'd never

28

eaten before, and I knew at that moment I'd never be full again. Her mouth on mine was everything.

I rolled her to her back, my hand lowering to her breast. An awkward squeeze and Mati pulled back.

"Denton," she warned, or was it a question? Either way, I pulled away, rejected. Flipping to lay on my back next to her, I stared up at the ceiling. Her fan spun around and around like the thoughts in my head. I'd kissed my best friend, and I liked it, too much. My dick strained in my jeans, and I curled to my side, my back to her in my embarrassment.

My hand slithers into my boxers, and I do something I haven't done since I was a teen. I whack myself off with the memories of my first kiss, the one kiss that changed everything.

+ + +

I'm on the road early after a restless night on a lumpy bed. I could stay at elegant hotels along my course, but I'm retracing steps, which means stopping at roadside motels instead. The memories come faster with each town I pass as I barrel toward Texas. It's going to be a long day, and I've already had two cups of coffee. I checked my phone this morning for any additional words from Mati but don't find any. For some reason, this irritates me.

At my first stop, I message her again.

Hey.

Master of words, mate, I tell myself after I hit send. I don't know how to start a conversation, which isn't typical. I'm a pro with the ladies, but then again, I don't do social media with them. I'm a one-and-done kind of man. I'll call if I want. I'll send a text if I wish. Most mornings-after, I don't do either.

I don't bother checking back in until later in the day. Nothing again.

Mati?

I tap enter. This would be so much easier if I had her phone number. I could text her; however, data reception is terrible as I cross to I-20E. *Hello Texas,* here comes more memories. Hours into the state, I see the signs for Dallas, and the turnoff for Denton, the town I'm named after

29

L.B. Dunbar

and the place I picked up my cousin, Tommy. His younger sister followed us the year after.

God, I'm tired, I think as I consider the journey my life has taken. Rockstar. Photographer. Model. It isn't that I don't have a good life, but I'm tired all the same. A little knocking in my chest tells me it's more than that. I'm lonely. *Fine, I admit it.* I'm exhausted from the endless struggle: women, appearances, forced conversations. Small talk is one thing I hate most, and yet I'm attempting to small talk Mati. Fuck that.

The next stop I make, I furiously type.

Whatever Chris has for me, I'd like to suggest you open it. I'm not interested in secrets. Full disclosure. So just crack the envelope and tell me what's inside. I can't even imagine the prize at the bottom of the box. And I apologize if I offended you by stating the truth of your appearance.

Tap.

Send.

Shit.

Here's the thing about social media messages, you can't erase them once they're sent, and this is one I'd like to take back instantly.

7

Secrets

[Mati]

The pub has an Oktoberfest planned in a few weeks, and we need a permit to close a portion of Main Street. This should be easy to achieve as my brother Charlie, is the current mayor of the city, but *noooo*, there are glitches in blocking off a part of the thoroughfare through the heartbeat of Blue Ridge. Plan B is to use the side street between our building and the one across the street. Plan C is to use the public lot behind us which is a whole other hassle. We need to figure out something.

It's already the beginning of September. October will be here sooner than we think. I'm hoping I'll be headed to a volleyball state championship a month later, but I keep those goals to myself. I have a secret. I want to be a college volleyball coach. Chris knew this and encouraged me to apply to a variety of places, but I didn't follow through. I always had an excuse. The kids. The pub. Where we lived. Chris's practice. With Chris's death, I slowly came to realize there are no longer as many things holding me back.

My son Jax works for my oldest brother Giant in the warehouse as head of direct sales. His twin brother Jordan works in his father's law practice, as an associate partner. Jordan was only an intern when Chris died, so my brother and Chris's partner, Charlie, took over his apprenticeship until Jordan passed the bar. Both boys are in relationships, although I wish Jax would marry Hollilyn, his pregnant girlfriend. Jordan married his college sweetheart, Maggie. I thought all twins did things in sync, but as they aren't identical, maybe not.

Besides them being secure, the pub isn't a career move, it's family, which holds me back in other ways. As the family ages, though, I can be replaced. Which leaves my home as the only remaining excuse. Originally, I didn't want to leave my house, but I've become more and

L.B. Dunbar

more willing as time passes. The place holds a million fond memories, and at times, those memories haunt me. As our second home, after our first apartment, this is where we raised our boys. Holidays. Birthdays. Anniversaries. Sometimes, the past pains me. Yet, I don't think I could move too far away. Blue Ridge is my home—the only place I've ever known. I'm forty-four, and change is scary.

Still.

I find I'm ready. I applied for the position of head of women's volleyball at Northeastern Georgia, some thirty minutes down the mountain. It would be a commute, but I don't want to get ahead of myself. The application is pending. I also applied to Dalton State, but I've recently learned they cut women's volleyball. I need to search for a few more applications, but first, I check Facebook.

A string of messages from Denton greet me, but the last one catches me off guard.

It sounds angry.

What does he have to be angry about?

Full disclosure. Secrets. What the…

My mind drifts back to being fourteen. We kissed, and we kept it quiet. I swore I'd take it to the grave. Marriage has all kinds of hidden truths. This one would have killed Chris. I laugh bitterly at the irony. Chris went to the grave first. He'll never know what happened, but I remember. I remember stopping Denton, thinking he was only looking for sympathy from me. He didn't want me; he wanted my comfort. This was confirmed two weeks later when he went out with Kristy Moseley, and they gave up their virginity to each other. I hated him. I hated how it made me feel, which is another secret I plan to have buried with me.

I'm not certain how to respond to his message, but it irritates me.

Denton, I work all day, so I'm sorry to respond so late. I'm not opening the envelope. Whatever is in there is between you and Chris, as Chris wanted it to be. I have no interest in disclosing anything or exposing secrets. Just give me your address, or I can give the envelope to Dolores, and she can forward it to you.

I've noticed once again he hasn't included where to send the letter. I don't like offering him Option B—his sister—but my patience wears thin.

The three bubbles appear instantly, and my fingers fly back from the keyboard as if he can see me.

Hey. Where do you work?

I stare at the question. *That's it?* Nothing else after all he said earlier?

I'm the varsity girls' volleyball coach for Blue Ridge High School. I also work for the BRMP.

BRMP?

Blue Ridge Microbrewery and Pub.

Ah, yes. Dolores mentioned her competition.

Competition? When Billy decided to open the pub sixteen years ago, we worried about the effects on the community, especially the diner run by Denton's sister. Billy and Dolores were friends, as Dolores was practically family, like Denton. Billy researched prior to opening to prove our pub wouldn't conflict with her restaurant. The diner catered to locals and the pub was intended to attract visitors. Blue Ridge was growing as a community, a little-hidden niche for artisans, and a blossoming tourist destination.

We aren't her competition, I defend.

Easy there, Spice.

Spice?

Yeah, your hair looks cinnamon. What happened to the paprika?

I gasp.

I did not have paprika colored hair! And if I'm a spice, what are you, Mr. Salt and Pepper? My lips curl in a knowing smile. When I was younger, my hair was rust-colored at best. With aging, it's lightened, and coloring helps. Also, he might have called me gorgeous, but I've seen him. He's aged well—*very well*.

Ha ha, he replies.

My shoulders relax. I didn't even realize how tense I'd grown typing to him, but his canned laughter eases me.

L.B. Dunbar

So, old BRHS? Wow, what's it been, twenty years?

Twenty-seven actually. There's a reunion this fall during the football season.

I don't know why I tell him this. It's only a reminder of how long it's been. I doubt he'd show. Twenty-seven isn't a milestone, but our twenty-fifth was canceled due to bad weather. Year twenty-six wasn't necessary with the death of Chris. Everyone returned home, except Denton. A high school reunion doesn't seem like his thing. I'd like to skip it myself, but I promised Cora I'd go.

A reunion? Whoa. I bet that would be interesting.

Thinking of attending? I don't know why I ask.

Are you inviting me? My brows twitch. What is he *asking*? I'll bite, I decide. He won't return anyway.

And if I were?

I'd be there.

My mouth falls open. He's kidding me; he has to be. Denton Chance would not come back to Blue Ridge for a high school reunion, let alone me. He has never returned.

It's not like it's a car ride away. I tease.

Stranger things have happened. Cryptic, but I let it go. It's almost midnight here, and I need to get to bed. I wish I could say get to sleep, but considering I didn't sleep last night, I'm doubtful peace will visit me tonight. I'm about to type goodnight when the bubbles appear again.

Can I ask you something?

Before I can answer, a second question appears.

Ever think about that kiss? Ever tell Chris?

I stare at the words. Has he been reading my mind? Will he jump through the screen ready to punk me? I look over my shoulder in the dark office as if that's a possibility.

No, and I'm not discussing Chris with you. I sit back in the seat, crossing my arms defiantly as the words blur on the screen. I can't talk about Chris with Denton. Not like this.

Can I ask you something else, then?

I shake my head. I don't want to keep talking with Denton, and I'm about to exit out the chat without a closing when another message pops up.

Are you lonely without him?

My eyes cloud again. I hate Denton, and yet I don't. He's hit a nerve I've been struggling with, especially as we crossed the one-year mark of Chris's death. I miss Chris, but I've come to terms with the fact he'll never be back. He'll never walk through our front door. He'll never enter our bedroom. He'll never climb into our bed.

So, yeah, I am lonely.

Yes.

I don't know why I offer this truth to Denton. Cora's been telling me I'm lonely for a while, but I brush her off. I don't want to admit my weakness to anyone. I'm not only lonely; I'm getting restless. I don't think I can date, but I feel like I need something.

Ever ease the pain?

The question comes as if conjured from my head, and yet I don't know what he's asking me.

I don't know what you mean.

You can't be that innocent, still, lion cat. My mouth falls open as I stare at the words. He can't...he couldn't...he doesn't mean what I think he means. I type the first thing that comes to mind.

Man, you have balls.

Yes. Yes, I do...and I like to use them.

Oh, my God. How did we get to this point? And, how dare he?

Good to know things haven't changed for you. If he stood before me, I might smack him. Using his balls is exactly what he did after our kiss, or rather, using his dick. He slept with my nemesis Kristy Moseley after I went out with Chris. *It wasn't a date*, I argued with Denton, but then again, it felt like one. We never went to the movies as just two people, unless the third had an excuse not to attend. Chris told me Denton couldn't make it. Denton told me Chris lied. Denton went out with Kristy three nights later.

Touché.

L.B. Dunbar

My lips twist. I don't like this turn of conversation, nor do I like the memory. Denton and I never discussed the kiss. I assumed it never meant anything to him. Secretly, it meant the world to me. It changed everything—in my heart. As for our friendship, I pretended nothing happened, just like he did. I decided he wasn't interested in me like *that*—as a girl. He was my first kiss, though, and I'm positive I was his. It was the only first we shared.

I don't know how to end this conversation. Strangely, I don't want to, but it's just getting too weird, too awkward.

I've gotta get to bed.

Alone?

I shake my head, a low chuckle rumbling up my chest. He's lost his mind.

Yes, alone.

Too bad. Wish I was there.

That's it. I close the chat by slamming the laptop shut. My mind races back to our youth, when he slept in my bed as a kid, when he snuck into my room as a young teenager. He came to me the next night after he had sex with Kristy—his cheek red and puffy from his dad. I followed through with what I'd done a hundred times. A washcloth. Ice. Tylenol. But that night, I refused to let Denton stay.

"Is it because of Chris?" he snapped. He'd been angry and distant ever since Chris and I went to the movies. Nothing happened. We didn't even hold hands. We didn't kiss. But it was still different.

"No," I argued back. "It's because of Kristy."

"Kristy? What does she have to do with anything?"

"You slept with her."

"So? It didn't mean anything."

"Too bad for her, then. She's telling everyone she's your girlfriend."

"She is not," Denton hissed. "Is Chris your boyfriend?" His voice whined.

"And if he is?" I teased, irritation in my response. He wasn't, though. I didn't anticipate Chris being my boyfriend. I'd wanted the kiss

36

with Denton to mean something, but after Kristy, my hopes shattered, and I couldn't forgive him.

"I'd..."

"What?" My breath hitched. Never had a question held so much.

"Never mind." Denton threw the washcloth on the floor and slipped back through the window.

He never returned. Chris and I started officially dating a few weeks later.

8

Upset and Whiskey

[Denton]

I've upset you. I'm sorry.
I'm still waiting for a response. I've crossed another time zone, and I'm an hour behind her. It's midnight, but she was awake. Now, she's ignoring me, or she's closed the chat in anger. I can see her, glaring at the computer, huffing away from it. I remember her spitfire.
Because of Kristy. I didn't hear it then. The jealousy. The hurt. I'd betrayed our kiss by sleeping with Kristy, but I only did it after they went on a date. She no longer let me come to her as my haven, because of Kristy. The girl I fooled around with too often in high school. The girl who followed me to California and I married when she told me she was pregnant. The girl who lost our baby and then lost me. I didn't blame her or the baby. I blamed her for using me to get out of Blue Ridge. The wrong girl went with me.
Because I did what Chris asked of me.
Bitter thoughts fill me. If I hadn't listened to Chris in the first place, if I hadn't agreed, my life could have been so different. So would Mati's.
"I took Mati to the movies."
"Without me?"
"Yeah, you don't mind, right?"
"Why would I mind?" I lied. I wanted to punch him.
"Just checking."
"Did you kiss her?" I teased, holding my breath in hopes he hadn't. Would he tell me? I hadn't told him.
"No, dude. We aren't like that." But he hesitated, and in the awkward pause, I knew everything. Chris liked Mati, just like me. I hadn't told her yet. I was still freaked out by my reaction to our kiss. Not the boner she gave me, but the fact I wanted to move fast as if I needed to race, or I'd never catch her.

How true it had been. I didn't get the girl.

When Mati doesn't respond to my message, I chuck my phone toward the end of the bed and roll to my side. I'm already in my boxer briefs, hoping for another night of self-soothing release with the help of her banter. Instead, I went too far—asking if she was alone, asking if she sought relief, asking if I could be in her bed. I'm losing my mind over her. Again.

I'm also repelling her. I need to be cool, but the closer I get to Georgia the more my heart races, as if I won't get there fast enough. Again.

+ + +

I haven't thought too much on my mother's situation, although she's the purpose for my return. Dolores said this was the end, and I'm torn with how I feel about her impending death. It's been so long since we've spoken. Maybe last Christmas. The one before. I can't even remember. I check-in with Dolores once a month. Maybe every two. I'm not certain there either. Mati says it's been twenty-seven years. Where did the time go? What have I been doing?

I can answer the second question, but I can't say I have anything to show for the years. Grammys. Honors. A great condo on the beach. Superficial things, which is what I think of my life as I reflect on it the closer I get to Georgia. I'm privileged, and I know it, but I sense I'm missing more important things as I wind up the mountains of Georgia—climbing, climbing, climbing—back to the past.

The forest around me is dark, the road illuminated from my headlights. I should be tired, but I'm wired. Sorrow is my companion.

I make a stop just outside of town. The space is spooky, but I know I can't pass it up. This needs to be my first visit. Death is the whole reason I'm here.

There's one grave I won't visit in this cemetery, but I feel its presence. Too soon my mother will lie next to him once again. I shiver with the thought.

L.B. Dunbar

Staring at the name etched in granite, I stand over a different tombstone.

Christopher John Rathstone.

Forty-four years old. Gone too young and I'm a year too late.

"I'm sorry, man." My fingers jiggle change in my pocket. I stopped at the liquor store just before I got here. Olde Benny's. The man must be a hundred years old by now, I think. Swallowing against the sharp sting, I take a deep pull of the Irish whiskey in a brown bag. Chris and I shared our first drink with this cheap-ass liquor. I wanted a taste of what my old man felt was more important than his wife and children. Chris, being loyal, said he'd share the experience with me.

The alcohol flows bitterly down my throat. I never understood the old man's love for this flavor, but tonight, I stand at this grave to toast my love for one of my oldest friends, not to recall my hatred for my father.

"I'm sorry I wasn't here." A car crash on a mountain road we knew well—a curve we risked a million times in the dark. A deer on the pavement and his life was taken. Poor Mati. At forty-four, she's too young to be a widow.

I didn't attend Chris's funeral. Too busy. The same excuse I used for my father's, although there was more bittersweet vengeance in my intention than the lie. My absence from my best friend's burial had to do with his wife. Her tears for him. Her sorrow. Her loss. It would have broken me all over again, just like the first time I gave her up. I'm a selfish man.

"You fucker," I curse. "You weren't supposed to die. You promised to take care of her forever." I pour a heavy dose of whiskey on the grass blanketing his permanent resting place, sharing another drink with him. Chris and I shared everything, especially our feelings for his wife. Only, I loved her first.

9

U-turn

[Mati]

I don't hear from Denton again, and I hate to admit, I'm disappointed. *Are you lonely without him?* While I first thought he meant to insult me, I've been thinking more and more about the question, wondering why he asked me. Is he lonely, too? Of course, I quickly blow off the thought. He's all Hollywood—rockstars, actors, and models. He can't possibly be lonely.

"Whatcha looking at?" Hollilyn asks me, peering over my shoulder as I stare at the empty chat after Denton's last comment.

I've upset you. I'm sorry.

I can't tell him I'm not upset, because I am. A smiley face seems trite. I don't forgive him for what he said. Instead, I'm confused by it all and my reaction to him.

"Nothing," I say sharply, dipping the phone into my apron. Most girls don't wear them, but I still do. I'm old, what can I say. I like the short apron with pockets for everything. I can't pull off sticking my phone in my back pocket as the young things do. They aren't supposed to have their phones on them while they're working.

Hollilyn bumps my shoulder, and I look up at her. Blonde hair. Blue eyes. She's the opposite of Jax with his dark hair and dark eyes. I like my son's girlfriend, although I didn't at first. She's a professional waitress, having worked several of the local establishments before settling at the pub for a time. Now she works for Dolores's diner as she believed waiting at the pub was a conflict of interest—fraternizing with the staff and such—as Jax works the business side of our craft beer distribution. My son, however, had been rather wayward with the waitstaff, dismissing the no-fraternizing clause, so I wasn't surprised when he ended up with her. I just didn't want it to be permanent. I like to think I don't judge, but I know I did in her case. Hollilyn Abernathy is from the other side of town, and at first, I supposed she saw my son as a means to move up the social ladder.

When she announced she was pregnant, my first thought was not kind, but she's grown on me. When I see them together, I see how much she worships my son. I wish I saw the same in him. I want him to marry her. The longer he holds off, the more wary I become that he's not in love with her. She moved in with him, but I'm not convinced that means anything.

Jax also works hard. As the chief salesperson for the Giant Beer brand, he travels often, and I worry the absence will take its toll. I want Jax to be happy. I want Hollilyn to be happy, and most of all, I want a healthy grandbaby.

Hollilyn still peers at me, waiting for an explanation. She doesn't accept *nothing* as an answer, and I'm wondering what she's doing at the pub. She must have met Jax for lunch.

"Just checking my phone for messages," I say too cheerful for me.

"Since when?"

"Since none of your business," I snap, but I'm teasing, hoping she'll let it drop. Her eyes open wide.

"Oh my gosh. Do you have a date? A secret lover? A *boyfriend*?"

"What? No," I admonish, blinking at how rapidly this girl's mind fires off possibilities.

"Who has a boyfriend?" my brother Billy asks as he rounds the bar. Tall, dark, and devilishly handsome, with silver streaks in his hair, hinting at his age. He has a perpetual twinkle to his dark eyes and a smile on his face, but inside, he's still hurting from lost love. He's the owner of BRMP, but tonight he's playing bartender.

"Mati," Hollilyn offers.

"I do not." My voice cracks like a teen.

"You bonking someone?" my older brother asks, winking at me like we share a secret. I make a face, scrunching up my nose. Then his expression sobers. "Never mind, don't answer that." As if I'd share my sexual goings-on with my brother.

"Bonking? What are you, a hundred? Who even uses such a word?" I chuckle, awkwardly trying to cover the fact I've been thinking about *bonking* for the past twenty-four hours, but no one needs to know such details.

"I was trying to be delicate, seeing as you're a female and all." He winks again. My brothers love to tease me about being a woman—the token girl child in the family—the one my parents wanted most, or at least, my mother did. Too bad I turned out to be such a disappointment. I'm not the debutante my mother hoped for. I didn't even have a coming-out party. I got mono around my sixteenth birthday, and the event was canceled. Thank goodness for semi-contagious diseases.

"Speaking of bonking. What number you up to?" I can't believe I'm asking this question, but I want to shift the spotlight off me, and there's nothing my brother likes to talk about more than his sex life. Billy keeps a tally of how many women he's laid since his divorce. That's all he's done, for nearly seventeen years—get laid. Most people say it's because he can't get over Rachel, his ex-wife. I think there's more to the story. In my opinion, he needs to stop *bonking* and settle down. Not quite as rebellious as our brother James, who disowned the family when his wife left him, but still a wild one, despite being forty-six.

"I can't even count that high." This is his new standard answer.

"You know what they say about a man who brags about the bedroom."

"What?" he asks, wiping some glasses and setting them on the bar.

"He's overcompensating for what he doesn't have."

"Ew…don't be disrespecting my junk. You're my sister."

"Oh my God," I mutter, walking away from him. Men are too much; brothers are even worse.

Hollilyn's been listening to our interchange, and she laughs. "Your family is so weird." Yeah, well, she wants to join it. I hug her and tell her I've got to get to coaching, hoping the subject of my *lacking* sex life is dropped.

+ + +

I hold practice and then head to Dolores's Diner.

43

L.B. Dunbar

She isn't our competition, I scream in my head at Denton. I hate that I'm thinking of him, but I can't seem to stop.

Do you touch yourself? He might as well have asked outright.

No, I don't. Okay. I don't. I just feel weird, and I also haven't been interested in…anything…until about three months ago. I suppress any urges, but with Denton's question, I'm a ball of fire, ready to implode. I want to be touched by somebody. It might have to be myself. Cora swears by the inner goddess.

I shake my head and will myself to think of something else, returning to Denton's competition accusation. Growing up next to us, the Chances were like honorary Harrington siblings. In return, we loved their grandmother, Magnolia. Her farm is about twenty minutes outside of town off Scenic Drive and thinking of her reminds me I owe her a visit. I try to see her every other week. She's always been good to me. On the other hand, I can't say I feel the same about Caroline, Denton's mother, but I do my best when I visit. My mama taught me to be respectful.

Denton's father, Kip Chance, was valued as the mayor of Blue Ridge, but that didn't mean he was esteemed by the community, especially our family who knew the truth of his behavior toward his wife and children. When he died of alcohol poisoning, no one was sad, although people attended his funeral—out of respect. Ironically, the man who wanted to keep alcohol out of our town died from too much of it. Shortly after his death, Billy opened the pub. The brewery was already functioning on the outer edge of town and a constant bone of contention for Mayor Chance.

Dolores eventually inherited the diner from her grandmother, who'd named it after her mama, Dolores. Originally, Magnolia saw the need for a coffee shop when people stopped on the scenic rail trip up the mountain. She also wanted a place to sell the McIntyre legacy: fried chicken and egg salad sandwiches. The farm kept the town fed in times of trouble, according to city lore, with their apple orchards and fields of miscellaneous vegetables. With hopes to pass her diner down to her daughter, it skipped a generation when Caroline's sights settled on a desire for higher society. Unfortunately, she went down a rabbit hole with her marriage to Kip Chance. Kip used the long-standing history of the McIntyre family as a stepping stone to be a socialite of the city, which isn't saying much as downtown Blue Ridge is only three blocks long.

Dolores, the granddaughter, however, follows in her grandmother's footsteps. She's a sharp woman, who's worked hard the past twenty plus years. She isn't an only child, but you'd think she is from Denton's absence. I like her, and for a while there, I thought she'd be my sister-in-law after sneaking around with James so often. We get along, although I wouldn't trust her with all my secrets. *Remember*, she knows everything as the owner of the town diner. Still, Thursday night's special is her famous chicken salad, and I love chicken salad, as well as I love to *not* cook for myself. It's a ritual for me to go to the diner on Thursdays. When Chris first passed, I needed the structure. Some habits dwindled. Some stuck. This one sticks.

Until I enter Dolores's Diner as I always do after practice and find Denton Chance—in the flesh—sitting at the counter. Twenty-seven years later, and I know it's him by the slouch of his shoulders and the curve of his back as he sits at the counter. That back I held as we slept as kids, but he's not a child any longer.

Ever want to make a U-turn on life?

This is me as the bell over the door, signaling someone's entrance seems to continue to peal in my head, and he slowly turns in my direction. One look at his eyes—inky black, like midnight over the ridges of the mountains—confirms who he is. His hair is cropped short with the addition of salt-and-pepper. His jaw holds stubble like it's been professionally applied, and he's tan—California tan—for September.

Sexy silver fox. He defines the phrase.

And my brain disconnects. I don't move forward.

"California," I mutter, and I search the wall for a map that does not hang there. That's where he ran after high school graduation. He got out of this town faster than you can blink, and never, ever looked back. He dumped his best friend and me.

I stare around the diner, bewildered.

Georgia. A map visualizes in my head, and I mentally count as if I'm passing highway signs. My fingers tick off the number of states in between the West Coast and here. Then another thought occurs. He never mentioned anything to me. Social media. He didn't say he was coming. He didn't even hint at it.

My brows pinch as his deep eyes focus on mine. His mouth crooks upward at one corner, and butterflies take flight in my belly so fast I nearly vomit them out on the tile floor.

Instead, I make another move.

That U-turn I mentioned—I pivot immediately. I don't run to him as my body twitches to do. I don't say hello. I turn in a semicircle and walk away, just like he did.

10
Your Turn

[Denton]

"Well, that went well," Dolores mocks from behind the Formica countertop. My back remained to her as I spun on the stool the second Mati entered the diner. I'd like to say I had a sixth sense about her presence despite all these years, but I didn't. The low whistle and *oh shit* of my sister told me Mati had arrived. She'd previously warned me Mati was a regular—every Thursday evening. A volleyball coach, I remember her telling me. I chuckle at the thought. She loved the sport and was darn good at it. She went all-conference, hoping to take her team to State until she broke her ankle. Scholarship revoked. She intended to go to Georgia State anyway. Heard she dropped out when she was pregnant.

I sigh with the memories and spin to face my sister again. I can't shake the image of Mati. She's even more gorgeous in person. Pretty, freckle-faced Mati with hair the color of a brilliant fall-turned tree and eyes a deep bark brown, looks the same, only...gorgeous. Without even being near me, the scent of pomegranate filters through my nose, like a distance memory. Her hair is longer than when we were teens. Her body is curvier but her face not so round. I recall the outline of her shape— solid, athletic, strong—and my fingers tingle as if it were yesterday and not twenty-seven years ago. The Mati I remember was fierce. The woman I just saw looked like she'd seen a ghost.

"That was horrible," I mutter, picking up my coffee mug and taking another dreg. The stuff is better than I remember. I stare at my sister. Two years older than me with blue-black hair, it's obviously a dye job. However, the darker color does nothing for her age. She's forty-seven, with excellent bone structure in her face, but the crow's feet around her eyes give away her age. We don't look much like siblings. She just told me to call her Lores. I think it has to do with the motorcycle man in her life, but I haven't pried too much. I'm not changing her name.

47

L.B. Dunbar

"Did you see how she looked at me?"

"She looked shell-shocked."

"She looked like she was going to get sick."

"Who you talkin' about? Mati?" A pretty blonde asks as she rounds the counter, her stomach protruding, arriving a few seconds before her. She's due soon from the looks of it.

"Hollilyn, this is my brother Denton. He went to school with Mati." The blonde stops behind the counter, her brow shooting up.

"Well, wasn't she lucky?" She winks at me, and I'd be certain she was flirting if it wasn't for the pregnant belly.

"Hollilyn *dates* Mati's son, Jax." Dolores rolls her eyes at the explanation. Is that what the kids call it nowadays when they're pregnant out of wedlock? The scowl on Hollilyn's face tells me she doesn't care for the explanation.

"Don't mind Mati. That look on her face is only temporary. When Jax told her about this…" She rubs her stomach. "…she had the same expression. Then she broke into tears." Hollilyn smiles. Dolores rolls her eyes again.

"I'm sure they were tears of bliss," Dolores mutters. I'm sensing there's a story here.

"Anyway, Mati's bark is worse than her bite," Hollilyn adds as if I don't have a history with the woman. I remember the girl who held me in her arms on her twin bed, rubbing over my head and kissing the bruises, soothing me like the child I was. She took her *bite* to her parents, who couldn't help me. Who would believe the mayor would do such a thing to his child?

"Denton?" Dolores questions, seeing I'm lost in my head.

"It doesn't matter. I'm not here for her. I'm here for Mom." I haven't even been to the house yet. Dolores knows it will be difficult to go back. I took a room at Conrad Lodge a few miles away.

"She's at Magnolia's." This is news to me.

"Why isn't she at the house?"

Dolores stares at me like I have two heads.

"The house was given to the state after Dad died. The new mayor lives there as the house was dubbed the 'mayor's house' by the state. Anyway, I think Charlie wanted to be close to his parents."

"Charlie?" I question.

"Charlie Harrington, mayor of the city."

I blink, holding my coffee mid-air. When did little Charlie become the mayor?

"My God, Denton, do you listen to anything I tell you?" Dolores's blue eyes open wide.

I do, it's just…I never let it stick in my head.

"When did he become mayor?" I ask, ignoring my sister's tone.

"It's a long story. He's in his third term, I think. His daughter is ten, and he plans to run for state representative."

Whoa. He has a daughter? And I never knew he aspired to be a politician. A little rich coming from a kid whose family ran an illegal brewery for most of their history. Then again, I never knew Chris would be a lawyer. Recalling Mati's face, I wonder if I remember anything correctly.

"Seems like I'm missing a lot around here."

"We're boring," Hollilyn replies as she returns from serving customers. She dismissively waves a hand before entering the kitchen. The diner is just what you'd expect in a small town. Exposure to the kitchen through a hot window, large coffeepots on a back counter, and an old-fashioned sitting counter with stools. Booths line the opposite wall in the rectangular space. This place is our history, at least on my mother's side.

"You know Giant runs the brewery now, and Billy manages the pub. Charlie is the mayor like I mentioned, and James, well, he left the family. That should bring you up to date."

I stare at my sister catching me up on the Harringtons in lightning speed. She always had a crush on James Harrington. He had a dark soul but loved hard, or so Dolores told me.

"What happened to James?"

Dolores glares at me, slowly shaking her head. "I'm reminding you, only so you don't make a fool of yourself. His son died. And, so did

Giant's wife, so don't be asking foolish questions of the family no longer living." Her hand rests on her hip as she admonishes me, and my heart sinks a little. The Harrington boys were like brothers, and it appears I've missed some of their sorrows. Something I'm not familiar with creeps under my skin. Guilt, perhaps.

"Jesus. I'm sorry," I mutter, as my sister continues to shake her head and turn away from me for an order. I'm not looking forward to heading back to Conrad Lodge, but I can't face my mother yet. Instead, I decide to hang out in the diner a little longer, really taking in the atmosphere. I notice the old beech-colored paneling, the cheap checkered tile, and a crack in one of the stools.

"You need to fix this place up," I mumble, to which hot coffee covers my fingers wrapped around my mug.

"Oops, sorry. Must be my dilapidated diner distracting me," Dolores snarks.

"I'm just saying, the place could use a pick-me-up." My eyes narrow at a wall of images. *Is that me?* I slowly rise, magnetically pulled to the photos, taking in a memorial of my years with our cousins. Images include Kit—wild-haired and singing her heart out on stage. Newspaper clippings of Tommy and me. Printouts of web stories. Framed concert tickets.

"You came to see us?" I turn to my sister. She didn't tell me, or I don't remember. It was nearly twenty years ago.

"You played Atlanta. A few of us went."

I nod, staring back at the tickets. "Who?" I ask, my heart racing.

"It was a girls' weekend. Gosh, I don't know. Probably Mati, Evie, Rachel, myself…" Her voice fades in my head. There's only one name I'm focused on. Mati. Mati saw me perform. I wonder what she thought of me on stage. I never knew they were there, but then something trickles through my memory.

"There's a group of girls here to see you," security tells me.

"When aren't there women?" Tommy snorts in our dressing room.

I dismiss them because I was married to Kristy.

"I'm sorry," I mutter to the reflection of my sister in the glass protecting the tickets.

"For insulting the diner?" She sighs. "Forget about it."

"For…everything." Dolores's eyes widen and then she pats me on the shoulder, without much affection for an older sister.

"Don't worry about it. You're here now."

I am, but I'm not staying. Ghosts are all around me.

11

A Team Sport

[Mati]

The girls' home opener is on Friday. It's been twenty-four hours since I saw Denton, but the town is abuzz with his return.

Kent at Duncan Hardware. "Did you hear Denton Chance is back?" *Yes, I did.*

Hetty at the flower shop. "Denton Chance is back. Have you seen him? Mmm…mmm…mmm." *Yes, I have.*

Shannon at Tom's Grocery. "Denton Chance is back. Weren't you two friends?" *Yes, we were.*

We aren't now though and haven't been for twenty-seven years. The thought makes me a little sad. What surprises me is I'm even sadder he's stopped all Facebook communication. I checked messages after our awkward moment at the diner, thinking he might make some smart-ass comment about my behavior, but the chat remains blank after his last post.

I've upset you. I'm sorry.

I've read those words a million times, interpreted them a hundred ways, adding innuendo that most likely doesn't exist.

"I know it's upsetting, but I think it's better if you don't go with me."

"Why?" I can still hear the whine in my voice, the desperate plea to understand.

"I've just decided to take the trip alone."

"But we promised we'd go together. A road trip to celebrate graduation. Cross country and back before college." This was the plan. Chris couldn't go because he didn't have the money. He didn't live on the Lane, like Denton and me. I offered to pay his way, but he didn't like that option. In fact, we fought over it. He wanted to take care of me and

didn't want me using my daddy's money to pay for his portion of the trip.

"I'm not going to college." Denton's declaration surprised me.

"Since when?" His face. I remember his expression. Blank. *"You never intended to go, did you?"* My voice dropped, a strange sensation settling over me.

"I've got to get out of here, Mati. You of all people know that."

"But I don't understand. Why didn't you tell me? Why don't you want me with you?"

"I'm sorry. I just need to go alone."

He couldn't look at me as he tore my heart out over a trip I'd been looking forward to for almost a year. The moment the idea sparked, I ran with it—planning, plotting, mapping. We were going to see the country by backroads, and I couldn't wait. My parents approved because it was Denton. They trusted him to take care of me. Three months of freedom before college. I didn't understand. The day after high school graduation he was gone, without me.

+ + +

I stand in the same high school he ran away from and coach my first game of the season. It's an exciting night, as I have high hopes for my girls. Admittedly, I might get a tad animated in my coaching, yelling out errors, and coaching encouragement to self-correct their positions. My setter has a shot at all-conference as does my libero. She's small like I was but digs deep for the ball. Hannah Cassidy reminds me so much of myself. I want this to be a good year for her, and the University of Georgia has been scouting her. So have a few schools in California. They're a long shot, but not impossible.

We win the game in two sets and I'm riding the high of a great start to our season. The girls take down the equipment as family and friends linger. The younger crowd will head out for a party. The older will end up at Blue Ridge Microbrewery and Pub. Some will drift to the true *bar*—bar—Ridge's Edge—at the end of town. It's more for locals, old men, and a few bikers. I'm looking forward to a celebratory drink or two when

53

L.B. Dunbar

I look up and find Denton among the crowd. Feeling propelled toward him, I take the steps to close the distance. My heart races as if I'm seeing him for the first time despite the familiarity of our surrounding. Perhaps it's the familiarity that accelerates my heart. We've stood in this gym a hundred times before, but this moment seems so much more meaningful.

"Hey," he greets me, and I almost giggle from nerves and the irony of the word. How very Californian.

"What are you doing here?" I'm skipping the formalities. Denton looks around the gym and then glances up at the banners hanging near the ceiling. His brows pinch and I'm certain he's reading his name. And Chris's. He shrugs and returns his attention to me.

"Heard there was a game. This is the *it* place to be tonight."

In small towns, we take our sports seriously. In this town, we take the winning sports most seriously, and I'm the winningest coach in the past eighteen years. Still, it makes no sense for this man, who ran from here faster than Dolores can make a milkshake, to be standing before me.

"We won," I say, and my face heats as I've stated the obvious.

"I noticed," he replies, his lip crooking like it did when he saw me at the diner. I suddenly feel ten feet too small compared to his six-two stature, and a million times the hillbilly I am. The other thing striking me and twisting my tongue is his voice. I haven't heard his voice in twenty-seven years, and it's not what I remember. Smooth. Edgy. Rockstar. His voice alone could melt panties, and I bet it did over the years. Of course, now I'm thinking about his mouth on panties, and his voice whispering things in places hidden on a woman, and I'm blushing even deeper.

Good Lord, I'm a mess. If I didn't know better, I'd think I was having a hot flash.

"Anyway, I wanted to see you," he says, and those butterflies in my belly—they explode. The teenager inside me erupts as well.

"You did?" I sound as awkward as I feel.

"The letter, remember?"

"Oh, right." My head nods. "Yeah, I don't have it with me." Of course, I don't, and I'm wishing the gym floor would swallow me whole at this point. I'm perspiring just from speaking to him.

Second Chance

"No worries." He looks down at his feet, and if we were standing outside, I expect he'd kick the dirt like he used to do as a kid.

"I also heard you've been visiting Magnolia, and I wanted to thank you." His grandmother. Dolores and Denton weren't allowed to call her grandma. It made her feel old.

"Oh, that. Well, you know how much I love her." I do love her. She's the grandmother I never had as my father's parents died when I was still young, and my mother's lived in southern Georgia until they each passed.

"I remember." Again, his voice is rich and rolls over the -r sound like I imagine his tongue might caress something, like an ice cream cone…or a woman.

Heat, again. I'm too warm. He's too close. He looks so good, as good as I remember, but even better. I'm so flustered by his nearness.

I don't know what to say next and he's staring at me, like he's waiting for me to answer him. Did he ask me a question? Thankfully, I'm saved by one of the girls.

"Coach, we're all cleaned up." In the time I've stood and stared at Denton, the girls have put away the equipment and the gym has thinned out. I take in the emptiness, and I nod at Hannah.

"Thanks, girls. Stay out of trouble." I blanket the statement to all the girls. I don't ride them hard on behavior because I give them respect. I understand they're teenagers, but I also reinforce how serious I am about the season. No funny business.

"Such a hard-ass," Denton says, and a snarky comment rests on my tongue. *Wouldn't you like to know?* "So, BPMP. You'll be there next?"

He's implying the pub.

"Yeah. I need to finish up a few things with Alyce, and then I'm heading out."

Denton stands before me, hands in his jean pockets, and tips up on his toes. For a moment, we're sixteen again. He's come down from the stands to congratulate me and we're making plans for an after-party somewhere.

"First drink's on me," he says, and I swallow a sudden lump in my throat. He used to say that all the time, and we'd laugh as most alcohol

55

L.B. Dunbar

at parties was free or stolen from his daddy. I don't have a response, so I give him a nod. How Californian of me, and I've never been there.

"I'll see ya there."

Denton nods back, and I've just experienced the most awkward moment of my life. Turning for the coaches' office long before he exits the gym, my heart races as I will myself not to look back at him.

"*Who* was that?" my assistant coach Alyce Wright blurts. She's nearly foaming at the mouth as she speaks. With short, subtle waves in her light blonde hair and big blue eyes, her disposition is more like a cheerleader than a volleyball coach. Thankfully, she has a competitive spirit, despite her perkiness, as the school insists I have an assistant. She's also an English teacher here and a few years younger than me.

"Who?" I ask, my heart still pattering so hard I throw myself into a chair in the coaches' office. We share this space with every other girls' team and the girls' PE teacher. It's really nothing more than a walk-in closet where I put my purse and jacket during practice.

"That…that gorgeous hunk of sex on a stick." Alyce speaks like she's never seen a man before. She's also not from Blue Ridge originally, so she doesn't know all our history. I don't even have to consider who she means.

"His name is Denton Chance. I went to high school with him." It's a bit evasive, and rather trite compared to the long-standing relationship with him.

"He looks like a rockstar."

"He was," I mumble and brace the armrests, waiting for Alyce's response.

"He what?!" A shriek-screech combination reminds me again of a cheerleader.

"He was in a band called Chrome Teardrops." Alyce falls in a chair opposite me. Her legs collapse as she clasps her hands against her chest.

"You're kidding, right?"

"I wish I was." Based on her reaction and the excitement of Denton's return whispered throughout town, I wish I was kidding. There is so much enthusiasm for his success and his return. Everyone is proud of him, and the behavior irks me.

56

"I'd totally do him. Think he'd do me?" My head had fallen against the hard back of the office furniture, but it tilts upward, my eyes widening at Alyce's brazen suggestion.

Is she joking? This is a side of her I've never seen.

"I'm pretty sure he'd do anyone, so you've probably got a shot." A gruff comment. It's not meant to insult her but to insinuate Denton is promiscuous. Realistically, I have no idea how willingly he does women. He might have a girlfriend. He might even be married, although I did check his relationship status on Facebook which said: single. But I've heard men lie about their status all the time on social media in hopes to lure in women. At least, that's what Hollilyn tells me. However, I don't think Denton needs to taunt anyone for attention. I also realize I'm instantly jealous of Alyce's willingness to *do him* as well as her eagerness to have him *do her*. My head falls back again. I don't know why I care. *I don't care*, I mentally tell the ceiling. "He'll be at the pub."

I don't have to look over at Alyce to know she's jumped up in excitement. I sense her enthusiasm, plus the little clapping she does. *Two. Four. Six. Eight. Who do we want to fornicate? Go Denton.*

"What are we waiting for? Let's go." Alyce smacks the outside of my leg and steps around me. I wish I shared her enthusiasm, but I just don't. I don't know what I feel, but after our awkward exchange on the gym floor, I'm certain I'd rather be mauled by a bear than face him.

"I think I'll head home." My heart sinks with the suggestion. I don't want to go home. I look forward to spending time with others, especially at the pub, where I'm the center of attention. I'm not trying to be vain, but it helps suppress the knowledge I'll eventually go home—alone.

"Oh no, girlfriend." Alyce sucks in a huge breath and I wonder when she started speaking like a teenager. "We go together. Wingman and all. Or wing woman, I guess, but that just sounds weird. Never mind. Team sport. I'm ready to set. You need to attack."

Now, she's using volleyball terms as euphemisms.

"What are you talking about?"

"I saw him talking to you, Mati. It's time. It's time to serve."

What the hell?

"Ace. Point. Match."

L.B. Dunbar

"Alyce?" *What the...*

"You need sex, Mati. Time to get back out there. Spike the ball."

"I'm not doing anything to the ball," I admonish, sitting forward to glare up at my overeager, sex-encouraging friend. And then I'm suddenly thinking things I shouldn't, like the young adults I coach, and I'm wondering about something Denton said.

There's no such thing as too big.

12

Waiting Games

[Denton]

After being in the old high school gym, memories flood my mind of Chris and me. We were all-star athletes—basketball was our game and the gymnasium was like a second home to me. I recall one night in particular, just the two of us after practice, still dribbling, still taking shots. We were waiting on my dad for a ride. I knew he'd be late.

"What do you think of Mati?"

"What do you mean what do I think?" The three of us had been best friends for years, much to her parents' dismay. Then again, I'd definitely started to notice the change in Mati's physique, and looking at her caused stirrings in my jeans I shouldn't be having about one of our best friends. There was also the incident in her room which we didn't speak of. Mati and I both ignored it as if it didn't happen. So I lied when I said, *"I don't think anything of her other than her being one of my best friends."*

"What do you think if I ask her out?"

"Where you going?" I ask—dense for a moment—before reality set in. Oh, he meant *out-out.*

"I thought I'd take her to dinner." He paused, his eye on the hoop as he shot, but his concentration was off. *"It's been hard with my mom. I just find it easy to talk to Mati."*

Shit, I remember thinking. *He wasn't playing some guilt-card. He really had been upset lately about his mother's breast cancer diagnosis and I understood all too well how good Mati was at comforting people.*

"I like when she holds my hand."

Shit. Shit.

"Have you kissed her?" I asked, trying to remain calm and still the shaking in my arms. I took another shot at the basket, but the ball wasn't even close.

"No, but I'd like to. Think that's a bad thing?"

Yes! *"No, but why Mati?"*

"Have you seen her lately? She's hot, but it's always been more than that. She's my friend first. One of my best friends."

I totally understood what he was saying, but still—Mati with Chris?

"Think she'd go out with me? Just the two of us?"

"Didn't you already go to the movies?" I snap, still a little bitter they went out a few weeks before without me.

"Yeah, but that just happened." He stops bouncing the ball, tucking it under his arm, and looks over at me. *"I want your permission."*

This stumps me. "Why?"

"Because it's always been the three of us, and I never want to lose either one of you. I just...I just feel this pull to be with her as more than a friend." He looks away, his cheeks reddening. *"Does any of this even make sense?"*

Chris had older parents, so speaking about his feelings wasn't something he was comfortable discussing with them. Any sex information we needed, we got from the Harrington brothers. Of course, that was a little too weird considering Chris might be using the moves we learned on their sister. Then again, I'd done the same thing...and it backfired.

"Yeah, I get it. Go out with her," I said, swallowing the lump in my throat. *"Just don't turn into some sap writing love songs about her and going all kissy face in front of me."* I started kissing the back of my hand, mocking them while remembering my own lips on Mati. I didn't want to think of them kissing each other but I didn't know what to say. I couldn't tell him I'd already kissed her, unless she said something, which I didn't think she had. She'd been as tight-lipped as me about it, pretending it didn't happen, which was further proof to me she wasn't interested in me like I was in her.

"I think I'll leave the love song stuff to you." He laughed, tossing the ball at me while I was still kissing the back of my hand. He'd recently learned my secret passion—playing the guitar.

"Yeah," I teased. *"I'll use the two of you as my inspiration."*

I sit up straighter in my seat. How prophetic that moment had been. The love I lost—and had to witness between them—became the basis of many love songs Tommy and I wrote together.

+ + +

The Blue Ridge Microbrewery and Pub wasn't here when I left, and it's quite a nod to the modern world compared to some of the other buildings still standing on Main Street. An old two-story storefront, I can't even remember what was in the original place. The walls have been stripped down to the brick and the hardwood floor finished in a dark brown. Neon signs here and there project some color into the dimness. Music and chatter fill the place packed with people.

I'm sitting at the bar, replaying my conversation with Mati in my head.

Could it have been any more uncomfortable?

The letter. I tried to cover for myself when I told her outright I wanted to see her. I shake my head as I lift the house beer to my lips. It's a fall brew, pub special, and it's good. Much better than the piss whiskey I drank a few nights ago over Chris's grave.

I'm swallowing down a mouthful when I'm slapped on the back. People sure do want to touch me in this town. I've been hugged by every old lady, given sympathy and prayers for my mother, and patted on the back by all the men who remember my father as the mayor. I cringe with each reference to him. I've also been approached a few times by teens and adults old enough to remember Chrome Teardrops although we were popular more than a decade ago.

As I turn to see who has smacked me, a hand cups the back of my neck.

"Where you been, fucker?" I'm astonished to see Charlie Harrington, the new mayor of Blue Ridge. He looks nothing like I remember, and yet his eyes are one-hundred percent Harrington. Soft brown, like bark on an old tree. He tightly smiles, like he's practiced the move more than once in his life. His hair grays at the temple and I chuckle with a thought. We've all grown older, only my memory holds us back.

"Is that how the local politician speaks to his constituents?" I scoff.

"Considering you aren't a local, I'll speak to you any way I like." He's teasing me as he takes a seat on the stool to my left. A warm hand still holds my neck, and I twist as much as I can to see a giant of a man standing next to me.

George Harrington the Second, nicknamed Giant as a kid, stands up to his name. He's huge. Solid shoulders, dark messy hair and a bushy beard with specks of gray in it. His eyes are all Harrington as well but they're harder, guarded, and I remember what Dolores told me. He lost his wife some time ago. His thick hand holds my neck a moment longer, before giving it a squeeze and releasing me. The force pushes me forward a bit, and for a second, I feel like we're kids again.

Giant is six years older than Mati, which seemed like a lifetime when we were children. He was in the military when we graduated from high school.

"Welcome back," he mutters, his voice deeper than I remember, and somber, like the weight of the world sits on those broad shoulders.

"Thanks," I mutter as he leans against the bar to my right. Anyone else surrounded by two Harringtons might be a little intimidated. I know I am as I've been sitting here having dirty thoughts of their little sister, who isn't little anymore.

Holy shit. Mati is all woman, curving like the backroads I took to get here. Her breasts are still large, and her hips round out to match, but her waist dips inward. She's an hourglass and I want to tell time by her. I take another gulp of beer as a distraction from my thoughts and the semi in my jeans. Sweat trickles down the back of my neck as if the two brothers know what I've been imagining.

"When did you get in?" Giant asks, taking a pull of his beer as if he doesn't really care for an answer, just making small talk. I hate small talk.

"Two nights ago. It was late, or rather, early in the morning." I'd slept like the dead—no pun intended—when I got to the Conrad Lodge.

In fact, I'd woken up shortly before I went to the diner to see my sister and have dinner.

"I heard about your mama. We're real sorry in Blue Ridge, Denton. She was a respected figure of this community." If it had been any other person than Charlie who spoke, I might have laughed in his face. Respected? She was a joke. She let her husband smack her, belittle her, and cheat on her. For what purpose? She didn't love him. She could have left him. But Charlie has a role to play. He's the current mayor and he needs to honor his predecessor, even if he didn't agree with his marital practices.

"Thanks, Charlie. I appreciate that." I inhale, calming my nerves at the mere mention of my mother.

As if I weren't already bookended by Harringtons, Billy walks the length of the bar and stops behind it in front of me.

"Holy shit. I wondered when you'd come in here. Heard you were back," Billy jokes. He's got a twinkle to his eye, akin to his brother Charlie, but he looks nothing like either of his brothers. Streaks of silver fill his hair while his thick scruff remains jet black. I bet he dyes it.

"This place is amazing, Billy. Congratulations." From the modern, rustic interior to the pulsing crowd, this place is no match for the diner. While I called it competition, it's nothing close. This place is in a totally different stratosphere than the rundown greasy spoon my sister owns.

"Yeah, well, about time you show your pretty face, man. How long has it been?"

Mati's words ring in my head. "Twenty-seven years." Saying the number out loud sounds like a long time, *too long*.

Billy lets out a low whistle. "Lot's happened since you've been gone."

I nod in reply, knowing there is so much he's suggesting as he leans forward to rest his elbows on the solid wood bar top.

"Gonna stick around a bit?" Giant asks. His eyes shift sideways to me, but his face remains forward toward the wall of televisions and beer taps behind his brother.

My first thought is the truth—*nope*—but I hesitate. "Been considering it."

63

"Don't be making promises you don't intend to keep," Charlie offers.

Oh boy, here it is. The road trip.

"And don't be going after something that could have been yours, but you tossed aside." With his insinuation, my head rolls to Billy. *What the fuck?*

"And don't be listening to either one of them," Giant adds under his breath with a deep chuckle.

"Good to have you back," Charlie jokes, tapping the edge of my tallboy with his and then taking a long pull of his beer. They might be teasing me, but there's something underneath their comments. A brother warning of *don't hurt Mati again.*

"Where's James?" I cringe the second I ask, recalling Dolores's cryptic comments about him.

"He's doing his own thing now," Giant offers of his younger brother, and Charlie lowers his head. I don't understand their expressions, but a judge's gavel just sentenced this conversation to life in prison.

"Oh, fuck." Billy immediately lowers behind the bar, slithering down the interior, and disappearing from view. Charlie and I both lean forward, looking over the wooden counter, as Giant lets out a deep breath beside me.

Charlie and I return to our stools and swivel in time to see an angry woman walking into the bar, and she's furrowing a straight line through the crowd for me.

"What's Billy's beef with her?" I ask, knowing before I finish asking what might have happened.

"Tapped that one too many times," Giant offers behind me, and I nod. I totally understand.

Kristy Moseley is my ex-wife, stalker extraordinaire, and a thorough pain in my ass. With her in high school—tapping that one too many times as Charlie just said of his brother—we were hardly high school sweethearts. More like the Bickersons. We had a constant love-hate relationship, leading to hate sex, and long spells of not talking to one another. When I cut Mati from the road trip across the country,

64

Kristy decided to hop in instead. I thought she'd be a good distraction from what happened with Mati.

Then she got pregnant.

I married her as the band started, but when she miscarried, we fell apart. Not because of a lost baby, but because we were lost souls in a city that welcomes them. Kristy wanted the fame of a rockstar husband but didn't want the reality of it, which included long stretches without one another. There were months of disconnect between my life on the road and hers in an unforgiving city. We were a statistic like other young couples at the birth of a band. Our divorce was inevitable.

I'd heard she came home eventually.

"Well, well, well. The prodigal star returns." Kristy saunters up to me in her heeled boots and skinny jeans. She hasn't aged well, and I feel a little sorry for her. Bleach-blonde hair fried on the ends from product overuse. Skin tight from too much sun—possibly fake. Thick false eyelashes and a touch too much makeup on her lids. She looks like a woman trying too hard, which reminds me of her as a teenager.

"Kristy," I mutter, wondering how Billy's doing behind the bar.

"And what does Blue Ridge owe the pleasure of the infamous rockstar's return?"

"My mother's dying," I blurt, harsh and quick. As much as I mean to hurt Kristy, a shooting pain stabs back at me.

Kristy's hard face softens as much as it can under her thick foundation, and she offers subtle grace with her sympathy. "I'm sorry. I'd heard."

In a small town, gossip could never remain quiet. The former mayor's widowed wife dying would be news.

However, Kristy's sympathy passes rapidly. "You're looking good, Denton," she says, and I want to hide behind the bar with Billy as she steps forward. *I will never tap that again.* Kristy has no boundaries, though, and her hand comes to rest on my T-shirt, inside my jacket. She slips it down my chest, heading for my waist, as her eyes close. A quiet tiger *rawr* escapes and I shiver, knowing her thoughts. This is her signature move, hinting at what she wants. How did I ever find this woman attractive?

L.B. Dunbar

A little cheer goes up near the door and my head lifts to see Mati walking in with her assistant coach. Our eyes meet instantly, but hers quickly turn away. A tight smile forms on her lips as she greets someone, probably congratulating her on her win.

As I stare, I realize Kristy still stands before me, her fingers hooked into the waistband of my jeans.

"What the fuck are you doing?" I mumble under my breath, directing my irritation at my ex-wife. She tugs, and I stumble toward her, placing my hands on her shoulders to steady myself.

"I'm actually looking for Billy."

"Billy?" I repeat, my voice rising a bit.

"We haven't seen him yet tonight," Charlie offers. Giant's presence fills the space behind me as if he's blocking something happening at my back—aka, his brother hiding behind the bar.

Kristy glances between us. "You're protecting him."

"How could I protect him? I haven't seen him," I say, offering the protection I refuted.

"You were always one of them." Her eyes narrow and I have no idea what she's talking about. I gently press her back from me, but she still has her fingers over my belt. My hand lowers to hers, prying her grip from me.

"Nice seeing you again," I say, acting as if I'm shaking her hand, a casual acquaintance instead of my ex-wife. Kristy doesn't shake back but pushes my palm off hers.

She turns to Charlie. "You tell Billy I'm looking for him." Then she spins on her too-high heels and stumbles. I can't help the curl to my lips and I hear Giant stifle a chuckle behind me. Charlie's the only one gentleman enough to reach forward and assist her. As Kristy rights herself, she walks toward a corner with a pool table, and Charlie twists back to the bar.

"In what polar universe does that woman think I take orders from her?" He lifts his glass and drains his beer.

Billy raises up from his haunches, only the top of his head peeking up from behind the wood counter. "Is the coast clear?"

Second Chance

"Only if you're on the West Coast, buddy." I chuckle at the reference. Thank God Kristy left California.

Remaining in his crouched position, Billy squat walks to the end of the bar and ducks behind a swinging door, which I'm assuming leads to a kitchen.

"She's right about one thing. You could have been one of us." Giant taps the edge of my glass with his. I glare up at him, not understanding his meaning, but the sentiment turns back toward the door. I scan the crowd as fast as I can, and then double back, my eyes racing over people's faces.

"She left," Charlie says, not even spinning in my direction, but knowing who I'm looking for.

"When?"

"When you had your hands on your ex-wife."

"Damn it," I curse loudly, reaching for my wallet to cover my tab.

"Don't worry about it," Charlie offers, setting his fingers around the bottom of my mug and sliding it toward him. "Might I suggest you chase *her*. For once."

I'd like to argue with Charlie—how I did chase Mati, how I kissed her, and she didn't reciprocate. Then she married our best friend, having babies with him.

My mouth actually opens, preparing to spill this history, when Giant speaks. "The stopwatch started, man."

Fuck them and their cryptic innuendos. I push through the crowd, pressing out the door into a chilly early fall mountain evening in hopes I won't have to run too far.

67

13

Between Cars

[Mati]

Cars can park in the angled spots along Main Street, but on a night like tonight, everywhere is full. So, I'm parked in the public parking lot, a gravel strip across the alley behind the pub. It's the location where we might have to host the Oktoberfest, but I'm not thinking of the event as I power walk around the side of the pub and cross the alley. I'm steaming with reckless energy from seeing Kristy and Denton together.

Why was he touching her?

Is he happy to see her?

Will he sleep with her?

A rush of emotion fills my being and my body thrums with irritation. It's all reminiscent of the first time I saw them *together* together. The image was scarring at best and heartbreaking at worst. I walked up on them at a field party. Denton's ass exposed to the air, his dick disappearing inside her. One of her legs over his hip, her skirt hiked up to her waist. Her breath hitched as he pounded into her, her back against the side of a pickup truck. She struggled to say his name in her false cries of passion. Fake because I can't imagine anyone ever muttering in a high-pitched squeal like her. Rutting pigs came to mind. I hoped it hurt his ears at the time.

I can be childish.

The image instantly returns, and I curse the memory. We fought about who knows what that night, and then he disappeared. I went in search of him because I was either still fuming or wanting to apologize. I can't remember the circumstances other than what I saw. Everything else was obliterated from my brain.

I wished I was her. The thought sneaks in like the hiss of a snake. A devil angel on one shoulder reminding me I was jealous. Jealous he'd been with her. Jealous she was with him. Jealous they were having sex.

Chris and I hadn't yet, and we wouldn't until after Denton left. I remained a virgin until after high school, unlike most of my friends. However, it wasn't long after graduation when the deed happened.

I don't want to think about that. I'm still riled from what I saw inside the pub. So riled, I hardly hear the crunch of gravel behind me before a hand grips above my elbow. I turn, right hook aiming for a body when it's stopped by a quicker hand.

"Settle down, lion cat."

"Don't call me that," I snap. Denton's mouth curls at my sharp retort and it fuels my anger. I struggle against the hold he has on my elbow and my fist. Instantly, my back hits a pickup truck and Denton's body hovers over mine, holding me in place.

"Easy," he whispers while I huff and puff into his chest, my own rising and falling and scraping over his abs. He's hard, rock hard in the midsection and I immediately wonder if he has a six-pack. The thought that he might makes me want to punch him again. *Goddamn him* for looking so good, smelling so good—sharp and manly—and feeling so good against me.

His hand releases my fist and lifts for my cheek. My head tips up and I swallow.

Will he kiss me?

Of course, he won't kiss me.

It would be silly of him to kiss me.

Do I want him to kiss me?

His thumb rubs over my lower lip and I part them, my tongue sweeping out to brush against the salty pad at the end of his fingertip.

I want him to kiss me.

"Mati," he whispers, his warm breath fanning down on me in the cool evening air. His nose lowers, the tip tickling over mine before he skims it to the edge of my mouth. I still, holding my breath, while my heart races within my chest.

"What's got you so worked up?" The twitch in his mouth whispers near the corner of mine. He's close but not where I want him to be. He's also teasing me. He knows why I'm upset, and I realize I have no right to be. Denton Chance isn't mine and never was. He was hers.

L.B. Dunbar

I don't respond to his question, willing my blood to settle.

"Don't be jealous." He smirks, and the curl of his mouth tickles mine. A shivering sensation ripples down over my skin, slinking over my body and straight to one part thumping faster than my heart.

"I'm not jealous," I say, but I don't recognize my own voice. Hoarse, scratchy, throaty. I'm so turned on by his nose stroking over my cheek and the tip of his lips nudging close but not quite to the edge of mine.

"Good. You shouldn't be." His fingers have left my face and slide down my neck, curling around the side. His thumb swipes up and down my throat and I feel the power in his hands.

Kiss me, my brain screams. I want to be the girl he pinned to the side of a pickup truck, wretched up, and slammed into. The heat between my thighs increases and dampness pools. He'd have no trouble entering me. I'm primed and ready. My eyes close with the thought.

"How long's it been, lion cat?" The question whispers over my lips and I swallow, knowing it's been too long since I've been kissed.

"Open," he demands, voice sharp, and my lids spring wide as my face heats. *What was I thinking?*

"You see me, Mati?" I do see him. His dark eyes peering down at me, deep as midnight over the ridges behind him. His face no more than an inch from mine and the prickle of his scruff teases me. His tongue peeks out and strokes over the lower of his lips. His mouth—his luscious looking, swollen mouth. *God dammit.* The throb ratchets up the beat to achy desire. "Do you see *me?*"

I don't know what he's asking. *Yes, I see him,* and I don't understand why he's not kissing me.

The thumb against my throat tightens—not in a threat—but more like possession. He could own me. I'd sell my soul to him, if he'd kiss me.

"Yes," I squeak, again not recognizing the smoky hush in my voice.

"I see you, too, Spice. Only you." I don't know why he's given me a new nickname, but I like it. I want to be spice. I want to be all kinds of spicy with him.

"What do you see?" My breath, now wheezing faster, mingles with his. His eyes roam my face, his thumb pressing under my chin, forcing me to hold his stare. He lowers his head and I pause, thinking his mouth will meet mine, but he slips to the right and skims my neck. His nose leads, tracing the vein exposed to him. If he were Edward Cullen, I'd be screaming for him to bite me. Instead, I will his teeth to take a nip. Just one nibble. It'd push me over the edge. I'm so wired, willing, wet, I could come from his closeness.

But he pulls back.

What? Nooooo...

His hand slips from my throat, and he releases my hip, which I didn't realize he held. He blinks and turns his face toward the pub.

"Need a ride home?" he asks, completely breaking the spell. His eyes return to me as if he wants me to read them—read him—and I can't. It's been so long since I've seen him, I don't know what he wants me to see. I no longer know the man before me.

"I drove here." I point in the general direction to my left although I hardly know my name let alone where I parked my black 4x4 truck.

He nods, and I ask the obligatory, "Where are you?"

He points to a white beast reflecting under the single light illuminating the gravel lot. It's got a dark strip down the hood and looks expensive.

"Rental," I scoff.

"Mine." He pauses. "I took a road trip to get here."

My heart drops. *A road trip.* I don't know how to respond.

"Want to ride?"

I shake my head at the invitation. The mood dies within me. I'm suddenly bone tired. The win. The upset. The rejection.

"Maybe some other time," I offer, slipping my hands in my jacket pockets. He nods and steps back, allowing me to press away from the pickup at my back.

"I'll wait," he offers. Does he mean he'll wait for a ride? He'll wait for me? "Your car…" His head tilts and I realize he'll wait until I find my truck. *I'm a fool.* He'll also wait until I enter it and drive off. That's when it hits me.

L.B. Dunbar

He wanted to go for a ride…

14

Road Trips

[Denton]

Road trips were what we did. Or rather, a ride was our thing.

When Mati no longer allowed me to stay in her bed, the night we fought over her reason—Kristy—she didn't stay away long.

Another night.

Another fist.

I stole my father's car to get away.

Pushing it down the drive, the tires crunched over the gravel. I got halfway down the path when Mati came out of nowhere.

"What are you doing?" she whispered, her voice still too loud in the silence of the mountain night.

"I'm going for a ride." I kept pushing, willing the tires to quiet but knowing the request was unreasonable. Fortunately, my dad was passed out and would not hear a sound anyway.

"Where?"

"Anywhere but here," I snapped, my voice terse, my muscles tense from pressing at the car.

"I'm going with you."

"Why?" I stopped, standing to my full height. I didn't need her sympathy any longer. She'd made herself clear and clarity settled deeper when she started officially dating Chris.

"Because...because..." She paused, licking her lips and looking back at my house—the Southern columned structure a symbol of status, and yet haunted within. Because you love me, my heart cried. "Because we can pretend we're running away."

Pretend.

"Fine," I huffed. "Get in and hold the steering wheel steady."

My anger released the more the car moved toward the Lane, the dirt strip joining three ancient homes—the Harringtons', ours, and the

Conrads'. Mati climbed to the passenger's side allowing me to hop in the driver's seat. I turned to her, preparing to tell her I didn't need her, but when I looked over at her, she smiled. A genuine smile like I hadn't seen in a long while from her. Her face lit up and I compared her to a dog, the ones eager to just ride in the car, wind on their face, not a care in the world. She wasn't a pup, though. She was beautiful, and I wanted to capture the sensation, capture her.

Instead, I turned the key, and the engine purred to life, breaking the silence of midnight and off we went. No destination in place. Just took a ride.

+ + +

My body still hums from the near kiss with Mati. I should have taken her against the truck like my body begged me. But I want Mati to recognize me. I want her to know it's me kissing her, not a ghost, wish fulfillment, or a replacement. I need her to see me.

The next day, I'm thinking of her and the first ride we took as I follow the road to my grandmother's house. I'm finally on my way to see my mother. Twenty minutes along the woods around Blue Ridge and a dirt drive pulls me back to my roots. Dolores and Shamus McIntyre, our great-grandparents, owned this farm. Their daughter, Magnolia McIntyre married Edwin Duncan and moved to town where she opened her diner, named after her mother. When Edwin died after a fall from a ladder, Magnolia returned to the farm for her parents' help raising her girls. Her daughters rebelled against farm life and married men who would carry them away.

My mother, Caroline, didn't get any farther than town, up to three full blocks from the original train stop and a strip of shops, including said diner. She climbed out of her farm girl background after she met Kip Chance at a community dance in Elton, a town at the base of our ridge. Love at first sight, she'd tease, keeping up the pretense of my father being a romantic man. Her sister, Rosalyn, married a preacher, Reverend Thomas Lawson Carrigan, a man travelling through the town, who stopped at the diner for a cup of coffee. He took her as far as Texas before settling down when the first of two kids came along.

Both children ran away from them.

I ran away from here.

Running seems to be a family trait.

I exhale as the dust whirls around my car. The precious beast will need a bath after this drive. I pull up to the rough patch of trampled dirt before the house and park. Everything looks...dilapidated. The large gray, clapboard sided home looks dirty with equally unclean white shutters, missing here and there. One window is boarded over. The sprawling front porch sags as do the front steps looking like they might collapse under the weight of another foot. A faded red barn in the background slants. It's picturesque if not a bit sad. Suddenly, I wish I had my camera which I left in my room at the Lodge. I don't take stills but sometimes, something in nature will take my breath, and I just want to capture the moment as best I can. Surprisingly, the farm setting feels this way to me, and I want to keep the moment. I've let too many moments pass.

Another memory comes to me of sitting in this driveway looking up at the house.

"You gonna be all right?" I asked as we sat in Magnolia's driveway. Chris stared at my grandmother's home.

"Yeah," he said weakly. It had been a rough week. We buried his mother. When it came to parents, Chris got the short end of the stick. Not in the love category. They loved him something wicked, but they had been older when they had their miracle child. His mother was diagnosed with breast cancer, but it was his father passing away from a heart condition in his sophomore year that surprised us all. His momma seemed to give up after losing the love of her life and passed at the end of our junior year. He wouldn't be eighteen until the end of the summer and he needed a place to live. Magnolia took him in.

"She's gonna love you, man," I teased, pushing at his shoulder. My grandmother already did love him like another grandson, probably a better one than me. I'd been using her home to practice the guitar, often

bringing Chris as my excuse to my dad. Chris would sit and chat with her while I played in a room upstairs.

"You know I love you, man." *His voice was sad, though he tried to add humor. Underneath the joking, there was a hint of truth. I was like the brother he never had, and he was the same to me. I trusted him with my secrets—the guitar, my dad's abuse, and my need to run away.* "I'll owe you forever for this."

"Quit being a sap," *I joked, but I appreciated the words.* "You won't owe me anything." *He might have been one of the only people to say he loved me in my youth. That would mean everything to me.*

"You've already given me everything I'll ever need." *His voice turns serious and I feel that old lump cutting off my airway. He's done this before—thanking me for letting him date Mati and keeping the friendship strong between the three of us.* "She's everything to me and she's all I have now."

I want to remind him he has me, too, so he doesn't need the doomsday attitude, but he knows the truth. I'm not sticking around this town. The second I get the chance, I'm leaving.

"You've got a golden ticket out of here," *he told me once. He had faith in me like no other. Not my father who hated my singing or my mother who didn't know my plan. Mati might have believed in me, but I didn't share my dream with her. It wasn't that I didn't trust her, it's just that Chris understood this secret better. He wasn't trying to talk me out of anything or ask me to change my goal. He wanted me to run with it and run I did.*

Finally, I exit the car.

"Who's there?" Magnolia bellows through the double screen door.

"Magnolia? It's Denton." One door swings open, and a little woman I hardly recognize as my grandmother crosses onto the porch. Her small frame looks like it's folded, and she walks with a cane, a tap, tap, tapping as she covers the wooden planks of the covered porch.

"Denton? I once had a grandson named Denton. He disappeared about thirty years ago." Her scratchy, shaky voice withers as she speaks. I can't see her eyes behind her pop-bottle sized lenses to know if she's teasing me. Somehow, I don't think she is.

"It's only been twenty-seven," I offer weakly.

"Twenty-seven? Well, that was practically yesterday then." She snorts. I'm not forgiven but she isn't angry. I step up to the stairs and she watches me like a hawk with those magnified eyeglasses.

"You look just like him," she mumbles, and I stop. I don't want to look anything like *him*. "You're crossing that grass with enough swagger to make a rockstar jealous."

"I was a rockstar," I mutter.

"I remember." She stuns me as I step up to the decking and stare down at her small stature.

"Well, don't just stand there. Hug me." I might break her if I embrace her, but I reach out and wrap my arms around her bony shoulders.

"Hmm...you smell like him, too." I pull back abruptly, noting she patronizingly pats my back.

"I don't smell like him." *He* smelled like whiskey and sweat.

"He smelled full of shit. And your excuse for staying gone for so long stinks like it, too."

"I haven't given an excuse," I mutter, but her hearing is clearly still sharp.

"Exactly," she responds. We stand in silence other than the crickets humming in the yard. Then it hits me. She means the fact I *don't* have one. I don't have a reason why I never called or came to visit her. While my father might have been an excuse to stay away, he wasn't a reason to skip a phone call.

"Well, get in there. It's gonna be rough." She throws out the words like we're going to work the fields around her house. Her once thriving farm isn't working any longer, and I suspect a realtor is just waiting to gobble up the property. Someone got their hands on a portion near town and turned it into a subdivision.

I hold the door for Magnolia and follow her inside. The moment steals my breath. It's as if I've entered a time warp. The place looks the same, sort of. Floral furniture fades to almost no flowers in the pattern. Worn wood floors attest to years of footprints. Browning wallpaper curls near ancient wood molding. Floor-to-ceiling windows brighten corners.

Surprisingly, the place smells lemony, and I wonder if the cleanliness comes from my sister.

Magnolia points up the staircase and I realize she can't make the journey. Last I remember, her room was on the first floor beside the kitchen.

"We would have put her in the parlor, but she wanted to be in her room. Says she can see the mountaintops from up there."

I climb the staircase, the creaking beneath my feet making me leery I might break one. Each crackle sends a prickle over my skin. My mother's room is at the end of the hall and I continue to feel like I'm being sucked into a vortex. A window before me threatens to pull me into another dimension. I reach her door and knock.

"Come in," a weak voice invites me. I enter and freeze at the picture before me. With the curtains pulled, the thick blanket, and the frail woman under it, death fills the room.

"Kip?"

The call of my father's name nearly brings me to my knees. She thinks I'm him.

"Mother. It's Denton." I stop a few feet from the bed, afraid to come closer, afraid as if she's contagious. It's cancer. I can't catch it, but I'm frightened and my skin tingles. She's so pale. Her hair greasy and slicked back from her head. Her blue eyes are dull like the room, and she squints.

"Calvin?" Her fingers twitch on the coverlet, inching their way to the edge of the mattress. I assume she intends to reach for me and I step forward, curling my hand over her pencil-thin fingers. She's cold, her skin like tissue paper, illuminating the blue in her veins on the back of her hand.

"Denton," I repeat. Is she delusional? Medicated? I don't know what to say or do next. *How are you?* is not something you ask the dying, so I kneel next to the bed and stare at her. Her eyes close, her breathing labors.

"It's been a long time." I expect her to call me *son*. I haven't heard the label in years. Has she forgotten me? Memories haunt me.

Get your ass over here, son.

Don't you give me that look, son.

I'll kick your ass from here to Texas, son.

My father meant everything he said. He did it for years. Then one day, I pushed back.

You'll pay for that, son.

I did. He went after her next. My head lowers to her hand, my forehead resting on her cold skin. Suddenly, I realize how warm I am. Her touch feels pleasant, like a mother's touch soothing a feverish child.

"I'm sorry, Mama." I don't know what to say to her, how to comfort her. I could give her a million excuses. The endless tours. The award shows. The band breakup. My modeling. My photography. None of it seems relevant. None of it will bring back the years.

"You came back," she whispers in her raspy, quiet voice. "I always knew you'd come back."

I came back, I repeat, but I don't know what to think of being here.

79

15

Massage Therapy

[Mati]

Doing yardwork over the weekend, I hurt my back. Pulling weeds. Churning mulch. Raking leaves. It's a process in the early fall of the mountains, and something I enjoy doing for the outdoor exertion, but it wreaks havoc on my body. I try to stay physically fit with volleyball coaching and all. I can't encourage the girls to keep in shape if I don't, but yardwork can be my downfall, especially with the gusto I used to yank, pull, and prod in my frustration over Denton. So, I call Hollilyn.

A little-known secret about Hollilyn Abernathy—she wanted to be a massage therapist.

"I like making people feel good," she once told me, although this might have been more information than I needed. She even went to school for it but didn't have the funds to continue the classes. Her dream had been to open a shop here in Blue Ridge, but we don't have the population for a large clientele. She would have to go to another city—a bigger one—with an actual spa, but she stayed here instead. A select few know of her skill, and she comes when you call. Thank goodness.

The trouble is, her belly is getting larger, being roughly two months out from having my first grandbaby. I'm excited, but sometimes it makes me sad to think Chris will miss the birth. He loved babies, and he talked about being a grandfather although I was nowhere near ready for this next phase in our lives. Jax got Hollilyn pregnant after Chris's death, obviously, and I worry he sought solace in Hollilyn but didn't mean to make it a long-term relationship. Fatherhood is forever, and Jax knows better than to leave this baby. Still, I worry about his commitment to the mother. Some days I feel sorry for her instead of my own son. I don't want him leading her on, but I also don't have evidence he is.

"Let them be," my son Jordan says of his twin. "Not everyone is marriage material." Jordan married his Maggie soon after he graduated college. Hollilyn's pregnancy has been bittersweet for Maggie as she's been wanting—and trying—for a child, whereas Hollilyn got knocked up on the first night. Again, too much information.

When Hollilyn arrives, she tells me to lay on the floor, on my stomach. She says she'll just kneel next to me. I feel bad having her get down to my level, but I don't know what else to do, and the knot in my back is tight. As she begins to work her magic, I'm slipping into the comfort of her deep-rubbing fingers and the silence of the room. However, I knew it wouldn't last long.

"So, who's the man from the other night?"

I want to play it off, but there's no doubt I made a small scene pushing my way through the crowd to escape the pub. I try anyway. "What man?"

"The one at the diner." It only takes a second to remember my turnabout when I entered and saw Denton the first time. "You look like you'd seen a ghost."

"In many ways, I had," I mutter into the circular pillow holding my face mere inches from the floor.

"He asked quite a bit about you and the Harringtons after you left."

I could ask Hollilyn how she heard, but the diner knows everything, and she works there.

"He lived next door to us as a kid."

"Ah, the boy next door." Her voice singsongs like she knows something I don't. I remain quiet. "Jax told me about him."

My head pulls up, forcing my back to curl, and a pinch radiates down my spine. I ignore the pain. "How does Jax know anything about Denton?"

"Said he was his dad's best friend. Actually, all three of you were best friends. He said his dad told him they were both in love with you, but the luckier man won you over."

Well, stick me with a hot poker and turn me over. My breath catches in my throat, and I choke as I speak. "What?"

"Jax told me one bit of advice his daddy once told him was treat women with respect but disrespect everything else if you want her bad enough."

L.B. Dunbar

Strange bit of advice coming from Chris who followed the rules to a T, including holding out to have sex with me until we graduated high school and I turned eighteen. Then asking me to marry him the second I was pregnant, wanting to do right by me. He went to my father and apologized, but also begged my daddy for my hand. I don't think Daddy would have told Chris no.

I'm still contemplating what Hollilyn has told me when she continues.

"Heard he left town shortly after you graduated high school. Followed his dream to be a rockstar. That's what Dolores says. But Jax thinks Chris asked Denton to leave."

"Why would he think that?" I'm completely flabbergasted by my son's opinionated accusation.

"I can't remember exactly." Hollilyn pauses and my body tenses, wanting to know more. It can't be true. Chris would never ask Denton to go. He loved him like the brother he never had. Their bond was strong. Not to mention, the three of us had plans—go to college together, and then we'd raise our families near one another. Chris felt just as betrayed as I did when Denton left. *Didn't he?*

The question rattles in my brain as Hollilyn hits a sore spot. She works at the tense muscles along my spine at the moment, and my thoughts wander back to the night after Denton disappeared.

"Why would he do this? Why did he tell me I couldn't go?"

"Maybe he didn't want some chick cramping his style on the open road."

I stared at Chris, disbelieving what he'd said.

"I'm not some chick. I'm one of his best friends."

"You're right. You aren't some chick to him. Maybe that's why he didn't want you to go."

"What does that mean?"

I'd been in my room all day, crying my eyes out over a lost road trip and my disappeared friend. Chris looked away from me, speaking to my bedroom window.

"It means…I just think Denton needed to go out on his own. Pursue his dream. Alone."

82

Did Denton think I'd be in the way? He toyed with the idea of starting a rock band with his cousin Tommy, but I never thought he'd do it. We were going to college. His daddy insisted on it. I still didn't understand. Denton could have told me anything. I would have supported his decision. Hell, I would have gone with him.

"He seemed pretty interested in you," Hollilyn speaks, and I practically feel the weight of her thoughts.

"Just spit it out," I snap, knowing she wants to add something.

"He asked if you were dating anyone." Another pause. "You know, Mati, I don't think anyone would say anything if you did go out. On a date."

I rock my head against the circular cushion. It isn't that I don't want to date. It's that I don't know how or what or who. I don't know that I have it in me, and yet I know I can't keep being alone. I'm lonely.

"I don't care what others think," I mutter, snarky but muffled by the cushion. It's not *really* true. I don't want to be judged when Chris was practically a hero to this town. Good husband. Best father. Fair lawyer. My worth is not wrapped up in Chris's achievements, but I also don't know how to measure myself without him.

I'm saved from responding further to Hollilyn when a knock comes to the front door. It's Sunday evening, and I'm not expecting anyone. My kids have keys as do their significant others and my parents. I want Hollilyn to ignore it, but she presses upward.

"I'll just see who it is." I feel guilty taking advantage of a pregnant woman, but I'm lying on the living room floor wearing only my underwear, a sheet over my lower half, and a body that feels like mush.

The door opens. I hear muffled words. The door shuts. Hollilyn quietly waddles back to me, and warm fingers dig into my back. The pressure is deeper than she gave a moment ago. The pads of her fingertips feeling thicker, firmer, almost callused. I groan under the touch.

"I'll just let myself out." Hollilyn's voice projects from across the room, and I lift my head, swiveling it to see her putting on an overlarge sweater. I twist, clutching the sheet to my chest to find Denton on his knees next to me.

16

Coaching

[Denton]

I don't know what I'm doing here, but after spending two days with my mother I needed to get out of the house. And I couldn't be alone. Once the blonde from the diner let me in, I stared from the front entrance at Mati on the living room floor. My eyes flicked between Mati and the blonde, brows pinching in question.

What the fuck have I walked in on?

The very-pregnant girl shakes her head with a sly smile as if reading my dirty thoughts. I'm not opposed to girl-on-girl action or two-girls-on-me, but I don't want to consider Mati in this position. Plus, isn't this girl pregnant from her son?

"Go get her," she whispers, leaning toward me as if telling me a secret. I slip off my boots and walk as quietly as I can toward Mati's body on the floor. I look back at Hollilyn—was that her name?—and she nods, her hand lifting with fingers flicking forward for encouragement.

I've given massages before. In fact, this might be one of my specialties after dating a masseuse for a short bit, years and years ago. Suddenly, I'm perspiring. I stare down at Mati's bare back and discover she has a freckle near the base of her spine. My fingers shake as I spread them, hovering an inch above her pale skin. I lower as if being forced, and instantly the tips of my fingers prickle with pleasure.

I'm touching her.

I'm stroking down her spine.

I'm feeling the vibration of her heart through her shallow breaths.

"I'll just see myself out." Hollilyn breaks the connection with her voice and Mati's head shoots upward. Instantly, she clutches the sheet to her chest, narrowly covering her large breasts, and glares at me.

"Denton," she breathes and I imagine her saying my name as I climb over her, connecting with her, filling her. I'm hardening in my jeans as I crouch on the floor and my imagination goes into overdrive with all I want to do to her. Missionary style. From behind. Ankles on my shoulders. Any position. All of them.

"Hey," I choke, her eyes nailing me in place. My fingers rest on her skin as if I can't remove them.

"What are you doing here?" She tugs the sheet higher, but it does nothing to disguise what I know lays underneath. She's still curvy, voluptuous even, in the breast category.

"I wanted to see you." The truth spills forth before I can stop it.

"What for?" she asks harshly, and I'd be taken aback if I didn't know this was classic Mati. Suspicious.

"What was going on here?" I redirect instead, pinching lightly at her back skin. Mati sighs.

"I hurt my back while raking leaves. Hollilyn is the town masseuse, so to speak. She's used to me pulling it. I'm getting old."

"Damn, here I thought I walked in on some girl-on-girl action. Kinky but strange with your son's girlfriend." I chuckle. "And you aren't old, Mati."

"Girl-on-girl," she says slowly before twisting in a way her back remains to me, but her elbows rise to hold her off the floor. "My God, Denton. You're incorrigible." There's judgment in her tone, but then she laughs. "I don't get it alone, let alone with a girl, and I'd prefer a man, thank you very much."

Her words startle me and run straight to my zipper region. Sound check. Did I hear her correctly? She wants a man.

My fingers return their attention to her back, working at the lower muscles.

"You don't need to do that. I should get dressed." She wrestles with the sheet, tugging it upward and bending her knees as if to stand.

"Let me take care of you." My fingers continue to rub, not letting her shuffling fluster me nor stop my attention. I don't know if I can remove my hands even if she begs me. It's as if they have a will of their own—*keep touching her.*

Her knees collapse, and she lowers her upper half back to the floor. "That does feel good," she admits quietly. My lips curl, and I continue pressing into the knot I feel on her lower right side. I massage in silence, letting my fingers speak.

Let me take care of you.

Let me make you feel good.

Let me keep touching you.

Eventually, Mati purrs from the attention, and I shift. My knees are cramping in the position I'm in anyway, not to mention the angle isn't centered. I slip a leg between her thighs. Mati stills.

"I'm at a better advantage like this."

Mati snorts, and I realize too late the innuendo in my statement. However, her dirty mind triggers mine, and I slip my knee higher. Mati's thighs separate, allowing for the broad curl of my leg. I'm an inch away from an area I imagine needs some extra attention. Then I notice her hips shift. I kneel forward, adjusting my knee to add pressure against her center. Mati's hands fist.

"How long's it been, Mati?"

"I don't know what you mean." Her eyes pop open. She moved the circular cushion out of her way and rests her head on its side against the floor. She isn't looking at me, but her eye shifts in my direction.

"Since you've had sex." I pause, rethinking. "Do you touch yourself?"

She chuckles sarcastically. "Denton, do you have any shame?"

"There's no shame in touching yourself, Mati. Is that how you get relief?" My voice lowers, the rubbing of her muscles turning more to strokes down her skin. My knee pushes forward, nudging her center to press back. She shivers. Her head gives a single shake.

"You don't touch yourself?" I tease, my voice drawing lower at the possibility.

"I don't...I don't know how." I startle at her confession but even more at her honesty. She's telling me she doesn't pleasure herself and it takes all my strength not to rip the sheet from her body and relieve her myself.

"Let me teach you," I whisper, leaning forward near her ear.

"You can't," she says, her face pinking. "This is so embarrassing. Why are we discussing this?"

I ignore her and kneel upward, reaching for a bolster pillow on the couch. The circular curve of the pillow will be perfect for what she needs.

My knee still balances against her core, but I'm sensing she won't get off on me. Instead, I remove my leg and set the pillow in its place.

"Get up on your knees." The demand comes out rough, my throat tightening at the thought of her on all fours and what I'd do to her on her knees, but this needs to be about Mati.

"What?" She swallows but does what I ask. Compliant Mati. Some things don't change. I push some of the excess sheet upward as Mati follows my lead and tugs the material forward. Her calves are exposed, along with her back. The sheet only covers her ass and her breasts. She looks practically Grecian in her attire and I want to be the gladiator to conquer her.

I slip the pillow into the space between her thighs, and gently push at her lower back, forcing her to lower on it.

"Ride the pillow," I command, watching as Mati keeps her forehead pinned to the floor. Her elbows bend for support.

"I can't do this with you watching," she mutters, her head rolling side to side.

"It's me, Mati. You can do this." I don't know why I encourage her, why I offer such torture as being a witness to this, but the need to be near her overwhelms me. "I'll leave everything to you. I'll just be the coach."

I straddle her spread calves, mine resting on either side of hers. I'm careful not to let my hard-on tap her ass but I'm so close—too close—and I ache to press the seam of my zipper against the thin sheet covering her. One hand on the floor holds me balanced over her, while the other reaches for her hip and presses downward. Then tugs up. Down. Up. I use her hip to form a rhythm, causing her to rock against the cylinder pillow.

"Oh, God," she mutters, her body slowly giving into the beat. Down. Up. I follow along, still using all my strength not to touch her with my straining dick. Mati's picking up the pace a little, but she whimpers.

"It isn't enough."

87

"Touch yourself." My voice growls. "Slip your fingers into the sheet. I can't see anything."

She needs to be aware I can't visually see what she's doing to herself, although I know every detail. I feel her movements, and my dick senses her warm presence. Her fingers fumble into the sheet, and the edge of her breast is exposed. Side-boob. A sexy treat. My mouth waters for a nipple, but I refrain, keeping my concentration on driving her into the pillow, increasing the friction with the touch of her fingers.

She hesitates, and the pause almost sends me to the moon. I imagine her first touch. The shock at the soft skin. The wonder at the wetness. The sensation of pleasure.

My God, I need to have a first touch myself.

Her confidence building, her rocking motion proves she does what I ask.

"Are you wet, Mati?" My voice roughens as does my force on her hip.

"Oh God, this is so wrong."

"Not wrong, Mati. Feels good, doesn't it? Just feel."

"So good," she mutters, her hips no longer needing my direction. She's rocking on her knees, humping the pillow and I risk the nerve to look down at her thrusting hips. Her motions set me too close to the edge. I need to be the one.

I pull the pillow from between her thighs and slide my bent knee underneath her instead. She lets out a cry of protest but doesn't stop her movements. My arm curls forward, wrapping around her waist. Her hand remains buried within the sheet while the other toys with the edge up top, attempting to hold it over her breasts. She's failing. One is almost begging to be released. Only her nipple remains covered.

"Keep stroking," I mutter, tugging her upward from the waist. I shift her until she straddles my thick thigh. Her back hits my chest, and my legs burn with the strain of kneeling as do my knees on her hard floor, but I'll suffer the pain. I feel her fingers pinned between my thigh and her heat. I roll my hips forward. She pushes back to meet me.

A dance. This is what we do. This is what we were once good at. This is us.

17

Dancing Around the Issues

[Mati]

The next couple of days pass in a blur. I work. I coach. And I try my damnedest to forget what happened with Denton. I blamed him moments afterward, but days later, I fault myself. What we did—what he *coached* me to do—was nothing like I'd done before. I didn't lie when I said I didn't get myself off. I don't. I always had Chris. We took care of one another. It wasn't always mutual—sometimes one or the other of us had it better—but we kept our needs between *us*. That was our marriage.

My ass in the air, humping a pillow, touching myself while Denton guided me from behind—was on a whole different level.

And I liked it.

When I shouldn't.

Because I felt guilty over what we'd done. What I did.

Yet, I played the scene on repeat in my head, and I even attempted the actions again as best I could nights later. Surprisingly, it wasn't quite the same without Denton, his voice in my ear, his hands on my skin, and this puzzled me.

I shouldn't be attracted to him so instantly after twenty-seven years. It was like I was a fourteen-year-old once again, filled with pent-up frustration regarding him.

"Penny for your thoughts," Billy calls from his desk as I enter his office to grab my purse. The waitstaff has a small area to hang their jackets and lock up personal belongings near the kitchen, but I have a locker in Billy's office. Perks of being his sister.

"They aren't worth that much," I sigh, closing the locker with more force than necessary.

"Sit," he commands, his forehead furrowing as he looks at me. I fold into a chair before his desk. His office isn't imposing, and the chair rests to the side, against a wall but still opposite him. "What's going on?"

L.B. Dunbar

I shrug, feeling the weight of my older brother's eyes. Of all my brothers, Billy is the one I'm closest to even though Charlie comes right above me in birth order. Billy and I are similar in that we both married our high school sweethearts. We fell hard for *the one* and loved even harder. Billy's loss wasn't quite like mine, in that he and Rachel divorced, but it didn't hurt any less for him. The difference is Billy almost immediately started banging women, while I've been a hermit toward anything sexual.

When I don't respond, Billy speaks again. "Seen Denton?"

"No," I offer too quickly, too loudly. "Why would you ask?" Defensive doesn't begin to describe my tone, or maybe it's guilt mingling in my question.

"He was here last Friday. We saw him chase after you after the whole Kristy thing."

"He did not," I singsong, and a thought occurs. "What was she doing here anyway?" I hadn't asked Denton yet about his ex-wife. When I heard they married, my heart ached, but I was deep in my own fresh marriage, preparing for the birth of twins. I didn't have time to ponder Denton's decision. He'd made his bed. He must have loved her. After all, he took her with him on the road trip and left me behind.

"She was looking for me."

My brows rise. "Why?"

The silence falling between us answers my question.

"*Nooo*. Billy, how could you?"

"I was horny." His honesty makes me laugh, and his fingers comb through his hair, forcing it to stand up a little. I'm not blind, so I recognize my brother's a good-looking man with the silver streaks in his hair and darker scruff on his jaw, but good lord, he needs to keep his dick in his pants sometimes.

Pot meet kettle? I think. Not quite apples to apples, I decide. "That's not an excuse."

His eyes narrow at me like he's trying to read something in my expression or tell me something. We're close but haven't ever mastered telepathy, so he's forced to speak.

"It's as good an excuse as any. You should try it."

"Sleeping with Kristy." I snort, knowing something like that will never be on my radar. *Thought there was a little girl-on-girl action happening here.* Denton's words make me shiver.

"Not that, silly. Letting loose your horny."

My mouth falls open. "Billy, I know it's difficult to remember sometimes, but I am your sister. I don't need to hear these things."

"And I don't need to know details about you either, but I know you're lonely. And it's human nature to have needs." His eyes narrow further if even possible as he glares at me with a knowing look. "Sometimes those needs belong with someone other than yourself. Do you get what I'm saying?"

I laugh. "Is this like an adult version of sex ed? Are you about to tell me how the birds and the bees work because I already know those things. Two boys, remember?" Motherhood should make it obvious I've had sex before.

"Listen, smart-ass, I'm trying not to spell it out in graphic detail with charts and diagrams but take it from a guy who has been where you are...alone...you can't have sex with just yourself."

"Why are we having this conversation?" I exhale.

"Because Denton is back."

If my brother Billy had smacked me upside the head, I'd be less confused.

"What does that have to do with anything?"

"That man is still the boy who loved you."

My mouth falls open. "He is *not*." I sound like a teenager, whining and all. "He doesn't even know me. We aren't the kids we used to be."

"Look, I'm not suggesting you need to fall in love again. Look at me." He taps his chest with both hands and spreads his arms wide like he's the master of greatness. "But you're an adult, and so is he. I'm just saying, if something happens, it happens. You can give yourself permission."

My lips twist. I hear what he's saying, and I nod. I'm listening, but I don't know if I'm where he suggests.

L.B. Dunbar

"Okay, enough about your sex life. Let's talk Oktoberfest a second. If I find out that bitch running the bookstore is behind our *not* getting a permit for the party, I'm gonna have some head."

First, I'd like to point out *having head* is my brother's problem, but I don't wish to open the book again on his sexual history. Second, Billy has it in for Roxanne McAllister for some reason. Maybe because she's the only girl in town who hasn't given him head. I don't know, and I don't want to know, but what I do know is she filed a noise complaint against us the first year she opened, and Billy hasn't ever forgiven her for it. Our pub is on the corner of Main Street and Third, and BookEnds—her bookstore—is across Third to the side of us. The noise complaint was all a misunderstanding. Personally, I like her shop and I'd love to do a books and beer night, but Billy will have nothing to do with the idea.

"I don't think she's the issue. Besides, I thought we came up with a Plan C. The gravel lot."

Billy swipes through his hair again. "Yeah, but it's more behind the pub and people have to cross the alley. I just don't understand the hold up. What's Charlie's worth if he can't pull strings for us?" He's being rhetorical. It isn't up to our brother to give us the street permit. He works hard enough as it is to encourage tourism while trying to keep the locals happy.

"If that chick has cock blocked this event, I'm gonna—"

A knock raps at his open door and Billy pauses his thought. "Hey boss, there's a girl here to see you," the busboy announces. My brow rises in the direction of my brother. Always something. Or someone.

+ + +

Once I'm home, I start collecting ingredients to make cookies. The volleyball team has a bake sale planned for the next two days to help cut the cost of uniforms, tournaments, and travel. They won't raise much, but it makes the girls feel like they "worked" toward something. I volunteered to make cookies to show support. I have nothing else to do, and Hollilyn offered to help me when she heard I made this commitment. She arrives with an apron that says, "Bun in the oven."

"Cute, right? I got it at Pearl's." Pearl's is a local tourist shop with all kinds of kitchen knickknacks and novelty tchotchkes. I laugh as I touch her belly. She's been sensitive to people reaching out to rub her and I don't blame her, but she's allowed me. Maybe it's the maternal connection. I'm the mother of the man who got her pregnant. Hollilyn had a different kind of upbringing. Small row houses line the other side of the train tracks, the ones putting Blue Ridge on the map originally. Her father was the town drunk. Her mother a floozy. It's a wonder Hollilyn seems so good-natured, although a bit ditzy at times. She's definitely grown on me.

As we start organizing what we plan to make—a monster cookie which includes oatmeal, peanut butter, and chocolate candies—Hollilyn pops the air with a question I had hoped wouldn't get asked.

"So, how did the other night go?"

I stop measuring and set the cup down on the counter. "You know, I should be mad at you for letting him in here."

"Why?" She looks up at me, and the innocence on her face proves she doesn't believe that she did anything wrong.

"It's just…it wasn't an appropriate time."

Hollilyn nods as if she understands, but then she shakes her head. "When would be an appropriate time?"

The question holds weight. I don't know if I'd have let Denton in if he'd knocked on the door and I was the only one home. Then my sex pulses and I realize I'm kidding myself. If I had the foresight to know what we'd do, I'd have yanked the door off the hinges and tackled him to the hall floor. This is my mentality after my brother's pep talk.

Give yourself permission.

Something niggles at my memory of the other night, though. It's what Denton said: *I'll just be your coach.* If he's willing, he just might be the person I need. I'm comfortable enough with him because of our history and I don't run any risk of connection because he'll leave eventually. The thought saddens me, but I know the truth. Denton is here for his mother.

L.B. Dunbar

Caroline battles lung cancer—ironic as she never smoked—received secondhand from her husband, who had a nasty habit in private. Among other nastiness, the town was surprised she caught this of all diseases from her husband. For Denton and his mother's sakes, I hope they can reconcile some issues before she passes. Once she does—and the inevitable is coming—Denton will leave. He has no reason to stay.

"I don't know if I'm ready," I say as way of avoidance. My lack of dating isn't something I want to discuss with my son's pregnant girlfriend.

"Mati, you're more than ready." She exaggerates as she speaks while rolling her eyes to the ceiling as if looking for divine intervention into my readiness.

"What does that mean?"

"It means, a little sex might take the edge off."

"I'm not edgy," I snap, proving her point, and she chuckles. "I wouldn't know the first thing about dating anyway."

"Who's talking dating? That's foreplay. You need to get right to the good stuff." I stare at this girl, rubbing her belly, looking like she swallowed a watermelon, which gives testament to her skipping the foreplay with my son and heading straight to business. I shudder. I should not know these things about my children. But I laugh.

"Let's just get to making cookies."

"You're so boring," she teases, reaching for her phone and turning on some music, but there's something to what she said. I am boring, and I'm bored. I'm tired of moping around, filling my time by a pattern of places to eat and places to be, instead of living my life.

With the music blaring and Hollilyn singing off key, I'm pulled into the rhythm, feeling a weight lift off me as I silently admit some truth to myself. I'm ready to start living, not just *being*. I follow Hollilyn's lead and wiggle my hips as I measure out oatmeal.

"Oh," Hollilyn drags out. "There she goes," she encourages, clapping her hands over her head and deepening the shake of her hips. I sway as I dump lumps of peanut butter in the mix, and Hollilyn sashays toward me. She dances in front of me a moment and I follow her lead. Arms up while hers go down, arms down while hers go up. Ever dance with a pregnant woman? *Awkward.* Then she reaches for the bag of mini-candies and pours the entire package into the mixture.

I pick up the metal bowl and fold the dough, moving in pace with the melody of the music. I'm beating the thick mixture around and around until I feel something at my backside. Peering over my shoulder, Hollilyn is twerking on me, her bottom up and bouncing into mine. I only know this term from my volleyball girls.

"What the heck…" I giggle as she presses her ass more and more against mine.

"Come on, Mati. I see you got some rhythm. Let loose a little." She stops and reaches around me for the bowl, slamming it back on the kitchen island, and returning to her pose. The music pulses louder after she turns up the volume and then she is leaning back into me…with her backside.

"Go, Mati. Go, Mati. You got this. You want this." Hollilyn works her cheer to the rhythm of the song and while I'm laughing—a good belly laugh—I find myself giving into her encouragement. I want to be carefree and laugh a little and dance. I sway and rock and let my hips move in a way they haven't in a long, long time. I love to dance. I'm good at dancing. And Chris didn't know how.

For the first time in a year, I push away thoughts of him and will myself to follow the lead of the music. I'm sideways to the island with Hollilyn behind me and I'm rediscovering movement I haven't felt in forever. My knees bend. My hips bop. Left, right. Left, right when fingers come to my sides.

"Don't stop, Mati." A voice too deep to be Hollilyn's speaks behind my ear and my brain screams freeze, but the guide at my hips keeps me moving. Denton undulates behind me, and as I glance over my shoulder, Hollilyn twerks against him now, forcing him against me. I laugh louder, and the noise sounds so foreign in my kitchen. I haven't laughed like this since I don't know when. I haven't felt this carefree in so long. And I can't remember the last time I danced.

My face heats but I keep the beat, continuing to chuckle as Hollilyn sings off key. Denton holds my hips, bending his knee behind mine, and moving us as one, like we used to do.

L.B. Dunbar

While Chris didn't know how to dance, Denton did, and we loved to dance together.

"What the hell is going on here?"

Like the needle of an old-fashioned record player screeching over vinyl, my son Jax's voice fills the kitchen and the music abruptly stops. As does our dance party.

"Jax, baby, I didn't hear you come in," Hollilyn says, stepping up to him to defuse what is obviously a raised temper. Her hand at his chest does nothing to alleviate the rising and falling of his upper body or the glare aimed at Denton.

"We were just making cookies," I offer weakly as if I'd been caught with my hands in the jar before dinner. I'm hyperaware of Denton's hands still resting on my hips as he stands partially behind me. He removes his fingers as the pressure of Jax's laser beam eyes bores into them at my waist. Stepping forward, Denton offers a hand.

"I'm Denton Chance. I was a—"

"I know who you are," Jax snides, refusing to meet the hand offered to him.

"Jaxson," I shriek. Just who the hell does he think *he is* and who does he think raised him? *Shake the man's damn hand.* But Jax stays still, his breathing calming, while his fists remain clenched at his hips. Hollilyn tries to lean into him but I can see she might as well be pressed against the brick outside my house. Jax is not budging.

"Jaxson George Rathstone, what is wrong with you?" The full name snaps him to attention, and he unclenches his fingers and reaches forward. A forced, single pump handshake is all he offers.

"What's going on here?" he asks the second he releases Denton's hand and steps back to Hollilyn. He still doesn't respond to her touch and my heart breaks a little at the rejection he's giving his girl who is working hard to settle him. In fact, I'm *a lot* disappointed in his behavior.

"I said, we're making cookies—"

"Is that what the kids call it these days?" he snarks.

Let me pause here to say if my son wasn't twenty-six, I'd slap him and send him to his room.

"Excuse me?" He at least has the audacity to look ashamed a moment and turns his head as if I *did* strike him. "The girls have a bake sale the next few days and I volunteered to make cookies. Hollilyn offered to help."

"And him?" Jax nods his head at Denton, ignoring his presence by speaking in the third person. "Why's he grinding up against you?"

"Easy there, son," Denton warns, gritting his teeth while he speaks to my adult child acting like a toddler.

"I'm not your son," Jax snaps, and I'm appalled at the sharpness in his voice. "I know who you are. You were a terrible friend to my father." At this point, I don't know who my son is. His behavior is beyond me.

"Jax, that's enough. You aren't being fair."

"Fuck fair," Jax spats. Now, I'm growing angry.

"That's enough. Why don't you take Hollilyn home?" I suggest, knowing I'm not about to reprimand my son in front of someone he actually *doesn't* know. However, I'll be ripping into him later. Hollilyn turns to me, distress in her eyes as she mouths, *I'm sorry.*

I don't really know what she's sorry about. She didn't do anything. In fact, she's been like a few other females in my life—Cora and Alyce—encouraging me to go for it, whatever *it* may be. I'm grateful for her five minutes of dancing because, truthfully, it's been enlightening and fulfilling.

"And what about him?" Jax asks, like a petulant child, and in my typical motherly response, I reply, "You worry about you. Take Hollilyn home."

Without another glance at me, or a hug goodbye, my son storms out of the kitchen, tugging his pregnant girlfriend behind him.

I take a deep breath, letting out my embarrassment at my son's behavior.

"I'm so sorry about that," I say, lowering my head and rubbing at my forehead as I speak. "I don't know where any of that came from."

Denton steps forward, his body in my space and I'm forced to look up at him when his fingers press under my chin.

"He's just looking out for his mama. But you didn't do anything wrong, Mati."

L.B. Dunbar

"I know, but..." I don't know why I'm offering a *but*, but I suddenly feel guilty, and I don't even know what I feel guilty for. I take another deep breath and then slowly exhale, hoping to switch subjects. "What are you doing here?"

"Would you be mad if I said I just wanted a little time with you?"

Not mad. *Not mad at all.* My heart races for a new reason. Maybe it's the flutters in my belly. Maybe it's the memories in my head. My response takes too long, so I ask another question.

"How did you get in here?"

"The front door was unlocked. Probably not the safest idea." Hollilyn must have left it open when she entered but then again, I'm not always the best at keeping things locked up during the day. At night, if I could hermetically seal the house, I would.

Denton's still holding up my chin, and my eyes drift to his lips. As if he knows I'm looking at them, his tongue sneaks out, just the tip, and swipes across the bottom layer. A part of me moistens. My lower region pulses to the rhythm of the no-longer-beating music, and a vision of Denton and me dancing some twenty-seven years ago flashes before me.

Prom night. Slow dance. Too close.

My chest rises as if I'm racing and I'm certain he can feel my heartbeat against the weight of his forearm near my breast. I'm near heart attack proportion. I didn't realize I reached out for his waist or my fingers curled into his belt loop. I might have tugged him toward me.

"It's been a long few days with my mother, Mati. Let's go for a ride." His voice lowers, and like the call of a siren to a sailor, I'm on board for his request. I swallow down his song. The epiphany I had moments ago about living life sings back to me, and I realize living life needs a little spark to ignite it. And Denton Chance might be the one to light my fire—cliché like an old-time rock song—but appropriate for the man before me.

"Okay." I swallow back the word and his fingers skate from under my chin to my throat, cupping around it again. I like this move, and a ripple projects down my center to my essence. He stares down at me a moment and then his fingers release me. His hand lowers to mine, and without another word, he leads me out to his car.

100

18

Stolen Moments

[Denton]

Chris and I had been friends since as long as I could remember. Chris and me...and Mati. While the Harringtons were my neighbors, a house filled with boys, Mati was the one I fell in line with because of our schooling. She's also the one I fell in love with and I remember the exact moment...

A river edges the back of our properties on the Lane. A dock existed off the Harringtons' property as well as a tree fort near it. Little Mati Harrington wanted to be part of the boys' club which included Billy, Charlie, Chris and me. No girls allowed. We were holding one of our regular meetings which really involved cookies stolen from our kitchen, thanks to Etta my housekeeper, and playing handheld video games. Some days we fished. Some days we swam. That day was one of those days. Off went our clothes, down to our tighty-whiteys, and in we went to the frigid water. Mati hadn't been included again and while we whooped and hollered in the cold river, the sneaky devil stole our clothes and our precious video games.

My dad would be murderous if anything happened to mine, after I whined I needed it. We had the money, but it was the fact I wanted something other than for my birthday or a holiday. I went to Magnolia instead and she had me work her yard to earn the money. This pissed him off even more and he hit me on the side of my head with the device once he found me with it.

Don't be crawling to that woman as if I can't provide for my offspring.

The second I saw Mati taunting us from the edge of the river, dangling the whole stolen lot over the water's edge in a giant butterfly net, I went for her. Mati didn't scare easily, so even as I pressed up on

101

the dock, trapping her at the end, and cussing at her to give me our belongings, she didn't flinch.

She slipped.

Her flatfooted tennis shoes went off the decking and the momentum took her forward. She didn't let go of the net, holding it like it could save her, until Mati and all went in.

I didn't dive for Mati, I dove for the video game, but all was lost. The concept of soaking electronics in rice hadn't been predominant then, and I wanted to kill Mati, but I was more concerned my dad would kill me.

"You little..." I barely bit my tongue at the same time Billy Harrington warned me to watch my words.

"She ruined my game," I whined from the river, holding up the precious item like it was the holy grail, of all things.

"And she'll get you another," Billy assured me. I didn't believe him. That wasn't the point. All I saw was the fury of my father.

"He's gonna kill me," I whispered.

"No, he's not," Mati admonished, and in that moment, I hated her. What did she know? "You can come to me if he does." Spoken like she could stop him, like she ruled the world, and fists would halt on her command, she nodded her head for emphasis—her wet, wild lion hair matted to her forehead. I ignored her. I vowed I'd never pay her any attention again.

But that night, after a smack that rattled my teeth and swelled the side of my face, I went to Mati. Climbed the trellis along her porch leading up to her bedroom on the second floor and crawled through her open window.

"See. See what you did," I whisper-yelled, pointing a finger at her through the tears. I shook with rage and hurt, but little Mati uncurled herself from her bed and guided me to it. She went for a washcloth in the bathroom off her bedroom and returned to wipe my face. She mothered me like my own mother was afraid to do after an incident. Then Mati crawled into the bed next to me, rolled me to my side, and wrapped her arms around me. She tucked my head into her chest, making me listen to her heart beat as she stroked my back and whispered her apology. She

promised to get me a new game and harm my father in a multitude of
ways. Fierce lion cat had no idea she couldn't really save me. It had been
all her fault—both the beating and the result—that night I fell in love
with her.

+ + +

The memory washes over me as we drive for a bit. Besides dancing, drives were another thing Mati and I did, and what I loved most was we didn't need to speak. Music played on the radio. In this case, my phone as the original radio no longer has reception in the Beast. We drive until I find an old turnoff for Bolton Lake. The Beast doesn't handle the terrain as well as an old pickup might, but within minutes we park.

When I open my door, Mati opens hers and hops out. I leave the headlights on to guide our way. I don't know where I thought we'd go, and I have no plan once we're here. Finally, I stop walking, pick up a rock and skip it out across the inky water. Mati pauses at my side.

"Sometimes I'd come out here and pretend you were going to meet me," I admit, surprising myself I tell her such a secret, and Mati gasps. I hold my tongue from telling her the rest of my fantasy—how we'd make a bonfire and kiss or dance to a song on the radio or make love to the lull of the lake.

"Is it strange being back here?" Her voice remains low as if she didn't want to disturb the night sounds of nature. Her eyes watch a second rock—skip, skip, skip and then plunk—into the black liquid. She's shorter than me, smaller than I remember, and with her arms crossed over her body it's like she's holding herself together. I want to reach for her, wrap her in my arms, but instead, I answer her question.

"Yes." I exhale, facing out toward the lake. "Everywhere I turn, there's a memory."

"And that's bad, right?" The question surprises me, and I twist to look at her.

"Not bad…just…overwhelming."

"It's been a long time," she says softly, her voice lowering as does her head. Mati kicks at the dirt with her toe and her hair falls forward.

L.B. Dunbar

My fingers have a mind of their own, and I reach for her wild locks which appear a little tamer as she's aged. Her hair is straight compared to the curls of her youth, and I brush thick strands behind her ear. Her head shoots up and my fingers pause on the side of her neck. Her throat rolls as she swallows and then she speaks. "It's hard to remember it all."

"I remember the most important things." I don't recognize my own deep voice as I stare down at her. My eyes trace over her face, her brown eyes sparkling with gold in the reflection of my headlights. My lips twitch and I want to taste her. I want to feel the Mati who held me those nights so long ago, have her press against me again, only this time as adults, with larger bodies and greater needs. Like the night I learned Mati Harrington was a necessity in my life. She would be my safe haven until I was eighteen.

"What's something good you remember?" she asks as my thumb strokes up and down the front of her neck, under her chin. I like this spot on her and I feel her voice tremble through the pad of my thumb.

I shake my head as I respond. "Football games and bonfire parties and swimming in the lake." One of our friends had a house on Bolton Lake, and it eventually became the party place. Mati's brow pinches at the answer, her head nodding to agree, but somehow, I don't think my response was what she wanted.

"What do you remember about being young here?" I ask.

"Oh, gosh." She chuckles softly, and the laughter trembles against my thumb at her throat. A vibration shoots through my arm to another part of me, jolted to life. "I live here, so everything is a memory, but then again, so much has changed."

I laugh softly as well. "Your son was right. I was a terrible friend," I say, sobering a little at the flash of old times in my head.

"I'm so sorry again for his behavior. Jax is…he's so much like me. Hotheaded, quick-tempered, stubborn, angry. But that's not an excuse. He's not a child; he's an adult, which makes it worse. He shouldn't have spoken to you like that."

"It's all right." My fingers release her throat. While I like the comfort of her skin, there's something holding me back. Mati is Chris's

104

wife. She has children with him. My hand falls to my jeans and my fingers tap my thigh.

"It's not all right. Jax and Jordan loved their father. We all did. We all grieve his loss, but it's time to move on." Her voice rises with each word. She speaks as if she's trying to convince herself.

"Can you move on?" I ask, turning my body in the direction of the lake again. I've faced death before—my cousin Kit's, my father's, currently the state of my mother—but I've never lost a spouse, not like Mati.

"Everyone tells me it's time," she whispers, and her words wrap around me like the mountain breeze. I twist back to her when I speak. "Time for what, Mati?"

"You to kiss me."

To say I experience a halt to the world spinning on its axis is an understatement. Everything around me stilled. The sounds in the trees. The lap of the lake. The wind in the air. I stare at her, disbelieving what she said.

"But you don't have to, if you don't want—" My fingers in her hair at the edge of her face stop her from speaking. In fact, I think she stopped breathing.

"Relax, Mati," I encourage, and she visibly lets out a breath. Her eyes lower to close. "Look at me," I demand, and they snap open. "Do you see me?"

I need to know Mati is aware it's me standing before her and not Chris. Not some memory of him, some apparition of him, not some wishful thinking to have him. Me. *Me.*

"I see you, Denton," she says, and it's all it takes to lose my self-control. My mouth lands on hers like a man starving in a desert—crash, bang, burn. It's awkward and sloppy and our teeth clash. I'm making a mess of this as if I've never kissed before, and yet this is the *second* kiss I've been waiting for since I was fourteen. Mati pulls back abruptly.

"Well," she says, rolling her lips inward. Her eyes lose their sparkle in the reflection of the headlights. "That wasn't what I expected."

I can't help myself. I laugh. Leave it to Mati to add more sting to an already sticky moment.

L.B. Dunbar

"I'm sorry. I don't know…that was…" I pause, lowering my forehead to hers as I spread my fingers in her hair, holding her head in place. "That was awful."

Mati tugs back, the force loosening my fingers and they slide down to her neck, gripping her before she steps away from me. Her face turns away and if I didn't know better, I'd think I embarrassed her. But this is Mati, right? She doesn't get frazzled. My brow pinches as my eyes outline the edge of her jaw, the curve of her lips and the point of her nose.

"Can I ask you something?"

"Sure," she replies softly, her head lowering to look at our feet.

"Will you dance with me?"

Remember Ren and Willard in *Footloose*—the original version? I was Ren. I loved to dance, and Chris didn't. He not only didn't know how, he didn't want to learn. He claimed he had no rhythm, while the beat lived in me. Call it a musician thing, but I love to move, and right now, I need to move with Mati in my arms. Dancing was another connection we had. She loved to dance as well, and while Chris didn't, he never stopped her from dancing with me. *Until one night he did.*

"Here?" Mati scoffs, the tension between us loosening a little.

"Right here seems perfect." I slip an arm around her waist and drag her hand in mine upward to rest between us, pressing her against me. I begin to sway, a beat filling my head.

"Has it been time for other guys to kiss you?" I ask, embarrassed to recall our failure, but curious if she's kissed others.

"Cora, Alyce, and now Hollilyn are all on the Mati-must-date bandwagon, but I haven't dated anyone. I don't know if I'm ready for that."

I nod as if I understand. "Maybe you just need a little practice. Like a trial period. You know, sample the experience…"

She stops swaying in time with me. "I think I got it." She sighs, and then she whines. "But not you, too."

"What do you mean, not me, too?"

"Are you jumping on the get-Mati-laid train?"

It's my turn to fumble and I step on her toes. "What?!" I choke.

"Never mind."

I stop us for a second and stare down at her. "Mati, if you aren't ready to jump in feet first, maybe just dip a toe in the water. See what you think. Pretend a little."

Mati's brow pinches and she looks out to the lake at our side. "I guess. I mean, I think I'm ready to try. I just don't think I'm ready for anything long term." I don't want to ask if she has someone in mind for her experiment, but I'm a willing man. If she isn't interested in long term, there's no one more temporary than me. With another song in my head, I twirl her around, making Mati sway with me again.

"I love that song," she whispers, and I peer down at her.

"What song?" I ask, confused.

"The one you're singing. 'Dancing in the Dark' by Ed Sheeran."

"I was singing?" I'm shocked. I haven't really sung since leaving the band ten years ago. I might harmonize when I'm listening to music at home, alone, but not outside, not in public. Not with others.

"Yep. In the car you were singing, too." She pauses as my brows raise. *I was?* "You have a nice voice. I don't remember it so deep, and I only heard you sing the one time."

The concert in Atlanta. The one I didn't know she attended. The one where I refused the admittance of a group of girls.

"I'm sorry about Atlanta. I didn't know you guys were there."

"It was a long time ago," Mati says, dismissing it with her tone.

"I'm getting tired of that excuse," I admit, and I am. Too much time has passed, and I've missed so many things. Leaving Blue Ridge behind because of my dad forced me to lose more than just him. I spin us in the glow of the headlights, and I twirl Mati away from me before tugging her back. Our movements are fluid, practiced, as if I've never left her and we're still teens…dancing in the dark.

When she turns in my arms, I hold her a little closer, her heavy breasts pressed against my chest.

"Can I ask you something else?" My voice breaks, nearly cracking like I'm a teen again and I swallow my nerves.

"Of course." She shrugs within my arms.

107

L.B. Dunbar

"Can I have a second chance at that kiss?" I really botched the opportunity, and with her asking me for it, I can't waste another minute. I need to take back what I lost and fix it.

"Okay," she hesitates, but I don't want her concerned. I won't mess up again. My hands release her waist, and my fingers cup her neck. My thumbs stroke over her skin, and she swallows, allowing me to relish the roll. She's nervous but she wants this, wants me, at least *this with me*, and I don't want to disappoint her.

"I've missed you, Mati," I admit, but I don't allow her to respond. I don't want to know if she never missed me. Not yet. My mouth covers hers—softer, sweeter, gentler—taking my time to press on the curves of her sensitive skin, tugging it back with mine. She wavers, but I continue. I'm still the man thirsting in the heat, but I use more self-control this time. I open, taking in more of her, and dragging out the pull of her bottom lip. She makes a sound, a low rumble, almost a purr, and I smile against her.

My wild cat. My spice.

My tongue stretches forward, licking the outline of her bottom lip, unlocking her mouth. When she opens, I press inward, searching, seeking, and I'm not disappointed when she meets me. The connection is a trigger, and Mati leans into me, her fingers fisting in my shirt. Her head tilts of its own accord and the kiss deepens as our tongues take over our dance. Mati is kissing me back, open-mouthed, and tongue-wild, and for a moment, I wonder if she's as thirsty as me. We drink each other in, hands beginning to roam. Mine slip from her neck to wrap around her, pressing at her lower back to bring her closer. Hers move to my biceps, squeezing at the muscle as if tugging me to her.

Within seconds, I slip both hands behind her thighs, never releasing her lips, and lift her upward. She squeaks into my mouth and I chuckle with the reverberation. Her legs wrap around my waist and I walk us to the hood of my car. Normally, I'd never set anything on it, but Mati is the exception. She's been the exception to everything, and this kiss proves I've missed out on so much more than I ever knew. I should have never walked away. I should have never listened to Chris. I should have taken her with me.

As her backside settles on the front of the Beast, her legs release my hips but remain straddled on either side of my thighs as I stand between her open legs. I want to take advantage of her in a million ways on this hood—entering her as we stand and then flipping her to bend over and take her from behind. My dick nearly weeps, but tonight, we won't get so far, and I know this the instant my hand lowers for her breast.

Subtler than the hungry fumbling of a fourteen-year old, I take my time to travel down her curves, pausing over the hill of one swell, and swiping a finger through the valley between them. Circling the heavy weight before palming the peak and covering the entire globe, I tug quickly, pinching an already pointed nipple and then Mati pulls back.

"Denton, I…" Her voice falters, and I'm propelled back to being fourteen.

"We can stop." I'd never rush her and pause when I realize speed isn't the issue. Something in her face tells me it's more. "We aren't doing anything wrong, Mati." I believe that. With my whole being, I know we aren't cheating. We aren't sneaking. We aren't anything. Chris is gone.

"Then why do I feel so guilty?"

And that's when it hits me. He isn't gone. Not to her. He's very present between us. She doesn't see me.

"We should go," I comment, ignoring her question. Another memory is about to be left behind.

19

Farmers Dot Come

[Mati]

After *that* kiss, the one that curled my toes, moistened my undies, and set my skin ablaze, Denton took me home. I shouldn't have told him how I felt, but his immediate rejection tells me he wants nothing to do with me. It's like the other night when he made me...you know...on the pillow and then he couldn't look at me. This round, he doesn't speak. Silence. Total silence.

While our drives usually involved no talking, music would play, and the lyrics filled the car and our thoughts. The other night, nothing. No music, just the sound of tires rushing down mountain roads and the wind whipping through open windows. Even my thoughts didn't speak. It was my heart which kept telling me: *You are so stupid.*

My head overruled my body, and my emotions got in the way. It was a good reminder why I haven't dated. I'd never be good at casual sex. I'd never be able to separate my feelings from the physical. It just wouldn't be me. I fall hard. I love passionately. I get involved. That's just me.

These thoughts follow me for days, especially as I drive to pick up Cora Conrad. Formerly, Corabelle Conrad-Devester. Corabelle lived on the Lane as a child, like my family and the mayor. The three estate homes lined a gravel drive set off by a private entrance from the main street. Her family owns the Conrad Lodge, a local resort which had fallen into disrepair over the years. Cora has been the strong arm behind a major renovation, along with adding a bakery run by her daughter.

Not friends as children, I strongly disliked Cora Conrad with her better-than-others attitude and her debutante wannabe ways, not to mention, she was nosy and a gossip. I especially disliked when she turned her daughter into a beauty queen, flaunting her daughter's success as if it were an accomplishment all Cora's doing. Then Chris died, and Cora wised up to the affair her husband, Stan Devester, Blue Ridge's high school athletic director, was having with the principal's secretary. Cora changed. She brought me an apple pie. Her condolences were genuine, and I found she was more like me than I remembered.

We both needed a friend.

Sunday after church, we plan to visit Magnolia and pay our respects to Caroline. Cora calls it "visiting." I call it an obligation, although seeing Magnolia is never such a thing. My heart aches at the changes to her once magnificent home. The gray clapboard looks dirty and decrepit. The white shutters are in need of fresh paint and a proper hanging. Her front porch sags. My brothers visit occasionally, but Magnolia will have none of their help.

"You're here to drink my sweet tea, not right my shutters." Somehow, there always seems to be an innuendo under that statement. Magnolia's house dates back to the post-Civil War era. I suppose the place would rot eventually like many of the classic homes scattered here and there in the area. The thought makes me sad.

"Heard Denton Chance is back," Cora says, her voice a little snide like she knows a secret I don't. "Also heard he's been seen at your house."

My head whips to Cora, blinking in disbelief a moment, before facing forward as I drive.

"Who told you that?"

"A little birdie." The tone of her voice tells me she's smirking, and I glance sideways to see I'm correct. The cat ate the canary with her expression.

"Who?"

"I'm not telling. In fact, I'm not speaking to you because you haven't even told me he was back, nor have you mentioned him coming to see you. I thought we were friends, Matilda Harrington Rathstone." And this is why we weren't friends as children, because Cora is persnickety. Of course, she's teasing me. Cora and I have had numerous conversations in the past year including some hidden truths of our relationships with our husbands and our current desires to move forward.

111

L.B. Dunbar

Cora took it upon herself to prove she was still desirable to a man about a year ago, but that's another story for another time.

"There's nothing to tell, Corabelle Conrad," I mock, leaving off the Devester as she removed it from her name. I won't sling shit back so far as to insult her by including Stan's name tacked to hers.

"Mati…" She pauses, smoothing down the denim on her legs. She's still in a transitional phase—her words—to life as a divorcée. The material feels foreign to her as she typically wore only dresses everywhere, and I mean everywhere. She's allowed herself jeans and even leggings over the past few months as an update to her wardrobe. "You can tell me, you know? I'd understand these things."

I'd love to tell her something if I understood it myself, but I don't. I don't know what to do, and I don't know how I feel.

Liar.

How I feel is I want Denton Chance. I want to do things with him, by him, for him. I want him in a way I don't recognize, and it scares me.

"There's nothing to tell," I repeat, my voice lower, signaling my confusion.

"When you're ready then," Cora offers, and this is why we are now friends. She won't press. She understands.

We pull up to Magnolia's house. My chest clenches at the sight, and then my heart leaps like I've been tossed in the river on the edge of the Lane properties. Denton's car is parked on the well-worn gravel drive. The same car he sat me on, stood between my thighs, and kissed me like I've never been kissed before. Chris and I kissed—a lot—and it was all fine and good, but Denton's kiss is on a different level. He was…he is…I can't find the words. My toes twitched, and my breasts ached, and I just felt him everywhere, yet needed more.

I open the door of my truck and hop down. I'm wearing jean shorts despite the fall chill with a bulky sweater on top and my cowboy boots on my feet. I look messy, but casual, and I like this combination. Coaching young girls keeps my wardrobe slightly in style. I shake my head. I don't even know why I'm considering what I'm wearing. I never think about these things.

We help ourselves up the front steps. Cora carries a box of muffins from her daughter's bakery. I made an egg casserole. We rap on the door and Dolores answers. She looks tired with purple rings under her eyes from tears or lack of sleep. Either way, losing her mother will be difficult. The McIntyre-Duncan-Chance clan has been a matriarchy for a long time. When Denton departs, Dolores will only have her grandmother remaining, whose days might be limited as well.

"Mati. Cora," she greets us, leaning in for awkward hugs and tipping her head for us to follow her. We pass the empty front parlors, the dining room, the grand staircase in the center of the house, and a breakfast nook before reaching the kitchen. The counter is littered with baked goods and when she opens the fridge, we see it stocked with piles upon piles of meals from well-wishing community members.

"We'll need a party to empty out all these things," Dolores says, not meaning to hurt anyone's feelings, but stating the truth. There is too much food for three people, which reminds me Denton is somewhere around here, making the total four. "Mama's resting; otherwise, I'd allow you up."

To be honest, I don't want to see Caroline and it's nothing against her, although I hold plenty against her. I don't do well with death and I don't do well with dying people I don't consider close to me, so going up to her sick room is the last thing I want to do. I'd rather spend my time sipping sweet tea with Magnolia.

"We understand," Cora answers for us, and I'm grateful she has more grace and manners than I. "How are you doing, Dee?"

"It's Lores," she corrects, and I blink up at her. "Rusty likes to call me Lores, so I'm trying to go by the new name."

I stare at her. *Rusty?* Does she mean Crusty Rusty from the same motorcycle club James joined? The same one where Cora's son is an initiate? Dolores can't possibly be hooking up with someone from the Devil's Edge?

"Rusty?" Cora asks, swallowing back the same thought as me.

"Rusty Miller."

L.B. Dunbar

Yep. Confirmation. *Aw, shit.* What is Dolores doing with him? But the question doesn't get asked when the room falls silent as we hear the tap, tap, tapping of Magnolia's cane.

"Ladies," Magnolia announces, greeting Cora and me. "Are those some of Apple's muffins?" Apple Jane is the name of the personae Jane Royston, Cora's daughter, portrays. She's a modern-day Betty Crocker, portraying the perfect housewife circa 1950, dressing in bright red dresses to set off her brunette hair and signature red lips. I've always considered the costume ridiculous. Her apple baked goods are her claim to fame.

"Yes ma'am," Cora chirps cheerfully, still proud of her daughter's accomplishments which, over time, Cora credits as all her daughter's doing. Cora has come a long way.

"Well, let's set up outside. Sweet tea, Dolores," Magnolia snaps at her granddaughter like she's a servant and takes her tapping cane toward the front of the house where a screened-in porch sits off the main parlor.

"I'll get the tea," Cora offers, seeing the exasperation, frustration, and exhaustion on Dolores's face.

Thank you, she mouths, swiping at a tear in the corner of her eye. Not knowing what to do with myself, I step over to Dolores, ready to hug her, but she puts her hand up. Comfort is the last thing she wants while touch is the very thing she needs. Good Lord, is that why she's with Crusty Rusty? I shiver as I shrink back from her raised hand.

"I think I'll keep Magnolia company." Exiting the kitchen for the long hallway leading to the front of the house, I see Denton cross the front yard through the double door entry screens. He stops. Notices the truck next to his car and turns for the house. I tuck myself behind a wall by the staircase, holding my breath and banging my head on the plaster behind me. The screen creaks open and then something slows it from slamming shut. Heavy footsteps stalk down the hall and I close my eyes as if it will hide me.

I sense him pass me. Rather, I smell him pass. Fresh cut grass. Fall leaves. All man. Suddenly, his presence is before me, but my eyes remain closed.

"Mati," he whispers, and I have no choice but to open to him.

"Oh, hey." My voice is too loud, my tone too cheery.

"What are you doing here?"

"I came to visit Magnolia and see your mother. Cora Conrad is with me."

"Are you two friends?" he asks, placing his large hand over my head as he leans toward me. My heart races, my throat closes. By God, I want him to kiss me. My teeth cut into my bottom lip and Denton's eyes follow the movement.

"Yeah," I whisper, no longer remembering what he asked. A thick thumb comes to my lower lip, tugging it free from where I hold it, and retracing where my teeth stung.

"Don't tease me, Mati." His voice is strong, the warning clear. He's a man who doesn't need to be trifled with. He can get any woman he wants. The thought irritates me.

"Why would I ever tease you, Denton?" I snap.

"Because that's what you do." He presses off the wall and steps back, pivots for the kitchen and leaves me breathless against the wall. Two seconds later, I'm still recovering, my thoughts racing to all the pranks we played on one another as children. Some were rather poor decisions with heavy consequences. Or was he referring to the other night?

"Nothing happened, huh?" Cora says, walking toward me with a tray of sweet tea in a pitcher and several glasses. "That how you got dirt on your lips?" she teases, but as she passes, I wipe a shaky finger over my mouth and fresh soil marks the pad of my thumb. I realize that's not the only dirty spot on me after being near Denton.

20

Bees Sting. So Do Women.

[Denton]

While I help myself to an apple muffin followed by a full glass of sweet tea, I can't wait to return to the yard. My skin buzzes knowing Mati's in the house and another part of me aches with need. Her words from the other night tamper my desire.

Why do I feel so guilty?

I can't help her with her emotions. Guilt is something I've been unfamiliar with until recently. Guilt at being gone so long. Guilt at letting friendships fall apart. Guilt at this house slipping into disrepair.

Mentally, I've begun making a list of all the things this place needs.

"See Mati?" Dolores asks, but I finish gulping my sweet tea before answering.

"Yeah, why?"

"You got that glazed over look in your eyes."

"I do not," I whine, sounding like a teen.

"When will you admit you love that girl?" Dolores asks, surprising me with her boldness.

"When will I *what*? What are you talking about?" I stuff another bite of muffin into my mouth.

"Twenty-seven years later and you still have a look of longing when it comes to her." Dolores shakes her head. "Here's my unsolicited advice as your older sister. Don't let more time pass. In a moment, time is slow. In a year, time went too fast."

What the fuck?

Sometimes I think Dolores is sneaking my mother's meds. She looks wired. Her blue eyes too bright. Her skin too pale. She's working too hard.

116

More guilt knocks at my chest. I haven't responded to her declaration, so she steps to the side, pats me on the shoulder as she passes, and says, "I'm going to check on Mother."

I slip out the kitchen door for the yard, but round the house to hear Magnolia speaking with Mati and Cora on the screened in porch.

"Did you see my grandson? He's a rockstar, you know."

"We know, Miss Magnolia," Cora replies politely, something all-knowing in her voice. I can't believe Mati and Cora are friends, but then again, people change, I suppose. I know I have.

Cora owns the Conrad Lodge where I'm staying but I haven't seen her there yet. The place seems pretty busy with the fall colors transitioning on the mountain trees. Tourism is a new draw to the area and a bonus for the community. The display will be beautiful and reminds me I need to start keeping my camera with me.

"He ran away from here," Magnolia adds, and I stiffen beside the corner of the house. "Just like his daddy. Looks just like him." My whole body goes board still. I hate the reference to *him*, and the comparison. Magnolia has said it many times passing me, as if she's shocked how much I look like my father. I've blocked him out so often I don't remember him as more than fists or fights. Still, I don't know what she means about running away, as my father never left Blue Ridge. Once he settled here, his roots were planted deep.

"I think he's rather handsome," Cora adds, fueling the conversation. Mati doesn't respond, and I find I'm holding my breath wondering what she thinks of me. I'm a little vain like that. *Does she also see* him *when she looks at me?* My heart weighs heavy in my chest with the thought.

"I don't think he looks anything like *his father*," Mati defends, and although I didn't kiss her by the stairwell, I want to kiss her now. "He's nothing like him."

Her voice rises, her defense strong, and I'm reminded once again of all the nights Mati saved me.

"Oh, no," Magnolia mocks. "Nothing like him. Shame about his daddy."

L.B. Dunbar

I'm worrying she's been sneaking Mother's meds, too. Either that, or she's going senile which is a possibility, although most days she seems rather lucid. She's eighty-something years old.

"Yes, Denton missed his father's funeral, if I recall," Cora speaks, reminding me of another shortcoming of mine. Dolores swears I should have attended. *The funeral would have given you closure.* In many ways, I think that's why I'm presently here.

"Yes, he did," Magnolia replies, sadness lacing her voice and I'm all kinds of confused. Magnolia hated my father, but she sounds like she's sympathetic to his passing. "Darn shame what happened to him."

I can't listen any longer. I have work to do. Cleaning the yard isn't going to make this place more presentable, but it's a start. It's also a good place to let my mind wander while my body works out pent-up frustration. I'm all mixed up about Mati.

For a guilty woman, she looked rather willing leaning against the wall by the staircase. Her lips moist. Her teeth nibbling the corner. Her breath hitching as I leaned forward. If she doesn't want me, her body hasn't gotten the memo.

I'm turning for the other side of the house when I hear Dolores's voice drift through the porch.

"Mati, Mother heard you were down here, and she'd like a word with you, if you don't mind." I step back, tilting my head for more information, but don't hear anything. A moment later, Magnolia speaks.

"Poor Mati. Caroline's doing all kinds of confessing lately."

I have no idea what she means.

+ + +

I'm in the side yard, raking dry, fallen leaves from the trees which border the property. Most farm homes have trees and bushes to block wind, hold off the dust of crops, and form natural privacy screens around the main house. This old place is no different. A blower would be the best way to get all the leaves to the center of the yard, but I'm finding the physical exertion refreshing. Not to mention, there's no gym in town and I need the workout. I'm hoping to hear from my agent any day about a shoot

118

I've wanted for years. The only weight lifting I've been doing is carrying Magnolia up the stairs to see my mother.

"Put those biceps to use and carry me up to see my daughter." A rather bold demand coming from a lady who typically tries to act prim and proper, but I would have offered anyway. She needs to see my mother.

My mind drifts, and again, I think of Chris.

"She's so mad at me," Chris said as we raked leaves in Magnolia's yard. Chris felt working around her house was his way of paying my grandmother back for taking him in. I didn't see why I had to be dragged into his unwarranted payment plan, and I also didn't want to be discussing him and Mati fighting. Ever since Mati got the idea to go on a road trip together, Chris started acting strange about the three of us as friends. He couldn't afford to go, although Mati had offered to pay his portion. They'd had a wicked fight about it.

"I just want her to understand I want things on my own terms. I don't want a handout from her which is really from her daddy. I need to work next summer to save up for college expenses anyway." I understood where Chris was coming from. I knew he didn't have the financial means that Mati and I have, although he'd received a small inheritance which he named his college fund. Still, Chris was uptight, and I likened it to him needing to get laid. He had some honorable desire to wait until Mati was eighteen before they had sex. I found strange relief in his chivalry. It meant they hadn't done the deed. However, I was a hypocrite in this area as I was fucking Kristy on the regular—then breaking up with her and then hate fucking her and then getting back together with her. It was a vicious cycle.

"She'll listen to you." The comment stopped me from raking a moment and I hold my breath.

Please don't involve me, *I remember thinking. I felt the weight of his eyes on me. He knew about Mati sneaking out her window to take rides with me. We hadn't exactly kept it a secret, although we also didn't feel the need to discuss it. Mati reassured Chris he was the one and only for her. I didn't even want to consider how she did the proving. Then she had the accident. It put the brakes on the rides, and Chris was almost*

L.B. Dunbar

relieved. It somehow brought them tighter, and I was feeling like the third wheel, even though I had Kristy. Still, when they had a little tiff, Chris would come to me to work magic on getting him back in her good graces. Some days, it was harder than others to play the game.

"What do you want me to say?"

"You know my circumstances. She'll listen to your reasoning. It's not that I don't want to go. I just can't."

"Are you telling her she can't go without you?"

Chris hesitated for a moment and my heart dropped. If he told her not to go, she'd listen. She'd follow his lead, but she'd also be pissed off. Mati had really taken the idea of a road trip and ran with it. Maps. Pinpricks. Plans. She was out of control.

"No, man. I'd never tell her not to go. I trust you with her. I know you'd take care of her." Somehow, there was deeper meaning in his words and the pressure of his eyes I could no longer ignore. I looked up at him, feeling like that look should have been burned into my memory forever. He was telling me something, but I couldn't read him.

Fingers tap my shoulder and I nearly come out of my skin, tugging the earbuds from my ears where music filtered through my head drowning out my thoughts.

"Drink?" Cora offers, holding up a glass of lemonade. I've been drinking too many sweet drinks here, and need to double up on the water, but it's well water and my taste buds haven't forgotten the sulfury, mineral taste.

"Thanks." I take the offered glass and guzzle the cool refreshment. I'm aware of Cora watching me, my chest on display as I removed my shirt a while back. It's hot work in the sun despite the cool temperature.

"Like what you see, Corabelle?" I tease. Her eyes appreciate my body without batting one of her fake-lashed eyes nor pinching her face in the typical judgmental way I remember from her.

"I've seen better," she snips, and I laugh. Little Miss Goody-Two-Shoes has never seen anything like my body up close in her life, but still, her snark is stimulating.

"Mati still with Mother?" It seems like a long time has passed and knowing Mati's attitude about my mother, I'm hoping she doesn't give her own confessions upstairs. My mama's been through enough—going through enough—it's time to let the past rest.

"Yes." Cora looks around the yard, her nose scrunching up like she smells something rotten. "You know, you could sell this place for a nice price."

I look up at the house, my eyes taking in the sagging roof and the caving back porch. The list of repairs grows.

"I couldn't do that to Magnolia. Plus, I don't need the money." I don't often gloat about my good fortune, but it's true. I don't need the funds. The royalties alone from our songs work in my favor, as do the modeling shoots, not to mention my own photography. I'm doing well.

"Maybe you should share a little here then." Cora's comment startles me, like a little slap on the cheek to wake someone up. I blink in the direction of the house.

"It might take a lot more than what I have to fix this."

"How about her?" Cora adds, and I stare back at her, uncertain of her meaning. "Got enough to fix Mati?"

"Mati's not broken," I defend, and then I reconsider. "Does she need money? Are finances bad since Chris…" The words fall away like the leaves of the trees at my back. *Does Mati need help?*

"Mati doesn't need money," Cora snorts with a humorless laugh. "She needs a man." Her eyes roam down my body, with no shame in pausing at my zipper region and then rolling back up my ripped abs.

"I'm man enough," I snap, my voice strengthening in defense. What the hell is she implying?

"Then I suggest you get fixing." One brow raises like I'm to understand her. I shake my head, dismissing her with a chuckle. Mati doesn't need mending. She's always been tough. She doesn't need a man, either. She made that clear the other night. *Or maybe it's just me.* It doesn't matter. I'm not giving into Mati unless she sees me and not some substitute for Chris. The other night she was pretending, like me, until her guilt caught up to her. Guilt for a man she's still hung up on, and I don't blame her. Chris was her husband. He was a great guy.

L.B. Dunbar

"What's going on out here?" Mati questions, her voice too high, her eyes laced with red. Has she been crying? I've never seen Mati cry. Not that I can remember.

Then a memory returns.

"Why can't I come with you?" Tears stream down her face. Of all the hurts we caused one another, not going on the road trip was the one that forced the crocodile tears to plop down her cheeks.

Because of Chris, I screamed in my head, but don't give her the truthful answer.

"I'm raking leaves," I say, stating the obvious and tensing my fingers around the rake handle. Mati stops at the sound of my voice, her feet tripping in the grass.

"I…my…you…" She closes her gaping mouth, licks her lips, then swallows. Her eyes remain magnetized to my skin. Over my abs, up my chest, down one arm at a time. I'm exposed to her in a new way. Not like she hasn't seen my bare chest before—as a teen—but as a man, Mati's mesmerized. Her chest rises and falls as her eyes widen and dilate. My skin quivers, rippling under the desire I observe in those eyes.

Her body definitely hasn't gotten the memo. She wants me.

To tease her further, I rub a hand down my chest, taking my time brushing off sweat mixed with bits and pieces of leaves clinging to my skin. I lower my palm, flattening it over my belly until I get to my waistband. I tug at my belt, adjusting myself only enough, so my dick unfurls, and the bulge isn't undisguised. My body likes Mati perusing me.

"Mati," Cora snaps, and we both jump with the sharpness of her voice, the motherly sound like we've been caught doing something, like making out.

I want to make out with her.

I want to make love to her.

I'm not even startled by my thoughts. I've felt this way since I was fourteen. Thirty-one goddamn years later, I still feel the same way, and it frustrates the fuck out of me. I drop the rake, ready to take her. Kiss the crap out of her and lay her down in the pile of leaves. But we have an audience, so I do the next best thing. I scoop up a handful of dead foliage and toss it in Mati's face. She sputters and coughs, her fingers swiping at her tongue as her gaping mouth got a taste of dried leaves.

"You didn't." She shakes her head, eyes narrowing, challenge accepted. Leaves fly at me, missing my chest and making a mess of the collection it took me an hour to rake.

I scoop up another handful and take two steps toward her. She tries to duck, but I'm quick, scrubbing leaves in her hair as she squeals. One hand protects her face while the other sticks out, trying to keep me at arm's length, trying to fight me off. Mati humorously screeches, and I'm transported back in time. Teenage games. Fall between our yards. Laughter. Then she snorts. This adds to her fit and Cora joins the laughter.

"Think that's funny," I say, scooping up a pile for Cora and her too polished face, too perfect hair. She screams as she runs, but I lunge, catching her, and sticking leaves down the back of her shirt.

Another round hits me in the back, some sticking to me as I'm sweaty. I turn to face Mati, who stands with both hands over her mouth. She cocks a hip, emphasizing her short jean shorts which I missed as she stood in my grandmother's hall.

"Oops," she teases, all false innocence. She turns her back, and I catch her around the waist before she gets away. My hand, full of leaves, heads for the front of her sweater, sneaking in the loose opening and traveling downward. I drop the leaves and cover a breast with a thick palm. Several things happen at once. Mati curls back, her ass hitting the hard-on at my zipper and the response causes me to nip at her exposed neck.

"Don't be a tease, Spice," I whisper at her ear until another pile of leaves tumbles over my head. I'm in a tug of war—both women vying for my attention—or at least getting a kick out of covering me with fallen foliage. Releasing Mati, I turn for Cora. I'm bending at the waist for more leaves when Cora screams.

"What?" I ask, standing upright, staring at her pained expression. Liquid fills her eyes.

"I think I was just stung by a bee."

"Where?" I step forward, feeling Mati at my side.

L.B. Dunbar

"My back."

"Are you allergic?"

"I don't think so," she says, and I don't waste time. Quickly, I drop the leaves from my dirty hands, bend again, and scoop Cora unceremoniously over my shoulder. I carry her into the house, feeling the weight of Mati's eyes stinging my back instead.

21
Not So Squeaky Clean

[Mati]

I should have rushed after Cora being carried over Denton's shoulder fireman style, but I didn't. Instead, I took my time to swipe leaves from inside my sweater and feel the tingle of my breast from where he squeezed me. I swiped at the bits and pieces of foliage under my clothing and then fluffed my hair to find more crumbs. Finally, taking a deep breath, I slowly pace toward the house, feet heavy, like a dead woman walking.

A dying woman spoke to me upstairs, and my eyes still sting from all she said to me...

"He's come home." Her chopping voice startled me like she was the smoker all those years instead of Kip.

"Yes, he has, ma'am." I didn't know what to say. Her fingers twitched against the coverlet, and the sensitive thing would have been to reach out and cover her hand, but I didn't. I offered words instead. "He came to see you."

Mrs. Chance rolled her head on the pillow, her once velvety black hair faded to a dull charcoal color. Her cheeks are hollow, and her lips blend with her skin. I'm not good with death like this, and I send up a silent prayer of gratitude Chris went quickly, without long-lasting suffering.

"He's here for you, too." Her voice was hardly more than a whisper, so for a moment, I thought I misunderstood.

"Pardon me?" I lean closer, certain I didn't hear her correctly.

"Take care of him like you always did. Don't let him leave without you this time." Two things race through my mind. She knew. She knew he came to my house, to my room, to my drive after each and every time her husband touched him. She knew! And she did nothing about it. The second thing was her nerve to think I let him leave or had a choice in not

L.B. Dunbar

going with him. I had no say. I never knew he didn't plan to attend college, and then he dumped me from the road trip for Kristy.

"I..." *My mouth opened and shut. How could I argue with a dying woman?* "Yes, ma'am." *I cringe as I acquiesce, but I'm not about to fight with her, even if I am stubborn.*

"He loved you so much."

Her words pushed me over the edge, and a tear leaked. I thought she meant Chris for a moment, but she rolled her head on the pillow before looking at me, her piercing blue eyes the same as her daughter's. "Denton loved you fiercely."

She had to be wrong. He loved me like a friend, like I loved him because I denied my feelings for him. He kissed me and then had sex with another girl. He was just a horny teen.

"Protect his heart more than anything this time," *she said, and then her eyes closed.*

For a moment, I feared I was witnessing the end, and it shouldn't have been me sitting with her. Denton or Dolores or even Magnolia, anyone but me. Thankfully, a nurse entered, checked Caroline's vitals, and excused me as it was obvious she wanted to rest.

I came downstairs to another bee's nest of confusion, all puns intended. Cora and Denton looked like they were flirting. Their laughter mingling in the warm afternoon. Her eyes admiring him. *How could she not?* I've never seen so many ripples on a man, so up close, and he looked...hot. Literally, sweaty and glistening, and it just turned me on in all the wrong ways. My tongue was three sizes too big and thickening, eager to lick him everywhere.

Then he had to act like a child with leaves in my face.

Then act like a man grabbing my breast and nipping at my neck.

And I liked it. I liked it too much.

I shiver as I climb the stairs, recalling his bite.

Don't be a tease. Twice he said that today, but I wasn't teasing him. I didn't know how to tease. I didn't even know how to flirt, but it was obvious Cora does. Her hand on his forearm. Her subtle coquettish giggle. My legs feel sluggish as I climb the stairs to the second floor. My heart sinks to my belly, as I hear laughter and whispers down the hall. I near the bathroom door, perched open a sliver, and knock.

"Cora?" Silence abruptly comes from the other side of the wood. Silence, other than the roar of the running water. I lean forward, my ear tipped toward the door. *Is that the shower?*

"Was that Mati?" Denton asks, and I hold my breath, waiting for an answer.

"Cora," I call out again.

"Don't come in." The deep male voice warns me, while a female giggle follows, and like having the wind knocked out of me, I'm hit with my mistake. I turn tail and race for the stairs. A million images cross my mind, including Denton and Cora in a variety of positions in a shower. I realize I've read too many romance novels and continue to flee without looking back.

+ + +

I can't go home. I don't want to be alone yet. Instead, I detour outside of town, seeking an all too familiar place. It's Sunday, a day many visit for the peace and serenity of the surroundings. The woods are quiet here, and I'm reminded of a Robert Frost poem. My wilder side wanted the path less traveled, but that was years ago. I took the one prominent and worn, and I followed it to this point.

I easily find the plot I'm looking for and stand over the granite stone.

Christopher John Rathstone

I've been here often, but retreated the past few months, knowing Chris isn't really in this place. He's above me and around me and in my heart, but not here. Not really. Still, I stand over his grave, my mind filled with a million things and nothing. I don't know what to say to him, how to ask his advice. He shouldn't be the one to give me guidance about dating, relationships, or other men. I fight the urge to question his death for the hundredth time. An accident. Something no one could prevent.

I loved my husband. He was my best friend. Yet, I've accepted he's no longer with me and the rare moments I've laughed lately with Denton

L.B. Dunbar

remind me how lonely I've been without Chris. It's felt good to laugh. It's felt good to even smile. I don't want to lose those feelings. They've been gone for too long.

I gaze down at the grass over Chris's grave. The cemetery takes care of the land, but a bottle of whiskey sits on the edge of his tombstone, and I curse the kids hanging out here to drink. Lifting the bottle to my chest, intending to throw it in the trash, I aimlessly stare at Chris's name.

What am I doing here? I wonder to myself. A chill runs up my legs as if someone touches the bare skin behind my knees and I shiver.

Chris? My brain teases, but I know it's not possible. For the longest time, I thought I heard his voice or felt his presence in our home, like the ghost limb of an amputee. A grieving support group online told me this was normal. The sensation would pass. Some people didn't care for that answer, wishing to hang on forever. I found relief in the concept. I felt like I was going crazy, and the longer I clung to the hope of hearing him, the harder it was to accept he was truly gone.

"I found Denton," I say aloud, speaking to the grass. "I don't know what to do with him, though." Then I remember the letter, the whole purpose for reaching out to him. I haven't given it to him, and he hasn't asked about it, but I need to take care of business. After the events of today between him and Cora, I need to give him his letter and move on.

I suppose I should thank Denton for the kisses he's given me. It's proven I'm ready to kiss again. Maybe not someone random, but *someone.* Someone who would make me feel desired, wanted, happy like Denton did in those moments. Denton isn't like Chris. He's more wild, carefree, spontaneous—all the things I've missed in myself, and the things I'd like to regain.

Taking a deep breath, I glance around the space void of other physical beings. My thoughts empty and I decide I need food along with the comfort of the living—my children.

22

The Trouble With Kids Is…
Kids Can Be Troublesome

[Mati]

I've tried to call Jax over the last couple of days, but it's clear he's avoiding me. Instead, I call Jordan. Of the two twins, he's more like his father, not only in that he's a lawyer but in his mannerisms. He's conservative, meticulous about details, and structured to a fault. It's one reason Maggie and he don't have kids. He wanted to wait, while she wanted to take a chance. Putting off trying has only prolonged the heartbreak for Maggie as pregnancy hasn't happened in five years of marriage.

"Hey, Mom," Maggie says immediately upon answering Jordan's phone. She's called me Mom from the beginning, and it warms my heart as I don't have daughters. Her own parents were thrilled she married Jordan but remain distanced as they live in South Carolina.

"Hey, Maggie. Have room for old Mati at supper?"

"You're not old and no need to ask. You're always welcome." Maggie sounds tired when she speaks to someone—presumably my son—and returns to me.

"Jordan says how about if we meet you at the pub?" The pub is the last place I want to go, but I agree because I suggested dinner. The other restaurant options in town include The Patio steakhouse or the diner, which isn't an option tonight. I accept the invitation and fifteen minutes later pull into the alley, find the employee spots directly behind BRMP full, and circle back for the public lot to park.

Crossing the alley and walking around the side of the pub, I see Roxanne outside the bookstore across the street. She's eclectic, a bit eccentric, and a whole lot of au natural, but as I've said before, I like her. I wave, and she waves back. I see nothing wrong with her.

129

L.B. Dunbar

When I enter the pub the first person to accost me is my brother Billy.

"Did you see that...that...*urg*...outside?" He nods toward the window facing the direction of the bookshop, and I admit I've never seen my brother so flustered. "She put in for a permit. She wants to host some kind of Booktober thing, selling books on the sidewalk." Billy's aghast at the thought, but I like the idea.

"So? Sounds fun."

"Fun? *Fun!* She wants it for the same weekend we have the Oktoberfest."

I shake my head, not understanding why we can't share the space. We don't want the sidewalk, we want the street.

"What am I missing here?" I ask, my eyes narrowing at my brother as he swipes a hand through his hair and tugs at the top. He's been acting strange the last week—distant and distracted—and I worry it has something to do with Kristy Moseley.

"Nothing. Just ignore me," he huffs, spinning away from the window. Now, I know something's wrong as he never wants to be ignored. He loves attention. But he takes a deep breath and asks, "What can I get you?"

"I'm meeting Jordan and Maggie here," I call to him, as I follow behind him while he walks the length of the bar.

"They're in the back corner with Jax and Hollilyn."

I stop. This should be interesting. Stalking to the farthest table in the corner, I slow my approach and swallow the lump in my throat. My boys are laughing. Their girls each slapping at them. Jax and Jordan tap beer mugs and then take a sip of their beverage. They look happy, healthy and whole, and I want to feel like them again. Chris and I would have completed the party—a six pack. Now, I'm a party of one.

"Mom," Maggie says, noticing me first and standing from her seat. She steps around the table to intercept me with a deep hug. "Don't be upset."

I don't know what I'd be mad about until I see the sullen expression fall across Jax's face.

"Hello, family," I say, trying to keep my voice chipper and my hurt down.

"Mom," Jordan says, standing to drag a chair from another table for me to join them and sit next to him. He's making a statement. He'll play mediator. Hollilyn sits on the other side of me.

"Hello, baby." Jordan doesn't flinch when I call him the endearment, even at twenty-six. "Jax," I say a little sterner, twisting my lips as I speak to my other son. Here's the thing about Jax. He's totally opposite his twin brother, and a little too similar to me—stubborn to the core with attitude and conviction rolled into one.

"You look sexy." Hollilyn compliments me, meaning well to loosen the tension, but Jax spits out his beer and Hollilyn turns back to him to mop at the table.

"Are those leaves in your hair?" Maggie asks, a smile curling on her pretty face as her brows rise. Maggie is a brunette, with soft waves and an even softer face, flawlessly natural in comparison to Hollilyn. Her brown eyes give away her emotions, and she looks both pleased and surprised as I tug at my wild hair to find pieces of foliage I missed.

"Oh, I was at Magnolia's today. Yard work."

"How's your back?" Hollilyn asks, and Jax scowls at her.

"Was Denton there?" Jordan asks, and now it's my turn for surprise. My eyes shift to Jax and back to Jordan.

"It's his grandmother's house, and his mama's there." My tone warns them to show respect, but a glance exchanges between my sons.

"How is Mrs. Chance?" Maggie asks, attempting to lessen the heavy air around us.

"She's dying," I blurt, insensitive in my own right.

"Mom," Jordan huffs before chuckling. He shakes his head in humor, but the weight of Jax's eyes press on me, so I turn to him.

"Spit it out," I snap because Jax has something to say and we might as well get this over. Without recognizing it before, I see so much of Denton in him it almost frightens me.

"I don't approve."

"Jaxson," Hollilyn whispers under her breath.

L.B. Dunbar

"And what exactly do you disapprove of?" I hold my breath, knowing his answer before he speaks. My fingers clench and unclench as I lean on the table.

"Of him."

"What about him?"

"Dating *you*." The stab going to my gut, I sit up straighter.

"Do I need your approval?" I've done nothing wrong, I tell myself, as Denton has said. *Give yourself permission*, Billy's voice filters in my head for support.

"No, you don't," Jordan interjects, aiming a glare at his brother. His hand comes out to cover mine, and he gives it a quick squeeze.

"I'm out of here," Jax says, slamming down his empty beer mug. He's halfway out of his seat with Hollilyn's hand on his forearm, and her unacknowledged attempts to soothe him tick me off.

"Sit down." I pause only a beat. "I loved your father—"

"Mom, we know this. You don't need to say anything," Jordan offers, ever the attorney trying to smooth ruffled feathers, but my mother hen feathers are cocked up, and I'm not letting my second twin pluck my fury. After a warning glare to his brother, I place a hand on Jordan's wrist as Jax's body returns to his seat.

"But he's gone," I continue as if Jordan hasn't spoken. "He was a good man, a great father, and adoring husband. And he died…without me."

Jordan hisses, and Jax lowers his head.

"And he asked me to carry on."

Jax's head lifts and Jordan turns to me.

"He left me a letter, spelling it all out, reminding me of promises we made to one another inside our marriage that is no one's business, not even either of yours." Jordan nods once, agreeing with me as he reaches for Maggie's hand. A sorrowful look crosses Hollilyn's eyes at the tenderness between a husband and wife. Jax does nothing to comfort her.

"If you don't want me to smile or laugh or enjoy myself…" I swallow the lump building in my throat. "Then I respect your wishes and understand you won't be coming around as much. Because I'm not dead, and I'm tired of feeling like I'm walking through water instead of enjoying the waves."

Jax has the decency to look away, his eyes closing at my words.

"I respect your feelings as my son, but I'd like you to respect mine, not only as your mother but also as a woman with years of life ahead of her—" I pause a second, taking a deep breath. "—alone, if I don't change, if I don't open up."

I might be treading a little too far into deep waters, exposing myself and my needs to my children, but Hollilyn's hand finds mine on the table and gives a squeeze of sisterhood. I glance at Maggie who nods, encouraging me as a tear slips from her eye. I draw strength from my daughter-in-law and Jax's girlfriend who should be my daughter-in-law, and it pushes me into drowning territory.

"And before you want to judge me, Jaxson, and anything looking like a relationship, I suggest you take a hard look at yourself and how you treat this girl."

"Mom," Jordan whisper-hisses. Hollilyn gasps and Jax stands, snarling, "I don't need this."

I stand as well. "I don't either. Sit down and enjoy your dinner. I'm going home. Alone."

Grabbing my purse, I step around my children and head for the door.

23
Broken Hearts and Doors

[Denton]

What a shitshow. First, the bee sting on Cora's back turned out to be nothing more than something poking her. Mother's nurse checked it out. *Dramatic much, Cora?* After the diagnosis, I decided to jump in the shower and rinse off the sweat and leaves stuck to my body. It seems Mati and Cora would be staying a while and I wanted to clean up. As I stood in the clawfoot tub, the curtain pulled around me, a knock raps to the door and hope spikes as did another part of me that Mati has followed me. The fantasy plays out where she removes her clothes and joins me without announcing herself, soaps me up, bringing me to the brink, and when I can't control myself any longer, I spin her around to bend her over, balance on the lip of the tub, and...

"Denton, I just want to put the antiseptic back in the medicine cabinet. Nurse Vivian says it goes in here."

The fantasy disappears when Cora calls out my name instead. I freeze, holding my dick in my hand. I feel like I've gotten caught with my fingers in the cookie jar which would be less embarrassing. A strangled tone escapes as I question, "Couldn't it wait?"

Cora chuckles and admits, "I guess it could have." Yet, the medicine cabinet mirror swings open, the creaking noise added to the running shower. I laugh nervously, nearly choking with the sexual energy of my hand on my hard-on while a woman stands on the other side of the thin curtain. The *wrong* woman.

Then another knock taps at the door.

"Cora?" Mati's sweet, hesitant voice forces me to release my dick, feeling the weight strain as it sticks out stiff and achy.

"Was that Mati?" I hush-whisper and panic strikes. *This. Cannot. Be. Happening.* The situation with Cora in the bathroom has all kinds of wrong written on it, so I call out, "Don't come in."

Second Chance

My fingers grip the curtain, and I stick my head out to see Cora's wide eyes shooting from me to the door.

"Oh, my heavens." A well-manicured hand comes to her pink lips, and a tense giggle escapes.

"What happened?" Did Mati walk in and notice Cora—or worse yet—see the outline of my body through the thin fabric giving away my hard-on?

"I think she ran away."

"What?" I reach for the faucet, turning off the taps, and spin for the curtain. Forgetting about Cora, I tug back the barrier. Cora stares at me, her eyes widening even more than moments before.

"Cora," I snap, leaning forward for the towel on the edge of the sink. I ignore her admiring gaze and gaping mouth to wrap myself in the threadbare towel. Stepping out of the tub, I slip on the loose rug and almost do the splits, landing the family jewels on the rim of the raised claw-foot. Righting myself, I press Cora out of my way as I race for the front bedroom—the one without a boarded-up window— overlooking the front lawn.

"Mothertrucker," I mutter, watching Mati run for her truck. I spin for the door, take the stairs two at a time, holding onto the towel at my waist, and reach the front screen door too late. Mati peels out of the gravel drive and takes off in the opposite direction of town. My palm slaps at the open front door to my side and the wood cracks. A loud snap reverberates around me and the ancient door splinters in the middle. A few ants scramble through the hole I've made, and I step back.

Curse words curse more words.

The stream of ants through the severed wood seems endless, covering the chipped paint along with the large splinters I've made. My shoulders fall as I realize I can't chase Mati.

"This house needs a wrecking ball," I mutter.

"This house needs some love," Cora counters behind me. I spin to face her, holding my towel while losing my pride after facing her naked, shampoo still dripping from my hair, and a semi-wood pitching the terrycloth at my waist.

135

"Yeah, I'll get right on that," I grumble, feeling no love for the house or my situation. I've been cooped up again, waiting, waiting, waiting, although I don't know if what I'm waiting for is my mother's passing or Mati's attention. Maybe it's both entwined together. Each day I sing softly to my mama while I also pine away, wondering when Mati will realize we did nothing wrong. We kissed. That's not a crime. And if it were, I'd steal more from her.

The sin lies in how much I liked it, how much I wanted more from a woman clearly not ready to go further. And if kissing were all I got from her while I stayed here, I'd take each lick, each suck, each nip, and store it in the memory bank along with the first one.

But for now, I have a front door to repair as I can't leave a house of women exposed out here. I really should move to the farmhouse, but I didn't want to leave Conrad Lodge yet. The resort room gives me respite from things I still try to ignore—my mother dying and my feelings for Mati.

After a call to Duncan Hardware—and a second shower—a new front door is delivered. Breaking the door with so much force reminds me of conversations I had with Mati as a teen. Staring after the busted door as Kent Duncan removes it, my stomach twists.

"You'll never be like him." *She exhaled as if astonished I thought such a thing.*

"But what if I am? What if I have a child and I get angry because he didn't pick up his shoes? Will I hurt him?" The genuine concern filled my head.

"You'll be a great dad one day, and you'll never hurt a child because of what Kip did to you."

I never had kids, though.

The current owner of the hardware store and somehow a cousin finishes the door install complete with a new handle and lock as the latch on the original door didn't work with the modern one. A big burly guy glances around the front entry and the parlor off each side of the extra wide hallway and whistles low.

"Good bones here but needs some TLC."

While the house has a solid foundation, many of the original elements are going to be lost if we start fixing things. I hang my head at hearing this comment for the second time in a few hours.

"I think I need a contractor." The list of repairs is long. Roof. Porch. Stairwell. Kent offers up two names and their numbers.

"I might be biased toward Duncan Construction, though. My brother Griffin owns it."

After thanking him for the recommendations, I retrieve Cora who has been waiting on the ride I promised to give her, since she owns the Lodge where I'm staying, and Mati ditched her. She's been busy talking with Magnolia and then sitting with Mother a bit so Dolores can rest. The weight of watching someone die is heaviest on my sister. When I look at Mother, I feel like I'm looking at a stranger. I don't know the woman with shallow breaths and hollow eyes lying in a bed. Then again, I remember the blankness in her stare as my father took his temper out on me.

"Kip, you're hurting him."

"Dear," he said through clenched teeth, *"shut your mouth or you're next."*

I'd swallow the beating to keep it from her until I could no longer take it and fought back.

An ache in my brain forces me to rub at my forehead. Dolores and I need to discuss the house and our grandmother before too much longer.

We could sell. That would be the easiest solution. Sell *as is.*

We could renovate and then sell, upping the investment and gaining a better return. My neighbor in California is an investor and might know someone who handles property like Magnolia's.

Either way, Magnolia cannot stay here alone. Dolores runs the diner which is another issue. It needs some upkeep as well. I'm overwhelmed with all the things crumbling around me.

Thinking of Garrett, I'm reminded of home. I want to go home—LA home—then I recall the side yard.

We were having a good time—throwing leaves at one another like kids—and the way Mati looked at me like she wanted to trace my abs with her tongue. A smile curls my lips with the thought. I'd let her have

137

L.B. Dunbar

her way with me as long as she sees it's me. Not because of lust. Not because I was a rockstar. Not because I was in magazines. But just because she could—and Mati did. Her eyes roamed my skin in appreciation, and her gaze sent shockwaves to other places, places ready to oblige her in all ways.

Then Cora had to bring things to a screeching halt, and I do mean screeching. I don't fault her directly, but her theatrics popped the mood and stole Mati's laughter. I haven't heard her laugh in so long and I hadn't realized how much I missed it. Her laugh was loud and strong like she really thought something was humorous or pleasant, and when she got going with the giggles, it could make you laugh as well without even knowing what was so funny to her. I miss that—that kind of laughter—and I'd forgotten it. Of all the things I remember about Mati, her laughter is something I shouldn't have forgotten.

I also realize Mati needs more care from me. Grabbing her tit like a bumbling teen wasn't exactly the way to win her into feeling *not* guilty.

Do I want to win her?

Is she a contest?

If I were still a hungry teen, I might respond with a yes. I remember the little things irking Chris about our continued friendship. The late night drives. The love of dance. The constant pranking. But Chris being Chris, took those things in stride. Maybe he also did it because he had Mati by his side.

However, Mati isn't a competition. I'm going home as soon as I settle things here. Don't get me wrong. I'm not rushing my mother's death. Surprisingly, she seems to be hanging on as the two weeks projected by the doctors passes. Still, I need to start thinking ahead. The house. Magnolia. The diner. But what about Mati? Do I just want sex with her or do I want all in? I'm not even certain it's a *me* question, but more of a Mati one. She needs to find herself, give in to herself. She's still young. She told me she doesn't date. She told me she doesn't touch herself. She's not a nun, though. She's too vibrant to be celibate, and I know just the man to help her with everything.

24

Open Doors

[Mati]

As I pull into my driveway, I see a light on in the front hall of my home. The etched glass in the front door gives nothing away other than the yellowish beams streaming through the design. *Did I leave the light on?* As I near the door, I stop, placing my forehead against the cold glass. It's so difficult to enter alone some nights. My palm flattens on the cool pane, and I take a deep breath. I'm startled when a palm matches mine on the other side of the glass, outlined by the light, and I smile a little, thinking it's one of the boys.

When Jax and Jordan were little, and Chris would return home late from his office, the boys would press their little hands to the glass waiting for their father. Chris would come to the door and rest his larger hand against the other side. The boys would squeal with delight, trying to reach for their dad through the solid panel. Assuming it's one of the boys, I turn the knob and enter the hall.

Then my voice freezes in my throat.

"Mati."

"Denton?" His hands slip inside his jean pockets, his head lowering sheepishly. "How did you get in here?" I ask, looking around the front hall as if I'll discover the answer.

"It's a small town, Mati. We all had a secret hiding spot with an extra key." So much for the false bottom on the underside of the flower box.

"What are you doing here?" An awkward silence falls between us. I don't invite him farther into the house. We just stand before each other in my narrow front hallway.

"I wanted to make sure you were okay."

I nod as if I understand when I don't. I take a step back, finding the wall for support. It's almost like we're in high school again. Me against

L.B. Dunbar

the lockers. Him talking to me from less than a foot away. My knees feel shaky as does my stomach.

"So." I swallow. "Where's Cora?" I hate that I asked. I hate how I sound jealous.

"Mati," Denton exhales, stepping forward. "Nothing happened." His fingers reach for my cheeks, hesitate a moment, and then return to his side. Still, his presence fills my space, his chest delicately pressing near mine. *So close*, I breathe.

"Sounds familiar," I say, my voice snappy. Next, he's going to renege his statement and tell me it didn't mean anything. It's Kristy all over again.

"Don't be like this." His voice lowers as his hands lift for my face, giving in to whatever held him back moments ago. My eyes shift toward his feet.

"I don't know how to be." I'm quiet as I speak. "I don't know how to feel."

"Just *feel*," he says, his voice sultry, deep, rustic, but I misunderstand his meaning.

"I mean, I understand Cora's beautiful and flirty and—"

"Mati." His breath caresses my lips as he exhales my name again. He's close enough I hear him swallow, but I continue, the roll building inside me.

"The other night. And then that kiss, Denton. That…kiss." I look up at him, my eyes filling with traitorous tears at the ache in my chest. *Did he kiss Cora?* "You pulled away and—"

His mouth crashes against mine, swallowing any other words and stealing my thoughts. Eager, energetic, all-consuming, his lips take mine, sucking and tugging, drawing me into him. I melt against his body as he pushes forward, pressing me against the wall at my back.

"How can you think I don't want you?" His words stutter between kisses.

"You couldn't even look at me after the other night after what happened on the floor, and—"

"Spice." He chuckles, pulling back and pressing his forehead against mine. "I couldn't look at you because your boob was hanging

140

out, pointing at me." His eyes lower, taking in the offensive breast. "Wanting me to take it in my mouth." His voice dips. "Begging me to suck it. Love it." A finger draws a line from my cheek to my neck. His hand momentarily circles my throat. Then his index finger slides downward, dragging the neckline of my overlarge sweater with it as it heads for the swell of one breast before resting at the tip of a ripened nipple, peaked and protruding through my bra. My breath catches.

"How can you think I don't want you, Mati?" His voice roughens, and a hesitant finger lowers to swipe at the seam of my shorts. My core pulses at the tease. "This is all I think about since I've been back."

Then he cups me, a full palm pressing against my covered sex and I gasp at the abruptness. He stills.

"I apologize. Maybe that's too much," he whispers, withdrawing his hand as if he's offended me as if touching me *there* crosses a line. Only my traitorous body follows his retreating fingers, erasing any lines drawn between us.

"Sweetheart?" he questions. My chest rises and falls, grappling for air I can't seem to bring into my lungs. His eyes search my face, questioning me. I don't know what to say. I don't know how to tell him what I crave. I need him.

He clears his throat. "Spice, do you want me to touch you?"

God, yes, please. But I don't say any of those things, partially ashamed of my desire. I roll my head to the side and nod as my eyes close.

"Look at me," he snaps as his hand returns to palm me between my thighs. "Do you see me, Spice?"

My eyes flit back to his. *I see him.* I see all of him—model beautiful with deep dark eyes and edgy cheekbones. Silver speckles mix with the scruff on his chin.

"All I ever wanted was to touch you," he says, and the words steal my breath. I inhale sharply before admitting a secret.

"I want that, too." Breathy and low, I hardly recognize my own voice in the confession.

"Just feel, Spice." He means physically and nothing more. "Ask me for anything."

L.B. Dunbar

"Touch me," I whisper, nearly in tears from the achy need.

Instantly, my loose neck sweater is tugged to my waist. Thick hands mirror each other as he cups each breast, squeezing over my bra and tweaking the nipples hidden beneath the fabric. My eyes close as my head falls back, but Denton demands I look at him again. The sharpness of his tone snaps open my lids, and I glance down at the attention he pays the heaviness of each globe. He pinches me, and I yelp, but the pain is a pleasure.

Fingers dip into each cup and tug the material aside, trussing me up like a call girl. I hate to admit, I love it. The weight. The roughness. His mouth suddenly savors one, lapping at it, sucking the nipple to a tight nub as if it could pebble even more. With a sharp release, he moves to the other breast, paying it the same attention. My fingers comb over his hair, holding his head against me. I never want him to stop, but then again, I want so much more.

As if reading my mind, his hands skim down my stomach, forcing the wide-necked sweater to my hips and then pushing at it to fall to the floor. Without breaking the suction on my breast, his fingers instantly come to my waist and unsnap my jean shorts. He releases my swollen nipple with a popping sound and his eyes lower, watching his fingers as they fumble with the zipper. He tugs at the denim, and I wiggle my hips, shimmying the material down a bit. Self-consciously my hand comes to the scarred skin at my belly, signifying the difficult birth of two babies.

"What happened?" he mutters, pushing my hand away and tracing over my scar. I don't want to answer. I don't want to bring into this moment the reality of an emergency C-section to remove the twins. Denton seems to understand my hesitation and his mouth returns to mine, resuming his journey lower. My head falls back, and my eyes close. Then his finger enters me, and my knees buckle. He pinches me at the hip, holding me upward.

"Sweet fuck, Mati. Your pussy is gorgeous like the rest of you." My eyes spring open, and I scoff. I should ask how he knows such a thing without looking, but he continues. "So wet, so wanting. My dick is begging to be near you." My breath hitches, and he peers up at me from his concentration on his finger filling me.

"What?" he asks, finding something on my face. "Don't like the dirty talk?" His lip curls at the corner. He's teasing me. I don't know how I feel about his naughty mouth. I mean, it's okay to read, but no one's ever spoken to me like this before. He positions the bulge stretching his jeans against his hand, slowly rolling his hips in time with his finger, mimicking how he'd enter me and pull back. In and out. Back and forth. He's literally having sex with me, with his finger, but *his dick wants in me.*

He leans closer to whisper in my ear. "Your pussy sings to me, and my dick wants to harmonize... slipping, sliding, separating you until there's only you and me." He draws back, and something fills his eyes. Something deep I can't read.

Okay, dirty talk works. It works just fine.

"Denton." His name comes out as a groan of need. He hasn't missed a beat in his rhythmic rutting, his hips moving in time with his finger filling me.

"It would feel so good, Spice. Me buried so deep inside you. You coating me." His voice drops an octave and a second finger joins the first. His breath hitches as he spreads me. My head falls forward, and I gaze down at his fingers entering me. His thumb finds the bundle of nerves, skin extra sensitive and a trigger for me. Pressing and pleasing, he's working me in a rhythm stronger than the beat of my heart. My fingers clutch at his shoulders as my knees tremble.

"Just feel. I got you, sweetheart," he mutters. "It's so much more than I imagined, Mati." My name is a lyric only he sings, and the beat at my core increases with the rapid pace of his fingers entering me, drawing me to the edge, and then returning to fill me.

My back presses to the wall, but I tip up on my toes. My fingertips dig into his shoulders as I feel the unfamiliar building inside. Flutters ripple through my lower abdomen. Thunder claps inside me and lightning strikes. I explode, lowering to my feet and clutching at him. I've been saying his name without realizing it—a song of my own.

"So gorgeous," he whispers, and I whimper at the loss of his fingers. He falls to his knees, and my hands clutch at the sides of his head. *What*

L.B. Dunbar

is he doing? He nudges my thighs to spread, and I gasp his name, curling my fingers around his ears.

"I can't go again," I warn. Yet, my jean shorts slip down my thighs along with my underwear and meet my sweater on the floor.

"You will," he demands into my soaked heat before returning his attention to my delicate folds. My fingernails claw behind his ears. I don't want to admit it's never happened before, but I've never had more than one orgasm at a time. I will myself not to think of Chris. It's only a second. A tiny pop in my bubble.

"Me," he growls against me, his mouth covering the scar signifying the Caesarean. This is too much, too soon. Then he lowers and exhales over me, the moisture of his breath meeting the heat of my core. "Me, Spice."

His tongue slices through already sensitive folds and my hips buck forward. Again, my body follows his retreat, wanting, needing more from him. I feel the curl of his lips against me before his tongue dips forward, licking and lapping. My eyes roll back at the sweet sensation. Teeth nip at my clit, already tender from his attention. His mouth turns aggressive, hungry, ravenous. "Make this pussy sing for me."

I'm aghast at his directness, but the curt demand makes my body obey. I come a second time with a scream. My legs fold, and I begin to slide down the wall. Thick hands grip my hips, pressing me upward, pinning me in place as he continues to savor me, sucking up each drip of my pleasure.

"Denton," I whisper. His lips slow, but he isn't finished. His tongue softens. His mouth gently sucks. A final lap and then he kisses me directly between my thighs. He pulls back, and his lips glisten as I stare down at him, brushing at his short hair with my fingertips.

"That..." My breath catches. "That was..." I can't speak. Denton rises slowly, forcing me to focus on the moisture coating his lips. With a salacious grin, he speaks.

"Yeah, Mati. *That was.*"

Quiet falls between us as he stands before me, stroking back my hair. His mouth comes to mine, and I taste myself on him. Guilty.

Decadent. Sweet. His lips are softer, telling me something I can't interpret. I don't know what to do next.

Shaky fingers reach for his belt, then unbuckling the catch on his belt.

It would feel so good, Spice. Me buried so deep inside you.

Instantly, his hand covers mine, and he draws away.

"Not tonight," he whispers. His lips find my forehead, and he kisses me, lingering on my furrowed brow. Suddenly, I'm conscious of standing before him with my clothing at my feet and my bra hiking up my breasts. I reach for the cups and cover myself, growing more awkward with each quiet, passing minute. Denton steps back and looks down at me. Another crooked grin graces his lips.

Do I ask him to stay?

Do I offer him a drink?

Do I admit I don't know what to do?

Coach me, my brain screams.

Knuckles swipe down my cheek until his fingers reach my throat, and he saves us both.

"Don't ever think I don't want you, Mati. You're all I've ever wanted."

25

Keepers of Secrets

[Denton]

Holy fuck. I take a deep breath and lower my head to the steering wheel. My eyes close and I want to squeal with glee like a teenage girl. I just ate the woman of my dreams, the girl I've wanted since high school, and she was amazing. My fingers coast under my nose, smelling her. Nothing compares to the taste lingering on my lips.

It was awkward there at the end, so I told her I'd see her later, just like when we were kids. I kissed her one more time and stole out her front door. Realizing time passes as I sit in my car parked down the street, I fire up the engine and head to the Lodge. I wanted to stay, let her finish unbuckling me and bury myself in her, but not tonight. One step at a time, I realize. Mati needs my reassurance especially when her hands covered her belly, and I lost her for a moment.

I don't need to know where she went. She called my name, but did she feel me? Did she know it was me kissing her, touching her, tasting her? I want to believe she did, but I'm not convinced she didn't slip in her thoughts and imagine me as someone else. Someone no longer present.

I have no idea what kind of marriage Chris and Mati had. I couldn't even guess, especially as mine was so short-lived and unhappy. Was he gentle with her like he was as a teen? Did he get rough with her, tease her, talk dirty to her? Did he keep it clean and missionary, or did he make her scream like she did for me? These questions fill me with doubt I never feel when I consider a woman. Then again, I don't put so much thought into most of them. I get in and get out, which is not what I want to happen with Mati. I want all of her, yet how fair would that be? I'm making lists and forming plans for the future, but my end goal remains the same—leave.

+ + +

I meet Dolores at Magnolia's the next day, and in the quiet of our mother's sick room, I mention the inevitable.

"What will we do with everything?"

"What do you mean?" Dolores asks, her eyes not leaving our resting mother.

"The farm. The diner. Magnolia."

Dolores's head shoots up to me. "Nothing will happen with any of those things. I'll take care of everything like I always do." Bitterness rings in her voice, and I understand. She's right. She's been here all along, but I'm here now. I'm not staying, but I'm here for the time being.

"Dolores, let me help you."

"How?" Dolores snaps, her hand reaching for Mother who lies there unresponsive.

"We could sell the farm. Use the money to improve the diner."

"And what about Magnolia?"

"We'll find her a place in town." The answer seems simple enough. She lived there once upon a time when her husband owned the hardware store, and she ran the diner.

"Denton, you can't move an eighty-year-old woman from her home. It will kill her."

"Dolores," I sigh, running a hand down my face. "Don't be so dramatic."

"Lores," she mutters under her breath, and I exhale again. I'm not calling my sister this name dubbed by the motorcycle putz who can't even bother to come here and comfort her. How did she get mixed up with Crusty Rusty anyway? I stare at my sister. Dark hair with a blue cast covers her grays. Her blue eyes are bright from exhaustion. We don't really look like siblings. We can pass as them but only upon a deep inspection. Dolores looks so much like my mother did once. Her hair. Her eyes. Her pale skin. My mother was always thin, sad, drunk. While my father was an alcoholic, my mother ran a close second to his ability to put away the alcohol. In her defense, she drank to disappear from him. Maybe it was to numb the effects of him.

"Why do you think she stayed?" I ask. Silence follows my question, and for a second, I wonder if I spoke out loud. I glance over at Dolores who continues to stare down at our mother.

"I think she was afraid to leave him. Maybe she thought she had no alternative. Where would she go? Back here? He took so much from her. She didn't go to college. She didn't have a skill. She was his wife. Nothing more."

"She was our mother," I add.

"I think that frightened her even more."

I pause, taking in my sister who peers at my mother. I don't know this woman any more than I know the woman lying on her deathbed. How are these people my family? How have I lost touch with them?

"He never…he never hurt you, right? I mean, even after I left. He didn't come for you."

"He never touched me. Insulted, yes, but never laid a finger on me." Dolores sighs, lowering her head. "He was nasty in his own right, but nothing like he was with you or with her." Her gaze returns to our mother. "He hated her in the end."

I don't want to know, and yet I feel it's only fair for Dolores to tell me.

"What happened?"

Dolores shakes her head. Her brows pinch and she lifts our mother's delicate hand to her lips. Her eyes close and I sense Dolores knows something she isn't sharing. I won't force her. I don't need the details of our father's abusive behavior. I lived it for eighteen years.

"You could have come to California," I offer. Dolores's head pivots and her eyes narrow at me.

"Don't do this."

"What?"

"Pretend like it would have been that easy, or you would have wanted me there."

"All you had to do was ask," I counter.

"All *you* had to do was ask as well." Cold runs through my body at her statement. I invited her to California. I did. *Didn't I?* I pause, thinking back as far as I can remember.

Shit.

"I'm sorry," I whisper. Her mouth opens to respond, and I expect her to tell me to *stuff it* like she did when we were kids. Then her lips close and twist. She's thinking, and I wait with anticipation for what she'll say next. When she doesn't speak, I let it go. We remain silent for the rest of the hour.

Eventually, Dolores leaves me alone with our mother. I lean back in the once overstuffed, now terribly uncomfortable, chair and kick my feet up on the edge of the bed. My head lolls backward. My eyes close and my throat vibrates. A soft, raspy rumble comes from my mother.

"Sing," she murmurs, her voice straining. *Was I singing?* I don't think I was. Humming, maybe. I hadn't even noticed. I look over at her to find her staring at the ceiling. Her fingers twitch again on the light blanket covering her, and I lower my feet, reaching forward to hold her hand. "Like him."

My father never sang.

Watching her swallow from the effort of speaking, I reach for ice chips in a cup on the nightstand. I hold one at her dry lips. She rolls her head side to side, letting the cool cube coat her cracked skin. When she turns away, I realize she's had enough. I'm returning the cup to the stand when she speaks again. Her voice is only slightly stronger.

"Calvin," she mutters. My brow furrows as I stand over her.

"Mama?" I question, uncertain what to ask. Her head slowly rolls again. Her hand begins fumbling with the cover, and I cup her fingers in mine. This time she squeezes as much as her pencil-thin fingers can tighten.

"Calvin." Her voice comes clearer. She repeats this a second time, her grip tightening.

"Denton," I correct, worrying once again she's delirious, calling out to me, but mixing up my name with Kip's.

Calvin? Who is Calvin?

"I knew you'd come back for me," she mutters, her fingers gripping. My mouth falls open to correct her, but the nurse enters to check on Mother.

L.B. Dunbar

"Miss Caroline, you settle down, honey," Vivian says, seeing Mama in an agitated state. The daytime hospice nurse is a godsend while Stephen is our angel during the night, as Magnolia calls him. Vivian pats my mother's arm, but Mama's eyes remain wild, her fingers squeezing mine.

"I don't know what she's saying." My voice cracks as I stand next to her, still holding her hand in mine. I don't understand. *Who is Calvin?*

"There, there, Miss Caroline." The nurse presses something on the attached IV and slowly my mother's lids lower. Her fingers go lax.

"Mama." Her name lingers between us, but she's out.

"Who's Calvin?" I ask Vivian as if she'd have an answer. Vivian juts out her lower lip, thinking a second.

"Never heard of a Calvin before. Then again, I'm not from these parts." Neither am I anymore, I think.

+ + +

"How's your mother?" Magnolia asks me as I trudge down the staircase. She stands at the bottom as if she waits for me. She's a prisoner in her own home as she can't climb the steps to visit her own daughter.

"Restless." I pause, staring down at the frail woman before me with her magnifying eyeglasses and her walking cane. "She called me Calvin."

Magnolia gasps. "She told you," she whispers, leaning toward me as if conspiring with me.

"Told me what?" I hush-whisper back to her, stretching forward to tower over her small stature.

"About Calvin." She straightens, and despite the pop-bottle eyewear, her eyes narrow at me.

"No. She called me Calvin. Who's Calvin?" For some reason, my heart races, and I inhale deeply, as if I can't catch my breath.

"Huh."

"Huh? That's it? What gives, Magnolia?"

"A *what* doesn't give, a *who* does."

I stare at her, even more confused than my mother.

150

"Okay," I exaggerate. "*Who* is he?"

"I'm only the keeper, not the giver of secrets."

Okay then, Magnolia has dipped into one too many meds today.

Pressing off the floor with her cane, she moves forward toward the front door and then detours to the parlor leading out to the screened-in porch. Guess I'm not playing escalator to her at the moment. She's taken to calling me such a nickname when I carry her up to see my mother.

"You're kind of slow, like an escalator. Not half as efficient as an elevator." I'm slow because she's fragile and I don't want to drop her walking up nearly two flights of stairs as the house has taller than average ceilings. I have to bite my tongue from telling her she should have installed an elevator then, instead of using me as her mule. If I spoke up, I'd sound like an ass, too.

I shake my head and turn for the kitchen. Hidden behind the open refrigerator door, Dolores digs through the stacks of casserole dishes and piles of plasticware.

"Don't we have any fruit? Just a simple apple would do." She's speaking to herself.

"Who's Calvin?" I ask, and she freezes. I sense it in her sudden quiet, nothing shuffling on the shelves. Slowly, she stands, her hand on the top of the lower door.

"She told you," Dolores whispers like my grandmother.

"No one's telling me anything. Mother was just calling me Calvin. Muttering how he came back, or I came back. I'm not even sure what she meant. I think she's looped." Which reminds me, I could go for a hit right about now, and I wonder if I have any weed left in the secret compartment in my car. This place has turned looney.

"Calvin was Kip's younger brother," Dolores says matter-of-factly as if I should know this, as if I should remember him. Only I don't. She closes the refrigerator door rather slowly, almost methodically and pauses a second with her palm on the yellow steel. Only her head spins in my direction. "He died when we were young."

Something isn't settling well with me and this simple explanation.

"Should I remember him? Are you a keeper of the secrets, too?" I tease, chuckling at the weird statement from Magnolia, but when her

151

L.B. Dunbar

eyes widen, I realize I'm correct. My sister knows more than she's telling.

26

Dear Old Dad

[Denton]

Excusing myself from Dolores, I decide to head to town. Her silence speaks volumes. She isn't going to share information with me, and I'll need to do some sleuthing myself. I'd love to go to Mati, but the time of day means she's coaching.

I find myself at the new mayor's office instead.

The place holds a two-fold memory. The positive one was first meeting Chris. I can't remember how old we were exactly—maybe nine or ten—but I remember leaving my dad's office on my bike, a tiff between us set me off too fast. I pedaled down the street with tears in my eyes and a sting in my chest. He hadn't hit me yet. That would come a year or so later, but his anger was already present. I stood on the pedals, pumping my legs to burn off the energy. When I came to the end of the street, I took the corner too quickly, and narrowly missed another bike. I hit a gravelly patch, and the force swept my bike out from under me. I fell to my side, the bike tangling in my legs.

"Are you okay?" a freckle-faced kid asked. His brown hair stood up in the air.

"I don't need help," I snapped, ignoring his offered hand and struggling with the bike. My shoelace wrapped around the pedal.

"You're bleeding." My leg was scraped from the small pebbles on the edge of the road, and I gripped my kneecap.

"Here." Chris handed me a handkerchief—an old-fashioned, honest-to-God handkerchief. "For your face."

I glanced at my scratched-up leg, burning from the gravel and then touched my face. Tears streamed down my cheek, and I didn't know if it was the pain of my injury or the ache in my heart from my dad. He didn't stare at my face but stood still, holding out a hand with the white square.

L.B. Dunbar

"Gotta be brave above all things," he said as I took the handkerchief from him and scrubbed over my face. "A little blood ain't nothing, but never let them see your tears." He nodded across the street to my neighbor, Mati. I cupped his offered hand, and he hiked me up to my feet. He reached for my bike and followed me as I hopped a little, getting out of the road, and keeping weight off my bleeding leg. I used the tearstained cloth to wipe off my leg, hissing at the sting. Feeling like I could add pressure to my knee, I stood taller.

"Hey, thanks." I handed the used handkerchief back to him.

"No problem," he said, smacking at my hand. Without thinking, we begin a small routine of palm slaps and fist bumps and then a weird wiggling of our fingers at each other thing. "Want some ice cream? My mama says ice cream cures everything." I snorted as my parents thought alcohol did that. "My treat."

Who could turn down free ice cream?

"I'm Chris. Chris Rathstone, by the way. I'm new here."

"Denton Chance. My dad's the mayor but don't let that scare you from being my friend."

His smile grew a little lilt to his lips. "Friends, huh? As long as you like basketball, we can be best friends." It was as simple as that. We were friends immediately.

My heart races as I step inside the antiquated two-story brick building. I ask the older woman at the reception desk if Charlie might have a moment for me. My heart continues to skip double time in my chest as I look around the outer office. Fresh paint and modern furniture do nothing to disguise the past I remember in these walls.

When I get home... The menace of my father's voice rings in my memory. I like to think I'm past the threat—the danger of ancient history—but being in this place forces the old anxiety through my veins. How can it be I still hear his voice so clearly? He's dead, I remind myself. He can't hurt me. I almost laugh at myself until the receptionist hangs up the landline and Charlie's office door swings open. His friendly smile is completely opposite any greeting I ever received from my father opening the same door.

"Denton," he greets me. "To what do I owe the honor?" He nods to signal me to follow him. Inside the official mayor's office, the old curtains have been removed and replaced with plantation blinds, which Charlie has open, allowing sunlight to stream into the dark place of my memory. The giant desk of my father's is gone, replaced with something sleek and modern. Charlie's contribution to the office, I assume.

Charlie formally points to a leather seat across from his desk, and I sink into it, surprised by the comfort. I've never been so relaxed in this surrounding. It takes me a moment to reconcile the older Charlie with the younger one. He sits across from me, official in his tie and dress shirt rolled to his elbows. He's business casual, but the spark in his eyes reminds me of the skinny kid running between yards with me.

"I'm looking for some information," I begin. "I thought it might be public record, or maybe you would just know something, being the mayor and all."

"I'm the mayor, Denton, not a wizard." He smiles at his own joke, and I shake my head. "Okay, so ask me, and if I don't know I can at least point you in a direction, I think."

"Not much confidence for a mayor." I chuckle.

"Why am I suddenly worried this is about Mati?"

His sister. Instantly, a vision of her naked and pressed against a wall fills my thoughts. I cough to stifle my concern that just from looking at me, he knows what I did to his little sister.

"Not Mati. Someone named Calvin. Calvin Chance perhaps. Did Kip have a brother?"

"Aren't these things you should be asking your family?" Charlie narrows his eyes, and for a moment I think I might be the only one who doesn't know the secret.

"Seeing as my family is a bunch of women who normally like to gossip, they are rather tight-lipped about this possible, mysterious uncle."

Charlie's hands clasp together as his elbows lean on his desk. He turns his head to the side.

"I'm familiar with the Calvin Chance case. His murder was an unsolved mystery around here some forty years ago."

155

L.B. Dunbar

Sitting up straighter, the leather suddenly doesn't feel as comfy, but rather stiff around me.

"What?"

"It's an old case. Nobody knows exactly what happened. An internet search might produce some general information, although the case is considered ancient by now. There might be some information in the archives of the library."

"How is it I don't know anything about this?"

"Again, it sounds like a question for your family, but you and I were young when it happened. I'm only familiar with it because it was a case still open when I first started practicing law. The statute of limitations on the investigation is open-ended in Georgia."

I don't know what this could mean, but I'm sensing something big is still a mystery.

Charlie says I can't have access to official court documents, but the case itself is public knowledge. I could head to my lodge room and fire up my laptop, but I'm thinking archives at the library might be a better place to start.

Ida Hildenbreth is still the librarian at Blue Ridge Public Library, and my guess is she's a hundred years old. Then again, she probably isn't, and I just remember her as already being old when I was a child. She's sharp as a tack, though, and instantly knows where to find the information which might interest me. I don't want town gossip or speculation, I tell her. Within minutes, she has me pulling up scanned documents from ancient newspapers and article after article about the mystery of Calvin Chance's murder.

Five years younger than his older brother, Calvin Chance served a tour of four years in the army, returned home only briefly, and reenlisted. Four years later, he returned home on a medical discharge to a hero's welcome. Three months later, his body was found in the woods opposite McIntyre Farm, my grandmother's estate. A gun wound to the chest was the cause of death. The news reports speculated he had a lover's quarrel, although he had no official sweetheart. Known to frequent a dance hall in Elton—the same place my mother claims to have met my father—the articles paint the picture of a playboy, a decorated veteran who knew how to attract the ladies. While there were no official suspects, the police deemed it could be any number of scorned women. After questioning, the mayor and his wife were cleared as suspects.

I sit back as I read this tidbit. Why would Calvin's brother and young wife—my parents—be considered in a murder investigation?

One article features a picture of my family. My parents stand with their arms around each other. It's a rare show of affection, one I later learned was practiced for the cameras. Dolores holds my father's hand on his right. I stand wrapped around my mother's leg on her left. I might be four or five years old.

The first family of Blue Ridge. *What a joke.*

Sitting forward, narrowing in on the image of my family, I see myself clinging to my mother at an early age, already holding onto her for love and protection which disappears years later. As I stare at the picture, I notice others standing around them, people I always considered nameless well-wishers or who worked with my father. As I zero in on the image, I realize the man to my left is dressed in full military uniform. His hand rests on the top of my head, but his face is turned toward my mother, not the camera. The image is grainy in black and white newsprint, but there's something about his face I don't need to see to comprehend. I've worn that expression myself—yearning. Suddenly, suspicions of the truth haunt me.

+ + +

I leave the library without concrete answers, yet I'm consumed by my speculation and find myself at BRMP on my fourth beer by six fifteen in the evening. The dinner rush is in full force, and I'm on my way to being hammered. I'll pay tomorrow for the shots between the craft brew, but I don't care tonight. I want my thoughts to disappear.

It can't be, I think for the millionth time, and then I knock on the bar top for another shot.

Things aren't bad until your ex looks good, and that's the stage I'm at when Kristy walks into the pub all hair sprayed up, stuffed into skinny jeans, and covered in a layer of makeup like icing on a cupcake. She

L.B. Dunbar

looks good in a blurry sort of way, which is bad. *So bad.* Noting my condition, she saunters right up to my barstool and spins me to position herself between my knees.

"Kristy." Her name slurs on my tongue, which feels thick and pasty.

"Denton." My name like nails-on-a-chalkboard, instantly recalling all the times she used it, and all the times I fell for it. *What was I ever thinking?*

Mati. That's what I was thinking.

Get back at Mati.

Only it backfired on me.

"You look good, baby. You feeling good tonight?" If I didn't know it was her, she could have been any woman, in any bar, propositioning me, and I'd laugh at the cheesy pickup line. Suddenly, pinpricks tiptoe up my chest, and I glance down to see the daggers of her fingernails over my T-shirt. "We can be good together, honey. Remember?"

Not good, I think.

Not like I was with Mati.

Now that I have memories of how things could be, I'll never go back.

Unfortunately, my hands have found Kristy's hips, and I'm tugging her to me. On the other hand, I consider I might be hanging on, so I don't fall off the stool. Either way, the position is compromising...not promising.

"Aw, fuck," I hear someone mutter at my side, and my head slowly rolls to see Billy Harrington glaring at me. He's standing on the wrong side of the bar. Statue still, arms crossing over his chest, he glares at me, which gives Kristy the perfect opportunity to kiss my cheek and then turn her head to face Billy.

"Hiya, Billy," she drawls, using her same screechy-screech on him. He's less affected than me, holding his frame tight as his jaw ticks. Is he jealous? Does he want her? Please, someone, take her off me. The smell of her perfume wafts over my nose which twitches. This is wrong. She is wrong. This isn't the scent I seek. Pomegranate. That's what I want.

"Kristy," Billy addresses her, his voice as tight as the expression on his cheeks. "Whatcha doing, Denton?"

158

"I'm drinking," I say as if he doesn't know. He's been the one serving me most of the evening.

"Is this what you want?" Billy asks, nodding only subtly at Kristy whose cheek still presses against mine, her eyes directed at Billy while I see two of him.

"I don't know what I want," I lie. I want his baby sister. I want her to comfort me, hold me like she did and tell me it isn't true. Tell me what I'm thinking about my parentage can't be real. My eyes close.

"That's what I thought." Billy nods. "Hand me your keys."

"I'm not drunk," I admonish, slurring slightly.

"And I'm not letting you leave here with her."

"Hey," Kristy pouts and straightens to face off with Billy. "Why? Are you jealous, Billy Harrington?"

"Hardly," he mutters, and I don't know why I find this funny, but I do. Suddenly, I'm laughing, bent at the waist cracking up, until my eyes tear and I know I'm on the verge of spilling my emotions all over the bar. I pull my phone from my pocket, handing it to Billy as well.

"What's this for?"

"So I don't do something equally stupid like call her." I swing back for the bar, disentangling my body from Kristy. I don't need to tell him who I mean.

"You don't need to call me, baby. I'm right here," Kristy purrs, rubbing her hand down the back of my head. I shiver, and not with desire. Billy presses between Kristy and me, and his voice coats my ear.

"You don't need to call her. I already did."

My eyes close again. I don't need to ask who he means.

27
Taking Care

[Mati]

I take a deep breath as I stand behind my brother positioned behind Denton. Elbows on the bar, Denton holds his head up with thick fingers as Billy says something to him. He's squeezed himself between Denton and sticky Kristy who had her hands on Denton—again—as I entered the pub. *What is it with these two?* I wonder for the millionth time. They were never good for each other, and yet something must have been good enough between them because Denton married her once they reached California. The only details I have of their divorce is Kristy's version which includes his desperate love for her but his desire for the rockstar road more.

"Billy," I say in greeting as I place a hand on his back. Billy shifts to look at me over his shoulder.

"He's all yours," he says, stepping back as Denton spins to face me. His eyes are a drunken glaze. His smile is too big, his face ruddy.

"Hey, Spice," he slurs.

"Denton, whatcha doing?" I rub a hand up his back, hoping to comfort what I suspect is pain over his mother's condition. I might not have the best relationship with my mother, but her dying would be one of the worst experiences of my life. I'd like to think Denton feels the same.

"Drinkin', lion cat. First drink's on me." He pats his lap like I should climb up and take a seat, but I shake my head, not appreciating his rude behavior in front of others for just this reason—Kristy gasps and my brother's brow rises.

"Actually," I emphasize. "I think it's time to go."

"Mati," he gasps in false surprise. "I didn't think you'd be so easy." He chuckles and turns for the bar. "Drink first."

"Listen, California." My fists come to my hips as one cocks to the side. "I'm not one of your hussies come to get some. I'm here to take your drunk ass to the Lodge before you make more of a fool of yourself." My eyes shift to Kristy. Maybe he wants his ex-wife again, but not on my watch. My brother called me for some reason. I shiver with thoughts of Kristy and Denton.

"California," he snorts. "We're a long way from California." His foot slips from the crossbar on the stool leg, and he lunges forward. Billy catches him at the chest as Denton's other leg falls forward to stop him from tumbling.

"I got it." Denton holds his hands upward. "I got it."

Billy removes his hands, spreading them wide to signal he released Denton, but still holding them close enough to catch him if he stumbles. It's evident he doesn't *got it*.

"Here's his keys," Billy offers, handing them over to me.

"She can't drive my car," Denton admonishes. "It's a stick. I drive." I'm going to bypass the insult that I can't drive a stick-shift vehicle. Billy intercedes anyway.

"No way, buddy. She drives, or you don't leave."

"Spice likes me to drive, isn't that right, Mati? I can drive all night long." The words come out like a song, and Denton moves his hips in a way to suggest something other than handling a car.

"I don't know what he means," I say, glaring at my brother whose lips cracks into a curve.

"None of my business." Billy smirks. My eyes drift to Kristy who has remained surprisingly silent during this interchange. Her mouth gapes open as she stares between Denton and me.

"You hooked up with him?" She squeaks.

"I did no such thing," I defend.

"But she wants to," Denton adds, wiggling a finger at me.

"I do not," I add more defensively. We are so not having this conversation before his ex-wife and my can't-keep-it-in-his pants brother.

"You so do, Mati. You just can't admit it yet." His finger taps my nose which I swat away. "But you will. Soon, sweetheart."

L.B. Dunbar

Oh. My. God.

"I think you should take care of him." I nod at my older brother whose face fights a grin.

"Sounds like you've got things handled," Billy says, the grin spreading.

"Yeah, sweetheart. Handle me." Denton's tone deepens, seductive and slurred. Not exactly a turn on.

"For the love of Pete," I mutter.

"Nope, name's Denton. Love of Denton."

It's my turn for my mouth to gap open.

"Holy shit," Kristy mumbles. "I always knew it was a matter of time."

My eyes narrow at her, ready to ask her what the hell she means but Denton cuts me off.

"Time. So much lost time," Denton mutters, swaying forward before Billy catches him at the chest again.

"Time you admit you love her," Kristy says over his mumbling.

My mouth falls open again and Denton's eyes narrow at his ex. His finger lifts for a tweak of his former wife's nose. "No can do," Denton says, his voice lowering while his head shakes. "I'm a keeper of secrets, too."

My brows pinch, and I glance at my brother at Denton's side for assistance.

"Okay, pal. Let's get you outside." Hoisting Denton's arm over his shoulder, my brother guides Denton out of the pub. Kristy remains at the bar, but I follow the scene before me. The diner's definitely going to be full of rumors tomorrow morning. This conversation will make coffee talk at every table.

+ + +

I should take Denton to the Lodge, but he falls asleep the second my truck purrs to life. I don't think I can carry him, nor do I know which room is his. Worse case is I leave him in my truck in my driveway overnight. I hope he doesn't puke, though. That would

162

be…unpleasant…to clean. I chuckle to myself with reminders of the boys when they were drunk in their teens.

Jax missed the toilet.

Jordan hit the front seat of Chris's car.

It wasn't funny at the time, but the memories of their drunk asses accost me. I turn for Denton only a second, his head pressed to the cool glass of the passenger window. Who takes care of him when he drinks too much? Does he do this often? Does he lose control? I refuse to let the last question linger. He wouldn't do such a thing. He knows better. He has to know better.

As I pull into my drive, I stare at him a moment longer, the truck still humming. He looks tortured even in his sleep, just like when he was a kid. I turn off the engine and place a hand on his shoulder. Gently pressing at him, I call his name. A smile grows on his lips, and his face softens.

"Denton," I say louder, jiggling his shoulder with more force. His hands flex on his thighs, his fingers stretching. Did he just groan?

"Denton," I snap, and his hand drags up his thigh to coast over his zipper region.

"Oh, Mati," he mutters, rubbing back and forth with the heel of his hand. The outline of a firm ridge shows along the seam of his jeans.

"Denton." I smack his arm, and he jolts awake, his palm still covering the bulge at his zipper. He blinks, his eyes having trouble focusing on me, but a devilish gleam dances in them. His hand lifts, coming for my cheek as his body leans forward. Anticipating his move, I outmaneuver him, but he's quick despite his drunkenness. His fingers curl around my throat.

"Don't pull away from me." His voice would sound sinister if I didn't know him better. There's an achy sound in his plea.

"Don't kiss me when you're drunk."

"I'll kiss you when I'm drunk. I'll kiss you like a punk. I'll kiss you here and there and everywhere." His eyes flit over my body, causing tingles to erupt as he outlines my breasts and leaps to my crotch before landing on my lips. He hasn't even touched me other than the grasp on my neck, and yet I feel him everywhere like he said.

His head swivels left to right, squinting as he peers out my windshield.

"You brought me to your house?" He turns to face me, and the fingers on my throat soften, his thumb stroking my skin.

"This is where I bring you," I mutter, recalling all the times he climbed into a different house, but still my house.

"I can't sleep with you here." His fingers slip from my neck and lift for his hair. His head falls back to tap on the seat as his fingers rake through his short locks. I'm taken aback by his comment. Does he mean *sleep* sleep, like when we were kids? Or does he mean *sex*-sleep? Because I can't sleep with him if he's drunk.

"Why do you do this to me, Mati?" he questions, interrupting my thoughts of actually having sex with him. Not tonight. Not here. But in general, what would sex be like with his hard body, covering me, burying inside me, knowing what I know of his hands and his tongue and his kisses?

He isn't looking at me as he speaks but staring out the passenger window at my house. The front porch light is on as is the front hall. It looks welcoming, but suddenly, I'm not certain I should invite Denton inside.

"I'll take you to the Lodge, now that you're awake."

With the mention of the Lodge, Denton opens his door and nearly tumbles out. I reach for him but miss and scramble to remove myself through the driver's side. By the time I've circled the truck, he's walking up the path to my front door. I need to double my steps to reach him, and I scoot around him to hop up on the stoop. Two hands come up to stop him. With me on the step, we stand equal in height. My heart races as my hands feel the cotton of his shirt, warmth emanating from him inside his open leather jacket. His own heart beats under my palm. His eyes search my face, but I consider he's having trouble focusing.

"Take me inside." His rustic, throaty voice drips over me like chocolate sauce on a sundae. *Damn it.*

"Nothing will happen tonight." I don't know if I'm saying it for his protection, as he's drunk, or mine, because I'm drunk on him, and don't trust myself. He scrubs a hand down his face before his eyes shift to the side.

"Take care of me, Mati," he restates, and something in the ache of his request breaks me. For a moment, I'm a young girl again facing a battered boy, and all I want to do is hold him tight to me, take away his demons, and promise to love him. Instead, I nod and turn to unlock my door.

Denton leads the way to my living room, and I'm relieved. He lowers with a heavy plop onto my couch and tips his head back, closing his eyes. Thinking he'll pass out, I continue toward my kitchen, fill a glass with water, and find some painkillers for the headache he'll eventually have. Returning to the living room, I place the items on the coffee table before I straighten and lean over Denton, brushing at his silver and ink hair. His hand shoots up and circles my wrist. He tugs my arm until his lips find my palm and lingers. His eyes flip open to catch mine. He slips my finger into his mouth and sucks hard a moment. Then he gives a gentle pull on my wrist, and I practically fall on top of him.

I right myself to sit next to him, our thighs pressed together, our shoulders touching. We remain silent for a few minutes, his warm fingers still wrapped around my wrist, but his head rests on the cushions again, and his eyes close.

"Rough day with your mom?"

"Rough life," he mutters. I stare at him, knowing what he means, yet also realizing his so-called life became much easier once he left Blue Ridge. He became a rockstar with money, fame, and females galore.

"What happened today?" I ask because I know something had to trigger his current condition. "Are you upset about your mother?"

"Upset?" He laughs without humor. "I'd have to care to be upset."

"That's cold."

"I'm cold, Mati. So cold." His eyes remain closed, his face to my ceiling.

"Is this about your father?" I absolutely understand his hatred of the man, but I also think with his father's death and Denton's physical absence it's something he should be able to let go of thirty years later. Then again, it wasn't me being insulted and beat.

L.B. Dunbar

"Yes." He sighs. "No."

I continue to stare at him.

"I don't think Kip was my father." Denton speaks so quietly I'm not certain I hear him incorrectly.

"What?" I shift to face him, and my knee lands on his thigh. His hand falls to my inner leg, but it's only resting there as if it's not actually touching me. I ignore the tingling of my skin under my jeans, as I wait out an explanation.

"Caroline keeps calling me Calvin. I thought she was just mixing up my name. When I asked Dolores and Magnolia what the name meant, who he might be, they were both surprisingly tight-lipped about him. Dolores did mention Kip had a brother named Calvin, though. I had an uncle I don't even remember."

My brows raise in surprise. I don't recall ever hearing about Kip's family. He rode into town one day, courted Caroline Duncan, married her, and melded into the history of Blue Ridge. That's the extent of my knowledge.

"Do you think he's your father?"

"I went to Charlie—"

"How would Charlie know?" His head rolls on the cushion, and he glares at me. I clamp my lips shut, allowing him to finish.

"Charlie said Calvin was Kip's brother. He was murdered in the woods near Magnolia's home. His case is unsolved."

I shake my head. "I don't understand."

"I saw a picture of them. Of us, as a family. Calvin was looking at my mother."

A *look* proves nothing. I sigh, noting his hand has begun to massage my inner thigh. The pressure feels nice, a little risky, and too thrilling for this conversation. He isn't making any sense, and I'm starting to assume he's drunker than I thought.

"How was he looking at your mother?"

Denton's dark eyes harden, turning midnight instead of soft coal. "He was looking at her like I look at you."

166

Heat breaks across my cheeks. Denton's palm creeps higher inside my thigh. My voice lowers as I speak. "I don't know what you mean." *How does he think he looks at me?*

"With longing." The words surprise me, and for a moment I'm lost in his eyes, the richness, the sincerity, the yearning. Has he wanted me like I wanted him? I'm not unschooled in modern dating practices. I know the other night meant nothing more than him making a statement— he set out to prove something with his dominance. I'm not complaining, just being realistic. Unfortunately, each touch from Denton reminds me how lonely I've been and how much I crave more.

The heat in his eyes is too much, and I look away. His fingers inch precariously close to my center, and while our conversation remains serious, my thoughts wander in other directions. Thick fingers dig into my denim-clad leg.

"It all makes sense now," he says, turning away from me and for a moment I think he's referring to us, but then he adds: "I think Calvin was my father. That's why Kip hated me."

It doesn't make any sense. I can't imagine Caroline cheating on Kip. She'd be too frightened. Then again, if she did have an affair, it could have been a reason for how he treated her. Not an excuse, though. Affair or not, there's no excuse. Nothing can forgive Kip's behavior toward his son, and eventually his wife. But still, his own brother?

"Denton," I whisper, covering his hand on my thigh, curling my fingers into his. The touch startles him, and his eyes drift downward to where our hands envelop one another. It's as if he didn't realize we'd been touching all this time.

"Mati." He leans toward me, a hand lifting for my hair, his lips seeking mine. I'm pressed backward until my hands touch his chest.

"Stop."

Denton stills, and we balance in this awkward position a moment. I can't kiss him like this.

"Make me forget, Mati." Lust fills his eyes. Sloppy, drunk lust. "Pretend with me."

As a child, he'd curl on my bed—me wrapped around him—and I'd hold him, hoping to make him forget for a little bit the horrors of his home. As if he could pretend he was part of mine. As adults, I have an idea he means more than a cuddle, but I can't go *that* far. Not tonight, not like this.

Using our enclosed hands, he drags mine to his zipper. There's no mistake in identifying the hard length, straining under the denim. Thick. Long. Bursting at the seams.

"That's right," he murmurs at me, his eyes closed, shutting out who I am as he flattens my palm against him. "Rub me off." He moans, but there's something in his tone that freezes me.

"Rub you off?"

"That's right, sweetheart. Take me deep, so I disappear."

Disconnect. That's what I hear. It isn't me he wants but a release. A distraction. And I can't be it for him. Irritation intertwines with my sympathy. For thirty seconds I see the rockstar in him. The man who got what he wanted but shut out the world to get it.

"Fuck you, Denton," I say softly, turning my head as I press at the firmness in his jeans, forcing him to release my hand. Balancing at a partially reclined angle, I feel like I'll fall at any moment. Fall into love with his pain. Fall into hate with his behavior. His eyes snap open, glassy and red, as he peers at me.

"That's what you want, isn't it?" His voice is hardly more than a whisper. "I want to fuck you, too, sweetheart. One day soon. I'm going to fuck you so hard I'll be imprinted inside your soul like you're in mine, and you'll never forget me, never want to forget me."

"I never wanted to forget you," I snap, ignoring the anatomy of him still straining against his zipper.

"Chris wanted you to." I feel myself lowering to the couch as Denton shifts his body. He shrugs, struggling with his jacket. Draping the heavy material over both of us, he curls behind me, molding me into his body.

"What does Chris have to do with anything?" Irritation turns to anger as Chris is brought into this conversation and we lay in such a comforting position. His voice turns drowsy and drifts off as he speaks into the nape of my neck.

"Chris has everything to do with us."

28
1991

[Denton]

It's prom night. Rented tuxedoes. Bright colored dresses. Dance music.

Chris and I planned the night. A hotel room down the ridge in Elton. Kristy and I would spend the night as we always do—hate fucking each other. We'd already gotten into a fight because my cummerbund didn't match her dress properly. Then she wanted a certain corsage, and Tom's Grocer didn't have the kind of flower she wanted, so I got her roses instead. She was pissed.

Chris, on the other hand, had everything planned perfectly—a romantic evening of taking Mati's virginity. I hated him, but I bit my tongue as I had for years.

"Hotel room. Check. Flowers. Check. Condoms. Check." Chris claps his hands, rubbing them together. I want to kill him.

"Sounds like you've thought of everything." I try to tamper the bitterness in my voice.

"I just want it to be special for Mati. She deserves the best." I don't miss the hint of glee in his voice, or the candor. He thinks he's better than me. I take a pull of the flask I have hidden in my jacket. In many ways, he's right. He deserves her. They'll settle down in a nice little house, with perfect little babies and become the next first couple of Blue Ridge—something I have no desire to be. I want out of this hellhole. A cross country road trip with Mati, and I'm out of here. I'll send her back here with my car, but I'm not returning.

Another song winds up, and Mati saunters up to us, bouncing on her heels. She's been dancing with some girls from the volleyball team. I'm happy to see her so energetic and springy. After her ankle injury, I worried she wouldn't recover for the simple things like dancing. The broken ankle fucked up her scholarship, though, and I don't think she'll ever forgive me.

169

"This is my song," she shouts, tugging on Chris's lapel. He lowers to kiss her, chaste and sweet, before glancing around to see if he'll be caught kissing his long-term girlfriend. He's not a risk taker like me. I've had Kristy in the boys' locker room and the girls' bathroom, both times while others could have seen us.

Mati's pulling at his tux coat, and while he stumbles forward with the force, he'll refuse her.

"Come dance." She pouts. She has the cutest curl to her lip, and I don't know how Chris denies her anything with that look. He's held out on sex with her, but one look like that from her, and I'd be buried deep, giving her whatever she wanted from me.

"You know I can't, baby," he says to her sweetly, just like that too soft kiss he gave her. Mati's a sexual being. I read it in her body language, and he's holding her back for whatever reason. Noble? Maybe. A gentleman? Probably. He's also an idiot for never learning to dance despite his inhibition. He's among friends here. No one will laugh. Too much, at least.

"I'll dance with you," I offer, slipping my flask in my jacket and shucking it for the back of a chair. This is the one pleasure Chris allows me. He'll let his wingman dance with his woman. He doesn't seem to worry about me in this capacity. Mati pouts one more time at Chris before reaching for me. She squeals with a little girlish whoop, so unlike her, as she pulls me toward the dance floor. Instantly, I forget Chris and Kristy and everything but the girl shaking her hips and raising her arms before me. We fall into a rhythm, letting the beat guide us, and we dance like stars trained to compete. I love how Mati moves, and it's another reminder of her sensuality.

The song shifts to a slower melody and the dance floor clears a little as the girls paired with girls find their dates, also refusing to dance to the heavier beat. A few couples step onto the floor, and Mati scans the room a second, searching for Chris. He'll slow dance if she asks him.

"Dance with me?" I suggest, holding up my hand and stretching out my arm. Mati smiles and slowly steps into my space. Hands come to my shoulders, ignoring the formal stance of my dance and my hands come to her hips. It's innocent enough except I can feel the curve of her

hips, the silkiness of her dress hugging them, and the possibility she isn't wearing anything underneath.

"Are you excited for our trip?" I ask, feeling the need to make conversation, although I typically find comfort in the silence of Mati as we take rides.

"I'm so excited," she says. "It's going to be amazing."

Just the two of us from here to the West Coast and back. At least back for her, not for me.

I spin us, and Mati leans into me. Her hands slip up to my neck and mine wrap around her waist, landing at the base of her spine. The tempo of the song is simple. A one-two step of ease and Mati and I fall in line. The song is about never letting go and always loving someone. There's something different about the way we move tonight, and my face lowers so my cheek presses next to hers, my breath tickling her ear. Her fingers dig at the curl of my hair near the nape of my neck. My hands lower to smooth over her hips. Mati presses against my chest. My lips can't help themselves, and they brush against her ear.

"Denton," she whispers, and my nose outlines the shell of her ear.

"Mati," I exhale into it. I've got a problem. One I've had for years when I've thought of Mati. One that's pressing into her lower belly because she's so tight against me. My fingers grip her hips, tugging her gently to me. She doesn't resist me. Her legs separate, and one slips on the other side of mine. I lift slightly, letting my upper thigh press against her core.

"Denton?" she questions, her voice low again. Our hips are in sync with one another. Back and forth. Back and forth. I want to let my head fall back and howl at the moon. She's driving me crazy, pressing against my leg, her thighs tightening around mine. My fingers splay outward, cupping her hips in my hands. Her fingers have crawled upward, tugging slightly at the hair near the nape of my neck. I'm so turned on.

I pull back to look down at her—bark rich eyes, a touch of pink on her cheeks, a gloss on her lips. My forehead comes to hers, our breath mingling, and not for the first time I wonder what it would be like to be lost in those eyes, looking up at me as I bury myself inside her. We'd move together like one, our dancing proves it.

L.B. Dunbar

Suddenly, I'm aware of a presence next to me. Pulling back from Mati, I see Chris standing next to us. The music, faded in my ears, rushes back to life around me. It's a new song, a fast one.

"Song's over," Chris says quietly, keeping his eyes on me. I release Mati, slipping one hand in my pocket to disguise the boner I have. My other hand rubs over my hair as my eyes lower. Shit. Chris looks pissed.

Mati's hand slowly slips down my shoulder and removes from me. She steps forward to Chris.

"I love this song," she says softly, trying to ease the tension between the three of us.

"I think I need a drink," I mutter, scrubbing at the back of my neck.

"I'll join you," Chris says, a slight hiss to his voice.

I follow Chris to a corner of the gymnasium and nab my jacket as I pass our table. The flask is nearly empty, but I take another pull before we reach the dark space. Chris turns on me once we're covered in the shadows.

"Don't take her with you." He rounds on me, the words almost spitting in my face.

"Don't take her where?"

"On the road trip."

My mouth falls open, and my eyes bug. He's got to be kidding. Mati and I have planned this trip for months. I'm shocked her parents agreed, but they trust me with her. Even her older brother James helped coerce them. Ten weeks. Almost as many states. Camping under the stars.

"I could never do that to her."

"Don't do it to her. Do it for me."

"What? Why?"

"I'm asking you not to take her."

"I heard you the first time, but I still don't understand."

"If she goes with you, she'll never come back." There's a plea in his voice, something I don't recognize. He's almost whining.

"Of course, she'll come back. She loves you." Dismissively, I wave at him.

"Look, I hate to ask. It's hard to ask." Chris understands all too well his circumstances. It made him humble which made him an even

172

better person. He was already the town's golden boy. He made all-conference for basketball and the all-star playoff team. He has straight As. He's president of the debate club, and he's going to college—pre-law—on a full-ride scholarship.

I snort. "Are you worried I'll steal her?" Sarcasm lingers, but she'd never cheat on Chris. I'd never allow her to cheat on Chris.

"Yes."

My mouth falls open for the second time, and then I straighten, crossing my arms over my chest.

"What's going on here?"

"I'm not blind, Denton. I know you better than anyone, even her. I see how you feel about her and how you lie to yourself, disappearing into Kristy—"

"You don't know shit." Over the years, I've had to defend my relationship with Kristy more than I cared to in order to keep up the pretense. I didn't love her. I liked her well enough, and we had a good time in bed together, but love? The emotion was reserved for only one girl.

"I know you have a talent. I know you're itching to discover it and be more. You'll go west, do great things, and never come back, and Mati'll stick with you because that's what she does. She'll fall in love with you for real."

Fall in love with me? It's been clear all along Mati loved Chris more. She loved me as the best friend. I'm a little surprised by his sudden show of jealousy. He's equally kept his feelings close to the chest, never hinting at this feeling.

"Don't you trust me with her?" Chris's brow pinches, and he looks away as if he can't admit his fear. She'll have more adventure with me—fulfill her wild spirit—but in the end, she'll want to settle down somewhere. She's hinted at it with all her talk of college and neighbors and babies in the future. That's not a life I foresee for myself. I envision small towns, late nights, and lots of road time. Mati would love it, but for how long?

L.B. Dunbar

"Denton, be real, man. She'll want things life on the road won't provide. Her daddy will only back her so far. You and I both know you need to leave. You've got to go, but don't take her."

Chris is still the only one who knows my passion—the guitar. He also knows how badly I want out of this town. If I make it—if the band I want to form with my cousin becomes something—Blue Ridge will only be a whisper of a memory to me.

"Even if she went with you, she'd want to come back. This is her home. Maybe it's why I've never said anything before. You take your rides together, but she never runs away with you. She comes home in the end." She goes to him in the end. I'd be kidding myself to think she'd ever love me like she loved him. I was the best friend, not the boyfriend.

"Do this for me, and it's the last thing I'll ever ask." Again, he's never asked anything of me. He's given me his friendship over the years, his unspoken brotherhood. I'd like to think I was doing some noble deed by honoring his request, but I wasn't. I was being selfish.

"What would I say to her?"

"Tell her you want to go solo." A weight on his shoulders seems to lift.

"She'll never believe me." Not to mention, it's going to break her heart. Mati doesn't need to leave Blue Ridge like I do, but she longs to see the world. Did I want to steal her away from him? Most days, yes. In reality, could I? No. What made me so loyal to Chris that I'd leave my soul behind and follow my dream? I was being selfish. He'd been my best friend through thick and thin, but I loved myself more than I loved either of them. I wouldn't survive any more of this town. I had to go with or without her.

"You've been good at keeping things from her for years. You'll be able to pull this off." Chris glares at me as if he knows my deepest, darkest secret. I'm in love with his girlfriend.

"Fine." I couldn't believe I was doing this for him. Was I making the ultimate sacrifice? My heart for his? In the end, it would be her heart I broke. "You better fucking take care of her."

174

"I will," he says, almost gloating that I'd given in. It was clear Chris and I could no longer be friends from that point forward, and we weren't.

The words echo in my head as I realize I've been dreaming of prom night. I'd missed him over the years once the friendship dissolved. Thinking back, I could accept he wanted to keep Mati because she was the only person he had left. When I went—and I would go—there would be no looking back on my part. Chris didn't have the means to follow me, nor did he want to leave. Blue Ridge was home to him and always would be. For me, I didn't look in the rearview mirror, even when my heart tempted me to glance back.

My eyes remain closed, but I rub at my throbbing temples. My back aches and I shift to find I'm almost falling. My eyes flip open, and I remember I'm on Mati's couch, in her house, *where she lived with him.* The room wobbles as I sit upright. I need some serious coffee. Light streams in through the front window and I see my keys on the coffee table, along with a glass of water and some pain pills. A crumbled scrap of paper gives me a phone number. Under it lies an envelope with my name on it. Instantly, I recognize the handwriting.

Damn him.

I swipe the envelope off the table and dial the number left for me. I'm assuming it's Mati's, but to my surprise, a male voice answers.

"Giant Brewing. This is Jax."

175

29

High School and Hallways

[Mati]

Fleck Denton and his *flecking* cryptic comments, just fleckity, fleck, *fleck*. My mind is out of sorts as I stand on the sideline watching the girls run drills.

"Jump at the net."

"Hannah, dig."

"Why is there a hole in the center?"

My voice cracks as I snap at the girls, taking out on them my feelings of inadequacy. He treated me like some groupie when all I was trying to do was take care of him.

Fleck him.

But then he has to be all crude, causing tingles in neglected places by saying what he said.

I'll imprint on you, your soul, and you'll never forget me.

As if I've ever forgotten him or that night—prom night—when everything shifted. The dance. The song. Chris and Denton had words. They didn't fight, not like my brothers who would throw a punch or two until Mama interceded and then they'd make up. Chris and Denton would argue, and within a day or two things were all good again. Not that time, though. Chris and Denton remained distant for weeks. The night before graduation, Denton broke my heart, and then he disappeared after the ceremony. I heard him drive off in the night, leaving me behind.

The mention of Chris last night changed everything. Like a splash of cold water, I woke up and wondered what I was doing sleeping next to a man who wanted me to act like a groupie. *Take me deep.* Not to mention, the implication of Chris as the reason things changed—the reason we lost Denton—haunts me and I recall what Hollilyn told me a while back.

Jax said his daddy told Denton to leave.

How could Chris do that? *Why* did Chris do it?

"Tanisha, jump," I yell, redirecting my thoughts to my middle and her lack of height at the net.

"You okay?" Alyce asks me, her arms at her sides as she stands next to me.

"What is she doing?" I bark, my head nodding at Tanisha. I think I growl.

"Not Tanisha," Alyce says. "What are *you* doing?"

I turn on my assistant coach, a glare beaming from my eyes until I see hers widen in surprise. Her head snaps back as if I've struck her, and I take a deep breath.

"I'm sorry," I mumble.

"What's going on?" Alyce lifts a hand to touch my arm, but I flinch back. I don't mean to be so cold, but I can't handle her tender spirit. I've been fighting tears all morning, after seeing Denton flat on his back on my couch, mouth gaping open, one arm over his eyes, the other dangling near the floor.

The scene also reminded me of prom night. Chris was hammered by the time we arrived at the hotel. He wasn't open about his plan, but the hints were there. We were both virgins. Prom night *was* the night, only it wasn't. He fell to the bed while I went to use the bathroom and when I returned to the room he was passed out—mouth gaping, arm over his eyes, another hanging off the bed toward the floor. I called James to come pick me up. He was the only one who wouldn't chastise me for where I really was as my parents thought I was at a friend's for the night.

"It's nothing," I respond to Alyce, looking away from her and staring out at my girls who look like they've never played volleyball in their lives.

What the fleck are they doing?

"Okay, take five," Alyce calls out, and I realize I've asked the question aloud. Crossing my arms, I pinch the bridge of my nose. "You," Alyce snaps, and I look up to see who she is speaking to, only to discover it's me. "Coaches' office."

I follow like an errant child, surprised at the strength in her tone and the directness of her demand. I pass her into the room, and she shuts the door.

"Sit. Speak."

While I take my seat, I glare up at her. "Well, missy, this is a side to you I haven't seen before."

"I have many sides, sister," she mocks in return. "Now, tell me what's going on with you."

We stare at one another in silence a moment. I'm the first to break away and lower my head to my hands.

"It's a man, isn't it?" Her voice rises an octave. "It's the man from the other night, right?" Her voice has reached an excited screech, and a little clap resounds in the small office. She's back to herself— cheery McCheerson cheerleader.

"It's nothing," I repeat, and I mean it. There's nothing to say or explain or happening. *Just nothing*. The thought makes me sad and a little hollow, as I put myself out there and then wanted to scrub myself clean after he spoke to me like he did. After his comment about Chris, he promptly fell asleep. How can men do that? One minute they're talking, and the next, out cold.

"It's never nothing with a man. Always something. Always trouble." Alyce shakes her head as she speaks, and I lift mine to look up at her.

"So much trouble," I mutter. Whatever Chris did, whatever Denton did, it's been a long time.

"Mati, you've got to give him a chance. You're out of practice, but—"

"What do you mean, I'm out of practice?"

"I just mean, it's been a long time since you've had to date, put effort into something."

"Marriage was effort," I defend, thinking of all the times Chris and I disagreed. We weren't the Bickersons, but we had our spats and married couple issues—finances and things.

"I'm sure it was, but dating is a different kind of effort."

"Who says anything about dating?"

Alyce's brow rises. "Friends-with-benefits is even more complicated. Why do you think that's a label on social media?"

I'm sitting upright, hands on my knees, blinking at her. "I'm not friends-with-benefitting either." *Does that even make sense?*

Alyce giggles. "Okay, look, anything you do, related to any man, from this point forward, is going to be complex. You had a familiarity with Chris. He was your husband. For *years*," she emphasizes as if I don't know this fact. "You'll be starting from scratch with anyone else. Starting new. The road might be bumpy at first, but the ride is worth the adventure."

Alyce's analogy hits harder than she knows. A road. A ride. An adventure. Life would have been all these things if I had been with Denton, but I never considered a life with Denton. Not really. Not until recently. Now, I think of him too much, but he isn't who I remember, and although I accept that people change, I don't want the rockstar. I want my friend.

"Maybe I just shouldn't date."

Alyce shakes her head again. "Maybe *not* dating has been your problem. You're out of practice like I said."

A subtle knock comes to the door, and we both look up at the window to see Hannah on the other side. Alyce opens the door.

"There's a man here for Coach Rath. I told him we had closed practices, but he says he has an appointment."

Alyce turns to me, a brow raised again. "What's he look like?" she directs back to Hannah.

"Tall and divine." Her face blushes. "I mean, he looks like a rockstar."

Alyce nods at Hannah. "We'll be right out. Tell the girls to run ladders." Hannah groans but it's just punishment for the laziness of practice.

Keeping a hand on the door, Alyce turns back to me. "Seems complicated has come a-knocking, Mati. Time to jump at the net," she teases, using her volleyball euphemisms again.

"I was never a middle," I correct her, grinning.

179

"Then dig, girl," she mocks with the reminder I was a libero, the player in the back, fighting for the ball. I'm used to complicated.

+ + +

I follow Alyce out of the office and walk directly to Denton. He looks mad—*flecking* hot, but mad. Well, I'm annoyed as well. Last night was a fail in the category of taking care of Denton. I should have held him on the couch, soothed him with words like I did when we were kids. I recall his assumptions about his father—another father. Things were certainly complicated, and I remind myself Denton doesn't need a relationship or friends-with-benefits or a date. He needs his friend, and I failed him.

"Hey," I say as I near him. I can feel the anger vibrating off his body, and I nod for the hall outside the gymnasium. I don't need a scene before the girls. In fact, I can't do this right now. I need to coach.

I continue into the hallway and spin to face him. He steps up to me, and suddenly I'm pressed against the trophy case across from the gym. His mouth crashes mine, and I can't breathe. He's consuming me as his lips capture mine, and I melt into him, although our mouths feel more like a fight than a kiss.

"I'm so pissed off at you," he mutters, nipping at my chin before returning to my mouth.

"Me? Well, I'm not too happy with you, either," I mumble into his lips.

"Why?" He releases me.

"Why what?"

"Why are you mad?"

"Because you were an ass last night." Denton pulls farther back and stares down at me.

"Did I hurt you?" His question startles me, as does the genuine concern.

"Only my feelings," I admit, looking down at my feet. My lips linger with the pressure of his, and I'd like him to kiss me again, but I realize where we are—our high school hallway. "I need to finish practice."

Ignoring what I said, Denton tugs me by the arm down the hall. He looks left and right as if looking for something. The building hasn't changed structurally in almost thirty years, despite updates to the decor. Finding what he must be looking for, he pulls me into an alcove near the library. My back hits the wall again, and his mouth finds mine. Kissing me, his lips devour mine like he hasn't tasted a favorite flavor in too long.

"I thought you were mad at me." I hardly get the words out as his mouth continues to move over mine.

"I am, but your lips," he mutters without breaking his attention.

"Denton," I exhale. "What are we doing?" His mouth sucks at my chin, traveling to my neck. His fingers have found their way to the place he likes to hold me. He covers my throat.

"I'm kissing you," he mutters against my skin before drawing back and peering into my eyes. "But we need to talk."

I freeze, stiffening at his words.

"What was that stunt with your son?"

I pull back. My hands gripped his biceps, but they slip to his chest, pressing him away from me. "What are you talking about?"

"You left me Jax's number this morning, to call him instead of you, for a ride."

My forehead furrows. "I did no such thing." Jax would rather punch Denton in the face than give him a ride.

Denton stands to his full height, glaring down at me. "What about the letter?"

"I didn't..." *Oh my God.* What happened? How did Jax find the letter? And why did he leave his number?

"Where?"

"What do you mean *where*?"

"Where was the letter and the number?"

"On the coffee table with the water glass and the medicine."

I step back from Denton, crossing my arms. Suddenly, a chill skitters over me, and I recall again where we are—in the halls of our high school.

"I didn't leave the letter or the number. I don't know what you're talking about." Or what Jax is playing at or why he was snooping in my house.

"I thought the number was yours. You left my keys and my phone but no means to get back to the pub. When I called the number, your son answered. I asked for you, not knowing if you worked at the brewery also, but he said you didn't work there. That's when he told me I called his number. I told him I didn't know it was his and I was looking for you." Denton combs his fingers through his hair. "After a few choice words, he asked me why I would be calling you. I didn't really feel like explaining everything, so I told him it must have been a mistake. A mean joke, Spice, but still a mistake."

My brows pinch as I continue to roam Denton's confused face. I agree with him. There has to be a mistake as Jax clearly didn't leave the number and neither did I. Another chill prickles my skin, and I suddenly feel like the halls are haunted.

"Could it have been Jordan?" I don't know why I'm asking Denton, as if he knows any better than me why one son or the other would give Denton the long overdue letter or leave Jax's number.

"How would I know?" Denton's right. He's been played by someone, but which one of my people did this to him?

"How did you get here?"

"I called the pub and told Billy to come get me."

Good Lord, soon the whole town will know Denton spent the night at my home. It's bad enough half the town knows he left the pub with me last night. *Complicated,* Alyce's word repeats. I don't know what else to say until I speak to a son...or two.

"I need to get to practice. I'm sorry about all of this, but I'll figure it out."

"Have dinner with me?" he asks, reaching for my arm as I turn away from him. "The diner."

Ugh. Not the diner, but something in the way he looks at me makes me agree.

"Meet you at six?"

182

30

The Not-a-date Date

[Denton]

I don't know why I'm nervous. It's Mati, and it's not a date. It's the diner but being seen with her will definitely make a statement. I sit at the counter, but I've already told Hollilyn I'll take a booth when Mati arrives. Hollilyn has been managing the place while Dolores takes time to be with our mother. I haven't been to the farm all day, and I need to give Dolores relief. I also have questions to ask Mother, but I don't know how.

"Hot date," Hollilyn teases as I swipe fingers through my hair again and she passes me to walk behind the counter.

"It's not a date," I retort. Hollilyn turns to face me, her bright eyes widening.

"Wonder if she thinks it's *not* a date?" Hollilyn nods behind me, and I spin to see Mati standing inside the diner door.

Goddamn. Mati wears black leggings with ankle booties and a fitted white sweater that looks soft and fluffy. It just covers her hips, and when she turns, it's going to hug her ass. I rub a sweaty hand down my jean-covered thigh and look at her hair, softly curled and falling in loose waves over her shoulder. She wears a touch of makeup which I haven't seen her wear before. The light covering highlights her eyes and covers the freckles over her nose and cheeks. Her lips are coated in a dull peach color, and she looks delicious.

I stand from the stool and cross the diner.

"You look gorgeous," I blurt like I've never been on a date before, but I remind myself it's not a date. It's Mati.

She pushes her hair behind her ear, blushing a little and looks away from me, but the smile on her face and the tug of her teeth at her lip tells me she appreciates the compliment. I wave toward the booth in the back. It's hardly private nor is the place fancy. I should have taken her

L.B. Dunbar

somewhere nicer, like The Patio, but I wanted casual, uncomplicated, easy.

Mati takes a seat, and I sit opposite her after throwing my leather jacket onto the bench. Hollilyn brings us each water, and I can't stop staring at Mati. It's like I'm sixteen, wanting her all over again, and fighting the feeling to reach for her.

"So, what's good here?"

Mati laughs. "You really don't know?"

"It's been a long time. The last time I ate here consistently was when Magnolia worked here." The comment is a reminder of the passage of time. I clear my throat. "I ate here my first night back, but I've been at the farm most nights eating everyone's generous casseroles." I rub my belly. "I'm gonna need extra workouts when I get home."

Mati's expression drops for a moment before a false smile curls those peachy lips.

Damn it. I shouldn't have mentioned LA.

"I guess I better not recommend the cheeseburger then."

I smile back at her, the grin just as weak. "I think that's what I'll have."

Hollilyn returns to take our order, and Mati's eyes follow Hollilyn's retreat, almost begging to go with her to the kitchen. The sensation to reach for her overwhelms me again.

"Mati?" I question, and she returns her attention to me. "Ever figure out what happened earlier today?"

"Surprisingly, Jordan is not answering my calls, but Jax gave me an earful."

"I'm supposing that earful wasn't pleasant."

"He's just…struggling, I guess. He was close with his father even though they were considerably opposite one another. Their relationship was kind of like you and Chris." Mati's eyes open wide in surprise at what she admitted. Clearing her throat, she continues. "I just mean, Jax always felt a little competitive with Jordan because Jax isn't similar to Chris like Jordan is. The lawyer, the married man, the solid guy. Jax is more restless and a little reckless."

184

"Is that how you remember me?" If she's comparing me to her son, she must think these things of me.

"Not restless in a bad way, just always knew you needed to get out. I didn't see rockstar coming, but then again, I guess we all had secrets." Mati takes a sip of her water, and I wonder what secrets she keeps. "Anyway, as far as reckless, I don't mean troublemaker, but Jax doesn't think before he reacts. I need to apologize again for whatever he said to you earlier."

I wave a hand at her. "He's just protecting his mama." The thought makes me smile. If Jax is like me, protecting my mother was what I did most of my young life.

"I think he's taking it a little far, especially as I can protect myself." Her voice quips tighter.

"Settle down, lion cat. No one doubts you. He's just being a good son." I turn toward the window a second and see three men pull into the lot on motorcycles. The first one, with his orange-tinted hair, has to be Crusty Rusty. The second is undeniably James Harrington looking harder than I remember with short gray hair and dark scruff. The last man I don't recognize, but he looks equally silver and menacing like James.

"Who's that?" I ask, interrupted by our conversation.

"That's Justice. He's the president of the Devil's Edge riding club."

"Is that James?" I turn back to Mati and see the pain in her eyes as she looks at her brother.

"Yeah." She glances back to me. "He doesn't associate with the family much."

"Is he in a motorcycle club?"

"It's a riding club, or so he says. One step up from casual cruising. One step down from hardcore clubs. I don't understand it."

She stares a minute longer before turning her attention back to me.

"Anyway, Jax is a good kid. Good man. Both my boys are." She pauses, reading my face as I read the pride in hers. "Did you ever want kids?"

"Once. Kristy was pregnant when we married."

Mati gasps. "I didn't know."

L.B. Dunbar

"We hadn't been trying, and she lost the baby after we got married. I made sure we didn't accidentally get pregnant again." The words sound harsh coming out of my mouth, but I don't mean them as rough as they sound. "Still. I think I would have liked children with the right woman." My eyes shift to Mati and back to the paper placemat before me.

"You never married again?" She hesitates with the question and my lip curls at the corner.

"No, Mati. I didn't marry again. I thought I was doing the right thing by marrying my pregnant girlfriend, but once we divorced, I realized I wasn't the marrying type. I had the road and the band, and I couldn't be tied down."

Mati takes another sip of her water, and Hollilyn arrives with a Coke for Mati. The aversion of Mati's eyes tells me I've said something wrong again.

"I feel like I don't know you anymore," she says when Hollilyn walks away. I smirk.

"I feel like you're exactly the same, only prettier than I remember." Her head shoots up, and instead of a sweet blush, confusion crosses her face, so I offer something else. My voice lowers as I speak, hoping to console her. "I'm no different than I was as a kid."

"You're nothing like that boy." I want to ask what she means, but our food arrives—two plates of cheeseburgers and a heap of French fries. Mati digs in almost immediately, and I marvel at the difference in her compared to the women I know in California: the models fighting to stay thin, the girls trying to impress with how little they eat. Yep, Mati is exactly who I remember—*herself.*

"What?" she mutters with a mouthful of food. I shake my head and take a bite of my burger with a smile on my face. Definitely going to need to up my workout when I get home.

We chat throughout the meal, reminiscing on what I consider safe ground—the farm, the river, the Lane. We don't mention Chris or Kristy, avoiding any memory that would involve either of them. When we finish eating, I pay for our meal, which Hollilyn insists I shouldn't since I'm family to Dolores. I remind her the place needs the money, and she takes the cash I offer along with a tip equaling the cost of our dinner.

I follow Mati to the parking lot, but I'm not ready for the evening to end. She hesitates next to her truck, and I laugh at the size compared to her stature.

"Why's it so big?" I chuckle as I nod at the S-10 4x4 truck in black.

"I thought there was no such thing as too big?" Her lips twist a little, and I recall what I said to her through social media. "After I got rid of the minivan, I didn't want to downsize to a car. Plus, this has better traction in snow."

I shiver with the thought of snow. I haven't experienced it in years except for photoshoots in Colorado.

"Mati and a minivan," I mock. She leans against the driver door, and I hover over her.

"Mom-mobile, I know, but very necessary."

"Big back seat, I guess." I pause for a moment, watching the wheels spin a little before she understands my implication.

"Oh, we didn't...I mean..." She's blushing and flustered, and I realize I don't want to know about her sex life with Chris, but there's a hint. She didn't have sex with him in her minivan. I eye the back of her truck a second.

"Let's go for a ride," I say, my voice dropping as I lean closer.

"I don't think you should kiss me here," she whispers as if people can hear her although the lot is mostly empty. Crusty, James and the guy named Justice are lingering on the edge of the lot, but not paying us any attention.

"Then where *can* I kiss you?"

L.B. Dunbar

31
Moon Chasing

[Mati]

I don't know how I agreed to this. One minute he's standing over me, flirting like the devil and the next he's driving my truck to God knows where. I don't even think he knows where he's going as it's been so long since he's been in the area. The only thing he asked me is if I had a blanket in the truck, and I blushed when I admitted I had two old sleeping bags. I never wanted to be unprepared in case I got stranded in the truck during a snowstorm.

"How did that subdivision get there?" he asks, passing by my neighborhood on the outer edge of town. It stands on a corner of his grandmother's former property.

"It's something Kip did shortly before he died. Somehow he obtained a chunk of Magnolia's property and rezoned the area for residential development."

His brow pinches. "How the hell did he do that?"

"I have no idea. He was mixed up with all kinds of characters shortly before he died."

Denton goes silent before he pulls off the main room for a faded two-tire trail on the edge of his grandmother's property. Her farm was once a viable poultry farm with a little bit of everything extra. Apple orchard. Vegetables. Local lore is the women of the McIntyre-Duncan line knew how to survive in times of trouble, like war and marriage. Chickens make eggs, and that's two meals right there: breakfast and dinner.

My truck bumbles and jolts over rough terrain which hasn't been visited in years. Denton doesn't seem to notice, his eyes straight ahead at the only thing we can see—unmowed meadows reflecting in the headlights.

"Do you know where you're going?" I tease, knowing he hasn't been on his grandmother's land in decades.

"Do you trust me, Mati?"

"Of course," I answer quickly, although I hesitate after I speak. *Do I?* Do I know this man, honestly? I think back to our conversation at the diner. He's so different than I remember, dismissing the loss of his child and the desire for more. Glancing over at his profile, I realize his tone is cooler than his reaction, and I take in his features—the edge to his cheeks, the scruff on his jaw, the curve of his nose. He isn't the boy I remember. He's a man, and despite his cool demeanor, I very much *do* want to know him better.

His head turns, and he catches me checking him out. The corner of his lip curls and then I see it in his eyes. *There's the boy.* The one I wanted without admitting I did. Suddenly, I'm wondering if he'll take me up against the truck. If he'll turn me into the girl I wanted him to make of me. The one with my skirt at my waist and him rhythmically pounding into me.

Quickly, I look away from him. I'll never be *that* girl. First, because I didn't wear skirts—didn't then, hardly do now. I wonder if that's the kind of girl he still wants. One in pretty skirts with a shrill voice. Then I think of how he kissed me in the hallway at the high school. I wasn't that girl to him then, the one he wanted to take up against a truck and fuck. I wonder if I'm that kind of woman now?

"Why'd you kiss me?" I blurt, turning back in his direction.

"What do you mean?"

"In the high school hallway. You said you were mad, but you kissed me like you hadn't seen me in years."

"I haven't seen you in years," he teases.

"I'm serious."

"So am I." He laughs like it's funny but my chest pinches. It's been too long, and I'm reminded again of the separation.

"Why didn't you ever contact us? Even if you wanted to leave Blue Ridge. Even if you didn't want me with you on the road—"

The sudden glare in his eyes as he takes a second to look at me stops my questioning.

L.B. Dunbar

"Let's clear up something right now. I had my reasons for leaving you behind, but make no mistake, I wanted to go on that trip just as much as you, with only you."

My heart leaps in my chest and nearly chokes me. My face heats as does another area of my body. The truck slows, and Denton puts it in park but keeps the engine running. He shifts in his seat, dangling an arm over the steering wheel and the other lands on the back of the seat.

"I wanted you with me, Mati."

"But that's not what you said—"

"I know what I said then," he interrupts me, swiping a hand through his hair and gazing out the front windshield. "I didn't mean it."

My shoulders fall, and I stare at him.

"I don't understand. Then why?"

Denton closes his eyes a second before lowering his head to get a better look out the front window at the dark sky.

"Let's check out the moon."

I'm thrown off by the statement and the abrupt end to our conversation, but the schoolboy expression on his face—the one that makes him innocent, sheepish, and cautious—has me sighing in frustration but agreeing.

"Okay."

We each exit our doors and Denton pulls the driver seat forward to retrieve the sleeping bags I told him about. He walks to the back of my truck and unlatches the tailgate. He spreads one on the bed floor before hopping up and leaning down for me. I take his offered hand, and he hauls me upward. I giggle at his strength before falling against him. As I land on my feet inside the truck bed, Denton looks upward to the late evening sky.

"I forgot how beautiful it can be," he whispers as if he doesn't wish to disturb the heavens above us.

"No moon or stars in Hollywood," I tease, quietly.

"Only rockstars and assholes," he says, lowering his gaze to me. He crouches down before taking a seat. Scooting back to place his back against the wall of the truck, he then pats the space between his spread legs. I follow his lead and crawl between his thighs. My body curls forward as I peer up at the sky until his arm snakes around my waist, and he drags me back to his chest.

"You're too far away, Spice."

My head shakes as I giggle, and then I melt into him, allowing my head to fall on his shoulder. We sit like this for several minutes, just moongazing. I can't remember the last time I did something like this. Just took a breath and looked up at heaven. Suddenly, my mind races to Chris. Is he up there? Can he see me? Does he know what I'm doing? Do I know what I'm doing?

"It's okay to miss him, Mati." I startle at the tender words in my ear. "But he isn't here anymore."

He isn't being harsh. His voice isn't detached like when he spoke of the miscarriage. He's speaking a truth I'm well aware of.

"I know that. I do. I do miss him, it's just that…" *Can I say how I feel?*

"You can talk to me. We can talk about him, if you'd like."

"Don't you? Don't you have things you want to say? Things you want to ask?"

I sit forward and spin to face him.

"I'll listen to whatever you want to tell me, but if all you have to say is how great a guy he was, how wonderful a father, a fair and honest lawyer…then I already know these things. First, because I knew Chris, and he'd be nothing less, and second because everyone who sees me wants to reminisce and tell me."

I exhale. He's right. These things are true.

"What I don't know is what kind of husband he was?" He pauses. "And I don't know if I can hear it, but I'll listen if you need to tell me."

"Cora's one of the few people who understands how I feel."

The warmth of his fingers on my cheeks tells me I can speak, but I don't have to. Despite the darkness, I see a spark in his eyes, a warmth of concern, but a steel strength that he'll take what I have to say.

"He wasn't perfect, Denton. He was a good husband. The best by most measures, but he wasn't a saint. We fought. We made up. We disagreed. We loved."

L.B. Dunbar

Denton's hands slip from my face, but I capture them, bringing them back to my cheeks.

"I loved him with all my heart while he was here. But he's not here anymore." My eyes don't leave his, and I will him to understand me when I don't even understand myself. "My heart has holes."

"What are you saying?"

"I'm saying, I know Chris is gone, and I know you'll leave, too…"

Denton's eyes remain on mine, his fingertips softly slipping into my hair. "Don't think about that yet."

"It's true, though. Why would you stay? California is probably very exciting. And warm." I tease without humor. The September air is cool in the mountains, and this empty field has nothing to ward off the slight breeze. I shiver, and Denton flips the second sleeping bag to cover my shoulders and drape over our bent knees.

"California is everything I wanted, minus one thing. It's larger than life and damning to the soul. It's parties and functions and fundraisers, and I loved it all for a long time. But I don't love it enough anymore."

My brows pinch as I look into his eyes. I wish the old saying were true: your eyes are the window to your soul, but I can't read his eyes. I don't know what he means because all I've known is what surrounds me.

"Ask me again why I kissed you today?"

My brow furrows deeper, but I ask: "Why'd you kiss me?"

"Because I'm jealous. I was so jealous every damn time I saw Chris steal a kiss from you in the hallway. I'm guessing he didn't do more than sneak them, though." His lip curls at the corner, and I think he's mocking me. Chris would never pull me into a corner and kiss the ever-living daylights out of me.

"He didn't," I answer too freely, my heart racing at his admission of being jealous.

"I always wanted to kiss you in that hallway. Make my own memories, of it being me to steal kisses, but I didn't just want to take a kiss or two. I wanted to steal your breath away."

My breath is robbed. It hitches at his words and my mouth gapes in shock. It's all the invitation he needs to lean forward and kiss me, only this time it's softer, sweeter, teasing. He's gentle as he sucks at my lower

Second Chance

lip and hesitant as his tongue tips forward to touch mine. He traces my upper lip before opening wider. The kiss grows in intensity, but he's taking his time, measuring each pause with greater strength, greater purpose. He's memorizing me, or at least, I'm memorizing him. Memorizing this. I want my own memories of him, whether it's a hallway or a hayfield. I want his kisses on my mouth, in my mind, and in my heart.

His mouth lowers to my chin, and his fingers find my neck.

"Why do you touch me like that?" I ask about the possessive cupping.

"I like to feel the vibration of your voice and the pulse at your side. I make you nervous, don't I? But you like it, don't you?"

He's not wrong on either count.

"Let me touch you, Mati. Let me feel what makes your pulse race." He nips the side of my neck, and I stretch to allow him better access. His hands find my hips, and he shifts me, so my back presses to his chest. His mouth isn't leaving my neck, and his nose nudges my sweater to the side to allow him nips at my shoulder. His hands wander over my waist to cup me between my thighs.

"Denton," I purr.

"Say yes, Mati. Just feel me."

I don't know if he means for me to actually touch him or feel what he's doing to me, but I have my answer as my hands slide over his raised knees and down his inner thighs.

"You first, Spice," he says, brushing one hand away, and I take the hint. I brace my palms on his knees as he slips a hand inside the waistband of my leggings. His breath exhales on my neck.

"You're so warm here, sweetheart," he whispers as his fingers creep lower, and then his breath hitches again. "So ready to be touched."

I shift my hips, and two fingers slip inward. My hands curl, cupping his kneecaps and my head falls back to his shoulder.

"Oh God," I mutter as he slides in and out of me.

"Feel good, sweetheart?"

"So good," I purr, my hips rolling forward, my inner walls clenching at him. I whimper as he drags to the edge of me, afraid he'll

193

L.B. Dunbar

leave my body, but then he lunges forward, and I'm so full. I cry out again.

"Should I try for a third?" Another finger joins the other two, and I worry for only a second I can't take him, but the position of my raised knees and spread legs allows him the stretch he needs to go deep. His thumb brushes the sensitive trigger just outside me, and I gasp.

"That's it, Spice. Take it. Take me." He nips at my neck, and I flinch at the pleasurable pain.

"Denton," I whisper, his name a hoarse warning. The flutters inside me ripple quickly to my center, and I fold forward with the clash of lightning inside me. I scream as he curls my hair in his fist and tugs my head back while his fingers fill me. He's touching something in me I don't recognize, and the second roll of thunder is almost instantaneous.

"I'm gonna go again," I call out. "I'm gonna come again."

"That's right, sweetheart. Two times with me." He growls in my ear, the tug of my hair possessive but tender. My senses overload and my body gives in a second time to the storm. Raining down on his fingers, I clamp my knees together, holding him in place between my thighs while my nails dig into his knees and my body gives over to the biggest orgasm I think I've ever had. If we weren't outside, under a heavenly sky, I'd see the same number of stars.

I fall back on his chest, and he slowly removes his fingers. Lifting them to his mouth, he sucks each one like he's savoring a treat. I want to be appalled. I should be aghast, but I'm not. I feel desperate like I want more than his fingers in me. The suction of his mouth over his fingers lingers at my ear and my skin prickles with need.

I spin between his legs and fumble for his belt buckle.

"Whoa there, Spice." He chuckles, but my fingers make fast work. He might have even shifted a little to help me. I don't care. Buckle unlatched. Zipper down. Palm wrapping around him inside his jeans.

"Push these down a little," I demand.

"Mati, you don't have to do this." But he's already working his jeans to his hips, setting free the miraculous appendage—in all its glory—this evening. He might have been mostly hard yesterday, but he's as stiff as an oak tree in my hand tonight.

"Let me…" I don't know what to say. Do this? Touch you? Have my way with you? "It's been so long, I just don't know…"

His hand covers mine, and a finger comes under my chin, tipping my face upward, forcing me to face him.

"Do you see me, Mati?"

"See you?" I choke, my eyes drifting downward despite my upward face. "How can I miss this?" I'm not mocking him, just astonished. He's large, larger than I've experienced, and he feels so good in my hand. My fingers wrapped around a sacred part of him, working him with strong tugs and gentle pulls. He chuckles softly and removes his finger from my chin. I catch his eyes, and despite the darkness, there's a spark.

"I see you, Denton," I say, sensing he needs to hear this from me for whatever reason. "I also want to keep touching you." His arms spread wide, and his hands fall to the edge of the truck. He rolls his hips again, and his dick jolts upward.

"By all means, lion cat. Touch me." By using my high school nickname, I'm suddenly wondering if he's trying to make memories again. For just a moment I wonder if he wanted it to be me against his pickup truck at sixteen and not Kristy.

"Don't go there," he whispers, and I fumble stroking him.

"I'm not going anywhere."

"In your head," he warns and then his breath catches as I stroke my thumb over the moist tip of him. "Damn it, Spice." His head falls back and his eyes close as I continue rubbing. I'm out of practice for handjobs, and I recall what a man likes second best to sex. I scoot back and lower my head.

"You don't know what's in my head," I warn.

"Tell me, Spice. Give me your fantasies."

I kiss the tip of him.

"Mati?" Denton whispers, but I'm on a mission. I don't have time to share my fantasy. The tip of my tongue circles the mushroom edge of him.

"Jesus," he hisses, and I smile. Opening, I draw him in, willing away random thoughts of random women. I can do this, I pep talk myself. I want to do this. I suck and I slurp and I feel like I've never given head

L.B. Dunbar

before, but Denton groans and his hand covers the back of my hair. He's muttering my name and begging me not to stop, and the feeling of control comes back to me. Empowerment. As I'm sucking him like my life depends on it, I realize I haven't felt this alive in a long time. And I let loose.

My tongue swirls around the stiff shaft, and I lap at the ridged edges. I suck the tip until my lips pop and then I take him to the back of my throat. He's deep and holding me in place.

"Spice," he mutters. "Pull back." But I refuse. I need to do this. He jets off, down my throat, and I swallow him and my pride. Tears sting my eyes as I release him and indelicately wipe at my lips.

"Sweetheart," he says quietly, his brow pinching as he looks at me.

"I'm okay," I lie, and instantly, I'm being tugged forward, wrapped in his arms. My ear rests over his heart, racing faster than normal, and I close my burning eyes.

"I'm sorry, Mati. I'm sorry."

I shake my head against his chest. His hand brushes back my hair, and I inhale his scent. Manly and mountain evenings. Moisture and fine mist.

"It was too much," he says, and I press upward to look at him, blinking away the tears.

"No, Denton. It was perfect."

He doesn't believe me, and I can't explain myself. I needed to know I could do this—be with another man—and there is no other man I want more than Denton.

"Let's just sit for a while, okay?" he asks, pulling me back to him.

I agree as he tucks himself away, and I sheepishly glance away. Fingers cup my throat and I twist in his direction. He kisses me briefly before folding me in his arms against his chest. We remain silent, looking up at the stars and I no longer wonder about Chris but see the brilliance of the pinpricked sky. Formations I haven't searched for in years materialize, and I realize it's similar to the moment with Denton. We're discovering a new constellation.

32
Secrets

[Denton]

Pissed off. This is my mood the next day despite an unforgettable evening with Mati. Everywhere I go, it's as if people give me the stink eye like they know something I don't. The donut shop for tar-tasting coffee. The grocer for some fruit for my sister. The service station for a tank of gas. It's as if they all hold a secret they know I don't know. I'm almost relieved to return to the dilapidated farm until I remember I have unanswered questions. I don't even consider my resting mother or the worry on Dolores's face as she sits beside her.

"Who is Calvin Chance? And was he in love with Mother?"

Dolores's head slowly looks up at me. She's tired beyond her years, and the strain in her eyes tells me our mama's death is going to take more of a toll on her. It's not that I'm heartless to our mother, but Dolores and she have a different bond.

"It's Mama story," she says, her voice low as her fingertips frame the corner of her lips for a second.

"Well, it sounds like it needs to be told to me."

Tears well in Dolores's eyes. "I…I don't know…"

"Forget it," I interject as her voice fades. I turn for the door, not paying a second of attention to my mother and stomp down the stairs. I need to do something, exert some energy somehow.

As I near the final baluster, I skip the last two stairs with one hop.

"Denton, don't jump down the stairs." The statement reminds me of a being a child, running through my grandmother's house, feeling like it was my own personal playground with two stairwells and an upper floor all to myself.

Magnolia stands at the edge of the hallway, near the staircase, and I almost plow her over in my quest for the outdoors.

L.B. Dunbar

"Not now, Magnolia," I warn as if she isn't the respected matriarch of our family.

"I think now is the perfect time." She spins on her old-lady heels and taps, taps, taps down her wide hallway to the parlor. The sway of her elder body leaves no argument. I'm to follow her as if I'm the errant child who skipped a few steps.

"Sit!" she demands as she takes her typical chair facing the direction of the drive.

My mouth opens, but she holds up a gnarled hand.

"I heard you upstairs," she begins.

"I didn't mean to raise my voice." It's something I'd say as a child. Her hand rises higher.

"Child, let me speak." Her hand lowers as does her head, shaking from side to side. "Being a parent is difficult, Denton. It's the greatest pleasure and the biggest pain in the ass. Children have minds of their own." Her eyes narrow behind the pop bottle glasses. "And they can't help who they love."

I fall back into the chair I sit in. This is one lecture I'm ready to hear from my grandmother.

"Your mother's dying, Denton. That doesn't mean she'll confess all her sins, though."

"But you know them?"

"Of course, I know them. I'm her mother."

I choke on the comment. My mother certainly doesn't know my sins, does she?

"Who's Calvin Chance?"

Magnolia looks away from me. "He was your uncle," she replies. Her hesitation prompts me.

"And who else?"

Magnolia turns back to me.

"Your mother met him first at that damn dance hall. She planned to run off with him, but he left without her. A military man. His brother swept in and took over. Kip Chance was a smooth talker." There's an edge to my grandmother's voice I've never heard before. "He worked his way into her heart, among other body parts, and her bank account."

198

Magnolia smooths down her skirt, ignorant of the dirtiness she portrayed in her words.

"A weak man feels big if he can bully his brother's girl into marrying him, making promises of wealth and power. Her broken heart fell for him."

"Mother didn't have any money," I say to fill the momentary silence.

"She had all the money. He wanted it."

I stare at my grandmother a moment before my eyes rove out the screen porch to the desolate land. The falling barn. The dried orchard trees. The overgrown fields.

"What happened?"

"He wanted to turn the property into subdivisions. Encourage more families. Grow the town. He'd be the hero. Then his brother returned."

"He was a hero." I recall the newsprint of Calvin in a uniform.

"He was. He wanted to be worthy of your mother, and that's why he left. He didn't know his brother would steal her. Calvin was too late."

I nod, looking out at the yard, but I feel the weight of Magnolia's eyes on me.

"What does this have to do with me? Why is she calling me Calvin?"

"You look exactly like him. Sound like him, too."

"Kip?" I mutter, leaning forward and resting my elbows on my thighs as I clasp my hands together. A growl fills my voice. I hate the comparison.

"Not Kip. Calvin."

My head pops up and my eyes narrow, trying to read this older woman and her statement.

"What are you saying?"

"We'll never know the truth. There weren't fancy tests back then. But she believed it was a strong possibility you were Calvin's."

"But that means—"

"We all have our reasons for decisions we make, Denton. I'm guessing Calvin never left her heart even though he left her behind." Magnified eyes peer at me through thick glasses. I swallow the bile in

L.B. Dunbar

my throat. Then, my father's treatment rushes through me. His hatred. His hands. I wasn't his, and he resented me.

"What do you mean I sound like him?"

"There was a lilt to his voice. An edge. And he could sing."

My breath hitches. No wonder my father didn't want me to learn the guitar. He didn't want to hear me hum. It was a hint I didn't belong to him.

"Did she tell Kip?"

"She did. And that was her mistake." Magnolia lowers her head. "She was more frightened of him then ever after."

"After what?" I snark.

"She planned to leave him, and he followed her." The rest falls silent between us.

"Calvin died," I add for her. If Kip killed his brother for his wife's infidelity, he got away with it. Power. He craved it, and he had people in his pocket to cover for it.

"That he did, and so she stayed. A real Daisy Buchanan." Magnolia's shoulders fall, the reference to a literary heroine who is weak and resolved to remain with the abusive, cheating husband after the death of her lover makes me sick. *Resolution* might have been the decision my mother made to remain with the man who killed her lover, who wasn't the father of her son. "He became mayor a year later, using the town's sympathy to play into his campaign."

We must accept the decisions we make. My mother made hers. I want to believe she still could have run away from Kip. It was her choice to stay. I didn't want to hate my mother, not on her deathbed. I'd already lost empathy for her when I was a child, and she didn't protect me. I tried to be a man as I grew and take the beatings to keep my father from her. As a teenager, resentment developed. I don't want to sympathize with her plight at losing the love of her life, but a niggling feeling develops in my chest.

"I'm telling you these things to give you peace at her death." I scoff in response, but Magnolia continues. "Don't you be seeking a deathbed explanation from her. She doesn't need to be prodded for admission of all her sins. Those are between her and her Maker."

200

I nod. I'll never have the full story. I'll never be able to change the past. I have a plate of misunderstanding and more resentment at the injustice of my childhood. Did she love Calvin yet marry my father? Not my father. Kip. Did she ever love Kip? When did she have the affair? Why? Again, I return to love, and for the briefest moment, I understand my mother. Her heart belonged to someone she could never have, and my thoughts leap to Mati. Maybe Mother and I were more kindred spirits than I imagined.

"You said Mama had all the money. How did Kip get the land for the subdivision? The one where Mati lives."

"I have a theory," Magnolia begins, pausing as she looks out at the land stretching as far as we can see. "When your mother told your father—told Kip—the truth. He blackmailed her. He threatened to expose her, and she'd rather save face than save herself. He would have hunted her down anyway. Who knows what goes on in marriages behind closed doors, but I'd bet she sold her soul, signing over things she didn't own to him. The land is in my name and wouldn't pass to Caroline and Rosalyn until I pass away, so whatever dealings he did weren't legal. Denton, I have no doubt you realize Kip Chance was an evil man. Caroline warned me not to fight him over that sliver of land. Thankfully, he died before he could get his hands on more."

I fall back in the seat again, staring out at the autumn meadows. I know what went on in their marriage. Excessive drinking. Domestic violence. Limitless infidelity.

"Do you want it back?"

Her head swings to me. "The land? What's a little earth when you might lose your daughter, instead? I'd have sold my soul as well to keep her here."

I understand her devotion to her daughter even if I can't understand why. My mother would have been so much better off had she left my father, and so would I.

33

Brotherly Love

[Mati]

I go to work the next day around eleven, and immediately, I'm accosted by Billy.

"So, what's going on with you two?" I want to say I don't know who he means, but the teasing gleam in my brother's eyes tells me everything. Not to mention, Denton called him after calling Jax.

I shrug.

I don't know what to say. Can I tell my brother I feel more alive than I have in a whole year? Can I tell him the guilt I feel at such a sensation? Can I admit I don't want it to end?

"Don't give me that shrug, little missy. I see the glow of..." He pauses, his eyes widening and his mouth freezing in place.

"Sex?" I finish for him, teasing him with the word, although I haven't done such a thing.

"These are things I shouldn't know," he says, straightening and pinking at the same time.

"Oh, and we should know each time you get laid?"

His arms defiantly cross his chest. "That's different. You're my little sister."

I match his stance and glare back at him. "Don't even think of using a double standard on me, William Forrest Harrington." Billy gasps as I use his full name. Our mother was obsessed with Roald Dahl books and all her children match the name of a prominent character in his stories. William is named for the short story "The Minpins."

"Matilda Brookes Harrington Rathstone, don't be middle-naming me."

I got my mother's maiden name as a middle name, and at least we are distracted from talking about sex.

"Did you stop by the house and leave Jax's number for Denton to call yesterday?"

Billy's head pulls back, the expression on his face morphing to confusion.

"Why the fuck would I do that?"

"I don't know." But obviously, Billy is aware of Jax's strong feelings against Denton. "What do you know?"

"Jax doesn't seem too fond of the ex-best friend hitting on his widowed mother, but who cares what he thinks, right?" Billy raises a brow, reminding me of our give-yourself-permission talk. "Now, Mother, on the other hand, she might be a problem."

My mouth falls open. "No," I question.

"Yes."

"How the hell does she know?"

Both Billy's brows rise. "Mati, Mother knows everything even though we're all in our forties. Plus, she met her ladies at the diner this morning."

I shiver. If Elaina Harrington knows anything about Denton and me, I'm in for a major grilling for information. Ignoring this probability, I return to my earlier question. "Denton found the letter from Chris and a crumbled note with Jax's phone number on it. I didn't leave either of them for him, and I don't know how he got them."

"Chris left Denton a letter?"

"Focus, Billy," I demand.

"Maybe he was snooping."

He could have been. "I don't think so." I pause a second. "But someone was." I eye the empty restaurant, wondering who's been in my house lately.

"Can we discuss the Oktoberfest for a second? It looks like Locals Only, the band we booked, bailed on us." The young band—a growing country music sensation and local favorite—would have been perfect for our night.

"What happened?"

"They got a gig in Atlanta. It's a 'bigger' deal." Billy air-quotes the word.

L.B. Dunbar

"Do we have a permit yet?"

Billy shakes his head before twisting it in the direction of the window facing BookEnds.

"It isn't her fault," I defend, getting tired of his blame on our innocent business neighbor.

"I know," he says, lowering his voice and his eyes.

Uh-oh. My stomach drops. "Now, what did you do?"

His head snaps up and his eyes narrow at me. "Nothing. I didn't do a thing." He stalks off, leaving me wondering what *that* was all about and a bit curious about the unusual shade of pink in his cheeks with a glow of sex in his eyes.

+ + +

Worse than facing my mother, I run into Cora.

"Why didn't you tell me, Miss Matilda Harrington?" Fists on her hips, she stops me in the freezer aisle at Tom's Grocery.

"Tell you what?"

"I thought we were best friends." The tone of her voice makes her sound like the ten-year-old child who annoyed the hell out of me. However, I admit, she is one of my best friends as an adult. Her tone softens when she speaks again. "Mati?"

I peer left and right before looking at her. "There's nothing to tell." But something in my expression gives me away.

"Did you have sex?" The word seems to echo through the aisle, possibly through the whole store. She said it loud enough it could have been projected over the loudspeaker. *Sex in aisle six.*

"No, I did not. And can you lower your voice, please?"

"Did you have sex?" she repeats in a hushed tone, mocking a whisper.

"Cora. I just said I didn't."

"But you look happy."

"Is sex the only means to happiness?" The blinking of her eyes and surprise in her face warns me of her answer. I'm on the verge of telling her I'm being sarcastic when she steamrolls ahead.

"Absolutely not. Men do not complete us, Matilda." I roll my eyes. I understand what she means, but Cora's self-discovery and self-sexuality stuff can get a little deep.

"Don't you roll your eyes at me. You are a strong, capable woman." My eyes flinch, eager to roll again, but I don't allow them. I know these things about myself. I feel the weight of truth in her words. Still, I'd like a man to complete me in another way. Thoughts of Denton have filled my head all day, especially after he kissed me goodnight on my doorstep like we'd been on a date instead of two people eating together at the diner or fooling around in a hayfield.

"I think I had a date with Denton Chance last night." The reality of what happened hits me. Were we on a date? Alyce talked me through what to wear and I got carried away by doing my hair and the touch of makeup. I told myself I just felt like putting in some effort. I wanted to look nice. I felt...pretty. Not that I needed to feel pretty, but I wanted to look good. For Denton. For myself. Oh, I don't know what I was doing...

"You think?" Cora stammers, hands coming to her hips again. "The whole town is talking about seeing Denton and you at the diner. Not to mention, he disappeared with you from the Pub after a run-in with his ex-wife."

"How do you know these things?" I ask, but it's rhetorical. I hold up a hand to prevent her from answering. "Why does the town even care?"

"Denton is a big deal. Rockstar. Prodigal son. Heartthrob." My eyes roll of their own volition at the last comment. "And you're...Mati Rathstone."

The name knocks the breath out of me. Does the town think I'm cheating on Chris? Do they see me as running around?

"I think everyone's been waiting for you to choose who you'd go for. I bet Kent Duncan. You cost me twenty bucks, Mati."

My mouth falls open a second, and then my voice rises as I speak. "What the... Are people taking bets on who I'll date?"

"Not bets. Just a little wager."

"Isn't that the same thing?"

"Pa-tay-toe. Pa-tah-toe." She waves dismissively at me.

205

L.B. Dunbar

"Cora!"

"Billy started it."

"Oh. My. God." Some days I hate my brothers. Cora holds up both hands.

"Don't shoot the messenger. I stopped at the wager of timing."

"What timing?" My eyes close. I don't know why I'm even asking.

"How long before you both admit you're still in love with each other?"

I shake my head. How can we admit we are *still* in love with each other? We were never in love in the first place. Love fell only on me, and it's my best-kept secret. Isn't it?

34
Fighting Words

[Denton]

"What's going on?" I ask as I surprise Mati at her home that evening. I lean in to kiss her, but she pulls back. This sparks my growing pile of irritation. I'm too high-strung from all the thoughts running in my head, and while I should have been at Magnolia's to sit with my mother, my car seemed to have driven here of its own volition.

"What's going on with you?" she retorts, a bark in her question at the tone in my voice.

"I'm sorry," I say immediately, stepping forward to cover her shoulders which bristle under my touch. I snap again. "What's this?"

I remove my hands, holding them upward as if I've been singed by her.

"Nothing," she mutters, turning her back to me and continuing down the hall to her kitchen. Her house is modest, laid out with small rooms, and I hesitate a moment as I remember this home is on borrowed land. Illegally.

"It's not nothing," I bite, unwilling to let the blasé response go. I'm itching for a fight, although Mati isn't the source of my anger. I just need to release this buzzing energy inside me. Learning my father isn't my father. Learning my father worked some illegal dealing to steal family land. Learning he might have blackmailed my mother to do so. I can't take more rejection or questions.

"Fine," she spins. "Everyone's talking about us."

"Who's everyone?" I ask, stunned at the outburst and offended expression on her face.

"The whole town."

My nose scrunches. "Who the fuck cares what the town thinks?"

"I do. I live here, remember?" There's a spark under those words and the flame reaches out to me, looking to set me on fire.

207

"I know that," I mock. My voice deepens, ripe with meaning. She stayed with Chris. However, it wasn't really her fault. Her eyes narrow.

"Of course, you remember. You left me behind." The venom in her voice is just as sharp as any slap, and I shake my head.

"I'm not doing this with you." *I'm not telling her the truth*, I warn myself. Not tonight when I'm already wound up about other things.

"Doing what, Denton? We never *did* anything, right? We aren't even doing anything now, according to you. *We aren't doing anything wrong*," she mocks in a falsely masculine voice.

"Lion cat, what are you talking about?"

"All those years ago. You had Kristy—"

"And you had Chris," I interject. Mati sighs as if she's exhausted by me. "And what about *now*? Again, who gives a fuck?"

"I do. I'm not some rock-star-on-the-road fling. One you can discard when you leave. I don't need the town talking about me seeing you or being seen with you."

"You're ashamed to be seen with me?" I'm shocked once again and still not understanding what the town's opinion has to do with anything.

"Denton, come on."

"No, you come on. I've known you almost my whole life. We were friends. What difference does it make if we're seen together?"

Mati stares back at me, her expression crippling before me. Her eyes softening with both sympathy and sorrow.

"You're right, Denton. What difference does it make?"

I can't read what she means, and I'm ready to ask when she continues. "I don't think we should be seen together. I'm not ready for whatever this is." She waves between us with a flick of her hand.

"Whatever this is? Why does *this* have to be anything?" The moment I ask, I know I've made a mistake. Mati's shoulders fall, and she looks away from me.

"I'm not one of your groupies, rockstar." Her voice drips with sarcasm.

"I never said you were. I didn't treat you like one either." I step toward her, but her cheek remains turned away from me. "Spice?"

"I can't do this," she mutters more to herself than to me. Her eyes close despite the pressure from my fingers under her chin.

"What is it you can't do? Is this about guilt? Are you still holding Chris between us?" My anger returns for new reasons, and this gets her attention. Her head snaps up in my direction.

"Don't bring Chris into this," she hisses.

"Chris will always be between us. He's the one who…" I can't tell her. *He's the one who asked me to leave.*

"What?" she barks, as my voice falters. I don't give in. "Yeah, that's right. Don't explain. You're good at that." Like lion cat claws, her words scratch deep as if I had a choice. I release her cheeks.

"You want an explanation from me? What about Chris? Did he ever explain things to you? What's it say in the damn letter he wrote me, Mati?" I know I have the letter, but I don't have the courage to read it. What if he tells me to stay away from her again?

"I told you I don't know."

"But he wrote one to you, too, didn't he? What's his say to you?"

She pauses, and I know I've pressed too far. Whatever he said to her remains in the sacred vault of marriage privilege, something between them I'm not privy to.

"Never mind, Mati." I sigh, swiping a hand over my head. "You know, I came here to talk about other things. Not this shit."

"This shit? Us?"

"There isn't an us." The moment the words release, I feel the temperature of the room plummet.

"That's right. There isn't." Her words hurt just as much as the ones I flung at her. I want there to be an us, but there can't be. I'm going home—California—and I can't wait to get back there as too many unknowns don't concern me here. I don't care about Kip, Calvin, a subdivision, or even a failing farm. I want out.

"I don't need this right now," I mutter, crestfallen in the woman I consider my safe haven which isn't a safe place after all. Turning to strut down her short hall, I ignore the wall where I pressed up against her, slid my fingers deep inside her, and split her open with my tongue.

"That's right. Run away like you always do."

209

L.B. Dunbar

I stop—take a millisecond of breath—and turn back to her.

"And what would I have stuck around here for?" The comment catches in my throat because standing before me is the one reason I would have stayed. More importantly, I had hoped to whisk her away from here with me. "I might have run away, Mati, but not from you. I could never outrun you. You've chased my heart and my dreams for almost three decades. And I didn't run, I sprinted because I knew if I didn't get away from here, I'd—"

"What?" she interjects, her breath drawing deep as her nostrils flare.

I'd steal you for mine. The words crush my heart and fill my dry mouth, but I can't admit them when she's looking at me like she wants to skewer me on a stick and roast me over an open pit. Heavy exhales of anger fall between us.

"You know what? It doesn't matter," she says, holding up a hand. "You have a lot going on with your mom and Dolores. I don't want to act like we can just pick up as friends like we were, and it will be okay when you leave again. I don't want to pretend."

"Things are different now, Mati. And the other night was certainly more than us being friends. We can stay in touch." I sigh, letting my fingers slip to her throat. I shrug. "I don't know…maybe you can come to visit me." The words fall from my lips without thinking.

"Don't say things you don't mean," she whispers, her eyes casting downward again.

"I do mean them." Recognizing I spoke with hesitation, it sounds as if I don't mean what I've said, but the second after the suggestion left my mouth, I find I do mean it. I want her to come to California and see me. I want to show her my life, share it with her. "I can show you around LA and take you to the ocean."

A spark of hope flickers in my chest and the heat of my anger settles into something else. A false smile from her stifles my enthusiasm.

"I can't take promises from you again, Denton." She tugs her face from my grasp, and her words claw at my chest.

"I'm not promising anything. I'm merely suggesting a trip, a vacation, a getaway."

"I can't," she says, her head shaking vehemently against the idea.

"Why not?"

"You don't understand," she continues, not answering my question, as her head continues to shake even more.

"Explain it to me." Her facial expression pinches and I brace myself for the strike.

"I think it's best some things remain left unsaid."

What the fuck does that mean?

35

Pillars Not Pedestals

[Mati]

I couldn't tell him how much it hurt me when he left without an explanation. Telling me all those years ago he wanted to go alone made no sense after all the plans we'd made, and then to take Kristy drove the proverbial knife deeper. It took time to forgive Denton. Maybe the sex I finally had with Chris served as the necessary distraction. Getting pregnant certainly realigned my priorities. Denton became an afterthought of yesterday while the future grew in my belly. Yet, deep inside, I still harbored a little salt in the old wound.

And true to Denton's history, he left.

I didn't break into tears although they teased my eyes. Instead, I slid to the floor, pressing my back against my front door, and tipped my head to rest on the cool window.

What was I thinking the other night, letting Denton touch me again and taking him in my mouth? I'd been caught up in making new memories and forgetting the painful old ones caused by the same man. Carefree, careless, he would leave as he should, and I didn't need the complication our situation provoked. I'd be the one left behind again. Denton didn't need the complication either. His mama was dying. His sister was distraught. His grandmother would be left alone in a big old decrepit house.

A tear escapes and I curse myself. I haven't cried this much since Chris died. I find I'm more weepy than upset, and I chalk it up to my personal news—an interview. I'm excited but nervous, and it would have been nice to share the jittery turmoil inside me with someone. Chris knew college coaching was a one-day dream, yet my one-day hadn't arrived. Children. Wife. A job close to home.

There was no longer anything holding me back. It was time to do something for me.

I couldn't say Denton was in my way. He'd not stop me from doing what I wanted. It was simply I couldn't open myself up to him. I couldn't share my excitement knowing he wouldn't understand it and leave for a different life—a bigger life—one that involved models and movie stars. He'd told me about his pending photoshoots. The ones that involved him on both sides of the lens. He was an artist in his own right, but his pretty face was still a commodity.

You can come to California.

It's as if he mocks me, promising me once again an adventure we never took together. I couldn't go now. I had my own life, and it blossoms with possibility, starting with the future interview. Northeastern Georgia decided to instate a women's volleyball program to their athletic roster, hoping to boost the attraction of the school. An opportunity like this couldn't be turned down. A chance to implement the program from the ground up? It was like a drizzle of caramel over vanilla ice cream on top of Apple Jane's crumble apple pie.

Damn Denton for stealing a little of my thunder by his aggressive attitude. I realize it wasn't intended solely at me. Like I said to him, he has a lot on his mind. Whatever was bothering him, he'd never take it out on me, but he'd pressed for a fight. He wanted to argue. In the past, he'd apologize, and we'd go for a ride.

I could wait him out, but for how long? Instead of giving in to Denton's whims, I need him to give in to me. My heart creaks open like a swollen door toward him, only to be slammed back with his behavior. My body had too willingly given into him. The attraction was an ache— an unfilled need. I didn't want to regret it, but my thoughts ran wild with concern. What was I doing with him?

I just want time with you.

Maybe I wanted time with him as well. Unfortunately, being with Denton seemed more than fulfilling some deep-seated desire. This was Denton—a man I'd always wondered about. What would his touch feel like? His hands. His lips. His tongue. Now that I knew, I wasn't sorry, but I was sad. I didn't want to be alone any longer. I wanted to share my life, live my life, and I foolishly thought Denton would be the one. One half of me yearns for him to stay, settle next to me finally, but the other side of me knows it isn't in his nature to stay put. He's proven it repeatedly—running is his skill—next to music and women.

+ + +

A few days pass before Cora insists I go with her to Magnolia's again. The girls have had back-to-back games, winning both matches and the hum of the interview ripples under my skin. These wins add to my existing stats, and once again, I consider we might head to the state championship. I'm in the midst of explaining this to Cora when we pull into Magnolia's crowded yard. Cora demands she drive this time, so I can't ditch her, as she claims I did previously.

Once again, I don't want to enter the sick room of Caroline Chance, but I do what I can in the kitchen. I organize casseroles, toss what is no longer edible, and wash dishes. As I'm drying, a familiar voice speaks behind me.

"Well, Matilda Harrington." The elegant, rich Southern voice of my mother drawls across the kitchen, and I nearly drop the glass I'm swiping dry.

"Mama," I address her like a child despite being a woman. While my mother couldn't handle my rejection of all things feminine, she also has a difficult time accepting I am a grown woman with my own children. Too often, she reminds me of Cora. They are cut from the same mold.

"It's been weeks since I've seen you." There's a question in the statement—*Where the hell have I been?*—but Mama would never curse. I typically visit my parents once a week; another ritual I fell into after Chris's death. Daddy could give or take my weekly dinners as he sneaks into the brewery or the pub often enough and we chat then, but Mama lives by rigid schedules.

"There's been a lot going on," I nonchalantly offer but cringe knowing it won't be enough of an explanation for her. I'm not ready to share my interview. She'll hijack the idea, and my confidence will wane before I even go for it. An interview isn't a promise of a job, I remind myself, and I don't need her reminding me of that fact, either. Nor do I need her telling me I should have stayed home. I didn't need to work. *Blah, blah, blah.*

"A lot or Denton?"

"Mama," I admonish, turning my back to her to hide the heat darkening my cheeks.

"The prodigal son returns…" Her voice drifts as if implying something scandalous, but I don't take the bait.

"Yes, he did. His mother's dying." I reach for the cupboard as I speak and set the glass on the shelf with a little more tap than necessary. "But he won't stay."

"You know I just worry about you. He broke your heart once before." She's referencing his leaving me and our road trip plans. "I don't want to see you shattered again." My mother was my rock when Chris died, so she knows what she speaks of. It was difficult for her to watch me fall apart as I'm not the type to break so easily. The scrape of a stool against the old linoleum tells me she's settling in for further grilling.

"How's Miss Caroline?" I interject, hoping to deflect topics to something more relevant.

"She's not going to last the night." The comment makes me drop the next glass I hold, which thankfully bounces in the metal sink.

"Mama?" I'm appalled until I see her face. As a woman who has buried both her parents as well as our Grandpa Harrington, she recognizes *the look of death* as she calls it.

"She held on longer than I thought she would." Mama smooths down her skirt, flicking at lint that doesn't exist. I'd heard from Dolores when they expected her to only last two weeks. It's been a bit longer than that. "Denton's return was all she ever wanted. Maybe grandchildren would also be on her list, but that clearly isn't happening. Poor Caroline."

My mother isn't being sarcastic or cruel. She's well aware of the pain Caroline suffered over the years, but she also knows Caroline burned her own bridges with her son and eventually her daughter. When Dolores inherited her grandmother's diner, she had everything Caroline didn't—freedom to be the woman she wanted to be. Independent. Self-sufficient. Respected. The town worshipped Caroline, but much of the honor came from empathy about her husband.

"How is Dolores?" I haven't seen her in the last week. She hasn't left her mother's bedside, and the wait for the inevitable must be draining. I scan over my own mother's physical form with a little more appreciation. She's a vision of health and propriety, with her ankles crossed, and her back ramrod straight as she sits on the rickety old stool. Elaina Harrington hardly looks her age, which is her purpose in life, second to hounding me about acting more feminine and Billy about his sex life. She's much more forgiving of the waywardness of my brothers. Then again, I haven't had cause to be wayward until the last few weeks.

"She's tired, and the worthless man she dates has come around once in a while which only upsets her more."

"Crusty Rusty?" I blurt, recalling the sight of him in the diner on occasion with James. My mother's eyes meet mine. She's having the same thoughts as me about my absentee brother. Mama misses him the most.

"He's not providing her any comfort in her time of need," Mama adds about Rusty, disapproval clear in her tone.

I can't argue there. I've wondered what Rusty's role would be in supporting Dolores—if he were even supporting her—but as I feared, it remains nonexistent.

"Dolores is a strong woman," I say in her defense, channeling some of Cora's self-empowerment speeches. I nod to further emphasize my words.

"Even the strongest of women need pillars of support sometimes." My mother's glare speaks volumes. She refers to me and the strength she offered when Chris passed. Women might be strong as columns, but no pillar stands alone. Then it's a pedestal, Mama would say, and she is adamant no person belongs on a pedestal, except maybe her. Saint Elaina.

"Mati?" The surprised groggy voice of Denton sends a jolt through my body. He looks exhausted, although the way his hair sticks up and his face has a crease on the side, it appears as if he just woke from a nap.

"Denton," I say, a little too breathless at his sexy, sleepy appearance and the way he returns my stare with a longing in his eyes. If my mother weren't present, I might run to him, despite our argument a few nights ago. I've missed him, and I hate how much it hurts to see him, want him, wish to hold him. Then again, he looks like he wants me to hold him. He steps forward as my mother turns on the stool, and then he stops in his tracks.

"Miss Elaina." He shifts toward my mother and envelopes her in a hug. A second mother to him, my mama holds him tightly in her smaller arms. My mother disapproved of my friendship with two boys, not because of who they were as people, but because they were male. She wanted me to be all girlie as a child. Denton holds a special place in Mama's heart, but she worried the apple wouldn't fall far from the tree and she didn't want me to end up with Denton, even if he was the mayor's son. She trusted him because she trusted Chris who trusted Denton. She eventually saw the man Chris would be, and despite my out-of-wedlock pregnancy, Chris fulfilled everything Mama wanted for me.

"My goodness, how you've grown," she says, all Southern sap and totally ridiculous as it's been twenty-five plus years. Of course, he's changed.

Denton pulls back and stares down at her. "I hope that's not an implication I'm getting fat." He rubs his belly while an award-winning smile beams at my mother. *Good Lord*, I think Mama's turning pink. "I have a photoshoot soon, and all these generous casseroles are doing me no good." A touch of Southern wavers into his statement, bringing back the boy who knew how to speak to adults with manners.

I blink as I process his words. *He has a photoshoot soon.* Where?

As if he's read my mind, his eyes jump to mine. "It's good to see such beautiful women on a sad occasion." The charm runs deep, and Mama blushes again, swatting at him like they're flirting with each other.

"Now, you," she teases, before pushing at her hair to fluff it, like I never do, and can't do presently with all my hair tugged up in a messy bun on top of my head. Mama's perfect coif hasn't even moved.

Denton returns to my mother. "It was nice of you to come to sit with Mother. I know she always valued your friendship."

Mama's mouth opens, and I pray for her to shut it. My mother never considered Caroline a friend but more a woman in need. Mama used to say she was doing her Christian duty by offering her shelter from the storm, but eventually, Mama prayed for an intervention like Caroline leaving Kip's ass. Again, she wouldn't have cursed; I just added that part.

"You know your family was special to me." My mother's response is said through gritted teeth, and I think Denton's been gone long enough to not realize mother's mockery. Mama wasn't ever in favor of Denton being one of my best friends, again not because of him per se. She was less in favor of finding Dolores in James's bed one night around the time they were eighteen. Mama would say God entrusts us to guide others for whatever His reason, and she felt the Chance children were her special divination.

"Thank you. I appreciate that," Denton says, making eye contact with me once again. There's a strange tension brewing between Denton and me as we focus on one another. Without breaking eye contact, I sense Mama's head moving back and forth, assessing us. Eventually, Denton stifles a yawn. "Is there any coffee?"

"Coming up," I say too cheerfully, but Mama's already out of her seat.

"Just let me get a fresh pot going, and then I'll be out of here. George is waiting for me." My parents love to brag that they've never spent a night apart from one another, but to clarify, Daddy has spent plenty of late nights at the pub before returning to Mama. She doesn't need to rush, but idle hands or something like that, she'd say, so she busies herself filling the coffee maker with water and measuring out fresh grounds before dramatically pressing the on switch.

"There." She turns a beaming smile at Denton although her eyes shift to mine. "Matilda, do you need a ride home?"

Suddenly, I feel like a child again, as if it might not be proper to remain in the house without her supervision.

"I'm with Cora," I offer.

"I thought Cora left," Denton says.

"She what?" I reply a little too strongly as Denton's mouth clamps shut.

"I can give you a ride home, dear," Mama offers, all sugar sweet and forceful. Her eyes do the shifty thing again as if she needs to get me out of the kitchen.

"If it's okay with Mati, I'd like her to stay. I can drive her home later."

"Now, Denton, honey, you need to stay with your mama. Matilda can ride with me." Mama's eyes focus on mine like I'm sixteen and can't make up my own mind.

"I'd like to stay," I say to Denton, ignoring the glare I feel burning the side of my head from my mother. Denton's lips quirk into a smile he's fighting, sensing the power play with my mother.

"Matilda?"

"I'll stop by soon, Mama." I step toward her and kiss her cheek, but she's quick. Her hands grip my upper arms, and she holds me near her.

"Pillars, Matilda. Not pedestals."

"Yes, Mama," I say, tugging myself free although I have no idea what she means.

36
Just Like Old Times, But Not Really

[Mati]

Denton offers to walk Mama out to her car, and I remain in the kitchen. It's as clean as it will be with its older cabinets and dull linoleum floor. I finish wiping down the counter as Denton walks back into the room.

"Thank you for saving me," I say immediately, grateful to escape a grilling ride home with my mother whose eagle eyes didn't miss the glances exchanged between Denton and me.

"Thank you for being here," he says, stepping closer to me, but pausing too far away. His hands slip into his pockets like he needs to keep them contained, so I take a step toward him. Reaching for his chest, I slide my palm hesitantly down the T-shirt he wears. The material is soft, but underneath is hard, firm, and flinching at my touch.

"I'm sorry about the other night." I'm not certain why I'm apologizing or what even happened, but we were definitely a bit unhinged. Arms envelop me and draw me into his chest. My cheek rests against the well-worn cotton, and I hear his heart racing.

"No, Mati. I'm sorry." A kiss comes to the top of my head, and his lips linger. "I'm all kinds of messed up by being back here." My own heart clenches with the sentiment, although I don't fault him. It must be strange to be back. Things aren't exactly how he remembers them. I'm different, for one thing. We're different, for another. "I'm so glad you're staying."

I pull back a little so I can look up at him, but I don't release him from my arms around his waist. "What can I do for you?"

"So many answers to that question," he murmurs before leaning down for the briefest of kisses—too quick, too tender. I don't want to let him go, but I swallow my desire and remember what my mama said.

She isn't going to last the night.

"How's your mama?"

"The nurses say it could be anytime. Everything is failing. She's heavily sedated in hopes to keep the pain at a minimum. She hasn't opened her eyes in days. She's still muttering things, but the sounds are completely indecipherable." His sad voice washes over me as his fingers come to my throat like they do, cupping me. His thumb strokes the side of the neck.

"Did she ever answer all your questions?"

He simply shakes his head as an answer, and a weak grin flinches at his lips. "Some things I'll never know."

We haven't talked further about his father—Kip, that is—and the possibility he wasn't his dad. I'm hoping in due time we will, but his mother is the priority tonight. My behavior toward him the other night was unforgivable, considering his circumstances. He came to talk to me, as he told me, and things got turned upside down. I repeat my earlier question.

"What can I do?"

"Would it be too much to ask you to stay? Mama's in her room, but I could set you in a room down the hall. Just knowing you're here waiting for me would mean so much."

"Of course," I respond immediately, without understanding how this will help him, but the sorrow in his voice makes me willing to do anything he asks.

We're silent as we climb the stairs, him leading the way by holding my hand. Our lack of words makes me wonder if we shouldn't be doing this, as if he's sneaking me upstairs because he doesn't want anyone to know I'm here. Cora pops into my head, and I wonder when the sneaky devil left, and why. *I'll be having words with her later,* I scold in my head.

As we reach the landing, Denton looks back at me and squeezes my fingers. He takes me toward the front of the house, which is the opposite direction of his mother's room.

"When I was a kid, I stayed here. I've slept here the last few nights. It was easier than going back and forth to the Lodge as I didn't know how things would progress with Mama."

221

L.B. Dunbar

I nod to acknowledge him. The room is disheveled. An unmade bed. A pile of clothes loosely draped over a chair in the corner. Two large windows with shades pulled to half-mast. It doesn't look like a little boy's room with the knotted white bedspread—literally, an antiquated spread which hangs to the floor. The double sized mattress sits on a white wrought iron frame with a spindled head and footboard. I don't know how Denton has fit on such a dainty, pretty thing. A faded circular rug covers the floor under the bed along with a pair of kicked-off shoes, a phone charger, and an open but off laptop.

"Do you mind hanging out in here?"

I still haven't spoken, a little afraid of my own voice. I shake my head again to show I understand but find my entire body quivers a little. Denton's hands rub up and down my shoulders before one hand comes to my throat again. He pauses there, his thumb stroking, his eyes focusing on mine.

"I'm so grateful you're here."

"I wouldn't want to be anywhere else." The words cause his eyes to enflame from a flicker to a full inferno. Instantly, his mouth covers mine as he crushes me to his body. His tongue lashes out, demanding mine twirl with his and I melt against him. He tips my head by a gentle nudge at my throat and the kiss deepens. His lips lead mine, dragging and drugging me. *I want this man.*

He pulls back abruptly but tugs my lower lip with his.

"I need to go." The reality of his situation catches up to me quickly and I feel foolish for my readiness to tackle him to the floor.

"Of course. I'll be right here."

"Thank you. This means everything to me."

+ + +

I find an old Harlequin paperback in the closet and use it to pass some time. Cora loves romance novels lately, although she preaches romance is dead. Offering too much information, she tells me she uses modern romance for self-titillation. I often hold up my hand, begging off details. I should call Cora, but I don't want to speak on the phone, afraid I'll

222

break the code of silence filling the old home. The place creaks and swells with the fall wind outside, but there is a strange comfort here. Ghosts roam these halls, but I'm not frightened. A nervous energy fills me, instead, as I wait for Denton.

Hours pass. I started out sitting on the bed I made up. Then I slunk to my back, but eventually I rolled to my side. It's in this position where my eyelids give up the fight to stay open and I doze. My mind drifts through images of the past. In no particular order, memories blur together until I recall how Denton would come to my room after run-ins with his father. The floorboards crackle and my eyes spring open to find Denton standing beside the bed.

"I'm sorry I fell asleep," I say, my voice low and groggy. My weight-laden body refuses to move.

"My mother's gone."

I reach forward for his hands which rest on his hips. He looks lost, uncertain what to do, where to go.

"Denton." My fingers wiggle for him to take them, and he eventually does. I scoot back on the bed, as I did when we were children, encouraging him to follow. His nostrils flare and I'm not certain if he's fighting tears of sorrow or something else. He folds down next to me and I wrap myself around him, tugging his head to my chest. He smells freshly showered and I realize his hair is wet. I stroke through the damp locks like I used to do to comfort him.

"I'm so sorry."

"Please don't," he whispers with a rasp in his voice.

"How do you feel?" I keep my voice as low as his.

"I don't know how to feel. I'm...I'm just numb."

My fingers slip to the back of his head, and I lean forward to kiss his forehead. Letting my lips linger, I press his head to me.

"Just let me hold you tonight." He's asking more than telling me. I wrap my arms around him, pinning him close to my heartbeat. His arms snake around me, tugging me closer, pinning me against him. Our legs entangle, and I hold him like I can't let him go. Like I won't let him go. I murmur to him like I did when we were kids. *You'll be okay. Everything will be all right.* My fingers move through his wet hair, stroking over his skull in a gentle massage.

"Mati?" he mutters into my breasts. Our bodies are a little different than the shape of us as kids, and his nose nuzzles against achy globes. "Stop talking."

I chuckle lightly, kiss the top of his head again and linger there as I continue to comb through his drying locks. Instead of speaking, I say the words in my head, adding the most important support I gave him as a nurturing child friend. *You'll be okay. Everything will be all right. One day you'll get out of this place, and it won't hurt so much.*

+ + +

We both sleep although I'm not certain for how long before my breasts are nuzzled by his nose again. We've loosened our hold on one another a little in our sleep, but Denton's face is still against my breasts, and he's moving side to side between them. At first, I think he's dreaming, so I whisper his name. Instantly, his hands clutch at my wrists, forcing them upward above my head.

"Denton," I squeak, more with surprise than admonishment. His fingers find mine, and he entwines ours together, dragging my hands higher over the pillow until they brush cool metal. Without breaking his concentration on my breasts, he rolls me to my back, following to press over me. He nips at one breast through my thin shirt. My fingers flex at the exciting scrape of his teeth, and he loops them around the spindles above me. A squeeze warns me to keep my hands on the wrought iron, and then he drags his open palms down the underside of my arms, along the side of my breasts to the hem of my shirt.

My mouth pops open about to speak, but he anticipates me. Lifting my shirt, he mutters into my belly.

"Don't speak."

I clamp my lips shut as his tongue draws designs over my skin, lapping and licking his way upward as he slowly follows the progression of my shirt. He still doesn't look up at me as his mouth covers one breast, again with his teeth, but his hands force my shirt upward.

"Off," he says to the breast, kissing the satiny material covering me. I release my hands only long enough to remove my shirt. He tosses it to the side of the bed, and my hands return to their captive position. As he tugs one cup to the side, my back arches, begging him to take my breast. I don't know what we're doing. I don't know that we should be doing this—here, now.

I question him once again by calling his name.

"Just let me pretend. For one night, let me pretend." His voice is so distant, so full of hurt and pain and question, and I can't deny him. His thumb and forefinger roll my nipple, tugging it taut. His tongue stretches to cover me, and then he opens wide, squeezing the achy globe as he sucks me into the heat of his mouth. My back arches again and I purr at the sensation. Wet. Tickling. He suckles before laving around the pert nipple. Then he nips me again, and my back shoots from the bed. Keeping me trussed up on one side, he pushes the material of the other cup aside and repeats the process. Lick. Squeeze. Cover.

He pulls back and presses my breasts together.

"I've always wanted to fuck your tits, lion cat." My mouth falls open at the admission, but before I can speak, he continues. "One day."

He releases the heavy weight of them, allowing them to fall to the side but trapped by the presence of removed fabric. His hands skate down my sides, and I shiver.

"Still ticklish," he mutters, more to his fingers moving to the waist of my jeans than me. He's outside himself, and I sense the disconnection, but I won't stop him. He might regret this tomorrow, but tonight, he needs me. I remember this feeling after Chris died. The desire to be close to someone at the same time not wanting anyone to touch me.

"Me," Denton growls, as his hands come to the button of my jeans and works it out of the hole. I worry for a moment I spoke aloud about Chris, and I stare at the top of his head, willing him to look up at me. It's becoming uncanny how he senses when Chris has entered my thoughts.

"Just let me touch you. Feel *me*." I nod to agree, but he's lost, focusing on my zipper which he slides downward at a torturously slow pace.

L.B. Dunbar

"You," I whisper, gaining his attention for a brief second. His head pops up. His eyes look wild. The darkness speckles with pinpricks of light seeping in from the moonlight outside. Otherwise, we are enveloped in black.

My jeans are forcefully tugged at the hip and I wiggle to help him slid them down my body. He presses kisses over my thighs and across my kneecap. He drags his tongue down my shin, and I'm grateful I shaved. He struggles only briefly with my skinny jeans at my ankles, and then he throws them to the floor. He reverses his attention, pressing kisses up my shins, circling my knee with his tongue, and drawing open mouth kisses over my skin on my thighs. His nose brushes against my core, and he inhales. The scent of my sex fills the room, and I buck at the attention.

He pulls back and scoots off the side of the bed. Quickly, he removes his T-shirt with one tug from behind his neck, and then he undoes his jeans. In only his boxer briefs, he climbs back over me to kneel between my legs.

"Only pretend," he tells me, like a warning, and I so desperately want to ask what he means. But my body sings for his attention. My skin hums from the bath of his lips up and over my legs. My core pulses— heavy, sluggish, deep—weeping for release. Thick palms massage up my legs once again before he hovers his body over mine. Balancing on one elbow by my side, he tugs the center of my underwear aside and impales me with two fingers. No prep. No warning. I buck off the bed, drawing his fingers into me, feeling full, wild, and ready. He drags them to the edge and then plunges forward again. I respond with a moan and clench, willing the digits to remain inside, and yet loving the teasing pull to release.

Denton's resting partially over me, attempting to hold most of his weight on the one elbow but his free hand repeats the motion of plunge and pull, back and forth. His other fingers pluck at my breast, sagging off to the side. He strums my center and tugs my nipple, and I realize he's touching me like he might stroke his guitar. I'm his instrument, and he's playing me. The telltale sign of fluttering butterflies crawls up my thighs. The pressure builds as Denton works me into sensory overload.

226

He rolls his hips, releasing my breast with a final pull and presses upward to balance on one hand.

He's sexing me with his fingers, but his dick is so close. Only stretchy cotton briefs separate us as his hips begin to thrust in matching rhythm with his fingers. He drags back before forcing forward, his hips keeping pace, his dick nudging me just off center.

"So close," he mutters, and I don't know if he means me and the building orgasm, or him and his dick near my core. Either way, I'm a bundle of desire—building, building, building—and then crashing.

My hips flex upward, my channel clenching to keep the thickness of Denton's fingers buried inside me as I ride the curls and curves of an all-encompassing orgasm. My back arches, my knees clamp his hips, and my body begs for more.

"Just pretend," he whispers as if he's reminding himself. He gives me what I need, working his fingers to draw out every drop of my pleasure before he removes his fingers and presses the covered tip of his hardness to my swollen core. He thrusts forward as if he wishes to enter but can't, won't. This is the pretend he means. Tonight should not be *the night* between us, and yet he needs to be close to me.

I meet his thrusts with my own, allowing my imagination to mingle with his. *What if…* My hands clutch at his back, expanding and flexing with each pulse at my entrance, wanting his admittance but holding back. My knees fall to the sides again, and I open as much as I can to him. My fingers find his ass, firm and flexing with each press forward. I squeeze, pressing at him to come closer, come inside. I'm ready to beg when his pace increases. He's pumping against me, and I'm afraid to speak, afraid to break the strained concentration on his face. A vein bulges along his neck, and I want to lick him there. I want to bite his shoulder. I want him buried inside me.

I don't realize how wild I am in response to him until I hear the bed creaking in rhythm with us.

Squeak, squeak, squeak, and then he stills. He's biting his lip and pressing so hard against me, I'm convinced the covered tip has entered me a little bit. I'd giggle at the concept of *only the tip* if I didn't think he looked beautiful and pained at the same time I feel wet warmth against me. He pauses, pressing against me, holding this glorious position and then he collapses. He blankets me a second, taking deep breaths against my neck. He slips to the side, and the moist cotton drags over my hip. His hand comes to my throat, fingers on my pulse point.

"Your heart's racing," he mutters into my shoulder before kissing it.

"That was…" My voice drifts. I'm not certain how to categorize what just happen. It was the best non-sex-sex I've ever had.

"Yeah." I hear the smile in his voice and the curl of his lips lingering on my shoulder. "That was."

37

You Frustrate Me

[Mati]

I awake alone. Denton's shoes are gone as is the pile of clothing once covering the chair in the corner. I pull the sheet to my chest before exiting the bed and find my clothing still on the floor. I haven't done the walk of shame since my short time as a college freshman, and this will be only slightly more embarrassing. I have no idea if anyone else knows I'm here or how things are progressing with Caroline. After Denton told me she passed, and we…well, we didn't discuss what was next for her or us.

Feeling slightly unclean wearing the same clothes as the day before, I slowly open the door. Down the long hall, the door to Caroline's room stands open. There's movement in the room which must have open shades as bright sunlight streams out into the hallway. I walk in that direction hoping to find Denton, but a heavy lump in my stomach tells me he isn't here.

"Hello," I say softly, peeking into the room. Caroline is gone. The equipment mostly removed.

"Hello." Vivian, the nurse, looks up from rolling a chord around her fist.

"Is there anything I can do to help?" I offer, feeling useless standing here watching her hustle around the room, but I have no idea how I can assist her.

"Hospice handles everything, honey. Miss Caroline was removed early this morning, and the machinery went next. I'm just doing a final sweep."

"Oh." I nod. "Have you seen Denton?"

"He mentioned heading to the Lodge."

"Thank you." The lump in my stomach weighs like a boulder. Slowly, I make my way down the staircase. No trace of breakfast or coffee consumption litters the kitchen. It looks just as I left it last night.

L.B. Dunbar

I have no idea how I'll get home, and I reach for my phone in my purse. *Maybe one of the boys can come to get me*, I think as I walk the wide hall to the front doors. Out of the corner of my eye, I see a figure sitting in the shadows of the front parlor.

"Miss Magnolia?"

She doesn't look up at me, and for a moment, I think she's sleeping sitting upright. I cross the room cautiously and then pause before her.

"Miss Magnolia," I repeat, lowering myself to crouch by her knees. Her pop bottle glasses mutate her eyes, but she blinks when I come into her view. "Miss Magnolia, can I do something for you?"

"A mother should never have to bury her child." Her elderly voice scratches as she speaks. I nod in agreement, but I'm not certain how to respond. "She should have had a second chance."

I continue to stare up at her from my position. Many would agree Mrs. Caroline Chance deserved a second round at love, but if what I remember from Denton is true, she had a few rounds at it and lost them all.

"What can I do for you?" I ask.

"I should have gone first. I'm older. I'm ready." She blinks, and a single tear slips down her cheek. I worry she's been sitting here all night, maybe witnessing the removal of her daughter's body.

"Where's Dolores?" I question, feeling like family will understand better how to handle Magnolia's grief.

"Rosalyn's coming," she says, ignoring my question. "Haven't seen my other girl in a long time, but now she'll come." Magnolia's voice turns bitter, and I recognize the name of Denton and Dolores's aunt.

"She should be here," I offer, hoping the words sound supportive.

"She should have been here a long time ago. Just like him." I don't have to ask who Magnolia means. She's referring to Denton and his absence from his mother's life even after Kip died.

"He's here now," I weakly defend.

"He's already planning on leaving. Got some meeting in New York City in a few days." Magnolia waves her hand to dismiss her grandson, and the lump in my gut bottoms out. Nausea rises to my throat.

"Well, let's take one day at a time," I suggest, reaching up to pat Magnolia's knee with strength I don't feel.

"One day at a time," Magnolia mutters as if speaking to herself, reassuring herself of the steps through grief. The stages of grieving and I are old friends. I stand, looking down at the frail woman I've always admired for her strength and dedication to family—a family that wasn't always loyal to her.

"You let me know if you need anything, Miss Magnolia," I offer once again, and she flicks her wrist to dismiss me. Her head shifts left, and she peers toward the enclosed side porch. The door remains closed against the cool air temperature outside, but sunshine dances through the screen.

I step away from her feeling guilty for not being able to offer her more support, but relief at finding a way out of this house of sadness. Seeing myself out to the front porch, I begin dialing Jordan's number when a red-haired man dressed in leather rounds the corner of the house. Crusty Rusty.

My heart swells a little with the hope he comforted Dolores in her time of need. Instantly, I think back to the comfort I offered Denton last night. I shiver with a combination of pleasure and disappointment at his absence. Watching Rusty, he walks straight to his bike and flips a leg over the seat.

Then he notices me.

Rusty Miller scans my body from toes to top and down again. His red hair sticks up a bit, and his facial hair is a poor mix between scruff and beard as if his jaw can't decide which way to go. He has some type of pox scars on his face, reminding me of the nemesis in the movie *Grease*. In fact, Crusty Rusty looks more *greasy* than crusty.

"Need a ride, beautiful?"

"Uhm…" This would be a bad idea. The worst idea ever. But I tell myself James is one of his club brothers, and I should be safe enough. James would never let something happen to me as his true sister. Then again, knowing nothing of the motorcycle club code of ethics, I doubt James's protection.

"I'm not certain that would be a good idea."

231

L.B. Dunbar

Crusty's brow pinches.

"You need a ride, right? Hop on. I'll take you to town." There's innuendo in the words I shouldn't read, and I try to tell myself I'm overthinking things.

"I live in the subdivision before town. Can you drop me there?"

"Anything for you, beautiful," he says, firing up the bike. I'm cursing myself as I step forward, knowing I should have just called one of the boys, but I also know I need to get off this property. I need to get away from the death lingering here. I need to remove myself from Denton.

He's going to New York City next week.

"Hang on, beautiful," Crusty yells as he kicks the bike into gear and screeches out of Magnolia's drive, spitting up gravel as we curve onto the main road. I hold onto the edges of his jacket, not wanting to wrap my arms around him or touch him any more than I need. The bike screams, and I realize it's been a long time since I've been on one. Not since James got his first one against Daddy's wishes before he went to rescue training.

We buzz right past my subdivision, and I pat Rusty on the back. "Hey, you missed my turn."

"You said town," he hollers back, and there's a strange twitch to his cheek like he's laughing at me. I don't really want to be seen in town on the back of a bike, one that belongs to a Devil's Edge, and more so the one belonging to Rusty Miller.

"Just U-turn up here," I yell, but I can feel the vibration of Rusty chuckling. He accelerates and races for Main Street. Turning into town, he slows enough to make sure we're seen by every person on the street— three blocks worth. He idles at a lower speed, but just fast enough I can't jump off, which is exactly what I'm thinking I'll do if he doesn't turn us around. As we pull up to a stoplight, the oncoming traffic turns next to us, and Denton's car passes by. My heart sinks as he does a double take before punching down his accelerator. Rusty ignores the light and U-turns while I scream. He guns it to catch Denton who must be going faster than the speed limit as Rusty certainly is. As Denton passes my subdivision, not giving it a second glance, Rusty slows and turns down

232

the quiet street. With a shaky hand, I point to the road he can take to my place and then holler which one is mine.

"The tan one on the left."

As he stops in front of my house, I hop off gracelessly, getting my foot stuck on the seat. I yank my leg with both hands and stomp my foot.

"Just what the hell was that?" I demand.

"Easy, beautiful."

"Don't call me beautiful and why would you do that?" Taking me into town was unnecessary. Rusty licks his teeth inside his mouth like he's cleaning them. Then he speaks.

"Had I known you were the wildcat, I'd have gone for you sooner."

My mouth falls open. "How dare you disrespect Dolores!"

"Dolores knows how things are."

I don't even want to know what that means. I know enough about James's behavior to assume Rusty and Dolores aren't exclusive although Dolores has dated no one else but Rusty for years.

"Rusty Miller, you need to be fair to Dolores."

He chuckles before responding. "Ain't nothing fair in this life, beautiful. Dolores knows that better than anyone."

My fists are rising to my hips, and I'm ready to give him a lecture like only my mother can produce when I hear another bike coming down my street. James doesn't even slow. He glides by, nods at Rusty, and continues to circle through the streets. Rusty's lips twitch with displeasure, and he revs his bike in response.

"See ya around, pussycat," he smirks, drifting his eyes too low on my body before lurching forward to follow James. I want to scrub myself all over from that look.

The slam of a vehicle door behind me turns my head, and I note a familiar SUV parked in my driveway. Jax stalks toward me.

Sweet Jesus, now what?

"What the hell were you doing?"

"Excuse me?" I snap, blinking in exaggeration at my son.

"First that Denton guy, and now Crusty Rusty Miller of Devil's Edge. Mama, what's going on with you?"

I stare at my son a second, mouth gaping in disbelief.

"There is no first or second here, Jaxson. I'm not running around with anyone."

"The whole town's talking about you and Denton. Some love reunited thing, and now this." He waves flippantly toward the street. "Riding on the back of Rusty's bike. Do you know what people will say next?"

"Jaxson Harrington, since when do you care what people think?"

While I don't care for the gossip of the town, I've also hardly had it directed at me. If I think about it, I don't want people talking about me as if I'm doing something wrong. Jax takes a huge breath and then exhales. "I don't give a rat's ass what the town thinks of me, but I do care what people say about my mother."

Well, it's nice to know he's still protective of me in some manner. As if it's okay for him to question my slut-itude, but if others suggest it, he's upset.

"You frustrate me," I mutter, recalling times when he was a child, and I just didn't understand why he'd do what he'd done. Toothbrush down the toilet. Gum in Sandy Eberstein's hair. A snake in the dishwasher.

"Mama, you frustrate me," he mocks back as his hands slip into his jacket pockets. We stare at one another a moment, eyes the same color as mine focus back at me.

"Miss Caroline died," I begin. "I was at Magnolia's and didn't have a ride home. I was getting ready to call Jordan when I saw Rusty leaving the house. I wasn't thinking, other than it was a few miles away."

A knowing look beams at me from my child, as if he's the adult. "Why'd you want to leave there?"

"I'm not a fan of death."

Jax nods in response. His expression softens. "What were you doing there in the first place?"

I pause, twisting my lips, thinking how best to explain myself to my son, and then rethinking—do I need to explain myself to my son?

"Miss Caroline was dying. Gran was there." *Close enough to the truth. No lie involved there.*

"It was Denton, wasn't it?"

"And what if it was him, Jaxson? His mother died! What's this thing you have against the man beside some story your father told you that I know nothing about?"

"Dad said Denton loved you like him."

I blink, utterly stunned at the revelation. "We were friends."

"Mama, don't be coy with me."

"I'm—"

"Dad asked him to leave town."

My mouth falls open again. "That's not—"

"He said he was going to lose you to Denton and he didn't know how he'd live without you. Told me I should always respect women but respect no one else when it came to keeping *the one*."

I recall what Hollilyn told me and I'm flabbergasted at this advice from Chris to our child. I'm equally stunned Hollilyn knew something so intimate between father and son as Jaxson seems to always keep her at arm's length.

"Why would your father say such a thing?"

"He said he knew one day I'd fall in love, but I'd find it hard to settle. Said I reminded him of an old friend in this manner. He told me if I wanted a girl bad enough to make her my only priority. Said because Denton left, it spoke volumes to his true feelings for you. He didn't make you his priority."

The words sting, although I try to find some sympathy in them for Chris. I'm puzzled by his concern that Denton would steal me and stung by his assessment that Denton's leaving meant I didn't matter to our oldest friend. He was probably right. Of course, he was right. Denton took Kristy, not me.

"It was all a long time ago, baby. None of it matters now."

"I don't want him thinking he can replace Daddy."

"Jaxson," my voice lowers. "No man would ever replace your father even if I took him as my hus—" I stop myself. I'm not thinking about marriage. I'm not even thinking boyfriends. Not lovers, not anything. I'm going to be alone for the rest of my life, and Denton's leaving proves this. Rusty's ride through town just double downed the possibility. No one would come near me if they thought I was a Devil's Edge chick. A saddening thought strikes regarding Dolores. Poor thing.

Jaxson isn't looking at me, but across the street, where I'm certain my nosy neighbors are watching me hash out life with my son in the driveway. I never wanted to live in this subdivision. Used to the Lane where three homes were separated by large yards, thick trees, and the peace of separation, the houses in the subdivision were too close together for my liking. Chris wanted to live here, though.

"Are you thinking of remarrying, Mama?"

"Honey, no. No, I'm nowhere near something like that. I'm just tired of being alone."

"Then why're you hanging out with so many men?"

"I think you're hurting for the wrong reasons, so I'm going to ignore the implication in the tone of your voice. If I'm dating a man, I have that right. I have the right to try him on like you've tried on many girls before Hollilyn."

"Please tell me it's not the same thing." A smile slowly creases his mouth, and he shudders.

"Don't be pulling double standards on me."

"Mama! Stop," he chokes.

"Besides, you have nothing to worry about. Denton Chance is leaving soon." *He always does*, I want to add.

"What if he wanted to stay?" I'm not sure why my son asks me this, and I'm frightened by my immediate answer. *I want him to stay*. This time I want him to choose me. But I have my own secrets, ones I'm not ready to share with anyone until I have definitive answers, which remind me the interview is in two days and I'll need to reschedule if the funeral is on the same date.

"Mama?" Jaxson's quiet voice pulls me from my thoughts.

"I'm not looking to turn back time, honey, if that's what you're asking. I wouldn't trade one second of my life with your father and you boys. But I still have time before me, God willing, and I'd like to do with it what I want."

The clear suggestion is: my time is mine.

Jaxson nods. "I guess we don't value time until it isn't ours anymore."

"What do you mean?"

"I mean like the baby coming. Everyone keeps telling me my time will no longer be mine. Everything I do, I'll do for him or her."

"That's how it should be," I say with a nod, my expression breaking into a slow grin.

"But I don't think I'm ready. I don't know if Hollilyn is the one. I didn't settle on her. It just happened."

"Oh, baby," I sigh. "I don't want you to feel you *settled*, but sometimes love just happens, in the strangest, most unexpected ways. It happens. Maybe the baby is your sign that Hollilyn *is* the one. But if she isn't, you're still going to be a father to a child with her, and you're bonded for life." My voice becomes harder, firmer, reinforcing the baby didn't ask to be born, and my son will live up to his responsibilities.

"I know," he exhales, swiping a hand through his dark hair, looking slightly like Chris but more like a Harrington.

"It's just jitters. You'll keep having them until the baby is born, and then you'll have new worries."

"You aren't making me feel any better, Mama."

"I'm not sugarcoating this for you, Jaxson. Parenting is hard work, and kids frustrate some days." My eyebrow twitches upward, and he huffs a chuckle. "But it's the most rewarding thing you'll ever do in your life as long as you *try* your best at it." I think of Kip Chance for a second. He never tried to be a father to his son, whether biological or not. He refused, and it made all the difference in the world to one boy.

"You know I'll try my hardest."

"And what about Hollilyn?"

"I'm trying there as well."

"Well, I guess that's all I can ask for her sake."

"Why you so worried about Hollilyn?"

"Because just like you, she deserves a happily ever after, and I don't want her settling for you because you settled on her."

"Did you settle on Dad?"

"Of course not," I say sharper than necessary.

L.B. Dunbar

"Did you love Denton back then?"

The question pulls me up short, and I don't know how to explain myself. *Did I?*

"I loved him differently than your father. Just like I feel differently about him now."

"Meaning?"

I exhale. "I don't even know." I don't know how to describe the emotions inside me when I think of Denton or how to explain the sensations I feel when I'm near him. I'm all kinds of confused, and I suddenly can relate to my child. To my surprise, Jaxson walks up to me and envelops me in his arms. There's no question I've loved a variety of men in my life: my Daddy, my brothers, Chris and Denton, but there's no love like loving my son. Both of them.

38

Life is a Mystery, So is Death

[Denton]

Shit. How could she be on the back of that asshole's bike only hours after what we've done? I have half a mind to turn around and follow them to her house, but the other half of me is too angry to deal with drama. I need to meet Dolores, and we need to get to the funeral home. I went to the Lodge to grab some clean clothes and something more presentable than jeans and a three-day-old T-shirt. I'd also ruined my last pair of clean underwear last night.

Last night. My dick jolts with the memory, but my heart weeps. I want Mati like I've never wanted her before, and I'm astounded at the strength it took to withhold ripping off her underwear and filling her. *Pretend*. The word whispers through my thoughts. We did pretend—for my sake. Mati gave me what I needed or as close to what we should do. Taking her during my numbness wasn't how I wanted to remember the first time with her.

My shoulders sag under the weight of the day ahead. There are so many unanswered questions, so many unknowns, beyond the funeral, and I'm worried about my meeting in New York. I've wanted the shoot with *Healthy Male* forever. Second to the sexiest man alive on *People*, a cover photo on the famous male magazine would boost my career and my ego at forty-five. Of course, one thing they'll want to discuss is the history of Chrome Teardrops and my exit from the band.

As I pull into the drive of Magnolia's home, I decide I need to take one day at a time. Holding my phone in my hand as I walk over the gravel, I scan the pop-up messages. The first text is from Mati.

Denton?

I curse myself for even opening the messenger app and note the time. She sent the text before I saw her on that damn bike with that crusty excuse for a human being. My heart thuds as I think of my sister and how

L.B. Dunbar

she's found herself in a relationship similar to our mother's. While there isn't any evidence of physical abuse, the emotional tug-of-war with a man like him has left just as many scars. Dolores doesn't see she deserves better than a biker who plays the field. I bite my own lip, thinking of Mati. She deserves more than a one-night stand and confusing sexual encounters like she's had with me.

I'm a dick, I think to myself as I enter the farmhouse for what I'm hoping will soon be my last time. Just the thought of New York City, the Ritz Carlton, and sushi has my heart racing for the days to pass quickly. Then I look down at my phone again. My screen saver is a picture of Mati which I took when she wasn't looking but gazing up at the stars the other night. So many unlimited possibilities; we joked as teenagers. Where did all the possibilities go?

"Mati," I say into the phone the second after she exhales my name upon answering. "How could you be on his bike?"

"How could you leave me without explanation?" There's more to her question than a simple disappearance this morning, but I can't drag up those memories.

"I left a note."

There's a pause lasting a little too long before she speaks. "I didn't see a note."

"It was on the nightstand, by the lamp." I left a note to avoid something like this very conversation.

"What did it say?" Her voice hesitates.

"It said, you should have read the note." I snort. She chuckles.

"I'm sorry," she mutters.

"So, tell me, what were you doing with Crusty Rusty?"

"I needed a ride home."

I shake my head. She's stating the obvious. However, if she'd only read my note, she'd know I was coming back for her. I'd never leave her hanging again.

"How are you doing today?" she asks, crashing into my conflicting thoughts. New York. Mati. California. Mati.

"I think I'm too focused on what needs to be done to know how I feel."

"Last night, you said you felt numb," Mati reminds me.

"Yeah, well, that was only a small portion of the night," I tease, and Mati's giggle proves she understands me. "I wish you'd read the note."

"Why don't you tell me what it said?" Her voice shifts, breathy and low. She has a sultry sound to her which I imagine she doesn't recognize.

"I wrote how I enjoyed waking up next to you and I hope to do it again soon."

"Before you leave," she mutters.

"What?"

"Before you go. To New York."

Shit.

"When were you going to tell me, Denton?"

The words *it's no big deal* rest on the edge of my tongue, but that would be a lie. This photoshoot could be huge for me.

"I just wanted to make it through the funeral."

Mati's silence speaks volumes.

"When do you leave?" Her voice lowers even more, and I don't want to imagine it, but I think I hear sadness in her tone. *Would she want me to stay?* The question sends a shiver up my spine. *I can't stay here.*

"The funeral will probably be in two days with the wake tomorrow evening. I'll leave the day after."

Mati gasps. "What about Magnolia?"

Magnolia, I sigh. My grandmother is one of the many things Dolores and I will need to discuss.

"I'll have to talk to Dolores."

Mati doesn't respond again.

"Look, I hate to go, but I need to find Dolores. We have so much to do today."

"Of course. Yes. Sure, you should go. Go, go," she states as if shooing a fly, or giving into the resolve—she wants me to leave.

241

39

Four Movie Buffs and a Funeral

[Mati]

The day of Caroline's wake, I have my interview. Coaching for Northeastern would be a dream come true, especially as I didn't complete my degree there nor did I get to use the volleyball scholarship I originally had to attend there. It wasn't all Denton's fault, but he felt guilty for weeks.

I'll work every day at Duncan's Construction if I need to, to have the money you lost.

It was a silly promise. My daddy could cover the cost. It was the loss of honor that hurt. That and my broken ankle. Climbing down the side of my house was becoming riskier, especially with a decade-old magnolia tree outside my window. Never truly sturdy enough to hold me, each climb through the branches was a short, thrill-seeking adventure. Until I fell.

Just jump. I'll catch you, Denton promised.

My foot lost its hold, and I tumbled to the ground. The scream woke my father. Denton hadn't caught me.

That's what you get for sneaking out, my mother admonished.

Maybe you're old enough to just use the door when you leave. My father winked. He never made assumptions about Denton and me. It's as if he knew what we were doing was innocent enough. Maybe he also understood I officially dated Chris and would never cheat on him.

I trust you to be making smart decisions with either boy, baby girl. You aren't one of my sons. Behave accordingly. The hint of a double standard never escaped me, but I appreciated my father's confidence in me.

I'd broken my ankle in two places that night. Volleyball playing became my history.

The interview was nerve-racking, albeit exciting. The aura of a college campus. The youthful energy. The thrill of the sport. Hope rattled in my bones and my body hummed by the time I was on my way back to Blue Ridge for the wake. Driving home from the interview, I reviewed every question and my answers, scrutinizing my responses.

Is there anything preventing you from moving closer to the university?

I cursed myself when Denton entered my mind. He wasn't a reason to hold me back. He wasn't a reason for anything. He'd be leaving in two days. Once he settled with his sister about his grandmother, he'd probably never return to Blue Ridge. My heart sank at the thought, but I knew it was for the best. Denton Chance didn't belong in our small town. He was always larger than life, and his return proves it all the more. He was meant to live outside our town.

I am still perspiring with nerves, although I thought the rest of the interview went well. I don't have time to stop at home, so I use a drive-thru napkin to wipe the sweat under my pits. Certain I smell of both perspiration and guilt, I don't have a choice but to enter the funeral home as I am—late.

Walking into O'Leary's Funeral Home, I notice Cora across the subdued room packed with townspeople. A few people I recognize seem more the type to attend a wake for the notoriety of saying they were there. A few others are the type to keep their eyes on Denton Chance for signs of any drama. Kristy Moseley becomes case in point. Denton's ex-wife clings to his arm as if she's holding onto a lifeline. The irony is Caroline Chance never liked her momentary daughter-in-law.

It should have been you, Mati, she said to me once upon a time.

"Where have you been?" Cora accosts me after making her way through the crowd. In the heat of the room, it appears the whole town has shown up to pay respects to their former first lady. While I never cared for Kip, he worked to keep Blue Ridge on the map, putting up small subdivisions like mine and trying to attract large businesses. The brewery is the bread and butter of the community, though, and Kip Chance always hated that fact. With Charlie as the mayor the last decade, he's shifted our economy to more small businesses and tourism.

"I had things to attend to," I hush-whisper, not caring for her accusatory tone with me.

We're very impressed with your winning record but also your philosophy for team sports and women's athletics. I'm not ready to share my little secret, but I smile to myself, nonetheless.

"What's that grin for, Miss Matilda?" Cora admonishes. I ignore her and redirect with: "Did I miss something?"

I don't care for gossip, but her expression suggests if I've missed something important.

"Denton needs you." First, I'm insulted with Cora's tone. She's eager to preach how a man should satisfy a woman, not be needy of her and make her feel her worth is deemed by him. Second, I'm shocked by her words. *Denton doesn't need me,* I think, my heart softening a little at the possibility. I know my way around grief, so I understand. He needs someone, but I can't narrow it down to only me.

As if he senses my thoughts of him, his head turns for the back of the room. He catches my eye, and I offer a weak wave. In return, I receive a head nod. *Ouch.*

"There are hundreds of people here," I point out, holding at bay my wounded heart.

"But he's only been looking for one person." Her brows raise as her arm loops through mine, leading me farther into the funeral home. I don't have a moment to pay my respects as the reverend calls our attention for a short prayer service. Shit, I'm later than I thought if the night has progressed to the prayer.

Cora guides me into seats near my family. Giant, Billy, and Charlie make a handsome lot in dark suits, lowered heads, and scruffy cheeks. I peek to the back of the room, hoping to find James on the periphery. Annoyance sparks when I don't even see Crusty Rusty. My heart sinks for Dolores, and I face forward to find Denton peering over his shoulder. He doesn't smile or even give me his Californian head nod. It's as if he's searching for someone but doesn't see me.

"You need to seize that man," Cora whispers, her voice a little louder than necessary and considering our surroundings, inappropriate.

Billy chuckles next to me, while Charlie leans forward to raise an eyebrow in our direction.

"He isn't a battle," I mutter out the side of my mouth.

"Love is a battlefield." My mouth pops open, ready to tell Cora we aren't talking about love when my brother begins to hum a few bars of the Pat Benatar classic and Cora holds her hand at half-mast to stop me from speaking. "I'm talking more about a *Dirty Dancing* moment."

I snort, and the noise travels. Billy knocks me in the shoulder with his, and I lower my head, acting as if I need to cough with a fist to my mouth.

"Nobody-puts-Baby-in-a-corner moment," I mock, not having the slightest inkling how this relates to me.

"More like an I'm-afraid-I'll-never-feel-again-how-I-feel-with-you moment," Cora mutters. I choke. Billy snorts. Giant reaches around Charlie and taps Billy in the back of the head.

"What the he...*heck*...do you mean?" I twist slightly, looking at the side of Cora's done-up face. She's an expert at makeup, unlike me. Pearls, black dress, she's all polished like a true Southern beauty.

"I'm just saying sometimes you have to be a little afraid of losing someone to recognize you may never feel like you feel right now again in your life." She drawls out the words.

From my seat, I see Denton at an angle with his sharp suit and sad eyes.

How can he look hot in jeans and tee or a tie and sorrow?

"I mean, that man wants you, and there's no denying he's hot as sin. And you want him. He's perfect for a test drive," Cora continues as if I don't understand her meaning. My eyes open wide and my face heats.

"Cora," I hiss.

"There's nothing wrong with a little ride, Mati, to see if you can still handle the road." Now Charlie chuckles, and I close my eyes as Cora's euphemisms take a wrong turn.

"Cora," I groan, warning her to stop.

"I'm just saying—"

"As much as I'm enjoying this *Steel Magnolia* moment listening to the two of you banter like Claire Belcher and Louisa Boudreaux, try to

245

remember where you are for a moment." Charlie's voice chastises us, as he leans forward like our mother did in church on Sunday mornings when the Harrington children misbehaved.

"Oh, and who might I be in this scenario?" I mutter to no one in particular, and Billy chuckles. "And what is this, movie hour?"

"You're turning into the grouchy one," Cora smirks next to me and sticks out her tongue at Charlie. I huff out a stifled laugh at her immaturity.

"When did he become so pious?" Cora leans into me, bumping my shoulder, as her voice lowers.

"When he hasn't been laid since Luci was three," Billy says quietly out the side of his mouth referencing Charlie's daughter, and I cover my mouth again to suppress another giggle. As if sensing our behavior, I look over at Denton but intercept my mother's eyes from where she stands behind Denton and Dolores in the second row. Her eyes narrow, and without looking at my brothers, I know we all straightened in our seats.

+ + +

The next day, the funeral is a difficult few hours for me. Memories of Chris's passing flood me as we listen to a sermon in church and then stand around Caroline's grave. My eyes drift across the cemetery to another plot, recalling another fall day, much like today—gloomy, rainy, lifeless. I don't focus on my own memories too long, though.

My parents provide the massive luncheon after the funeral at their home to show their respects as long-time neighbors to the Chances. Keeping my eyes on Denton, we circle each other like a practiced dance. As if attracted like magnets, we find each other, pass with a soft touch to the arm or swipe to the lower back, and then move on.

We haven't spoken in two days. I sent a text, and hours later he answered. His reply I missed, and it was late when I responded. We cross, miss, and continue marching forward. Our communication attempts are a metaphor for our relationship. We've been friends-with-feelings, missed our chance, and continued on opposing paths.

Our lives are so different. I'm hopeful of the volleyball coach position. He still wants his modeling career. Once again, we orbit one another, but just once I'd like to collide. I want to hold on and dig in and connect on a level I know I'll only achieve with him. Like Cora said, the *I'm-afraid-I'll-never-feel-again-how-I-feel-with-you* sentiment. My breath hitches with the overwhelming possibility it's true. I'll never feel again how I feel when I'm with Denton. I don't want to lose another second without him.

It's almost laughable when I think of the time we've lost, but then I look up and see Jax, his hand on Hollilyn's stomach. He leans forward and kisses her in a rare public display of tenderness. With the vision of my son, spreading his fingers over his future offspring, I'm almost shattered by the realization I wouldn't change a thing in my past. If everything happens for a reason, Denton and I just weren't meant to be. But what's the reason for his return to me now then?

40

Put a Ring on It

[Denton]

I've finally made my way to a swing in the yard. I should check on Magnolia and Dolores, but I'm too exhausted. Five minutes, I tell myself. I can't look at Dolores again. She looks so worn and empty, and I don't know who to hate first. My mother or her douchebag boyfriend, who really isn't a boyfriend but a sex partner. I shiver with the thought. Watching Dolores, I can almost see the weight on her shoulders. She knows she's got to keep the pieces together once I leave. The diner. The house. Our grandmother.

Just let me handle things like I always do, she snapped at me. I realize the timing of our conversation could have been better. I'd just gotten the call from my agent, informing me of *Healthy Male* and I wanted to tamper my own guilt at leaving so quickly by pressing the issues at hand.

This is the recognition I'd been waiting for, I argued when I told her I was leaving.

Why? Why is it so important for the world to give you appreciation but not the people here? The people whose opinion should matter the most.

I scoffed, ready to tell her there wasn't anyone here whose opinion I cared about, but Dolores waved a dismissive hand at me. *Never mind. I don't expect you to understand.*

I wanted to continue arguing, but our grandmother entered the room with tears in her magnified eyes, and the discussion came to a halt.

As I sit on the swing, one I sat on a hundred times with Mati, I realize I'm wrong. There are people here who matter to me. Mati immediately comes to mind, and I search her out across the yard. My eyes drift to her son, Jordan and his wife, Maggie, so like Chris and what I pictured of Mati when they were young. They work the crowd like seasoned society members, and I wonder if Chris ever aspired to be mayor before Charlie took the title.

Was that the reason he signed off on illegal contracts with my father?

I shake my head, refusing to think of the complicated shitshow behind this funeral.

My eyes float over a stream of people to find Jax and his girl, Hollilyn. She's a ball of energy, and her swollen belly reiterates the metaphor. She's been the backbone of the diner the last week, and I know Dolores is eternally grateful. Staring at her round stomach, my heart grieves for other losses. The children I've never had. I don't trust I would have been a good father, but I see what I might have missed when I watch Mati look at her boys. With a woman like her at my side, I could never be less than the man she expected. Then again, she didn't have expectations of me. She had Chris.

Chris. Death. Hollilyn. Life. The circle goes around and around, just like Mati and me during this luncheon. I find myself drawn to her like she's my sun, but then I'm a lost planet or an asteroid, shooting off in other directions. I search her out to ground me, to know I'm orbiting around these people I don't recognize or don't know, but she's still there: the center of my universe. The one constant. A brush of her hand or a tender touch to my back and I feel restored, like I'm realigned.

"You creeping on my girlfriend, now, old man?" The gruff, masculine voice stirs me from my thoughts, and I blink as I realize I'm staring in the direction of Hollilyn. She sheepishly smiles, but the coy look isn't for me. The look of love belongs to the man who hands me a glass of amber liquid and takes a seat next to me on the swing seat. Jax snorts as he grips the edge of the worn wooden slats and the rusty chains creak. Without a word, we both look up at the discolored S-clip holding the swing to the equally dull wooden support. I don't look in his direction when I answer his snarky question, but return my gaze to the yard, not focusing on any one thing.

"Young blondes who are pregnant and madly in love with someone aren't my thing."

Jax huffs next to me.

L.B. Dunbar

"Yeah, and what is your thing?" I turn for him, but all I see is his profile. Masculine, edgy jaw, and the same colored eyes as Mati. The distinction between the twins lives in their eyes. Jax is more Harrington.

"Someone over forty with lion colored hair and a personality to match." I chuckle at the appropriate description of his mother.

"Huh. I might know a woman like that." Both of us awkwardly laugh, a certain tension waffling between us. Knowing he doesn't like my interest in his mother, I reassure him of my future.

"Yeah, well, don't worry about anything. I'll be leaving tomorrow." Jax's head swings and the weight of his eyes burrow into the side of my head, but I refuse to look at him. I don't need his smug face telling me it's a good idea I'm going.

"What if she asked you to stay?" His question surprises me.

"Know something I don't?" My eyes shift to him and away.

"I know her heart hurt for a long time after my dad died. I don't want to see her go through that again."

"I'm not dead," I mutter.

"Nope. And that's worse because it means you're making a conscious choice to stay away when you could come back." The idea lingers between us. *Choice.* I never felt I had any other choice than to leave this town. I don't see returning to it a decision either.

Jax coughs as if he's clearing his throat, preparing for a speech. He isn't done with me yet. "I also might know a thing or two about losing a parent."

My head swings back in his direction, but his eyes remain on the dirt a foot before us. His loss was nothing like mine. He had a great father. Without knowing Chris during his fatherhood years, I just know he was the man. My dad was an asshole, and as for the loss of my mother, I think I lost her so long ago I'm numb to the current situation.

"I know it's not really the same," he begins as if he reads my thoughts. "I mean, I don't know much about you, but for me, it was hard to lose my dad." Jax swallows. "I loved my dad, and I know he loved me, but I wasn't Jordan. I didn't become the lawyer and follow in his footsteps. I didn't marry the first girl. I've been a bit more reckless." Jax swipes a hand through his hair. "A bit more of a player."

I chuckle a little. I definitely know about that.

"Dad used to say I reminded him of his best friend from when he was a kid. A bit wild but with a big heart deep inside." It's my turn to swallow hard, and I'll punch this kid if he brings me to tears. I haven't shed one yet, but I feel a prickle in my nose and the sting behind my eyes.

"I talked to my mom about you." His voice lowers, as does his head, and the seriousness of his tone makes my breath catch. My heart races. "I want to be candid with you which will make me sound like an insensitive ass."

Here it comes, I think. He's going to tell me to stay away from his mother and get the fuck out of town, just like his father.

"I feel a little sorry for you, Denton. You may have fame and fortune. California and beach babes. But I bet you never missed your dad. And I feel sorry for you that you didn't have that kind of relationship because I'd take my dad back over fame and fortune." I understand what he's saying, but he's right. I didn't have a relationship with my father, and I took fame and fortune to compensate for the lack of positive attention. Great lot it did me. I'm just as alone, but I have money. Sarcasm chokes me. "I'd never trade that kind of relationship."

I nod. I'm not certain if I'm supposed to respond. Am I to tell him he's correct? Does he want my recognition of what he already knows about me? I had a shit relationship with my father. *So, what?*

"As a peace offering, I'd like to give you something you may never have. My child's going to have lots of grand-uncles, but I'm talking about something more specific. Someone my child can call his own."

I snort. "Like a step-grandfather?"

"Let's not get carried away." Jax patronizingly pats me on the shoulder a little rougher than necessary. "More like a replacement piece." My forehead furrows, and he grimaces. "How about more like a thread…something that will weave you back to the area. Keep you in touch this time."

We remain silent a second, and I swallow back the rest of my drink, dismissing the burn in my throat and the continuing sting to my eyes.

"Do you think she's in love with me?"

L.B. Dunbar

Following the line of his vision to Hollilyn, who is rubbing her belly, but peering over at Jax, I chuckle at the obvious expression of her affection. Her face pinks and a shy smile forms on her face, brightening her cheeks.

"What's not to love, right, kid?" I chuckle. He's arrogant, and I expect a similar retort. Instead, he sounds uncertain of himself when he asks me: "Think I should marry her?"

"Do you love her?"

A small smile curls his lips, mirroring the woman beaming back at him. I'd say he does love her, even if he doesn't see it.

"Yeah," he sheepishly admits, his head lowering to break the connection between the two of them.

"What would your dad say?" I'm not sure I'm qualified to give advice on marriage, so I defer to Chris.

"Put a ring on that and never let her go." I chuckle, imagining Chris's voice saying such a thing.

"Yeah," I sigh, seeking out Mati in the crowd of people milling in the yard.

"Maybe you should do the same." My head swings back to him, but I take his meaning. To say I'm shocked is an understatement.

41

I'll Never Feel How I Feel With You Again.

[Denton]

I'm exhausted by the time I finally make my way to Conrad Lodge. A night away from the farmhouse is long overdue. I've just removed my dress shirt and T-shirt when a knock on my hotel door stops me from unbuckling my belt. I didn't order room service, so I have no idea who it could be.

"Mati?"

"May I come in?" she asks, lowering her eyes. Mine roam over her attire. A camel colored trench coat hangs open to reveal she still wears the black wrap dress she wore to the funeral. The dress hugs her curves in all the right places, and I hadn't missed her shapely legs above high heels. She looks sexy despite the dreary purpose of the clothing. I wave her into the room.

Closing the door, I turn to see her immediately remove her coat, and the curve of her backside draws my attention. Her dress clings to her, rounding over her shapely hips but dipping inward at her waist. Her long, lion-colored locks hang to the middle of her back, and she twists to look at me over her shoulder. The pose is photograph worthy, and I want to capture an image of her like this forever. I also want to ravish her. My dick twitches as I inhale a deep breath. Ravishing cannot be her purpose.

"Want something to drink?" I offer, returning to the glass already half filled with scotch on the nightstand by the bed.

"Nah," she scoffs. I twist in a way to plop myself on the bed, propping myself up against the headboard and crossing my ankles. I notice Mati has already taken a seat on a gold upholstered chair kitty-corner to me. Sipping the sharp alcohol, I watch her over the rim of my glass. She smooths down the skirt of her dress. Then she straightens up, and her fingers tug at the thin tie at the side of her waist. She's fidgety as she asks, "How are you doing?"

"Never been better," I lash out. I'm exhausted. I've hugged and kissed too many strangers. I had the strangest conversation with her son. And I've spent the day staring at her, wondering what she wants from me, *if* she wants something from me.

What if she asked you to stay? I can't imagine Mati asking me such a thing. She stays quiet as I take another sip of liquor. My eyes remain on the V at her breasts and the subtle heave of her chest, knowing I'm focused on her.

"It's been a difficult few days," she says, her eyes drifting to the closed curtains.

"What are you doing here, Mati?" I don't want to talk about the funeral. I don't want to talk about my mother, my father, my best friend, or her sons with him.

"I…I wanted to check on you. You worked the crowd today, but I know how hard it is to keep it together."

"Let's not compare death stories, okay?" I mutter, looking into my glass at the last drop of amber liquid. My mother's passing isn't the same as her husband's.

"I just thought you might be keeping things tight to the chest—"

"That's what I do," I interrupted.

"I know, and I know you're hurting when you can't explain it." She sighs. "But I'm here for you." Her eyes pierce mine, but I don't know how to express my feelings to Mati. I don't know how to feel about anything as there have been too many things *to feel* lately.

"We don't need to keep secrets," she says, and I blink.

"I didn't realize we were. I thought you just wanted to talk about my feelings."

Her brows pinch, and her eyes shift to her knees. Her hand slips under her coat which she laid over the arm of the chair. Standing abruptly, coat in hand, she passes the end of the bed, keeping her face forward.

"I think I've made a mistake," she mutters. As she draws near the corner of the mattress, I scramble over the coverlet and wrap an arm around her waist when my feet hit the floor. She narrowly escapes the short hall to the door, and I tug her to the wall, pinning her against it face first. My chest presses into her back, my hips flexing to hold her still. The coat over her wrist slips to the floor as her hands raise to protect her face from hitting the plaster.

"What secrets do you keep, Mati?" I whisper into her neck, breathing in her pomegranate scent, drawing in deep breaths, making myself high off her fragrance. My nose nuzzles her delicate skin, and my palm cups the spot under her jaw, feeling her swallow under my hold. My lips pucker below her ear.

She hasn't answered me other than an increase in the pulse at her vein and the press of her backside as if she's searching for me. I thrust forward, letting her know what she's doing to me. Her tight dress. Her long hair. Her fruity scent.

"I'll ask again. What are you doing here, Mati?" Without giving her time to answer, the hand at her throat slips downward and into the V of her dress. The material gives easily, and my fingers dip inside her bra to cover her breast. I squeeze, instantly feeling the peak of her nipple against my palm. I hiss at the hint of black lace bra.

"I'm afraid I'll never feel again how I feel with you," she mutters as if the line was practiced.

I hum against her neck as my fingers massage more aggressively at the weighty globe in my grasp. "What does that mean, Spice?" My lips begin a trail over her skin, and I nip her just above her clavicle. Her knees buckle, and she whimpers. "What secrets do you keep?"

"I loved you." The words freeze my lips, my mouth open against her neck but no longer pressing against it. My hand stills as well, holding her breast in my palm. "That first kiss meant everything to me."

I pull back and spin her to face me. "What?"

Bark brown eyes met mine, questioning if she should continue. I focus only on the color that has haunted my dreams for almost thirty years.

"I know you're leaving, but I'm afraid if I don't take the chance I never took before, I'll lose out. I'll lose you." She exhales, and her voice lowers. "Again."

She pauses before adding, "And I wondered if you'd like to take a chance with me?"

L.B. Dunbar

I fall to my knees, my fingers fumbling with the tie at her waist. Instantly, the dress falls open, and I'm met with black panties that match the bra and set my dick weeping. Cut like a V over her most precious part, the material curves upward over her hips. It's the sexiest thing I've ever seen next to the demi-cup bra with lace that hardly contains her up top.

"Did you wear this for me?" I address her while I open my mouth to exhale a heavy breath over her center. "What were you planning to happen tonight?"

If she answers me, I don't hear it as I remove the scrap of lace material and cover her pussy with my lips. My tongue snakes out instantly, devouring her, dulling the words in my head.

I loved you.

She couldn't have meant them. She loved Chris. Refusing to think of him, I plunge deeper, wedging my jaw between her thighs and slipping one leg over my shoulder to open her to me. I want this orgasm from her. I want her to come on my cheeks, my tongue, my lips...my dick. The thought increases my attention, lapping, and licking, sucking sensitive folds before delving two fingers into her wetness.

She cries out my name and her other leg collapses. She shatters over me, and I quickly pull back. I want this to happen again, and I stand, crashing my mouth over hers, forcing her to taste herself on me.

"Was that what you wanted to happen tonight?" I mutter against her mouth as we collide over and over with lips searching and seeking. Her head rolls against the wall behind her. "What other fantasy did you have?"

"I wanted you to take me like you took *her* against the truck."

I pull back, my eyes shifting over hers. "What?"

"I saw you," she says, her voice lowering. "When we were sixteen or so. You had Kristy up against a truck and—"

My mouth covers hers. I don't recall the memory, but even more so, I don't want anyone else in this room but us.

"See me," I murmur as I tug her thigh upward to rest near my hip. I'm still clothed, but I press into her, my dick straining behind the silk suit material.

256

"I do see you," she says into my ear. It's all the assurance I need. I spin her and gently push until she falls to the bed.

42

Pretend With Me

[Mati]

My back hits the mattress, and I bounce a little. My dress falls completely open and my legs spread, laying myself bare to Denton who stands at the edge of the bed fumbling with his belt.

"Take off the dress," he tells me in a voice I don't recognize. Deep. Rugged. Demanding. I sit up and slip the rest of the material off my shoulders. Dragging it behind me, it pools on the coverlet. I also remove my bra, keeping my eyes trained on his the entire time. The bedside lamp is still on, keeping nothing in the dark. Denton can see everything about me. The gash above my pubic line, the one marking the removal of my boys.

"Did it hurt?" he asks, lowering his body and forcing me back on the bed. His lips cover the line and a tear leaks from my eye. My head shakes, but he isn't looking at me. He's tracing over the scar with tender kisses before trailing lower and slipping a finger inside me again.

"Only us in this room tonight, okay?" he says, speaking to his finger entering my body. I nod again but realize he needs to hear me.

"Only us." He looks up then and his lip curls as he adds a second finger to the first.

"You are so beautiful, lion cat." The term of endearment from so long ago brings another tear and concern etches his brow.

"Ignore it," I whisper. "I want this." I do. I want this more than anything. I meant what I said. I'm afraid I'll never feel this way again. It will never be how it is with him *because of him*. This man I've loved differently and separately from my husband, all those years ago. This man my heart aches for now, and my body craves. I will not let another opportunity pass.

The depth of his fingers has me reaching for the edge again, but I want more than those digits. I scoot back on the bed, encouraging him to follow me.

"Can I tell you a secret?" he mutters, returning his fingers to me. "I wanted to take you up against a truck. And a tree. And in the damn river. And the lake."

My breath catches. "I've fantasized about your breasts. How they'd taste. How they'd feel. And your pussy, Mati. I just knew you'd weep. So wet." He emphasizes his words by adding a third finger to the mix, and I feel stretched as far as I can reach, but it isn't enough. I want more. I want him, *inside me.*

"Denton," I whimper.

"What do you want, Spice?"

My hands find his biceps, and I tug upward. I want him over me.

"Come first, and then I'll bury myself deep inside you. I'll fuck you like you've never been fucked before."

The crass language pushes me over the edge, and I explode. I'm still coming as he climbs between my thighs. The tip of him brushes through sensitive folds, and I peel off the bed. I'm ready to go again, and I don't even recognize the sensation. I've never come like this before.

"I'm clean," he states, and I fall back. For a moment, I'm outside myself. Is this really a conversation we need to have? I'm assuming I'm clean as I haven't been with another man—ever. And I haven't been with anyone in thirteen months. He stares down at me.

"Me too," I whisper, and he chuckles.

"I know. I just wanted to let you know about me."

"I don't know about these things." My voice remains low but my thoughts race with the realization he's been with so many women.

"Only us tonight," he reminds me. "See me."

"You're all I see," I tell him, keeping my eyes on his. In an instant, I'm filled. One deep, slow thrust and the hairs on his balls tickle my ass. My eyes roll back in my head. He's thick. He's long. He's so much more than I thought he would be.

He draws back, and my legs wrap over his hips. My hands find the perfection of his ass, and I press at the firm globes, willing him without words to stay inside me.

"Denton," I wheeze, nearly begging him to remain, but the drag to my entrance and the rush to fill me again bucks my hips and I let him lead. He plays my body like the instrument it is under his attention. I'll do anything he asks as long as he keeps doing what he's doing to fill me, to make me feel whole.

You can't keep him, my heart reminds me, but I quickly squash the negative sentiment. Tonight is about tonight.

One hand comes under my thigh, and he hitches it higher, my kneecap practically coming to my chin. "I wanted to be gentle with you, but I don't think I can. You wanted me to fuck you against a truck." He thrusts into me with each straining word. "I'll take you deep into this mattress. We'll make that our first memory."

My God, I think. I'll never be the same after this evening.

And I'm not. Denton fulfills his promise to bury me in the mattress as he stiffens, and warmth fills my channel.

An hour later, I'm exiting the bathroom, and he corners me against the wall again. With a sharp kiss and a little maneuvering, he slips into me again. He makes love to me against the wall until I can hardly stand. It's not a truck in the dark woods but a bright room in a hotel. He's slow but rhythmic, and the pace makes my legs quiver.

"I can't take it," I whimper.

"You can. You'll take all of me. All night," he commands, sliding back, threatening to leave my body, and then slamming upward, burying himself to the hilt. He guides me, moving my hips in ways to take him deeper.

"Just dance with me," he mutters as he kisses a path along my clavicle from shoulder to shoulder. Dancing is what we do. He hums a tone and his hands lift mine above my head. His hips set a new pace, and I discover we actually are dancing, joined as one. I've never felt anything like this before. My mind wants to drift, making a comparison I shouldn't make, but true to Denton, he catches me.

"See me," he murmurs against my neck.

"Only you," I reply before opening my mouth and seeking his. My fingers cover his scruffy jaw, and I plunge my tongue into his mouth. The newly familiar feeling tickles my belly.

"Almost there," he groans as he pulls back, lowering his eyes to watch himself enter me. I sneak a peek as well, and the visual undoes me. Waves of bliss shatter through me. I clutch at his neck, keeping myself in place against him. "Good girl, Spice."

He jets off inside me again, and I squeeze at his ass with one ankle. My leg wraps over his hip, holding him inside me, relishing the pulse and the warmth of him. Keeping himself inside me, he lifts my other thigh and walks us backward half a step until he sits on the bed. I straddle him, and we fall back on the bed.

"I'm spent," I softly groan, spreading kisses over his cheeks and his forehead, working down to his nose.

"We'll sleep a bit before round three." I chuckle as he softens inside me because I think he's kidding. He proves me wrong in the early hours of the morning.

+ + +

I'm lingering on the cusp of sleep, wondering if one can die from too much ecstasy. I've had sex three times in one night which is more than I might have had in a week of marriage. I don't want to think about Chris, but random thoughts float into my head and then drift away.

I've had a one-night stand, with my high school crush, twenty-seven years after high school. I want to giggle with the naughtiness of it, but then I want to cry, knowing Cora was right. I'll never feel this way again. And I want to feel it again. And again. Anyone who says once will be enough is lying. I can't imagine how I'll go on knowing it can be this good, but never with him. My eyes flip open to the hotel clock on the nightstand.

3:43 a.m.

At some point, we turned out the light and the night grew wilder.

"Let me fuck your tits, Mati." I didn't know what he meant until he straddled my upper body and pressed my breasts together, sandwiching

261

his heavy dick between them. His body rocked, and his fingers squeezed. I didn't think there would be anything in this position for me, but I was wrong. My body responded to the naughtiness, and my hips rolled into nothingness. The orgasm crept up my thighs, threatening as it tickled my sensitive core. Denton's thrusts grew more uncontrolled, his massage near to hurting me, and yet I was so turned on I couldn't think straight.

"Ready sweetheart?" I didn't know what he was asking me, but then he stilled, and sticky wet liquid covered my chest. Denton rubbed his fingers through the substance, painting my breasts and tweaking my nipples before leaning back to enter me with his coated fingers. It was the most indecent and indescribable thing I'd ever done, and I'd do it again in a heartbeat if he asked me.

"You're so perfect, Spice. That was a million times better than I imagined it to be, and I've imagined it so often."

"That was..." I replied.

I should be embarrassed or shocked at his admission, that he's fantasized about my breasts and doing what he did, but my fingers brush over sensitive nipples, peaked with the memory, and I smile to myself. I want to commit it all to memory and yet I know I'll never be able to replicate it all in my head. It will never be as good in fantasy as the reality.

3:47 a.m.

We only have an hour before he has to leave. The airport is in Atlanta, and he has a drive to get there. Then he's off to New York, returning to the high-profile life he leads. He'll go back to California, and I'll become a memory for him like he said.

A finger traces down my bare back, and I shiver at the tender touch. I don't turn for him. I'm afraid to look. I don't want to see regret in his eyes. Lips kiss down one vertebra at a time until he comes to the top of my ass. He flips me to my back and presses more kisses over my hip. The hardness of him is down near my calf, and I bend my leg to brush over the length.

"You little minx." He kisses across the scar low on my belly.

"I thought I was a lion cat."

He pauses to look up at me. It's dark in the room, but somehow, I can make out his features. His eyes spark despite the lack of light.

"Yes, definitely a wildcat. So wild." He slips over my legs and brings his body flush with mine. The tip of him points at my entrance, but he's making no attempt to enter me. Instead, he rests on his elbows, brushing back my hair and staring down into my face.

"I'm not pretending with you," he says, and I return his stare. I don't know what he means. My eyes don't leave his, trying to read his thoughts. He can't be telling me the truth.

"Don't let me go. Not yet," he says, kissing me softly, nudging the tip of himself between swollen, overused folds that want to take him again. "I want to love you one more time."

My breath hitches when I understand what he means. He doesn't want me thinking outside our little box. This will be our final round. He glides into me, tenderly taking his time. He's softer in his movements, sweeter in his words. We're making love, and a traitorous tear leaks as I unravel under him, like a slowly opened gift. I want to savor the unwrapping, knowing in my heart this is the last time we'll be together.

"I lied," he says, his neck beginning to strain with the slower pace. I'm struggling to get there as my thoughts fight my body. "Maybe we can pretend one more time. Pretend you love me, Mati."

I swallow as I'm overwhelmed by the depth of him in me. The strength of our connection. The intensity of the moment. I don't need to pretend. I know how I feel.

"I love you, Denton." His eyes close and he presses forward. A pulse. A release. Warmth quickly fills me. Then I'm cold.

He didn't say the words in return.

His head lowers to the crook of my neck, and he breathes deep. I didn't come, and suddenly my tears are the release I lacked. *Shit.*

"I need to go," he says into my skin, and I'm projected back to being seventeen. Only this time, I already know all the reasons he's leaving me. I don't like them any better now than I did back then.

43

Do Apologies Through Social Media Really Count?

[Mati]

Three weeks.

That's how long Denton has been gone. He never responded to my text.

I didn't want to say goodbye.

He never called.

Three days.

That's how long it took before I broke down and searched him on social media.

Post: **Enjoying Costa Rica with my girl, Freya.**

A beautiful older woman accompanies him in a tropical setting, and I realize she's the famous Freya Holstrum, a Swedish model, who hardly looks like she'd aged, other than the tight skin at her eyes. My heart sinks. It's Kristy all over again. For years after Denton left, we'd read about him and saw images splashed across magazines of his success—and his seductions. This actress. That model.

I shouldn't be upset. I'm the one who snuck out of the room after our night of pleasure. I just thought…I shouldn't have thought.

"You okay, Coach?" Alyce asks as we stand on the sideline watching the girls run wind sprints. The gym is my reprieve, where I usually lose myself, but today I seem extra aware of Denton's absence. I should be cursing Tanisha for not touching the line or Hannah for not quite making it to the mark, but I don't have the energy.

"I'm good," I lie, not taking my eyes off the gym floor.

"Want to talk about him?" I'm about to ask her who she means, but it seems silly to pretend. *Pretend.* I simply shake my head. There isn't anything to say. Denton chose his path like he always has, and I need to focus on mine.

"How was the interview?" Alyce changes subjects.

My head pops up, and I peer over at my assistant coach. "What interview?"

"Come on, Mati. You put me down as a reference."

"They called you?"

"I think that's how it works when you apply for a new job." I hold my breath, but Alyce smiles. "I think you'll make a great college coach."

"I don't know anything yet." The callback for a second-round interview came a few days after Denton left. With the girls on track for playoffs and a good shot at states, I'm an excellent candidate for Northeastern. At least in my own head.

"You'll hear from them soon."

"I don't want to get my hopes up." I've already done this to myself in more areas than one.

"Well, I'll keep mine up then." Alyce pats my arm before she hollers at the girls for cheating as they run.

+ + +

My days continue pretty much the same as they did before Denton. It's strange to think there is an *after*-Denton, just like there was an *after*-Chris. How could I lose both men? Both halves of my heart. I remind myself, I lost Denton long ago. Actually, I never really had him.

Enjoy the ride, Cora told me and using a euphemism of hers, that's what Denton was—a test drive. Am I ready to drive again? Nope. Not at all, because after-Denton Mati is heartbroken in a totally new way compared to losing Chris. Chris is gone forever. Denton is still out there. Still living, still loving, possibly filling someone else. I shiver with the thought too often as I lay in bed remembering all we did together.

On another Sunday, Cora and I make a visit to Magnolia's. Not surprisingly, Magnolia is sad. Her house is empty. Dolores has returned to her small home near town, giving herself the distance she needs from the sorrow of the farmhouse.

"It's quiet," the older woman says, staring out the window. "No one singing here anymore." Her screened-in porch is closed off with the decrease in temperature, so we sit inside the parlor. October came with a vengeance. Snow is predicted, and Billy is having a panic attack about what the possibility could mean for our Oktoberfest. We've already had the issue with entertainment. Much to Billy's excitement, we finally received permission to block off Third Avenue between the pub and the bookstore, squashing Roxie from hosting her Booktober event on the same weekend. I have no idea what he has against her.

"What can we do for you?" Cora asks, playing a better visitor than me to Magnolia. My mind keeps wandering up the staircase to a room now vacant. Bodies entangled on a bed. *Pretend*, he said.

"They want me to move. I may have trouble seeing, but I'm not deaf. I've heard them discussing what to do with me as if I need *doing with*." Magnolia practically pouts like she's a child. Her daughter Rosalyn came to the funeral minus her pastor husband and invited Magnolia to Texas.

What would I do in Texas? Magnolia snapped.

I hadn't known Denton and Dolores wanted to move her. Since he left, I assumed the responsibility of Magnolia fell to Dolores, like it had for the last twenty plus years.

Cora's eyes meet mine. As single women ourselves, we sympathize with Magnolia's plight. She doesn't want to leave her home, the only home she's known her entire life. Cora refused to leave hers. She kicked Stan out instead. I never left mine. However, I can understand why Dolores may wish to move Magnolia closer to town, where it would be easier to keep an eye on her. From what I can see, though, Magnolia is still sharp as a tack. The stairs are her only danger zone.

"So, you've heard from Denton?" Cora asks, and my eyes narrow at her, finding her question insensitive. She already asked me if I'd heard from him, and I hadn't.

"No, Denton doesn't call me. He's too busy being famous again." Magnolia scoffs before reaching for her warm tea. "He's like his father in those respects. Always wanting approval from a bigger sea than the pond." My lips twist as I contemplate if she means Kip or Calvin. Kip certainly wanted his moment in the limelight as the town mayor, but what about the military hero? He wanted something more himself.

"Yes, he must be busy," Cora smirks, not believing her own words. The entire drive to Magnolia's she admonished Denton and his lack of communication with me. She's seen the images of him on social media. He and Freya spent a week in Costa Rica. Cora believes he's home now. I've given up stalking him, but she's become a vulture for information.

Who needs men anyway? There are other ways to find pleasure in life.

Chocolate and wine are the only things that come to my mind, but I know that's not what she means. I'm not ready for what Cora means. I've tasted Denton, and I'll go back to starving myself of all things sexual. I don't want to be with anyone else. I won't be able to separate the physical from the emotional. Being with Denton proved this to me.

My phone pings and I excuse myself. Hollilyn is one month out from her due date, and I'm on alert for her labor. I was early with the twins. I enter the kitchen and find it's a notification from Facebook. Did I set those up? I don't even know how to do such a thing, but I enter the app and find the message.

Mati Harrington? I'm pretty certain I have the right woman. It's Denton Chance. If you have a second, can you message me back?

There are so many responses I could make. I could not respond, but the message will haunt me. I could ignore it like he's ignored me, but I know I can't be so vengeful. I could cuss him out which is what he deserves, but instead, I decide killing him with kindness will make it all the better.

Denton Chance? I don't know if I recall who you are. High school all-star athlete? Famous rockstar? Photographer wannabe? Cover model? Which one are you today?

Instantly I see the pop-up for a response, and I hate how I hold my breath waiting. The pop-up disappears and then returns.

Touché.

That's it. That's all he has to say. I spin to return to Magnolia and Cora when another response fills the screen.

He's the one who's sorry.

I pause in Magnolia's wide hallway. My eyes lift to the ceiling. I sigh in frustration. I don't want his apology. I want an explanation.

L.B. Dunbar

Sorry for what? There are so many words I could type to follow the question. For making my body sore and my heart ache? For giving me more than I expected in our one night together? For asking me to pretend when all of it was real to me? For leaving me behind again?

I opened Chris's letter. My throat clogs and my eyes sting. *I can't do this.* I don't want to know what Chris told him. None of it will matter, and something takes hold of me, knocking the air out of my lungs—guilt. Guilt for giving into my attraction to Denton all these years later. Suddenly, I feel like I've cheated on Chris. And I know one thing for certain…

I don't want to know what Chris told you.

The response is almost immediate.

It's big, though. Really big.

Is he joking with me? I'm not doing this with him. I don't want to play into his childish games of *how big?* I know how big he is, but his body parts aren't the topic of this conversation.

What Chris said is between you and him.

A response takes a few seconds.

I understand. Just accept my apology, for everything.

For everything? I question but refuse to ask. I can't hear him tell me he made a mistake. My guilty cup already overflows. Let me own my poor judgment of giving in to my lust for him.

Pretend you love me. I didn't have to pretend. I'd been pretending my whole life that I *didn't*.

+ + +

I've upset you. I apologize.

I curse myself when I check social media later that night. I abruptly left our conversation when Cora called out to me asking if everything was okay. She knows I'm on baby watch for Hollilyn.

Hey.

The message comes through almost immediately as if he can see I'm on social media and I flinch back in the dark office. If I get a new job, this office will be mine, but better yet, I think I'm ready to move.

Second Chance

Something smaller. Something without maintenance. Something outside of town.

Do apologies through social media really count? Way to get to the point. I sigh as if he can hear me through the computer. Social media needs sound effects.

How is Blue Ridge?

What are you doing? I exhale again.

I'm asking about town.

Why? I don't understand. Honestly. Why does he care? He left. He didn't look back just like the first time.

Because it seems easier than asking how you are, worrying that you'll say you're good and better without me.

I blink. I blink again. Well, way to get right to the point, Denton. My heart races. Can I answer him honestly? Can I tell him I miss him? I'm in a fog without him. I'm not better with him gone. *Come back.*

Blue Ridge is fine. BRMP Oktoberfest is this coming weekend. I decide avoidance is best.

I heard there's a big playoff game this weekend and a high school reunion of sorts.

Right. The reunion where football players from the class of 1991 will return to be honored and two men will be missing from the lineup. Chris Rathstone (Rath) and Denton Chance. The boys' football team isn't in playoffs yet, though. The only playoff game is...

How do you know about the volleyball team? I know the answer before he needs to answer.

Dolores and the high school's sports page. My shoulders fall, realizing he's been in touch with his sister and not me, but then again, it seems to be the way of things for him. He'd been in contact with his sister all along, but the sports page?

Stalking me?

A smiley face emoji follows.

In rapid succession, I post and then he does.

How was Costa Rica?

L.B. Dunbar

Can I ask you something? *Oh no. Not this again.* If he wants to know if I'm lonely or touching myself or thinking of him, he should be here with some answers.

It's getting late. I need to head to bed.

Alone? Does he seriously want me to answer that? My irritation grows at the accusation. I'm not the one who ran off to Costa Rica with a top model when I was supposed to be in New York.

How do you know about Costa Rica? Stalking me?

I'm not answering. Instead, I type: **I've got to go.**

I can explain. *I can explain. Nothing happened. It didn't mean anything.* I've heard it before from him.

Nothing good ever comes from a statement like that. I'm thinking the conversation will end, and almost hoping it will. I'm too exhausted to emotionally spar with Denton. Hurt. Betrayed. Confused. I don't understand life outside of marriage, commitment, and loyalty.

Forget that question, then. You said it was getting late. Am I too late?

Too late for what, I wonder, but I don't ask. **Was this your question?**

It is now.

I don't know. *I just don't know.*

Goodnight, Denton.

Dream of big things, Mati.

44
Oktoberfest or Lovefest

[Mati]

"Holy crap," Billy whoops, pulling the tap to fill another mug with the house specialty. Oktoberfest is in full swing, and after the noon football game, highlighting players from the class of 1991 with a special tribute to Chris Rathstone—the Rath—the celebration has moved to the Fest. Billy's serving beer faster than his hands can move with the help of his ever-faithful staff. We've been trading off turns as barkeep, so Billy can work the crowd, patting backs to greet people and thanking them for attending. To my surprise, Roxie McAllister mingles in the crowd, her eyes wandering to my brother who occasionally searches for her it seems.

Well, what is this? I wonder, but I don't have time to question things because I've got more beer to pour.

The evening draws to night and the entertainment should begin soon. Billy's been evasive about the replacement band he found.

"Don't you worry about it," he told me as we went through the final checklist. Billy had been onto me, knowing my mind wasn't one-hundred percent into the festivities. I let him assume it was Denton, which wasn't far from the truth. He'd been messaging me through the remainder of the week, switching to text messages instead of social media. He never asked if he could call me, and I chalked it up to modern conversation. No one wants to talk on the phone anymore.

My other reason for the lack of focus is the result of the second interview. A nerve-racking third round will occur. The committee wants to watch me coach—*live*. After dozens of tapes, cut and spliced to highlight my best efforts, the decision group wants to see me interact with my girls. Unfortunately, they hadn't made the game the night before which projected us into the final round. The committee planned to attend the state finals the first weekend of November. *No pressure.*

L.B. Dunbar

My thoughts dissipate when the first stroke of a guitar hits the darkened stage. The outline of bodies can be seen but no one recognizably definitive.

"Ready?" I hear projected over the crowd in a rough Southern drawl and for some reason my skin prickles with anticipation. If this is how the lead singer sounds with only one word, panties are going to melt tonight. Billy jumps up on the dark stage and heartily pats someone on the shoulder. He leans into the man, and holds a moment, speaking to his ear. I wish I could see who he's speaking with but I'm too short and too far back, standing behind our makeshift bar for the evening.

"Hello fellow beer drinkers," Billy addresses the waiting audience, and the crowd goes crazy as lights flip on to highlight the stage. "I want to thank everyone again for being here. We...wow...there are just so many more of you than we expected. We're humbled and honored, and we hope you enjoy the treat we have for you tonight. Our first booking was a local country band, who couldn't make it." The crowd begins to boo and hiss, but Billy waves his arm, suggesting the crowd simmer down. "It's their loss and our gain, though. They have no idea what they were missing, and to be honest, I'd rather listen to these guys play. You're in for a real treat as we welcome...Chrome Teardrops."

"Hey," someone yells at me, and Clyde nudges my arm. I look down to see I'm letting the tap run, the mug I'm holding overflows with beer which covers my hand and drips to the floor. I hadn't noticed. My eyes can't move from the stage. A hand covers mine on the tap and pushes it back to stop the stream. Another hand takes the too-full mug from me. I still can't move. Beer sticks to my fingers.

"That's...how...what..." I mutter to no one as the band starts into a classic rock ballad, originally sung by a female. Kit Carrigan. Her brother does the song just as much justice if not more in his smoky, rough Southern drawl. It's rock with a twang of country.

"That's..." I try again, pointing a shaky beer-coated finger at the stage and looking to my left. Billy's rounding the bar.

"Don't freak out."

"That's...Tommy Carrigan," I practically scream. Tommy Carrigan, silver fox extraordinaire with his slicked back, chin length hair

272

of silver and ink streams. His jaw has the right layer of scruff, equally salt and peppered, and his body... Let's just say, forty never looked so good on a man in a black T-shirt. Singer, guitarist, and songwriter for the band affiliated with his sister—the band which includes his cousin. My mouth falls open as I see Denton step up to the mic and fall into harmony with his cousin as if they haven't missed a day in the decade the band has been dissolved.

My mouth waters. My eyes fill.

Denton Chance is back.

"Go," Billy says, placing a hand on my shoulder blade and pressing me forward. "He came back for you."

"He did not," I snark, my voice whining with the statement.

"He did so," Billy mocks in reply, typical of our voices when we were children. My head turns for the stage, and I freeze.

"I can't...I can't go up there." While I'm excited to see Denton standing in the flesh before the crowd, in his hometown, performing in a way he never has before, my heart won't allow me to take one more step closer to him. He left me. Again.

And he never mentioned he was coming back.

My arms cross, defiant and stern.

"If you don't march your ass up to that stage, I'm hiking you over my shoulder and carrying you to him," Billy barks, giving my shoulder another shove, only this time it isn't as gentle as the first one. "He's showing you a grand gesture or something ridiculous like that."

"I'm not going," I say, but my eyes can't leave the stage. He looks good. *So good.* He's in his element up there, strumming away, and smiling for the ladies who have pushed their way to the stage. Without seeing her, I'm certain Kristy Moseley has made her way to the front of the line, taking credit for being his once-wife.

He cut his hair, and the shorter look gleams under the lights, a hint of silver mixed with the almond shade. He's let his beard grow more than normal. He claims he doesn't like the scruff despite the modern popularity, but it fills in nicely, emphasizing his age, but also heightening his appeal. He's sexy as fuck, as the saying goes, and just the thought makes me clench my thighs. That mouth has been between them. That jaw scraped over them. He licks his lips before stepping up to harmonize again, and I'm melting. I know that tongue…

"Get. Up. There." Billy growls.

"I'm not making a scene. He's singing. He's the entertainment. I'll speak to him when—"

I'm cut off when the song stops and immediately my name projects through the lingering final chords.

"Is there a Mati Harrington in the house?" Voices lower and people shift as Denton calls out again. He shields his eyes against the stage light pointed upward to highlight the band and scans the crowd. Suddenly, I'm lifted around the waist.

"Billy," I yell.

"Help me get her up there," he barks to the nearest man. Griffin Duncan is a big guy, which makes sense considering his profession as a builder. He grabs my ankles, which kick out at my brother, hoping to be free of his constraints. Together, the two men hike me level with the bar before Griffin places my feet on the sticky surface, holding them down, so I don't jump. Billy pushes my body upward.

"I hate you," I mumble down at my brother as the partygoers eventually realize the commotion in the back is me. Whoops and hollers begin as I smooth down my dress and stomp my cowboy-boot covered feet on the wooden surface under me. It doesn't feel very stable, so I'm afraid to move. I'm also caught in the glare of eyes up on stage, begging me to listen to him.

"Mati Harrington." My name is a smile in his voice. His lip curls up at the corner.

"Guys…" He turns to the man at his right and nods to another sexy silver fox sitting behind a drum set. "This is Mati."

A knowing smile comes from the drummer, who I recall is named Hank Paige. A smack to the arm comes from his cousin.

"Hello darlin'," Tommy drawls into the mic, and the ladies in the crowd begin to scream. *Shit, is that sexy.* But my eyes haven't left Denton.

"Blue Ridge," Denton begins, pausing to take a deep breath. "I haven't been a good son to you." Old neighbors and long-ago friends settle a bit, understanding his meaning. A few *awws* pop the tension thickening the air. "But I owe this girl an apology more than any of you." He laughs, and the audience chuckles a bit.

"I made a promise once, but I broke it. I left her behind."

Oh my God. My heart races and my hand lifts to cover my own throat. The vein in my neck pulses double time.

"I actually made a promise to two people." Denton sighs into the microphone. "So, I'm here to make good on the second one."

My heart beats so fast I swear anyone near me can hear it. My throat clogs and I can't swallow.

"I read the letter, Mati."

No. No, no, no.

Words project in white against the dark curtain behind him. In a familiar scrawl I've read for almost thirty years is a single statement.

Take care of her.

Warm liquid rolls down my face and creeps around the corner of my mouth.

Damn Chris.

And damn Denton.

Drumsticks tap three times and a guitar strums, reawakening the awestruck crowd. Tommy Carrigan's voice rouses the people into a song about caring for someone. I remain in a haze.

For all the town to see, my husband has given his permission. My *dead* husband gives his blessing to his best friend. Take care of me.

As the song plays, Denton speaks into the mic over the melody.

"This promise I intend to keep."

275

45

Take Care of Her

[Denton]

As the words behind me fade to black, blending with the curtain at our back, and the song continues, I notice Mati jump down from the bar and race away from the concert.

Shit.

Tommy lifts an eyebrow at me, but I shake my head. I'm good to finish the song. The guys are counting on me, and I owe them so big. After the stint in Costa Rica, I fired my agent. I don't need gigs that falsify my age—or me. That's not the point of growing older and accepting who I am. I do accept my age, and I'm good embracing it, not hiding it or aging me. I've already lost enough time in my life. I don't need to fast forward to life when I'm older. Unless that life includes Mati.

With her in mind, I begged the guys to do me this favor. Go home with me and help me win the girl—the right girl. Of course, the groveling to her included groveling to them. My head down and my apology prepared, I asked Tommy and Hank to meet me at a casual place near Hank's new home in St. Gabriel.

"I need a favor," I started.

"What?" Hank asked, implying he wanted to know more.

"Why?" Tommy narrowed his eyes, questioning my motives.

"It's about Mati." I didn't need to explain too much. They both already knew about the girl I loved, the best friend who asked me to leave, and how I left her behind. Hank always thought I was a fool for letting her go. Tommy said it was a sign of the greatness we would produce together. We did have a good run of things.

I explained my predicament. The photo shoot in Costa Rica. The hint that Mati misunderstood. The strange, sudden, unexpected need I had to return to my hometown to be with her. And then I opened the letter.

"Chris was my best friend. Whether it was him or me, we both looked after her. It was like a secret code between us. I never took advantage of her or our friendship once he started dating her. I bit my tongue and buried it in other girls instead. The final straw was him asking me to leave, and me warning him to take care of her."

"Now, it's your turn," Hank mumbled, looking down at the tri-folded paper between us on the table. One line is all it reads: Take care of her.

"What does this have to do with us?" Tommy asked, and I didn't blame him for his suspicion. I'm the one who left the band. That's how they'll always remember things. Not Kit being diagnosed. Or Hank too drunk to play. Or Tommy so out of control as a control freak.

"I need to woo her."

"What the fuck?" Tommy's head shot up

"He means he wants to win her back." Hank smirked.

"I know what the fuck it means," Tommy snapped. "But what does it have to do with us?"

"Her brother is hosting an Oktoberfest. He runs a pub, and he needs a band for the party."

Tommy's eyes narrowed. "You want us to get the band back together, for you?"

"I think it's—"

"If you say sweet, I will pummel you," Tommy warned Hank. I waited a full minute before exhaling in defeat. I knew it was too much to ask.

"Never mind," I sighed at the same time Hank said, "I'll do it."

"What?" Tommy and I say in unison with two different octaves to our voices.

"Look, I love Midge. Wholeheartedly, absolutely, one-million percent, and I would do anything if I lost her, so if I had a chance to win her back..." His voice lowered, and his eyes connected with mine. I sensed Hank would have also liked a second chance with a certain someone else in our lives, but that relationship was never meant to be. Midge to him was my Mati. The right woman.

277

L.B. Dunbar

"Fuck," Tommy *muttered, combing his fingers through his chin-length hair. It's a wonder he can still pull off the look. I've had to trim my hair to nearly a buzz cut, and it accentuates the gray every damn day.*

"Fine."

"What?" I blinked as if the motion would clarify the word.

"Fine. I'm in. But I'm warning you. You better take care of everything."

And I thought I had, right down to the letter—literally. What I didn't predict was Mati running.

The song ends, and I quickly remove my guitar. I give Tommy a sympathetic look, but he's already nodding for me to exit the stage. I hand off my guitar to a guy waiting in the wings. Tommy not only came through for me. He stepped it up another notch like he always does.

"Ladies and gentlemen, as my wingman leaves me to chase the girl, hope you don't mind that I brought another family member with me. Did you know Denton and I are cousins? Well, this punk ass is married to my niece. Welcome to the country, city kid. Gage Everly, everyone."

+ + +

The music fades behind me as I race to the edge of the street near the outside bar. Billy got the permit he wanted, and the space on Third Avenue is packed from brewery to bookstore.

"Where did she go?" I call out as I'm racing to Billy by the bar.

"Toward the alley."

I run in the direction of the alley behind the brewery. Scanning the dark parking area, I see a head bobbing between vehicles, making way for the back corner of the gravel lot behind the alley access.

"Mati," I yell, weaving between cars to lessen the distance between us. She picks up the pace, but her shorter legs can't outrace me. I quickly catch up just as she comes to the side of her truck and reach for her upper arm before she can touch the door handle of the vehicle.

"Mati." Her name huffs out as I'm out of breath.

"What?" she snaps with all the spice in her as she spins to face me.

"Stop running."

278

"Why? You're always running," she reminds me. "You left this town, your family, me." She jabs at her chest. "When will *you* stop running?"

"You're right." The admission stops her. Her eyes widen, stumped that I'm giving her credit.

"I'm…" Her lips clamp, and she tugs at her arm, but the force isn't enough to loosen me. I step forward, crowding her space and pressing her back against the driver door.

"I have something for you," I say. "I figured it was better to deliver in person." Pausing a beat, I lean forward, my fingers combing into the soft locks on the side of her head. I want her eyes on me. Her heart with mine. *See me*, I whisper.

"An apology. I'm sorry."

Tears streak her cheeks and my thumbs stretch to swipe at each drop.

"What about Freya?"

Freya? I think, and then I remember the message about Costa Rica. "Freya? Oh my God, Mati. No, no." My fingers delve deeper into her hair, holding her head, so she looks at me. "Nothing happened."

Mati's eyes close as I speak. "We were both duped. My agent didn't tell me I'd lost the 'Fit over Forty' article until I arrived in New York. My shoot was repositioned to a couple's shoot for another magazine."

"But I saw the post. You said hanging with your girl."

"You're my girl, Mati. Tell me I'm not too late."

"Why…why are you here?" Her teeth chatter as she speaks.

"I wanted to see you again. And I wanted to tell you I'm sorry in person." I lower my face toward hers. "And I want to touch you one more time." My lips lean for hers, but she stops me with a flinch.

"It doesn't work like this. You can't come and go as you please."

"Coming is all I plan on doing." Mati stiffens under my hands.

"You didn't…just make a joke of things."

My head tilts, and I reconsider for a second. A smile I can't contain breaks across my lips.

"Actually, I didn't, but it's good to see some things haven't changed. Still have a dirty mind."

L.B. Dunbar

"I do not—"

I cut her off with my mouth, swallowing her sharp tongue and relishing in the fight she gives before giving in to me. Her tongue swirls with mine, and my hands tighten in her hair. I tug, pulling her into me. Then my hips press forward, and I hear the soft thud of her body against her truck.

"I am…" I begin. "…in love with you. I always have been, and I always plan to be." Liquid-filled eyes stare up at me and the intensity of the moment has me nervous she doesn't feel the same, so I flirt with her. "And I'd really like to be dirty with you, too."

She gasps. "You are incorrigible."

"And you are who I want to be *in*. Because I'm in love with you," I repeat, holding my breath as my heart beats in rapid succession with each passing second, she doesn't say it back to me.

It's okay. I can wait. I've waited this long.

"I already told you I love you," she says softly, her voice hardly more than a whisper.

"That was pretend, Mati, I want—"

Cool fingers cover my lips. "That was real to me."

The words surprise me. I kiss the tips against my mouth, needing a moment to digest the possibility. *Mati loves me?* "You're freezing, sweetheart."

Reaching around her, I tug open her door and hold her hand as she steps up to the seat. Then I watch as she scoots over on the bench and I climb in after her. She pulls the key from a pocket in her jean jacket and hands them to me to start the truck and warm the seats.

"Is this real?" she asks me as silence swarms around us with the growing heat.

"Yes," I say, turning to her. "I'm back."

For some reason, that's all I need to say before she's on me. Her arms circle my neck, and her body forces me into the door at my back.

"Oof."

"Sorry," she mutters against my mouth, but I don't want her apology. I want her naked and underneath me. My fingers fumble with the front of her dress until I can get my hands inside. Slipping each into

280

her bra, I force the material away from her to cup each heavy globe and squeeze them together.

"I fucking love your tits, lion cat."

She purrs, and I chuckle before taking her mouth with mine again. She struggles to get her leg over mine, pinning her thigh against the seat. Her other leg curls around my hip, and I press her back until she's under me. We grind a few minutes, my jeans tight as her dress slips upward. We aren't graceful, and with my height, we don't fit well on the bench. I pull back, dragging her with me, and make her straddle my lap.

"Is this a fantasy?" I tease. Suddenly, I feel like a teenager again, fumbling around in a pickup truck, trying to make things work.

"Well, it was supposed to be up *against* the truck." She giggles and I still.

"Sweetheart, if you want me to fuck you against a truck we better be in the middle of nowhere where no one can accidentally see me taking care of my girl."

"Denton," she breathes out.

"So, for now, I'll have to please you *inside* the truck. Besides, it's fucking freezing out there." My fingers climb her inner thighs, reaching for the promised land.

"You're just a wimp, California," she mocks. My other hand tugs one of hers to the seam of my jeans, holding her palm over the bulge beneath.

"Good golly, I hope I'll be enough for you, being a wimp and all." But I've already got her nearly begging me. Her hand takes over and works at my buckle while my fingers dip into her underwear. I curse at her readiness, and my fingers easily slide into home.

"Yes, please me," she whispers, and I intend to do everything I can to fulfill her wish.

46

Coming and Going

[Mati]

Struggling in the limited space, clutching each other as we race to a finish line, I'm a mix of emotions—from the startle of seeing him to the shock of Chris's letter—not to mention the passionate workings on the bench seat of my truck. Once we simultaneously release, I slump against Denton, letting him hold me as our breathing softens and steam covers the windows of the heat-filled cab. Only seconds pass before a knock on the driver's side window has us both sitting upright.

"Shit," I mutter, noting our precarious position. Denton has slipped out of me, and he hastily moves me aside, righting his jeans while I tug down my dress. He powers down the window enough to see my oldest brother on the other side of the fog-covered glass.

"Mati," Giant addresses me, not even glancing at Denton. "You okay?" My big brother and I aren't especially close although we share one thing in common—we both lost a spouse to death. His was to cancer. Mine the freak accident. Giant has become protective of me because of this connection, understanding my lacking desire to date, at least until recently.

"I'm good," I say, my breath still ragged and a little anxious at being caught seconds after a sexual act by my brother.

"Billy wants to know if you're coming back." My head swings to Denton, who's been watching me while my brother speaks over him.

"I probably should," I offer sheepishly, feeling a bit awkward about having sex and then running off to work again. Denton's hand covers my thigh and squeezes.

"I should get back to the band but save a dance for me." He winks, and I want to tell him my dance card will only be filled by him. He grabs the latch to open the door and then leans back to me.

"Kiss me," he whispers, wanting me to make a statement. Despite his public apology and his declaration before the town, he needs me to accept him before my family. I lean forward and press a chaste kiss to his lips, but he reaches for my throat with the tender grasp I've learned to love and draws me back to him. Not as impassioned as moments ago, it's still intense while brief and makes the statement he needs.

He's with me.

He nods at Giant as he steps out of my truck and heads back to the festivities. Giant reaches over the steering wheel to remove my key from the ignition.

"Holy shit," he mutters, swiping at the heat on his face. His deep dark eyes find mine.

"You know what you're doing, baby sister?"

"I think so," I reply, although I sound uncertain. My body knows what it wants but the rest of me, I'm still a work in progress when it comes to Denton.

"He hurts you again, and I'll kill him this time." Giant might be big, and his tone sounds mean, but he's too gentle to kill anything other than out of necessity, like hunting.

"That won't be necessary."

"Think he'll stick?"

"I hope so," I say, and simply admitting my doubt makes me wonder. My head's back to overruling my heart. Giant reaches out a hand, and he tugs me forward to exit the truck. To my surprise, he pulls me into an embrace that's rare for the oldest Harrington sibling. He's always come across a bit unaffectionate, making us wonder how he produced two beautiful daughters.

"Follow your heart, Mati." I nod into his broad chest, melting into the unfamiliar warmth of my brother.

"I want to believe he'll stay," I offer.

"If he's smart, this time he will. He was always meant to be with you."

I pull back and look up at Giant, a little surprised by such an admission. There's no doubt my brothers have a fondness for Denton because of his upbringing, but they easily welcomed Chris into the fold.

"You all loved Chris," I remind him. However, in the past month, my brothers have hinted they always thought Denton would be the man added to the family.

"We did. We also knew Denton needed you. Things happen in the order they happen for a reason, though." I'm certain he means the death of his wife once he finally returned home from his military duty. Married young, they had a strange relationship, one that seemed a touch disconnected and a bit cold, but I'm not one to judge, nor do I know what went on in private between them.

"Think Denton's here for a reason, then?" I ask, curious what it means since Denton crept back into my life.

"I think Denton's here for you."

+ + +

"Dance with me," Denton's gruff, sleepy voice tickles from behind my ear. His arms encircle my waist, and he kisses me on the side of my neck. We've gone from zero to sixty with the public affection, and I'm a little nervous about people's reactions. Then I remind myself I don't care what people think. I spin in his arms, and he tugs me to the dance floor. The song is upbeat although I don't recognize what Gage Everly is singing on stage with his wife's uncle. Regardless, Denton leads me like he did all those years ago, and I decide it might be best to follow his lead in all other things as well.

We cuddle on the bench seat as we take a ride near midnight. Billy tells me I'm free, and I'm emotionally wrought, so I'm relieved to leave Oktoberfest. I don't even know where Denton is staying, and I'd like to offer my house although I think it would be awkward bringing him to the bed I shared with Chris. Sensing my worry, he doesn't even pause as he passes my subdivision, but continues down Scenic Drive, heading for Magnolia's.

"Be very quiet," he says as if he's sneaking me into his house past curfew. After closing the front door and setting the lock, he presses me into the wall and kisses me silly. We might never make it upstairs, and

I'm okay with remaining in the dark hallway as long as his mouth keeps torturing mine like it does.

When he pulls back, his forehead lands on mine, and he whispers while he speaks.

"I'm not dreaming, right? You're really here, and I'm kissing you, and I'm going to take you up those stairs and have my way with you. No pretending."

"No pretending," I say as his hands skim down my arms and he envelops both my hands in his. He tugs me from the wall and guides the way toward the staircase.

"I promised Magnolia I'd stay here tonight, although I warned her I was coming in late. Tommy should come to visit, too, as she is his grandmother as well, but he said he'll see her tomorrow. He's staying at Conrad Lodge."

"And where are you staying after tonight?" The question escapes before I consider the pressure it puts between us, suggesting the possibility we really aren't real.

"Undetermined," he states, giving my hand a squeeze. I don't feel reassured, but I'm not passing up another night with him.

He leads me into the same room we slept in the night his mother died. Closing the door with a soft click, I suddenly feel nervous. Denton comes up behind me, slipping my wool lined jean jacket from my shoulders. The night was cool, but the heat of drinking and dancing kept people warm enough. Now, my skin pebbles with a chill I don't attribute to the temperature. Heated hands rub down my arms as Denton stands behind me. He peppers my neck with kisses until his palm finds my throat. He tips me by the chin for better access to my skin.

"I want you again, Mati. I always want you," he whines as if he's confused by the sensation—as if it's a bad thing.

"Do you want to stop…" My voice trails as he nips me.

"Never! Never gonna stop wanting you, never did." His hands slide forward and unbutton my dress while his mouth continues to sprinkle kisses over my skin. He lifts my hair, travels along the nape of my neck until he reaches the opposite shoulder. Pushing my dress, the material falls to my hips, and I wiggle for it to drift to my feet.

L.B. Dunbar

"Spice, you are so fucking gorgeous," he curses, kissing down my spine and spreading his palms over my waist. "I want you like this."

I don't know what he means until he walks us forward to the edge of the bed.

"Lean forward, sweetheart." I do as he says, my palms hitting the knotty material of the bedspread. His foot comes between my feet, and he taps left to right, so I spread my legs. "Ever do..." He stops, and I know he wants to ask things we shouldn't discuss. In time we'll need to talk about Chris, but not now.

"I don't want to replace him," he says, standing behind and trailing fingers up and down my spine. His voice lowers, and I should look over my shoulder at him, but I don't. Instead, I focus on my fingers digging into the coverlet.

"I know," I whisper.

"I just want my own time."

"Me too," I say instantly because it's true. I'm the lucky one. I will have had them both. Denton might only be a blip, but I'll take the time he gives me.

He returns to kissing me, massaging my skin to bring us both back to the present—where we don't have to feel guilty. We don't have to repress things. We can just be us. It doesn't take long before the kisses grow rougher and our breathing heats. Hands grope, and my backside grinds against his jeans. Shoving my underwear to my feet, Denton tells me to step out of them.

"I'm still wearing my boots," I say.

"Keep them on." It's a bit awkward, but I do as he says. "Crawl up on the bed."

My sex pulses and a sultry scent fills the room. I'm so wet, I feel the moisture on my inner thighs. Doing as he asks, I kneel on the edge of the mattress, spreading enough so he can step between my booted feet.

"Fuck me," he mutters, and I'm about to make a joke that that's the plan when two fingers delve into me. I lurch forward, but his free hand grips my hip and draws me back. I'm stretched in a way I've never been. *I'll never feel this way again*, whispers through my head. He releases my hip and the sound of a belt buckle crackles in the room as fingers continue sliding in and out of me. It's a heady combination. A song between us.

And then we dance as he takes his time to enter me from behind. Torturously slow, he fills me until his balls tickle my thighs. My fingers clutch the bedspread as my back arches, forcing me to hold him deep inside. The angle is different. The feeling complete. And I want to answer his question.

No. I've never felt like this before.

"Spice," he growls as he pulls back and then thrusts forward, holding my hips so I can't escape the force. He sets the rhythm, pummeling into me in the sweetest beat. His palm skitters up my spine until he finds my hair. Twirling it in his fist, he gently tugs, and I tilt back.

"You're the greatest fantasy," he mutters, and I don't even know what he means, but I smile to myself. Releasing my hair, his hand skims to the front of me, reaching lower until he finds the sweet spot. I'm on sensory overload. He's touching where I need while filling me, and the orgasm flies through me. I scream into the bed covers unashamed, and yet surprised with myself. I've never come like this, and I instantly want a repeat.

"Give it to me, Spice," Denton groans, but I don't think I can get there again.

"No, fill me," I command, and Denton stills. The different position enhances the pleasure of each jolt, each pump, as he spills inside me.

"You dirty girl," he chuckles into my back.

"Some things never change," I giggle.

"Some things thankfully change," he says, pressing kisses on my shoulder. "Forever."

+ + +

The next morning, I wake alone, feeling spent and spoiled. Denton knows how to take care of me.

Taking care of my girl.

He called me his girl last night, and my face splits as I smile a ridiculous grin to myself. My hands spread over the sheet and I look for a note near the lamp on the table.

Nothing.

This really can't be happening again, can it? I freeze. I don't want to let negative thoughts take me. He says he's back, although I have no idea for how long.

Test ride, Cora called him. I don't want a test. I'll just take the ride—however long it lasts, wherever it leads. I dress in my walk-of-shame clothing and try to tiptoe down the stairs, only my boots tap on the hardwood and a stair or two creaks. As I step off the final step, facing the front door, a voice startles me from behind.

"Mornin', Mati."

Shit. I nearly come out of my skin. My eyes close in shame as I'm wearing the same dress as yesterday, even though Magnolia didn't see me. I'm also trying to sneak out of her house.

"Miss Magnolia," I say, spinning to face her and speaking with my most cheerful voice. My tone drops instantly as Magnolia examines me from behind her magnified glasses.

"Don't you Miss Magnolia me." I'm bracing for a mile-wide lecture about propriety and scruples and a woman's dignity. "I'm to deliver a message to you."

Sweet Lord, this is going to be awkward.

"Let me see if I get this correct." Her head tilts, scanning down my dress-clad body. "He said as you aren't particularly good at finding notes, he wanted me to tell you to meet him at the diner."

I blink. I blink again.

"What?"

"Denton is meeting Dolores this morning, no doubt to discuss me, and what to be doing about me." She pifts with a dismissive wave. "He said to meet him at the diner when you wake. I'm to wait here for that other no-good-grandson turned rockstar who promised to visit me sometime this morning." She leans forward as if to give me a secret. "I have two grandsons who are rockstars. World famous but can't tell time worth a damn. Don't they have people for these things? How long is a girl supposed to wait?" She shakes her head, and I laugh.

"I have no idea, Magnolia." I pause as I slip my hands into jean jacket pockets. "So, the diner you say?"

"Yep, don't keep him waiting," she says, reaching out to pat my arm. "He's already waited long enough."

I chuckle to myself, wondering how Denton got to the diner, but I have my answer as I park before the quiet restaurant in the center of town. Stepping out of my truck, I spin in time to see his fancy classic car racing for the exit of Blue Ridge and the highway down the mountain.

L.B. Dunbar

47

Side-lined

[Denton]

"Hey," I say, holding open the door to the diner with my back. I watched Mati exit her truck and then take a seat on the bench before the diner. Her head spins from me to the street and back.

"You...but..." She's pointing from me to the center of town, and I chuckle.

"Spice, whatcha thinking?"

"I just watched you leave."

The teasing smile on my face falls, and I step forward, forcing her to scoot over on the bench. Grabbing both her hands in mine, I find them freezing again.

"I'm right here, sweetheart." She nods in response, confusion on her rosy cheeks in the damp, cool mountain morning. "Come inside, okay?"

It's like I'm leading a wild animal, waiting for her to pounce or try to flee.

Focus on me. I set her on a stool and round the counter for a mug of coffee. Serving it up to her, I return around the counter and take a seat next to her. I spin her, so her knees come between mine, and I reach one of her cold hands, rubbing it between my fingers.

"I thought you left." Her voice sounds a little dull, and I want to envelop her, draw her into me, and light the fire I know this woman has inside her.

"I told you I planned to stay."

"For a night," she whispers, but there's a question in her statement.

"For as long as you'll keep me, Mati." Her eyes widen, and she slips her other hand into mine.

"I need to be serious for a moment, and I only want to mention this once. I have things to say to free myself, and then I hope we can let it

290

go." I take a deep breath, and Mati's fingers close over mine, giving me an encouraging squeeze. "I think Chris wanted us to be together...and strangely, I think he put Jax's number and the letter together before me on the table in your house. I wanted you to take care of me that night, just like old times. But I think Chris was reaching out, because he couldn't smack me upside the head, and tell me it was time I finally took care of you."

I bring our collective fingers to my mouth and press my lips against her fingers. "I'm here to take care of you, Mati. Follow you, wherever that leads."

"Denton, I...I don't know what to say." Her brows furrow and her expression shows she questions my decision, but things are settled.

"You think I'm crazy, don't you? About Chris? Like he *haunted* me or something."

"No, I...I think...I don't know what to think, but I definitely know Chris is no longer with me. Maybe he does want you to be here. But is this really what you want? You couldn't wait to get out of this place."

"You're right. I couldn't wait to go, but not to leave you behind. I wanted to go on that road trip, Mati. I wanted you to be with me...forever. And Chris knew it."

"What are you saying?"

I'm not certain I should share my secret, my guilt. I don't want to sound as if I'm trying to tarnish Chris's memory or his intentions. He loved her as much as me, but I don't want any more secrets.

"I'm saying Chris asked me to go, without you."

"Why?" she whines, and her voice rings out like the memory in my head of her at seventeen.

"Because he knew I loved you then like I still love you now."

Tears spill from her eyes.

"I don't want to upset you. I just want to have this out here. One final secret revealed." I swipe a silent tear trailing down her cheek. "Can you forgive us both?"

More tears fall in earnest as she bites her lip and nods. I lean forward and brush my lips against hers, soft and light, before pulling back. She

L.B. Dunbar

giggles for some reason, and I relax as the tears fade, and her face brightens.

"Who was in your car?" she asks, wiping away the last bit of moisture on her cheeks and twisting for the door.

"Dolores. I'm giving her some time off from life. We decided to give the diner to Hollilyn for the time being."

"Hollilyn? She's ready to pop any day!"

"She said she has a month."

"Do you see how big she is? That baby won't wait."

I chuckle at the stress in her voice. I love how animated she is. *I love her.*

"Calm down, Grandma."

"Ugh. I don't think I'm ready for this."

"Well, get ready." I'll never be a grandpa. I've never been a father. The two concepts have never concerned me until this moment. Have I missed too much? "Anyway, it gives me time to fix the place up. I'm hoping Dolores will stay away a while. I'd like to spruce it up in here and then sell, maybe to Hollilyn." I take another look around at the old paneled walls, the chipped tile floor, and the dated Formica countertop.

"You'd sell the diner? Out from under Dolores?"

"I don't want her to feel tied down anymore. I'd just like her to have some freedom. Once she takes it, she might not want to return."

"Stranger things have happened," she reminds me, her voice quiet, still a little untrusting of our situation, a little unsure of my staying put.

"It took me too long." It's true, but I'll take as long as I need to prove I'm not going anywhere. "I'm also going to rehab Magnolia's. Let's just see what happens with her. She needs some supervision, that one. And I could use the project seeing as I won't be America's next top model."

"What do you mean? I thought the shoot in Costa Rica…" Her voice dips and I realize we have one more thing to clear the air about.

"The shoot was for *Mature Life.*" Mati's nose wrinkles and she looks adorable.

"What's that?" Her voice drags, and I laugh.

"A magazine for the seasoned reader." Mati gasps and her fingers cover her lips.

"You aren't old! What happened to 'Fit over Forty' and *Healthy Male?*"

"It went to someone not forty." I wave dismissively. "It doesn't matter anymore. I realized on the way to Costa Rica I was fulfilling the wrong dream. Or maybe my dream just changed. I'm allowed to do that, as a *mature* man." I air quote, and we both laugh.

"You're definitely seasoned," she drawls, leaning toward me and tickling her fingertips over my peppered jaw.

"You know it, Spice." I take her lips and plan to show her how seasoned I can be. Grabbing her at the waist, I lift her to the counter and scoot to the stool she vacated. Positioning myself between her dangling knees, my hands climb her thighs and spread them.

"Denton," she whimpers as I pepper kisses on her inner thighs, dragging her to the edge of the countertop. "People will see." Her eyes shift to the large diner window with the blinds at half-mast. The closed sign will surprise people, and I'll need to make an announcement about the new management, but I have other things on my mind.

"Still ashamed to be seen with me?" I tease. We established all this last night. The kissing in front of her brother. The dancing at the party. "Those windows are frosted, and the door's locked."

"Not ashamed. I just don't need everyone to know our business." Her voice catches on the last word as I nuzzle my nose over her moistened underwear.

"*Our* business. I like the sound of that." I ignore her concerns as I blow heat on her sex. "But if they are going to talk about us, we should give them something to talk about. These need to go."

"Denton," she purrs both admonishing and encouraging me as I wiggle her underwear down her legs.

The delicacy of the day will be à la Mati.

+ + +

Two weeks later, Mati coaches the girls' volleyball state championship game with her team. It's a packed house, and my girl is a local hero. The parents love her. The fans want this win. Her girls are determined to make Mati proud, but the pride shows in her face when the final ball drops and the points fall in favor of Blue Ridge High School, making her the winningest coach in their history.

Mati was excessively nervous about this game, snapping at me a time or two in the days before it. Then like a mischievous kitten, she'd saunter up to me and apologize, curling into me for comfort and a little bit more. I was always happy to oblige.

So, I'm not concerned as I struggle through the crowd, hoping to get to her for our own congratulatory kiss until I near her and find two men in suits along with a woman in dress pants and a crisp white blouse.

"Congratulations, Coach. And welcome to the team." My brows pinch as my head volleys between them. I watch as an older gentleman shakes hands with Mati. Her face beams with excitement. The glow is more than this win. "We look forwarding to seeing you next week in Elton."

I freeze, taking in the logo on the jacket of the second man. Northeastern Georgia University. My eyes shoot to Mati's.

"You're leaving." The words blurt out of my mouth, sharp and shocked. In an instant, I sense the truth. Mati had her own dream, and these people are handing it to her. She keeps her eyes from me as she shakes another round of hands.

"I'll see you next week." The extremely tall woman in the group furrows her brow at me before recognition crosses her cheeks. Turning away, she follows the men to the exit. Mati and I step toward one another at the same time.

"You're leaving," I repeat. "But I just got here." *Shit.* I know it's the wrong thing to say. It's the worst thing to say, but I can't help myself. My chest burns. I'm giving up a lot to return here, and it's all because I want to be with her. But now, she's leaving? *What the fuck?*

"Well, I…" Another group of congratulatory people finds Mati, and I step back, allowing her to be swallowed up by her Mountain Cat family. These people want to touch her, tease her, but I wonder if they know she's about to leave them behind. She's going to leave me behind, and as much as I know I deserve it, my heart hurts.

"Hey man, great game." Charlie pats me on the back as if I'm worthy of his cheer. I didn't do anything. I watched my girl coach to victory, but there's no way in hell I'm going to watch her leave me.

"Yeah, good game," I mutter.

"You okay?" Charlie asks, his eyes narrowing on me.

"I think I could use a beer. Let Mati have her moment here."

Charlie nods slowly, looking from his sister to me. "You aren't running, are you?"

"Fuck no," I say. She's the one running from me.

48

Play Fair

[Mati]

I lose Denton in the sea of people. Call me selfish, but I let go of his reaction. This is my moment, and I absorb it all. The parents. The girls. The people. I love this town, and I've loved this job. Guilt coils around me, but I'll leave BPHS with the right people to take my place. Alyce Wright, for one. We had a long talk about this opportunity for me, and as much as I'd love to take her with me to join my coaching staff—how fun is that to say—Alyce doesn't want anything other than teaching English and living here in Blue Ridge.

"I'm where I'm finally meant to be. I'm good here," she told me. It's been a good place for me, too, but I've always lived on the cusp of wanting a little bit more. More adventure. More something. This is my road trip, and I'm not turning it down.

When I arrive at the pub, the place is packed. Everyone's excited about the girls' win, and I smile with girl-power pride. Women's sports deserve some limelight and considering we have a better winning record than the football team, I'm thrilled. Making my way through the crowd, I find Denton sulking next to Charlie. Charlie's shaking hands with people, playing his mayor part and absorbing some congratulations as my brother.

"She did all the work," he credits. "But I'm very proud of her." *Ah, Charlie.* Always trying to play fair.

"Hey," I say as I step up to the two men. Behind them, the television screens show highlights of the game. *Eek.* Seeing myself on the big screen—my face scrunched, my mouth wide open as I scream—I don't have a great winning game face, and I'll need to work on the look.

"Hey," Denton says. Hurt is written all over his face, and my shoulders fall. Finding out at the game wasn't how I wanted to tell him my news. I realize I kept this from him, but I also kept it from everyone. I didn't want to share until I had something worth sharing.

"We need to talk." My head lowers. I really don't want to do this here. I don't even want to do it tonight. I want to revel in my last minutes of pride for Blue Ridge High School. To my surprise, Denton's hand comes to my lower back.

"It can wait," he says without conviction, and he tugs me to him by my side. He kisses my temple. "Congratulations."

Charlie's watching us, although he shouldn't be surprised. Denton came to our family dinner a week ago. Every touch was confirmation Denton and I are together, but suddenly, I'm not so sure.

"Why the long face?" Billy asks as he walks toward us. His head volleys between Denton and me for a moment before he tilts his head to the kitchen door.

"I'll give you ten minutes in my office. Don't do anything on the desk. I don't need images I should never see in my head looking at the hard surface each day."

"That won't be necessary," Denton replies, but I interject. "William Forrest Harrington, would it kill you to remember for five minutes I'm your sister and a woman and speaking to me in such a way isn't appropriate?"

Billy chuckles. "I wasn't speaking to you. I was talking to him." He winks at Denton, who slowly smiles back at Billy. Is this some kind of guy code? As if I'd have sex on my brother's desk. Then again, the idea doesn't sound too awful. I shake my head. Denton and I need to talk.

Billy looks from Denton to me again. "Well, get it over with so you can enjoy the party." I hate how my brother can read me.

Instead of the office, I lead Denton up the stairs to the private party room on the second floor. The space is closed off this evening because the only party is in full swing downstairs. As we enter the vacant area, illuminated only by the dim streetlights outside the bare windows, Denton spins on me.

"Two weeks," he reels. "Two weeks and you didn't say anything. Explain. And then tell me why you didn't mention it before." He settles back on the edge of a table, his arms crossing over his chest.

L.B. Dunbar

"Would it have changed things? Would you have decided not to return?" My heart drops to my belly. It's one of the reasons I didn't mention it. Caught up in the newness of our relationship and the tenderness of his return, I didn't want to say anything which might jeopardize him leaving me.

Denton swipes both hands down his face. "I just want to understand what's happening."

I explain how weeks before his return I applied for college coaching positions. "I just felt ready to do something different, maybe something away from here. But I still have my family." I continue with the interview process and the schedule of when they each took place: his mother's wake, two days after he left, and finally the call that came a few days before the game tonight.

"We'll be offering the position to you. I thought you'd like to know in advance, so it isn't overwhelming when you win the state championship." I appreciated the head's up and the vote of confidence from Keli Stratham, the only female representative on the interview committee. She'd been a college coach for years until settling on Northeastern Georgia to be near family.

"My whole life, I've given up things. My volleyball scholarship," I say, to which Denton's face falls, but I lift a hand to stop him from interrupting me. "My college education when I got pregnant. Then my body to my boys. Motherhood. Working for the pub. I'm not begrudging any of those decisions or circumstances. I wouldn't trade most of them, but it's also my time. Does that make sense? Coaching at the college level has been my dream."

Denton closes his eyes. He nods slowly although I'm not certain he does understand. He ran off from this town, sacrificing our friendship, but nothing else. He followed his heart from the start, but my journey has been twists and turns on a different path leading to this point. *The road well-traveled.* Whether he understands my reasoning or not, I can't give in to the sorrow on his cheeks. I'm still too high from the win and the offer. It's a good night for me.

"Don't be like this," I speak softly, stepping toward him and tiptoeing my fingers up his chest. He looks away from me toward the neon lights reflecting through the windows. My hands come to his waistband and gently tug. His mood isn't budging, so I take it to the extreme. Pop goes the button on his jeans.

"Come on, Mati. Cut it out." His head shoots back to face me, but I'm already lowering to my knees. He needs to know I didn't keep anything intentionally from him. I want him even if I don't know how he'll fit in this new plan.

"Get up," he demands without conviction because I have his zipper undone and his dick released. My mouth surrounds him with velvety heat, drawing him deep until he gives into a quick, sharp release. He's unknowingly given me comfort from the tension leading up to the final game and the wait for the interview results. Hopefully, his release will give him the assurance he needs. I want him.

"Sweet fuck, Mati. I wasn't expecting that." He sighs, as he offers me a hand to lift myself off the hardwood flooring. I chuckle as I stand, wiping at my lips. He scrubs a hand down his face before tucking himself back inside his jeans.

"I'm never gonna win any fights with you, am I? Especially if you play dirty." He smirks at me, a hint of teasing restored to his hard-edged expression.

"I didn't know we were fighting or there was something to win."

"Why didn't you tell me?" His voice softens.

"I didn't want to say anything to anyone until I knew something concrete. I didn't purposely keep it. I just…" I shrug, uncertain I can explain my reasons.

"Do you not trust me?" He reaches for my hips and tugs me between his legs.

"I do. I just wanted this for me. And I didn't want to bring it between us."

"Nothing's coming between us," he whispers, taking my lips with his. My libido heats. Having a taste of him makes me want other things from him, but he draws back too quickly.

"We can't keep any more secrets, Mati. Everything needs to be open for this to work."

L.B. Dunbar

I nod, but I'm worried. Will we work if I follow my dream? His forehead lowers to meet mine.

"Look, I'm sorry. I overreacted. I'll go wherever you go. You're where I want to be."

I pull back, glancing up at him. *Can he mean what he said?* He just moved home.

"You're just saying that because I gave you a blow job," I tease, covering the nerves racing through me.

His palm flattens over my heart and then slips up to my throat. "I'm saying it because I love you and I'm not missing out on any more time with you."

I swallow the lump in my throat at his honesty.

"They're setting me up with an apartment near the university, but I could still come home some nights. It's only forty minutes away."

"Home is wherever you'll be, sweetheart. Maybe you could make a little room for me in your new place, and there's always space for you at Magnolia's."

He's made hints before tonight that he'd like us to live together. What's unspoken is how he doesn't want to move into my place. Rehabbing Magnolia's will be a messy job, but one he wants to be in the midst of while it happens. He says he'd like me to help him make decisions about colors, paint, tiles, and more. He wants us to make her place a home again.

With a more solid plan in place for my future, I'm ready for another step. "I'm selling the house."

Denton's surprise is hardly contained. His face softens as his eyes beam with delight. Then his smile falters. "How will your boys feel about that?"

"I understand it's where they grew up, but they don't live there anymore. It's gonna be hard, on all of us, but I'm ready. More than ready. This is my second chance."

His smile returns. "Mine too, sweetheart."

With his good mood restored, I rub my hands up and down his arms, looking left and right in the empty room. "So…think you could make love to me quick to celebrate my victory."

His eyes widen. "Here?" he teases, lowering his mouth to mine. "What if people see us?"

I giggle as I shrug.

"God, I love your dirty mind," he says, working at my pants and pushing them down my hips.

"I love you," I say, and the rest of the night becomes another victory.

49

House Rules

[Mati]

Announcing my new job and my plans to sell the family home after twenty-five years of living in it went exactly how I expected—rough.

"But you love the high school," Jordan reminds me. I do love the high school girls, but I'm ready for more of a challenge. Fortunately, Jordan understands the financial aspects of selling. I'm taking a job forty minutes away, and I'll have a new place to call my own. I don't need the expense of upkeeping a house.

"We have a guest room any time you want to come home," Jordan offers, patting my hand like I'm the prodigal mother running away.

Jaxson, on the other hand, says nothing. He doesn't glare at Denton, who sits at my side, his hand on my lower back as I explain the details of my job and my decision to sell the house. I expect Jax to blame Denton. He's already cussed Denton out for leaving and hurting me again, reminding him of *their conversation.*

What conversation? I asked as Denton and Jaxson stared at one another outside my mother's home before the Harrington family dinner a week before the championship.

You promised you wouldn't do it again, Jax accused.

And I'm not, Denton reminded him.

"This is my choice. Remember? My life. I'm tired of being alone and feeling like I'm underwater. I want to swim." Denton glances at me, not understanding the metaphor, but I only look from one son to the other. Jax doesn't meet my eyes. When he does look up, he glances directly at Denton, nods once, and then excuses himself from the dinner table where things were discussed as a family for most of my boys' lives. I'll miss these moments, but they were moments already lived, and new moments need to be made.

+ + +

It's ridiculous what kind of *stuff* you accumulate over twenty-five years in a house. A few days after my announcement, the boys come over to help me go through their old rooms, the basement, and the garage. Denton offered to help, but I told him I thought it would be better if it were only the boys and myself for a bit. He's been surprisingly patient and understanding. I think he's also relieved. It's not as if he doesn't recognize my life with Chris, but he doesn't want to witness it, and he doesn't want to feel like he's replacing it. Together, we're taking a new step.

"I'd like to buy the house," Jax says after a day of filling boxes and trash cans.

"What?" Jordan and I say in unison.

"My apartment isn't big enough for a family." He chews his lip as he speaks, his eyes darting everywhere but at his brother or myself. "I love this house." His voice cracks as he offers this truth and I reach for his arm.

"Honey—"

"I've been to the bank, and I'm waiting on approval for a loan." I swallow a lump in my throat. I don't know what to say. It isn't like I want to take money from my son, but I did plan on a little nest egg from the sale. I look at Jordan for an explanation. He and Maggie already own a home on the other side of town. They selected a large, older home with multiple bedrooms for all the children they planned to have and haven't yet.

"I'm assuming you two have already talked." I release Jax and shift my attention from one son to the other.

"I think it's a good move for Jax," Jordan defends his brother.

"Does this mean you and Hollilyn are getting married?" I want to swallow the question after I ask it, as I promised myself I wouldn't pressure him anymore about his relationship. Hell, I'm the one practically living with a man.

"Mom*ma*," Jax drones. I raise a hand in surrender.

"Fine. Sold."

"Really?" Jax and Jordan say together. It's uncanny sometimes how twins work in sync.

"Yours. I'll talk to Charlie. I haven't selected a realtor, so this saves us both any fees there. I just want a fair market price."

Jordan's smile fills his face as he claps his brother on the back. He's proud of him like he's finally growing up and acting responsibly. Jax's grin comes slowly, his eyes filling with realization.

"I'm gonna be a father and own a home."

"You're going to be a wonderful dad," I say, reaching for both his hands and giving them a gentle squeeze. "And a great homeowner."

Jax nods as he steps into me, and I hold my son like I haven't in years. Another pair of arms encircles us both.

"Family hug," Jordan mumbles, and my heart warms. I love my boys, and they love me.

+ + +

Denton arrives around dinnertime with a pizza and beer.

"You can't bring me fucking Coors. I distribute Giant Brewery Beer. That's our competition," Jax admonishes, and Denton looks to me for support as the room falls silent. Then I hit Jax on the back of the head, and Jordan laughs.

"He wishes Coors was his competitor," Jordan snorts. He took an offered beer and thirstily drinks before pulling free of the bottle with an exaggerated *ah*.

"If you weren't my twin, I'd disown you for that," Jax pouts as if betrayed by his brother.

"If you weren't my twin, I wouldn't have to always save your ass," Jordan teases.

The two of them remind me of Chris and Denton as kids. I slowly smile at Denton, stepping forward to give him a hesitant kiss in front of my boys. "Welcome to my world."

"I'm happy to be here," he says.

After a rousing hour of my boys nagging each other, they excuse themselves and leave me to my boxes. Denton sits beside me on the couch.

"Is it weird?" he asks, and I look around me. It is a bit nostalgic, but I've let the guilt go. It's been over a year. I have a new job coming. I have Denton staying. I'm ready to step forward.

"It's going to be different." I laugh.

"So, I talked to Magnolia."

"And?" I hesitate. I wanted him to ask Magnolia's permission, not just assume it was acceptable for me to stay in her home with him.

"She says she has no problem with you moving in, but we can't share a room."

"What?" I shriek.

"House rules, no person of the opposite sex in our bedrooms, especially as overnight guests."

I pout as I take a final pull of my beer. I don't want to be separated from him any more than I have to be. Commuting to and from the college will be enough of a distance and some nights I'll be staying there instead of coming back to Blue Ridge.

Suddenly, Denton laughs. My brow furrows deeper.

"You should see your face. I got you so good." He leans forward, slapping his knee like he pulled one over on me. I set my beer down with the empty pizza box and finished beer bottles on the coffee table.

"You..." I hiss, pressing at him on the shoulder. He catches my wrist and pulls me down on top of him. We shift until we line up. His legs spread, and I slip between them. Our upper bodies press against one another. I swipe a hand over his temple. "You are so bad, rockstar."

"Hmmm...actually I'm so good, especially when I'm with you."

His mouth takes mine, and I have to admit he's right. He is so good *for* me.

Epilogue
Gratitude

[Mati]

A week before Thanksgiving, Hollilyn goes into labor. To my surprise, she asked me if I'd be in the delivery room with her and Jax. I don't recall all the details of giving birth to my boys, as I was prepped and sedated for the emergency C-section, so I accept the offer with honor. As a witness to this miracle, I thought I'd be more squeamish, but I held it together for Hollilyn and Jaxson, and their beautiful baby boy.

Christopher Jaxson Rathstone.

"We'll call him CJ," Hollilyn announces, cooing over the head of her sweet baby as Jax positions an arm around her and a hand on the baby's back. They form a circle of life and family. My heart swells with pride.

Hours later, Jordan and Maggie come to visit, and I feel for Maggie. She wants a baby so badly. Jordan rubs Maggie's back as she rocks the babe in her arms. He kisses her temple as a silent tear trails down Maggie's face.

"He's so beautiful," she says.

"One day," Jordan encourages, but I'm thinking after five years, they may need an alternative to their current plan.

Denton arrives with the biggest teddy bear I've ever seen. Hollilyn laughs as he struggles through the door and Jax swears at the size.

"No such thing as too big," Denton says, winking at me. Setting the oversized stuffed animal in the vacant rocking chair in the corner, Denton stares at CJ in Maggie's arms.

"Want to hold him?" Hollilyn offers from her position in the bed. She looks tired but happy. Jax appears surprisingly calm, and Denton glances at the new father for permission.

"Go ahead, old man." The insult comes with a chuckle.

Denton takes the baby, juggling a little as Maggie lays CJ in his arms. If my womb could produce again, I might spontaneously become pregnant looking at the vision before me. He's a vision of seduction mixed with sexy daddy. Denton sways, his hips jutting left and then right like he's dancing with the baby. A hum fills the room and the rest of us quiet. Denton's finger strokes over CJ's little fingers which open and close around Denton's thick digit. A lump fills my throat as he breaks into a soft lullaby about angels.

"I thought you didn't like children," I say as the song ends and CJ sleeps in Denton's arms.

"I never said I didn't like them, just didn't have the right girl to have them." His eyes meet mine for a moment and my chest pinches. I love this man.

Jax clears his throat and stands, coming over to stand next to Denton.

"So, uhm…" Jax scratches at the back of his neck while staring down at the baby. His other hand slips into his back jeans pocket.

"You're kind of old to make a godfather," he chuckles awkwardly, and I hold my breath, wondering where he's going. He hasn't exactly been accepting of Denton before and after his return. "But, I was wondering…since you're sticking around…if you'll play the role of grandfather, instead. My dad would have liked that."

The tears in my eyes match those of Hollilyn. This is a big step for Jax. His acceptance of Denton means a lot to me, and this gesture is an olive branch. Denton grasps the opportunity. His smile grows as he looks down at the baby and then lifts him to kiss his forehead.

"Granddad Denton? I like the sound of that."

+ + +

We gather for a Harrington Thanksgiving with quite a few additions. With Dolores still absent, Denton brings Magnolia and joins us for a day of gluttonous eating and drinking. Beer is in abundance, but Denton brings scotch, and I'm waiting for things to get ugly between my father and brothers. Drunk Harringtons are rowdy Harringtons.

L.B. Dunbar

Dinner is laid out buffet style as our family has grown over the years. This year, Giant's girls don't make it home but promise to be here for Christmas. Charlie's daughter is still a star as she plays the piano for our entertainment, and Denton makes some new fans when he accompanies her. Billy remains surprisingly quiet throughout the holiday, but he wears his smile like a pro. He's a master at masking himself. Something's up with him, but I can't put my finger on it. My brother James remains silently absent, and a hole remains for my mother. However, a grandbaby steals the day's attention until after dinner.

With stuffed bodies and warm veins from alcohol, Jax stands before our congregated family in the large open plan family room.

"I'd like to make a toast." His brother groans, but I smile as I curl into Denton on the couch. I'm pleased they've made amends with one another, and Jax's suggestion to call Denton Granddad makes my old womb flipflop.

"To Grandma, of course, for an amazing meal." He holds up his tumbler in the direction of my mother who blushes like the flirt she can be while waving a dismissive hand as if she doesn't love the attention.

"To Grandpa George, for the finest beer." The Harrington boys cheer a little too rambunctiously over the family legacy, and CJ breaks into a wail.

"And to Hollilyn, the mother of my child. Who could have predicted this is how it would end?" He nods to his son in her arms, and she pinks, recalling the one-night stand I'm sure they both never expected to last longer than one night. "But if I would have known the path would lead me here, I would do it all over again. I only wish I'd met you sooner, so I hope I'm not too late to ask." He lowers to his knee before her in an overstuffed chair, and Hollilyn breaks into tears. I lean forward, covering my open mouth with both hands. "Will you be my wife, and share the rest of my nights with me?"

Hollilyn struggles to stand from her seat, and Denton pops up to take the baby from her arms. With another hand, he helps her upright, and Hollilyn looks like a bobblehead as she nods and nods and nods.

"Yes, yes, yes," she says, staring down at the ring Jax holds up to her. I recognize the piece. I wore it proudly for twenty-five years. It's time for it to bring love and commitment to another couple. However, Hollilyn bypasses the ring and goes for Jax's neck, wrapping her arms around him as she sobs against him.

"I love you," I hear him whisper to her, and she pulls back to kiss him with a little too much gusto for a family gathering.

"That's how they got in trouble in the first place," Billy says from next to me, nudging me in the side as his brows wiggle.

"Jaxson," I snap, clapping my hands and sounding every bit like my mother. I cringe with the thought, and Billy chuckles further.

"As if you don't kiss him like that." Billy winks at me as he nods toward Denton and I peer up at him, looking down at me while he holds CJ. The intensity of his gaze matches the heat of the room. Promises of kissing me *like that* whisper from his look.

+ + +

Hours later, we find ourselves inside my old room.

"Is it weird being in here again?" I ask. I'm curled on my side while Denton nuzzles into me, his head at my chest, his arms around my waist. There wasn't a choice, other than to stay. Too many of us were too tipsy to drive, and Mama demanded we all spend the night. It was just an excuse on her part. She gets to feed us all breakfast in the morning and prolong the gathering of family.

"Not weird, just different. Better, actually." He mutters to my breasts, his voice sleepy and buzzed from too much scotch. "I never thought I'd be so thankful to be back in this bed."

"Yeah," I say, for something to say.

"I'd come here to escape, and you never turned me away. Now, I lay here without running." He pulls back and looks up at me. "Thank you."

"You don't need to thank me. I love you," I whisper, leaning forward for a soft kiss, but he doesn't let me go so easily. His mouth chases my retreating lips to capture them with his. Within seconds, the kiss turns hot, filled with memories of longing and lonely nights. I'm pressed to my back as Denton maneuvers his body between my thighs.

L.B. Dunbar

Suddenly, I'm fourteen. He's going to go for my breast at any moment, and this time, I'm not going to turn away.

"I love you, Spice," Denton says, pulling back slowly. His eyes search for mine in the dark room. "I have something for you," he says, pressing upward and then hopping from the bed.

"What are you doing?" I giggle as he fumbles through the room and I hear him bump into the desk by the window.

"Fuck," he curses, hopping on one foot while trying to retrieve something from his bag. He hobbles back to the bed and then falls to his knees next to it. I prop up on one hand, my heart racing.

Unfolding a pamphlet, he spreads it on the mattress between us. Excitement fills his face as he smooths over the paper and lays a second sheet next to the first. It takes me a second to realize the large paper is a map.

"Mati Harrington, will you go on a road trip with me?"

I gasp, covering my lips with my fingers as I stare down at the crinkled paper. It's the original map, one I highlighted with different colored circles, marking places to stay and places to stop. The smaller piece of paper is from a notebook with blue lines and lists the details of our original plan.

"I didn't take the original adventure, so I saved the plan, hoping someday we'd get a second chance." His eyes peer up at me, filled with hesitancy as his hands coast over the paper again. "Hopefully, it's not too late."

"I'd love nothing more than to take a road trip with you."

A smile breaks at the corner of his lips. Then the paper floats to the floor, and he hops back to the bed, framing his body over mine. The map forgotten, his mouth finds mine.

"Thank you," he whispers. "Thank you for giving me this time."

"You have all my time," I giggle, continuing to kiss him back.

"You have all of me, Mati." And then he proves to me just how much of him I have.

310

Epilogue 2
[Dolores]

Runaway

"Just go, Dolores," my brother says to me. I stare at him, not even able to blink. Even though Denton is two years younger than I am, he looks better than I feel. Rock star. Model. Photographer. He's lived a life while I've spent mine here—in Blue Ridge, Georgia.

"I can't just leave," I admonish, brushing back my hair. It needs a cut and a wash. In fact, I can't remember when I last showered. Since my mother's death, a steady stream of well-wishers have stopped by at all hours to check on me.

I'm fine.

"Dolores." My brother sighs. It's a crime that men age well. At forty-five, he still has sharp cheekbones, bright dark eyes, and a smile that'll warm a room. I could hate him, but I don't. I understand why he ran away when he was eighteen. Our father was a miserable man. Still, it isn't lost on me that I was the one left behind to hold together the pieces of an already cracked vase. The diner. The farm. Our mother. Our grandmother. The list has been endless for twenty-seven years. And I'm tired.

"You can leave. I'm here now."

"Until you decide to leave again," I snap, causing Denton to flinch from his seat on a stool. He sits opposite the counter, the one I've been drawing circles on while we talk. He's right about this place. The paneling is dated, and the floor looks dirty even though it's clean. Grease permeates everything. Dolores' Diner is run down, and so am I.

"I deserve that," he says, lowering his voice, "but I have no intention of leaving. I finally have Mati in my life, and I'm not letting her go."

Matilda Harrington Rathstone had been my brother's fantasy girl his entire young life. As best friends, he gave her up to their other best

311

L.B. Dunbar

friend, Chris Rathstone—Rath—when they were young, but Denton got his second chance with her.

I nod in response to my brother because I don't know what to say. He disappeared again the day after our mother's funeral. Although he called me, promising he would come back, I didn't have much faith in him. When he left at eighteen, he left. To my surprise, he took my calls occasionally, but he was always busy. The road. The band. The women. He didn't listen to me about our father's death, our mother's illness, or our grandmother's declining health. All those things fell on me—the dutiful daughter.

"Look. I'm giving you my keys." Denton slides a ring of keys across the Formica countertop. "Take the Beast and drive. Get out of town. Get away from here. Get the fuck away from Rusty."

My head shoots up at the mention of Rusty Miller. Crusty Rusty— a member of the local motorcycle club Devil's Edge and my lover-with-only-lover-benefits for the past ten years. I can't even call him a friend, and he'd never allow me to call him a boyfriend. In simple terms, he's been a sex partner to me and a few other women in the area. I cringe at that thought. I typically defend my relationship with Rusty, what little relationship I can call it, but watching my brother get the girl of his dreams leaves me questioning my own sensibility in regard to Rusty. Slowly, I'm realizing I want a little more for me.

"Can't just go. Just drive and disappear." I wave a hand dismissively toward the front window of the diner. I open at six a.m., but Denton showed up and locked the door, pulling the blinds and turning the sign back to CLOSED.

"Yes. You can," he emphasized. "You can do this, and you should."

"Where would I go?" A teeny-tiny niggling of a possibility tiptoes over my chest. *Could I do this?*

"California," Denton says, his voice rising an octave, and he double taps his hands against the counter. *Bah-dum-dum.* "I'm giving you my keys. Car. Condo. It's on the beach."

Denton lowers his head to peer up at me. "Ever been to the beach, Dolores?"

I sigh. Yes, I've been to the beach. Bolton Lake is only a few miles from here, but somehow, I know the lake isn't the beach he means.

"The ocean," he clarifies as if reading my thoughts.

"Of course." I weakly smile. "When we were kids." I can't say I fondly remember the experience. It was one of the few times we took a family vacation. Like so many family outings, it ended poorly. Daddy drunk. Mother a close second. Denton getting in trouble. Had Daddy started hitting him by then? I don't recall.

"A real ocean," Denton teases. "The Pacific."

I chuckle. He's so full of himself and California. My eyes roam his face. He's going to find it difficult in this small town. Everyone will be in his business, especially when that business includes Mati, a beloved daughter of society and widow of the well-respected Chris Rathstone. Yet I see a twinkle in his eye, and a certain brightness fills his face. He looks...happy. I'm not certain I know the emotion, but if I could recognize it, I'd say Denton wears it.

"You just got back here," I remind him. His month-long absence left everything to me again. The after-funeral effects, the diner, the farm, and our aging grandmother, Magnolia. "I can't leave you."

"Yes, you can," he repeats. "In fact, it might be better for me. I need to dig in." He spreads his hands over the scrub-worn counter and then folds his fingers like he came across something sticky.

"You don't know the first thing about running a diner."

"I have Hollilyn."

"She's ready to have a baby any day," I shriek. My assistant manager and flirty waitress is due to have her first child in less than a month.

"Let me worry about that," Denton remarks.

"And then there's Magnolia. She doesn't know what to do with herself now that Mama's gone."

"Already working on that as well." He winks, actually winks, as though he knows a secret, but he isn't sharing with me.

My head tilts, and my hip juts out. I stare at him again. He fought so hard to be nothing like our father. In many ways, he isn't him, yet all I know of my brother relates to his fame and fortune as a rock star success. He looks like our dad, but not exactly. We look like siblings, but only if you look closely. His once black hair has specks of silver while mine is dull and almost a burning-charcoal color. I don't have the energy for my typical dye job, the one that gives me a hint of blue mixed with glossy black. We share similar facial bone structure, but while his is more model worthy, mine is because I forget to eat. Our eyes are the biggest difference. His are midnight while mine are a daytime blue—my mother's eyes, everyone tells me. I view the world just like her: loveless.

As if magnetically attracted to his keys, my fingers stretch as the tips tap on the countertop. My eyes focus on the metal strips with crooked teeth. *Could I do this?*

In answer to my unspoken question, my brother slides the ring within my reach. The metal hasn't touched my fingers, but they twitch as the pull grows stronger.

"Do it, Dolores." He dares me. "Run away for a while."

"I'd need to go home. Get some clothes. Close my house. Say good-bye to Magnolia."

Denton reaches into his back pocket and pulls out his wallet. My eyes widen at the wad of cash stuffed in it. He pulls two bills and then fumbles with a card. Two Benjamin Franklins and a gold card.

"I can't take your money," I admonish. I'm not some charity case. I have my own income, and my own home paid for by said income. I'm an independent business owner, for heaven's sakes.

"Consider it a loan then. I don't want you stopping as you pass go. Here's two hundred dollars and a card to get what you need."

I chuckle because he can read me. As if he knows I might take his offer but then second-guess myself when I get home to pack my things. My hand smooths down my hip, the feel of my waitress uniform suddenly constricting me. My podiatric-approved shoes with instep support weigh heavy on my feet. Sensing my inability to move, Denton pushes the keys the final distance, and I curl my fingers around the cool teeth. He stands and walks around the counter to envelop me in his arms. I've hugged a hundred people since my mother's death. The people of this town respected her as the former mayor's widow, even if they didn't respect the previous mayor.

Denton squeezes me, and I want to feel what he's offering, but I don't. I learned long ago to distance myself from physical affection. I can give it easily because it has no effect on me.

Yet.

The comfort of my brother's arms and his praise in my ear—"I believe in you. You can do this."—do something to me. I blink, but I won't cry. I haven't cried since my mother's funeral, since even before her diagnosis. I don't cry. It shows emotion, which I don't allow myself to feel.

I weakly pat Denton on the lower back. "Thank you."

He pulls back, his hands framing my face so I'm forced to look him in the eyes.

"This is going to be good for you," he says, his voice encouraging.

"I'll be fine," I reply quietly, giving a nod in agreement. I'm always *fine*.

+ + +

Want to read more about Dolores Chance? *Wine&Dine*

Want to jump ahead for more Harrington hotness? *Silver Brewer.*

Stay up to date on all sexy silver fox shenanigans in Love Notes.

+ + +

Thank you for taking the time to read this book. Please consider writing a review on major sales channels where ebooks and paperbooks are sold.

More by L.B. Dunbar

Road Trips & Romance

3 sisters. 3 destinations. A second chance at love over 40.

Hauling Ashe

Merging Wright

Rhode Trip

L.B. Dunbar

<u>Lakeside Cottage</u>
Four friends. Four summers. Shenanigans and love happen at the lake.
Living at 40
Loving at 40
Learning at 40
Letting Go at 40

<u>The Silver Foxes of Blue Ridge</u>
More sexy silver foxes in the mountain community of Blue Ridge.
Silver Brewer
Silver Player
Silver Mayor
Silver Biker

<u>Sexy Silver Foxes</u>
When sexy silver foxes meet the feisty vixens of their dreams.
After Care
Midlife Crisis
Restored Dreams
Second Chance
Wine&Dine

<u>Collision novellas</u>
A spin-off from After Care – the younger set/rock stars
Collide
Caught

<u>Smartypants Romance (an imprint of Penny Reid)</u>
Tales of the Winters sisters set in Green Valley.
Love in Due Time
Love in Deed
Love in a Pickle (2021)

<u>The World of True North (an imprint of Sarina Bowen)</u>
Welcome to Vermont! And the Busy Bean Café.
Cowboy
Studfinder

<u>Rom-com standalone for the over 40</u>
The Sex Education of M.E.

The Heart Collection
Small town, big hearts - stories of family and love.
Speak from the Heart
Read with your Heart
Look with your Heart
Fight from the Heart
View with your Heart

A Heart Collection Spin-off
The Heart Remembers

THE EARLY YEARS
The Legendary Rock Star Series
Rock star mayhem in the tradition of King Arthur.
A classic tale with a modern twist of romance and suspense
The Legend of Arturo King
The Story of Lansing Lotte
The Quest of Perkins Vale
The Truth of Tristan Lyons
The Trials of Guinevere DeGrance

Paradise Stories
MMA romance. Two brothers. One fight.
Abel
Cain

The Island Duet
Intrigue and suspense. The island knows what you've done.
Redemption Island
Return to the Island

Modern Descendants – writing as elda lore
Magical realism. Modern myths of Greek gods.
Hades
Solis
Heph

L.B. Dunbar

A Sip of *Silver Brewer*

A long and winding road

[Letty]

Where the hell am I?

I'm losing the GPS on my phone, and I feel as though I've passed the same copse of trees three times.

Who can tell?

Birches, maples, and cedars surround me, and those are the trees I recognize. Everything is a sea of thick bark and greenery, but soon, this forest will be ablaze with golds, reds, and oranges. The changing season is the reason for my rush. I need to secure the property before winter so the ground can be broken first thing next spring.

Working for Mullen Realty, I've climbed my way up from assistant office manager to assistant seller to commercial real estate agent. Not exactly my career choice but it's been a steady income. When I didn't have a job at twenty-four using my college degree in English, my mom made me go to work for my uncle, a real estate mogul in Chicago. I'm now forty, so I guess you could say I settled into the family business. Uncle Frank prides himself on buying and selling, and what he wants is to buy this godforsaken property in Georgia and sell it to a hotel company who wants the space for their next lodge-like resort and spa.

As the only vehicle in sight while I wind through the curving roads, I'm waiting for Jason to jump out with his creepy hockey mask and start swinging a chainsaw at me at any second. I might have mixed a few horror movies together, but that's the scene in my head as I weave along the narrow drive. I'm not even certain I'm in the correct county, let alone the right state anymore. I need Blue Ridge, Georgia, but all I've seen for miles is tree trunks and foliage, and occasionally, the inconspicuous marking for a turnoff. From the office, Marcus tries to assure me I'm in the correct place.

"There are only two tire tracks leading to nowhere," I say into the phone, struggling to drive the rented Jetta over the rough terrain.

"That's it. You're in the right place. Don't mess this up," his gruff voice barks through the speaker.

I hit a bump, and the phone jostles out of the cup holder to the floor. *Dammit.*

I can't risk reaching for it, and I'm too afraid to stop until I see the place I'm destined to find.

Harrington cabin.

I'm not certain what I expect. I've been told it's rustic, but I don't know if that means quaint or just plain rough. Either way, Mullen Real Estate wants the property.

"I think I'm almost there," I shout, as the phone lies facedown on the passenger side floor. I can't hear Marcus's reply. He's not only my assistant but one of my best friends, and he knows this acquisition is important to me. I'd prove myself as a skilled real estate buyer if I can book this deal. I'd also solidify my position in the company and earn myself a cut of the business.

Partner.

The word echoes through my head. The sound has a nice ring to it.

Olivet Pierson. Partner.

As the dirt road narrows, I see light at the end of the tunnel of trees. A clearing of sorts opens before me, and I slow even more than the five miles per hour I've been driving. As I break through the lane, a vision of masculinity stands before me. With his shirt off, the bare back of a muscular being slings an ax over his shoulder, splitting a piece of wood standing upright on another log. The thwack isn't heard inside the car, but the thunderous power in which he cracks the wood seems to vibrate under my vehicle and into my foot. I'm frozen at the appearance of his rippling back, sweaty spine, and low-slung pants that suggest he wears boxer briefs by the sliver of waistband exposed. In red. The hair on top of his head is short, trimmed close but not military style to his skull, while a bush of facial hair covers his jaw. My eyes focus on his profile as he stands and straightens, then quickly turns to see my car. Deep, dark eyes narrow, zeroing in on me in anger. He drops the ax and raises his hands, his mouth opening, but I don't hear what he says.

I'm blinded by the gleam of sunlight bouncing off his firm chest, a sprinkle of hair in the shape of a V between the flat plains of his pecs and above the slow hills of his abs. More hair leads south, dipping into the red band exposed above his waistline, and my mouth waters until two large hands hit the hood of my rental car, and I notice his mouth move as he shouts.

"Stop."

Oh. My. God.

My foot slams on the brake, causing me to jolt forward and narrowly missing the bridge of my nose on the steering wheel. I stare out the front windshield, taking in the appearance of the man I almost hit. He's a mountain of a man, someone I envision people wrote tales about long ago. He's lumbersexual by modern standards, and then I note his hair again. Cropped and charcoal. It isn't black but more like the smoky color before the coals are ready. A perfect blend of dusty silver covers his head and jaw. He's a silver fox, but from the size of him, he looks more like an angry grizzly.

"I'm so sorry," I mutter as I place the car in park and scramble to remove myself from the rental. My ankles twist as the heels I wear can't balance on the uneven dirt beneath my feet. I clutch the open driver's door for support, expecting to fall and knock my chin. How many stitches would I need? Is there even a doctor out here? A hospital nearby? Oh God, I might bleed to death.

Then I take note of the puzzled man before me, still leaning against my hood.

Staring at him, I'd die a happy woman.

However, the vibe coming off him is anything but pleased. His chest heaves as his eyes nearly disappear while he squints at me.

"Who are you?" He emphasizes each word as he speaks. I certainly can't use the statement "I was in the neighborhood" because I doubt you'd find another human being within miles.

Oh Lord, if I screamed, would anyone hear me? If a tree falls in the woods, does it make a sound if no one is around to hear it? My thoughts are out of control.

"I'm Olivet Pierson, and I'm looking for George Harrington the second. Is this the Harrington cabin?"

I'm here for the land, but the cabin catches my sight. The two-story building is of medium size, balanced with a window on either side of a single front door, standing open and inviting. A heavy metal overhang shadows the porch, which runs the full length of the cabin. The weathered gray structure with the deep black shingled roof doesn't look worn. It appears brand new. With a small yard and a forestry backdrop, the place looks quite homey.

"How did you get here?" His gruff voice returns my attention to him. His curiosity causes him to look up over the back of my car, staring down the pinched lane I traveled.

"Are you George Harrington?"

His head swings back to me, and his lips twist. Pressing off my car, he turns for a cloth on the pile of wood and wipes his face with it. Absentmindedly, he travels down his chest, or rather purposely, as he must know I'm watching his every move. I'm practically salivating as he takes his time to swipe across his broad pecs and dip to the trail leading lower. He pats himself with the cloth over the zipper region of his pants, and I flinch. My eyes flick upward, and his lips mockingly smirk.

I can't say it's a smile. His face looks far too serious for such a thing. Crinkles mark the edges of his eyes, and his cheekbones are well-defined. He might have been teasing me, but his face gives nothing away.

"So…" I repeat. "Are you George?"

"You must be looking for my father," he states, tossing what I realize is a white T-shirt back onto the pile of wood. He picks up the ax, and I try to catch my breath. I'm gripping the open door for support, peering at him as he turns his back on me and lifts the wood-chopping instrument. The sound of a splintering log resonates loudly around us, echoing in the deep quiet. I take a second to look around me, no longer lost in the woods, but noticing the beauty of various shades of green. Steeples of pines and broad sweeps of maple whisper in the breeze with a glorious blue sky as its backdrop. The landscape is breathtaking, and the silence reminds me this is the perfect location for a spa and resort. Secluded. Rustic. Peaceful.

Thwack.

Another log splits, and I shift my attention back to Mr. Lumbersexy.

"Do you know anything about the property?" I ask, interrupting him mid-swing. He doesn't miss the log, but it doesn't crack. The ax bounces back, and the log topples to its side. When he turns on me, the move is aggressive in nature, yet I find I don't fear him. His mouth opens, but I speak.

"I'm told it's owned by George Harrington II. A Miss Elaina Harrington on Mountain Spring Lane told me how to get here. Told me I'd find him here." I pause as he glares at me. I stopped at the original address given to me by the office. Mountain Spring Lane was a dirt strip with three impressive antebellum homes along the private drive. Old money covered the white paint of each house.

When he doesn't speak, I continue. "It's a beautiful piece of property." I turn my head as if I'm noticing the land, but all I can concentrate on is the weight of his eyes on me, knowing he's following the twist of my neck as I gaze around me.

"What do you want?" he snaps. The gruffness of his tone snaps my attention back to him. Maybe Grumpy is a better name for him instead of Sexy Lumberjack.

"I'm looking to discuss purchasing the land."

The ax slips from his hand while his other hand fists into a ball of knuckles. He's scary, but again, I don't fear him for some reason.

"It's not for sale."

"Everything's for sale, Mr...." He still doesn't offer his name, but I'm sensing I'm in the right place, so he must be George Harrington.

"Listen..." He pauses, and I offer my name.

"Olivet Pierson. Mullen Realty," I say, walking around my door and closing it. Reaching forward for his hand, I realize my palm already sweats with the anticipation of touching the paw of his. The closer I get to him, he appears even bigger, and we stand in contrast to one another. He's bare chested in wood shaving-covered pants and rustic work boots while I'm wobbling in my heels with a pencil skirt, blazer, and uncomfortable blouse.

His eyes glance down at my hand, but he doesn't reciprocate and reach for mine. Instead, he crosses his arms, puffing out his barrel chest and producing two large biceps, flexed in warning.

"Cricket," he begins, but I correct him.

"Olivet."

"This place isn't for sale, so you can just reverse out of here, hopefully without backing into an unsuspecting tree, and return to wherever you came from." All those words in his definitive tone add up to one: *Leave.* But I'm not going anywhere without the security of this property signed on a dotted line.

"Now Mr. Harrington," I say. Lowering my hand, I place both on the hood of my car. The problem is I'm still looking *up* at him, so I'm not really in a position of authority to talk him down. This always looks good in the movies, but it's clearly not working with my five-foot-seven stature compared to his six-foot-plus-too-many-extra-inches height.

"Giant," he states, and I stop.

"Excuse me?"

"Everyone calls me Giant."

"Well, Mr. Giant—"

"What do you want with the land?" he interjects, his voice still thunder deep but not so menacing.

"I work for Mullen Realty in Chicago, and we'd like to acquire this property for a resort—"

"A resort?" he huffs, his arms falling to his sides as he interrupts me. He turns his large head to the side, giving me a view of his profile. Strong facial features, a sharp nose broken at least once, and a tic to his jaw as he concentrates on something in the distance. "Do you know anything about this property, Cricket?"

"Olivet," I correct. "And yes, I do. I know it's a fine piece of land situated perfectly for a beautiful resort that will offer people peace and tranquility away from their hectic lives." I ramble off the future brochure sure to include such words to entice potential visitors. The serenity around us reminds me I'm not far off from my speculation.

L.B. Dunbar

He harrumphs, crossing his arms again. Not as fierce as the first time and more casual in nature, he shakes his head as though he's laughing at me. Only he isn't laughing. "It's not for sale."

I dismiss his words, considering what he would look like with laughter on his face. Would his cheeks glow? His mouth spread? I bet he has white teeth. A smile and a good chuckle might set him on fire. He's already larger than life in size, but with a good guffaw, he'd be bigger than thunder. A Greek god of sound and stature.

He's staring at me, and I realize I've taken too long to respond. I eye the cabin behind him. Rustic is one word for it. Cozy, graying, inviting. I rid the possibility of seeing the inside from my head. *He probably hides bodies under the porch.* I chuckle with the thought. He's fierce but not fearsome. There's just something about him. My head tilts, and my eyes pinch. I decide to change tactics. A new appeal.

"If it's a matter of money—"

"I don't need money." He scoffs, cutting me off and glaring at me again with a look of offense. "There isn't enough money in the world for me to give up this place."

My mouth pops open. "So, you are George Harrington the second?"

"I told you, I'm Giant, and I think we're done here, Cricket."

"Now, Mr. Harrington—"

He turns his back to me, that beautifully muscular back. My mouth waters, and I want to kiss up the river of his spine and along the flexing plains of his shoulder blades, which is absolutely ridiculous, considering he's a stranger. Besides, I've sworn off men. Pretty men with fancy names. *No thank you.* Although this man isn't pretty. He's weathered and worn like the cabin behind him, and for once, I'd like to be a little less straitlaced and buttoned-up. The collar of my blouse itches.

"Name your price, Mr. Harrington," I shout to his retreating back. He's abandoned the wood pile and stalks toward the low porch. Without touching the first stair, he steps up to the platform, swallowed by the shade of the overhang. My eyes are fixated on two firm globes filling out his Carhartt pants. *Oh my.* Within seconds, he's disappeared inside the cabin, closing the door on my proposal.

Well, that certainly didn't go as planned.

Continue Reading: _Silver Brewer_

(L)ittle (B)its of Gratitude

There are always so many people I'm thankful for in this journey, but a few stand out for recognition:

Tammi Hart – for giving me the starting block for this story and then sharing secrets to help it go for a "ride." I love the result and hope I've gotten your vision correct.

The admins of Loving L.B. – Krista, Tammi, and Sylvia – for keeping the doors open and the group running smoothly. I am eternally grateful.

Shannon Passmore – I think I should stop counting how many covers you've made for me (but I think it's 18), but this one, le sigh…here's hoping a sexy silver fox removing his shirt works.

Melissa Shank – I believe people come into our lives for a reason, and I couldn't have predicted five years ago (eep!) that in 2018, my reasons became most clear. I needed you and you have taken my journey to a new level. Thank you for talking me through the stories and off the ledge more than once.

Karen Fischer – Another person who has gratuitously come into my life and helped each book become better and better.

For all the girls (and a few guys) in Loving L.B. – for enjoying the "ride" with our sexy silver foxes, encouraging me when I need it most, and cheering me on when I'm at my best. I love you all.

For Do Not Disturb Book Club and the active authors within our little group, thank you for all your support, sharing, and just being awesome people. And to Alessandra Torre Inkers, another author group with open arms and supportive people, who pick you up when you need it most.

And finally, to the ultimate sexy silver fox in my life, Mr. Dunbar and our own brood of children: MD, MK, JR, and A. Looking forward to 2019 – the year I cross the line to 50 years old! You all make me feel 100 while keeping me 25. Much love to you.

About the Author

www.lbdunbar.com

L.B. Dunbar has an over-active imagination. To her benefit, such creativity has led to over thirty romance novels, including those offering a second chance at love over 40. Her signature works include the #sexysilverfoxes collection of mature males and feisty vixens ready for romance in their prime years. She's also written stories of small-town romance (Heart Collection), rock star mayhem (The Legendary Rock Stars Series), and a twist on intrigue and redemption (Redemption Island Duet). She's had several alter egos including elda lore, a writer of romantic magical realism through mythological retellings (Modern Descendants). In another life, she wanted to be an anthropologist and journalist. Instead, she was a middle school language arts teacher. The greatest story in her life is with the one and only, and their four grown children. Learn more about L.B. Dunbar by joining her reader group on Facebook (Loving L.B.) or subscribing to her newsletter (Love Notes).

FB: https://www.facebook.com/groups/LovingLB/
NL: http://bit.ly/LoveNotesfromLBDunbar
IG: @lbdunbarwrites

+ + +

Connect with L.B. Dunbar

Printed in Great Britain
by Amazon

81689778R00190